KAIGHLA RISES

Evryn, the Light

For my children—
May you always return to your own inner Light

"When they saw Eve talking to Adam, they said to one another, 'What sort of thing is this luminous woman? For she resembles that likeness which appeared to us in the Light.

'Let us lay hold of her and cast seed into her, so that, being soiled, she may not be able to ascend into her light... But let us not tell Adam... Rather let us bring a deep sleep over him. And let us instruct him in his sleep to the effect that she came from his rib, in order that Adam's wife may obey, and he may be lord over her.'

But Eve, being a force, laughed... She entered the Tree of Knowledge and remained there."

-"ON THE ORIGIN OF THE WORLD"
NAG HAMMADI LIBRARY

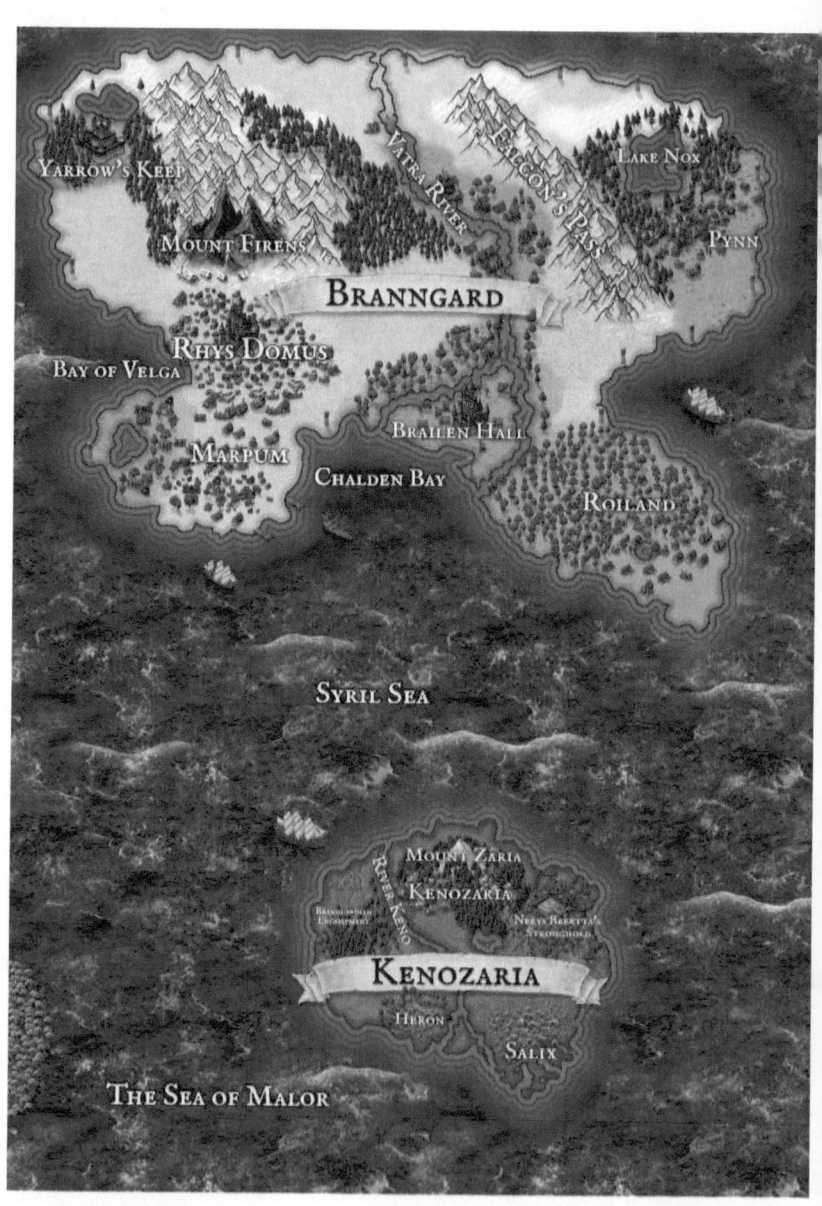

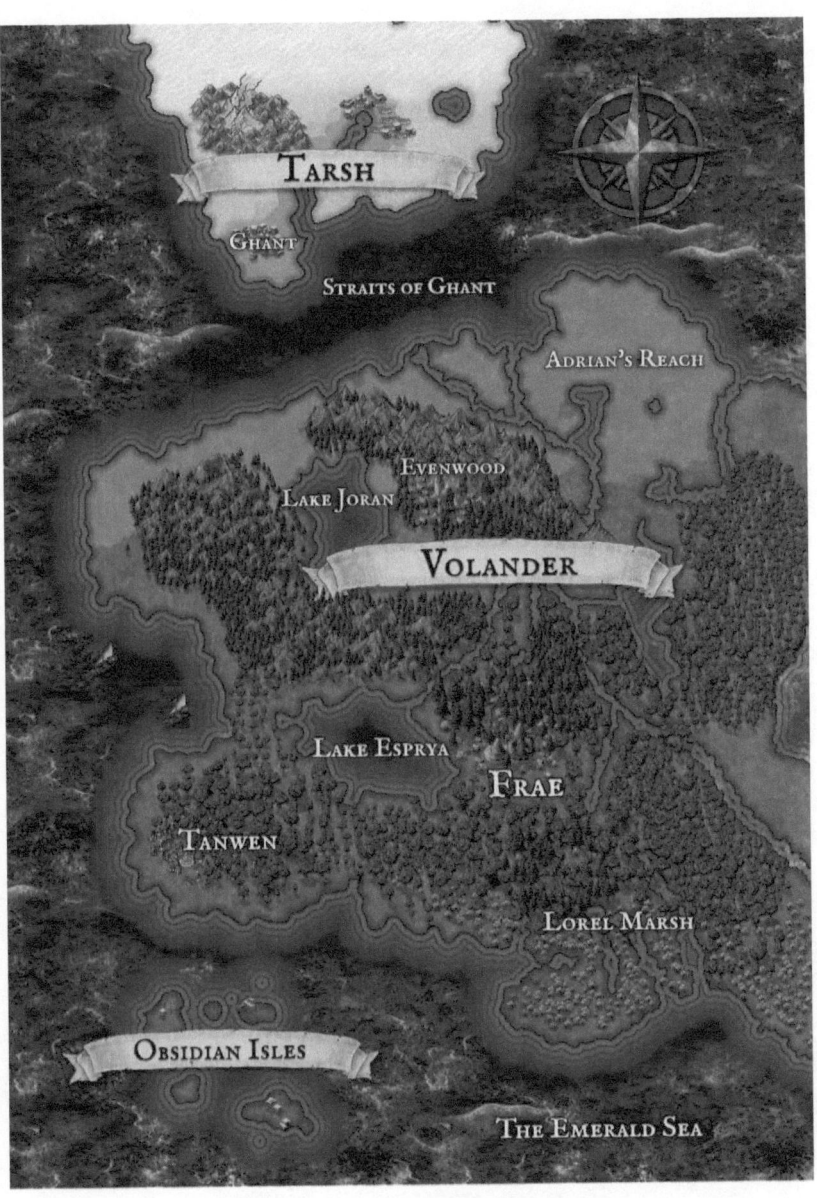

TARSH

GHANT

STRAITS OF GHANT

ADRIAN'S REACH

EVENWOOD

LAKE JORAN

VOLANDER

LAKE ESPRYA

FRAE

TANWEN

LOREL MARSH

OBSIDIAN ISLES

THE EMERALD SEA

SCAN FOR CONTENT WARNING

I

Summer

1

Evryn

I'm running east through the moonlit woods, dodging roots and rocks. I expect to hear the sounds of warfare behind me, to smell the village burning, but aside from some shouting down the mountain, all seems eerily normal.

I trip on an exposed root and fall, skinning my knee. I wince in pain as I pick tiny stones out of the scrapes.

What next? I ask the ether as I try to catch my breath. No one responds.

Aunt Tabitha? Nothing.

"Papa!" I call out audibly this time. But Papa doesn't respond, either.

I stop in my tracks. The whispers have *never* gone silent—not once in twenty-six years. Whatever is happening to Kenozaria, even my ancestors are shaken by it.

I stand for a moment, weighing my options. Aunt Meryn in Salix would welcome me, but that's a three-day hike south through the mountains, down into the valley, and through the marshlands. I'm not even sure I remember the way. Plus, I have no food or water, no weapons, and I'm ill-dressed to spend even one night in the mountains, let alone *several days* out in the open.

Mount Zaria's peak looms behind me, the Syril Sea rages in the north, and ahead, there are dark trees, only trees, as far as the eye can see. There must be some villages on the east coast that would be happy to shelter a child of Chief Korina Freya, and they can't be more than a few hours away. But then, people who are willing to shelter me may also be just as happy to hold me for ransom. It's a risk but it's my best hope of survival, so I run ahead through the pines until I can't take another step.

Just before dawn, I collapse against a tree trunk—breathless, bone-tired, and freezing. I close my eyes and try to calm my racing heart.

I awake abruptly to blinding sunlight and a rough hand over my mouth.

2

Evryn

Yesterday morning

"Don't pull the thread so tight, Rue, or you'll snap it," Mother admonished me.

'Rue,' she calls me when I disappoint her. Rue, like her regret that she didn't take Tabitha's expelling concoction sooner. Rue, the herb that failed her.

I laid my sewing down on my lap and sighed, drawing a sound of disapproval from Mother.

The morning light filtered through the curtains, falling across the remains of breakfast. It's quaint, our little cottage—the only home I've ever known. Eight months after rue failed my mother, I was born next to the hearth on a rainy afternoon.

Twelve years later, Papa finally succumbed to the fever that had been plaguing him for days. I lost what little remained of Mother that day, too. To escape the gnawing grief, she threw herself into her duties as the new chief of the Sanctum, so the rearing of the little ones

5

fell to me and Aunt Tabitha.

Ari stepped out of his room, yawning and pulling a shirt over his head. The middle child, the wildling, Ari has always straddled the line between this world and the next, and not always with grace. I've lain awake many nights, begging the gods to release him from the grip of fever or to relieve the pain from another broken bone.

"Happy morning to you, my dear." Mother smiled when she saw him, inviting him in for a kiss on the cheek. I am her eternal regret, but Ari is her *dear*.

She loves you, you know, Papa whispered.

She could show it, I thought.

"Where are you going this early?" Ziva asked Ari as she scrubbed away at the dishes. When Papa died, she was little more than a year old. She called me "Mama" longer than I should've allowed, and she's still never far behind me.

"Wear something warmer. It's cool this morning," Halline commanded as Ari grabbed the door handle. She should have been born first. Always the picture of poise in a sea of chaos, my little sister. If any of us resembles Papa, it's Halline.

"Can you bring back some water from the well when you finish... whatever it is you're going to do this early?" Mother asked Ari from the chair next to mine.

"Yep," he said, stepping through the front door, winking at me as he closed it behind him. I laughed under my breath. I knew *precisely* where Ari was going. Lyra's Bright Ceremony was that evening; he must have been heading out to prepare her gift.

I couldn't help but think of the morning Torek went out to prepare my Bright gift. The rose opal he gave me still hangs on a leather string around my neck. But Torek is gone now, like Papa and Aunt Tabitha.

After they brought his charred remains back to the village, I stayed in bed for a week, until one cold morning when Halline came to my room, carrying a tray of cider and some stewed potatoes and carrots.

"I don't mean to alarm you, but you're starting to smell, Evy," she said, laying the tray down on the end of my bed and crossing her arms the way she does.

I sat up and sighed weakly, putting my face in my hands.

"I know it hurts, darling," she said, sitting down next to me, gently pushing my dark, messy hair behind my ear and stroking my cheek. "But I promise you'll feel a *little* better if you bathe. And you'll make your family feel a little better, too."

"Hal, I *can't*," I moaned, pulling the covers over my head.

"Let's make a deal," she replied, standing up to rummage through my drawers for clean clothes. "You take a few bites of this stew and then wash off that stench in the hot bath I've just prepared for you, and I'll eat the rest of it and tell Mama you did. Deal?"

I took her up on the deal, and she was right: I did begin to feel better.

It's been six months, but losing him hurts more deeply than any other loss. Because unlike Aunt Tabitha and Papa and the others whom I've loved and lost, Torek's voice is missing from the cacophony of whispers that guide me day and night. Had it not been love? That would explain why I can't hear his whispers: only blood or true love can connect two souls across the chasm of death.

The sound of the oven door closing loudly brought me back to the moment. I forced Torek's memory from my mind and busied myself, helping Mother and Halline prepare our contribution to the Bright Feast.

It was sunset when Ari came back in, covered in wood shavings and sweat, carrying a big bucket of water.

"There's another outside," he said, setting the bucket down on the counter next to Halline.

7

In thanks, Halline handed him a small dish with a slice of cinnamon cake fresh from the oven. He took a bite and swooned.

"I assume your little excursion went well?" I asked, tousling his hair.

"Oh yeah. She's gonna love it," he replied with a mouthful of cake, wiping his brow and smiling as he walked into his room to strip off his filthy clothes.

Halline stood over the feast we'd prepared, assessing, it seemed from the look on her face, whether we'd made enough.

"It's *fine*," I assured her. "We're not the only family cooking."

"Yes, but we're Ari's family, and Ari is Lyra's betrothed."

"*Supposed* betrothed," Ziva piped up from a chair in the corner, looking up from the book in her lap.

"Ziva, put that book away and come help," Mother said, annoyed. "And we will do our best to show our support for Lyra. We love her, betrothed or not," she said, wiping her hands on her apron and brushing her long graying hair away from her face.

"Speak for yourself," I said, drawing another sound of disapproval from Mother.

In fairness, it's nothing personal with Lyra. I've never much enjoyed the company of other girls. I feel so out of place among them, uninterested in the glib happenings and mindless gossip that seem to consume their daily thoughts. And they don't much understand me, either. So, I prefer the company of the trees.

People may not understand me, but they respect me well enough. I am Chief Korina Freya's eldest daughter, after all, and my mother is a force to be reckoned with. It's generally assumed I will vie for her position when she passes into the Bright Lands, but I have no such design. Halline, maybe, or even Ziva. But not me. All I want is to build a simple home of my own, to plant things and watch them grow and commune with my ancestors in peace, and enjoy the simple pleasures of raising my own family—if I ever have one.

But that's not enough for my mother. *Nothing* is enough for my mother. I wish she could love me as I am—not as Rue, the private disgrace, or Evryn Korina, the heir-apparent, but as myself: plain *Evryn*. But she makes sure I know that I am not what she hoped I'd become, which is an upgraded version of herself, and I've given up on trying. So, I am "Rue" more often than I am "Evryn" to her.

As the night began to settle in, we all headed down to the village green with our gifts and food in hand.

The feast was lit by candles and set atop three long oak tables, each large enough to seat fifty people. The table was spread with unique dishes for the occasion from each family in the village. There was Halline's cinnamon cake from our grandmother's recipe and Minara's famous roast duck, Rayyan's squash and pumpkin pie, and many others—all to celebrate Lyra and the other Bright girls, who sat at a separate table, positioned longways, facing the others.

Lyra was always the most beautiful girl in town, just as her mother, Minara, had been when she was young. On that night, though, Lyra was positively *breathtaking*, her chestnut hair glistening with perfumed oils and topped with a wreath of wildflowers.

Ari beamed at her from his seat at our table, something Mother didn't fail to take note of.

"That girl will be the death of him," she said quietly to Halline at her side.

"Mama, can't he just enjoy the night?" Halline asked.

"She's so pretty! Even *I* can hardly look away!" Ziva remarked from her spot beside me.

"All I'm saying is that a young man shouldn't be so smitten with a girl, at least not so openly," Mother said, taking a bite of roast chicken. "He should let her worry a bit! Keep her on her toes!"

"They're the same age, Mother," I pointed out. "And she won't be a girl much longer. Just a few hours more."

"And wasn't Papa just as smitten with you, Mama?" Halline asked, taking a sip of mead.

Mother sighed and closed her eyes—her only admission of defeat—so we dropped the subject.

Just then, Mother's oldest friend, Rayyan, approached her from behind. "Hey, it's a party! Lighten up, Korina!" Rayyan laughed. "You look like you did on my wedding day—like it was the end of the world!" Mother eyed her for a moment before rising and embracing her, and the two went off to gossip with their friends at another table.

Ari sat awhile longer, watching as Lyra accepted gifts from friends and family throughout the village—dresses with a more flattering cut than the simpler ones she'd worn as a girl, aromatic oils to keep her skin soft and supple, and jewelry to enhance her beauty. Then he summoned his courage, taking a long drink of strawberry wine and a deep breath.

"You can do it, little brother." I smiled, patting him on the back. "Be brave!"

He gave my shoulder a gentle squeeze before standing up from his seat. As he approached Lyra's table, the smile that spread across her face was unmistakable. It was clear that they are deeply in love. When Ari offered her his Bright gift—a delicately carved wooden dove—she admired it and thanked him sweetly before placing it to the side with the other gifts she'd received. Ari offered her his hand and she took it, blushing, and rose from her seat before walking around the table to embrace him.

I thought that was the end—just an invitation to dance. But then they stood face-to-face, and Lyra pulled him in, placing her forehead on his and her hand on the center of his chest. Ari did the same, and the two took a few deep breaths in tandem.

"I guess it's official now," Ziva whispered excitedly.

The couple then walked together down to the dancing ring. The small band struck up a lively tune, and the two began to dance. Soon, other couples joined in the merriment.

"Here he comes," Halline said under her breath, tilting her head toward Koyran, who was approaching our table, holding a small bouquet of wildflowers. He's been smitten with me since we were children and has never accepted Torek as my true mate. It was *always* going to be Torek.

"Blessed Bright, ladies," he said, turning to me and handing me the flowers.

"And to you, Koyran," Halline replied for me, kicking me under the table.

"Uhhh, thank you for the flowers."

"Evryn, would you care to—"

"My sister is not well tonight, Koyran," Halline cut in, saving him the embarrassment of yet another rejection.

He looked down at his feet and back at me. "Forgive me. I know you may still be mourning Torek."

"Thank you for the invitation, Koyran. I'm honored by it, but I'm not ready," I said.

That's my girl, I heard Aunt Tabitha whisper.

Koyran turned away, defeated. He began to walk away from the table, but Ziva stopped him, standing up so fast she nearly knocked over her cup of mead.

"Koyran! Wait! I'd love to dance!" she cried, running after him. Koyran smiled weakly and took her hand before walking her to the dance ring.

"You won't be able to make that excuse much longer, you know?" Halline said, patting me on the shoulder.

"Milking it as long as I can," I mumbled under my breath as Halline stood to accept an invitation from Ayfa, Rayyan's daughter.

Sometime later, Lyra and the other Bright girls left the dance ring and began walking toward Mount Zaria. The music stopped, and everyone rose to follow them up into the hills.

When we reached the clearing at the top of Mount Zaria an hour later, the full moon was at its peak in the night sky, casting long pine tree shadows. A bonfire was raging in the center of the clearing. Mother and the other members of the Sanctum took their places next to the bonfire, decked out in their Bright garments. They embraced Lyra and the other girls, one by one.

"We are gathered to witness the Bright Walk of these beloved daughters of Keno and Zaria," Mother said to the hushed crowd. "No more will each think as a child, dress as a child, live as a child. With the guidance of her ancestors, each girl will enter into the second phase of her life—her Bright years, the years between girlhood and full womanhood."

Lyra and the other girls were about to receive the greatest gift of all: access to the wisdom of their ancestors and other loved ones who'd passed into the Bright Lands. Atop Mount Zaria—*only* atop Mount Zaria, and only during a full moon—Kenozarian women can hear their ancestors whispering to them, guiding them, giving them advice, and helping them make important decisions. All but me and Aunt Tabitha, apparently.

Like Tabitha, I didn't have to wait for my Bright Ceremony, and I don't have to visit the mountain or wait for a full moon to commune with my ancestors. I've been hearing the whispers every day for the twenty-six years I've been alive. They're my constant companion, and I can hear them everywhere—especially when I'd prefer silence.

I hear them best at dawn, as the mist rises from the mountains, or when the young trees lean to and fro with the wind. Sometimes it sounds like they're standing right beside me, whispers heavy with urgency.

Aunt Tabitha taught me when to listen to the whispers and when to ignore them.

"They can't know *everything*, after all," she would say, smirking.

Tabitha taught me, too, about the best herbs for quickening a lover's seed or repelling it—or at least trying to.

"Not even the strongest herbs can stop fate," she would say.

It could be Tabitha's herbs, or it could be fate, but I have never carried life in my womb, despite the eager attempts of my lovers and my own desire for a family one day. Sometimes I think Mother is right: maybe nothing good can take root in me.

"Your mother knows nothing of *true* goodness, Evryn, neither its roots nor its leaves," Tabitha would say, kissing my forehead when I used to come to her crying, once again, over Mother's incessant criticisms. Aunt Tabitha was honeysuckle and spring rain. Mother is all thorns and frost.

Mother turned to Lyra, who was the first girl in line. "As we uplift Lyra, daughter of Minara, she humbly opens her mind and heart and requests the guidance of her ancestors and the protection of Keno and Zaria," Mother continued. "Repeat after us, Lyra."

Lyra began reciting the ancient words along with Mother and the Sanctum.

"Zaria, make me a blessing to my people, a supportive friend, a loving companion, and a bulwark of refuge to my family, just as your mountain stands strong above us. Keno, help me to move without fear or force. Teach me when to rush forward and when to take my time, just as your river moves according to your wisdom."

Lyra began to glow, liquid amber radiating from the center of her chest throughout her body.

"Ancestors, share with me your sacred wisdom so that I may be a lamp unto my people. Guide me in serving our community with honor and integrity."

There was a low hum beginning to swell in the air. Lyra's ancestors were drawing nearer to her, bending low from their home among the trees atop the mountain. We could all feel it in the prickling of the hair on the backs of our necks.

Lyra removed her ceremonial dress and threw it into the bonfire, along with the flower crown and the purifying herbs she'd been carrying. Her naked skin radiated a warm glow that enveloped her and vibrated with her every move.

Ari sat silent, dumbstruck. "She's really something, isn't she?" he murmured to me. I smiled and took his hand in mine, squeezing it.

Lyra began to walk around the bonfire, thanking her ancestors for their invitation. With each cycle around the dancing flames, she walked faster and faster, glowing brighter and brighter still. Soon, it looked like she wasn't walking but *gliding* above the soft earth, being pulled around and around by an otherworldly force. Suddenly, she threw her head back, with only the whites of her eyes showing. She was chanting in an ancient tongue, receiving the wisdom of her ancestors from her own lips.

Having completed her thirteenth circumambulation, she fell to the ground as her mother and the other Bright girls came to her side to clothe her with a new dress. She was still in a trance-like state, unable to walk without assistance. Her first and most powerful communion with her ancestors was complete.

The ceremonies for the other four girls continued, much like Lyra's had. When everyone had received guidance from the Bright Lands, it was time for us to head back down the mountain to the village. Lyra and the others would spend the remainder of the night on the mountain, processing the wisdom they'd received.

Ari took one last look at Lyra, who stood staring into the fire, unaware of him, drunk on the flurry of whispers surrounding and filling her.

Suddenly, I felt a tightening sensation spread across my chest.

They're coming, Aunt Tabitha whispered.

Who's coming? I asked.

Just then, a sound erupted far below us, on the western edge of the village—a child crying in pain. Turning, we saw thousands of torches marching from the shore, across the River Keno, and heading toward our village.

Evryn, don't go home! Papa whispered urgently. *Run into the forest.*

3

Lukin

Three Days Ago

The sun was high in the sky when we disembarked from the ship into the dinghy. The land before us was a lush garden of emerald and pine in a sea of sapphire.

The journey from Branngard should have taken only a week, but we'd been at sea for three weeks, pushing hard against the wind—east, then south, then east again. Some of the men called it a bad omen, but I'm not sure I believe in omens, good or bad.

After everyone came ashore, we marched inland to a small plain and got busy setting up the tents while the camp followers collected firewood. It took all afternoon and by the end, we were exhausted and drenched in sweat, but the scouts reported there were no streams nearby to wash in and drinking water was in short supply already. So we headed back to our tents and removed our soiled sailing uniforms in favor of the starched and pressed marching ones we'd packed away in our boiled leather cargo bags.

As I stepped out of my tent into the cool breeze, a glint of sunlight off some metal drew my attention. At the edge of the encampment stood Akkar—the Torch of Branngard himself, decked out in his full splendor. His fine bronze armor, emblazoned with the flame sigil of Branngard on the breastplate, gleamed in the afternoon sun. A cape of rich, wine-red velvet hung from the back of his armor, flapping wildly in the wind. A crown of gold stood atop his cropped, dark hair, and he gripped a golden staff, as tall as he is, in his right hand.

As Akkar walked proudly through the ranks, accompanied by his security attaché—known as the Shield—the rank and file bowed our heads in reverence. Wherever the Torch of Branngard goes, Rhys goes, for the Torch of Branngard is the voice and heart and might of Rhys.

Only a few steps behind Akkar, a priest carried an ancient, leather-bound book atop a plush, red velvet pillow. The collection of all the wisdom Rhys has bestowed on his people through the Torches of Branngard, *Rhysvox* is forbidden to all but Akkar. Only his highest priests can even carry it.

Draven stood beside me, awestruck, as always, at the sight of the Torch. "I'd sell me left hand to have one look inside that book," he whispered as the procession passed by us.

"But not your right?" I asked, mockingly.

Draven punched my arm. "That mouth will be your downfall, Lukin, I swear it. Who can imagine what depths of wisdom are written there?"

The truth is, I *don't* care to know what *Rhysvox* says. If you've read one holy book, you've read them all. But to have traveled as I have and been given the opportunity to learn what I've learned is a privilege not often bestowed on most Branngardians.

My destiny was sealed before I could spell my own name. My uncle, Akkar—still just a humble priest back then—came to Yarrow's

Cairn to deliver the news himself: his uncle, the previous Torch of Branngard, had received a vision that I was to help bring the Light of Rhys to a new shore. We didn't know which shore it would be until one summer day a decade later when my father's men brought a young man to the cairn who had been taken captive while fishing off the coast of Kenozaria.

A tiny island southeast of Branngard, Kenozaria was known for two things: the richness of its soil and its people's simple-minded hospitality. They welcomed all visitors to their shores with open arms, under the condition that they respect the laws of Kenozaria—laws Akkar and his predecessors had no intention of honoring.

After my father's men had attempted to question the young fisherman and found his language incomprehensible, they'd brought him to my father, the lord of Yarrow's Cairn. In the end, it was decided that he should learn our language and tutor me in preparation for our eventual arrival on those shores.

The fisherman, Ferwyn Kestra, was a small, stooped man. He was soft-spoken and slow to anger, and he wore only rough-spun linen and a simple hat he insisted on removing whenever my mother and sister entered the room. The guards, servants, and even the stable boys taunted Master Ferwyn for his gentle demeanor and simple dress and marveled at how Kenozarians continued to populate their sparse little island if all the men were as soft and comely and demure as Master Ferwyn.

Though I taunted him alongside my friends, I inwardly marveled at Master Ferwyn. Through him, I learned how to speak the flowery Kenozarian language, so very different from the harsh, guttural tones of my mother tongue. I also learned about Kenozarian values and customs, and what they loved and feared. He taught me about their two gods—the lovers Keno, the river god, and Zaria, the goddess of the mountain—and their love that had created everything we see and hear and touch.

Master Ferwyn taught me to interact with nature rather than attempt to subdue it. I learned to hear the music in a river, to appreciate the silence at dawn. He also taught me to admire the unique, subtle magic of a woman's mind, rather than breaking her spirit like so many of the men around me often did. By watching him, I learned the importance of giving myself a few moments to consider my options instead of reacting in anger, like my father did.

When I reached my twentieth year, grown enough for battle, it was determined that I had learned all I could from my simple tutor, so my father saw fit to end Master Ferwyn's life.

"We can't have him escaping and informing the Kenozarians of our intentions," he said when I dared to question his decision. When he saw how much it bothered me, he scoffed. "You'll have to become comfortable killing friend and foe alike if you are to fulfill your destiny, son."

In short, I have been preparing for this moment all my life.

After we'd settled into camp and everyone had feasted—if salted pork and sprouted grains with warm ale could be called a feast—one of the members of the Shield came to our tent.

"The Torch would like a word with the captain," he said, addressing Draven as he opened the tent flap.

"And the Torch shall have what he requests," Draven replied happily, pushing my uniform coat into my chest as I exited the tent.

As the Shield and I walked through the camp, I got a better look at the surroundings. The plain we were camped on was butted against a ridge of high, jagged cliffs. I could just make out shrubbery on the cliffside in the faint light of the setting sun. I knew, thanks to Master Ferwyn's drawings of the island, that the Keno River lay half a day's march east, and the village and sacred mountain not much further.

My thoughts came to a halt along with my body when we arrived at Akkar's tent.

"Lukin! Oh, what a pleasure it is to see you, Nephew!" Akkar beamed when I entered the tent, embracing me and standing on his tiptoes to kiss my cheeks. After he sat back down in his chair, I took the seat he offered me opposite his desk.

He had stripped off his armor and finery and sat wearing a simple wine-red tunic and pants. In the candlelight, he looked more tired and worn than ever. His caramel skin gathered in bags under his dark eyes.

"The hour is late, Uncle" I began. "We could talk strategy in the morning if you prefer?"

Akkar flung my suggestion away in the air with his hand. "Nonsense. I'm a spring chicken! Rhys, be blessed!"

"Rhys, be praised," I replied in the customary way.

Akkar poured me a glass of wine. The Torch of Branngard is forbidden from partaking, but it doesn't stop him from lavishing it on others. "We'll begin our march tomorrow just after sunset. It will be a full moon, so they'll be gathered together atop the mountain for their heathen festivities. It's the perfect time for a surprise arrival."

I nodded in agreement.

"Now, let us discuss what we shall do once we've properly intro-duced ourselves to the villagers, shall we?" Akkar asked. "Your tutor, before his unfortunate death, told us of their easy way of welcoming guests to their shores."

Unfortunate death was one way to put it. "And if they *aren't* pleased to see us?" I asked.

"We are here to brighten their dark lives, to teach them a better way to live!"

By whose standards? I couldn't help but think of Master Ferwyn and his humility and kindness, but I decided against speaking my thoughts. "Yes, Uncle," I replied, then took another sip of wine.

"Most such heathen peoples are not so inclined to change their way of life, it's true. Unfortunate, but true. Still, we won't give up on them so easily."

"Yes, Uncle."

Akkar sat for a moment, pondering. "How much do you know about the origin of Branngard, Lukin?"

"About as much as the next sailor, I'd say."

"Oh, no! That won't do!" Akkar scolded me. "You are a Velga, my boy! You must know much more!"

"Yes, Uncle."

"Go on now. Tell me what you *do* know."

"Well, I know the peoples of the world lived in chaos and fear and darkness before Rhys revealed His Truth to the first Torch, who wrote His words in *Rhysvox*, which gave us order and stability." That line has been drilled into me since I was old enough to repeat the words, just as it has been for every Branngardian child.

He smiled. "Yes, but do you know *how* Rhys brought the Light?"

I shook my head.

"Before the time of man, the earth and the sky and the sea were ruled by a host of gods and goddesses," Akkar began. "Rhys was one of the gods of the earth—the god of fire and light. One summer day, Rhys saw a beautiful sea nymph dancing across the waves and fell instantly in love with her. Her name was Ilaria, and she was well-known for her predilection for seducing earth gods and never allowing herself to succumb to them. Rhys cleverly succeeded in wooing her, but before she would give herself to him, she made him promise her one thing: to never stop her from going to the sea when she wanted to, without question."

Here, Akkar snapped his fingers at a Shield, who came near and bent down to receive his orders before turning promptly and leaving the tent, then returning with a priest. When the priest entered the tent, he bowed low in greeting to the Torch, ignoring my presence, then walked behind Akkar to lift *Rhysvox* from its pillow. He ambled back around and kneeled, dropping his head in reverence as he held the book up to Akkar.

Akkar took the book from the priest and dismissed him, then began searching for the correct passage, thumbing delicately through the yellowed pages of *Rhysvox*. I sat for a moment, pondering on the theatrics of that little display, all of which could have been expediently avoided had Akkar simply stood up and retrieved the book on his own. But damn me and my cold impiety, as Draven would say.

"Delirious with love for her, Rhys agreed to her demands, and the two of them set up their home far from the sea, where Rhys could work his fire magic," Akkar began once he'd found the page he was looking for. "The two lived in pleasure and companionship for many years, wiling away their eternal days in conjugal bliss. But one winter day, as the sun god raced to bed early, Ilaria made her request: she needed to visit the sea and promised to return by spring.

"Remembering his oath to her, Rhys refrained from asking any questions. He embraced her and sent her on her way. But as the days grew shorter and darker, Rhys became more and more agitated. *Why must she go to the sea after all this time? What—or who—is calling her there?* he wondered. He tried to busy himself with his work, but after a month, he could no longer hold back his fury and decided to look for her and settle his mind, once and for all.

"'You are my lover, and I am yours,' Rhys called out as he approached the sea. 'Come to me and let us away, back to our home!' But Ilaria did not appear atop the waves. Once more, Rhys called out to his beloved, beckoning her to join him. When she still did not come, his anger and jealousy were aroused. 'I shall decimate the sea to show her the error of her ways,' Rhys declared. With that, he set the sea ablaze. Within moments, all the creatures of the sea and even the sea gods began rising out of the foam, roasting alive."

Here, Akkar paused for effect, so I tried to appear invested.

"Ilaria came to him finally, but not from the sea. Rhys turned to see her standing behind him, hand in hand with Ghan, the sky god of rain and wind. Upon seeing them together, Rhys exploded in a fit of fury so powerful it annihilated all living things, including Ilaria and all the other gods.

"For millennia, Rhys walked the dark plain of the earth alone, ruminating in his heartbreak. With each passing year, the rage and grief within him became stronger, increasing his power until, finally, he was ready to create a new world, even more beautiful than the one he had shared with Ilaria.

"He set upon his new world one people to rule all others, a people who would ensure his glory and renown were never forgotten again—a people who would spread his light far and wide and teach all others to honor his greatness. And he named them Branngard, the keepers of the flame."

Akkar stopped reading from *Rhysvox* and turned to beckon the priest back from where he stood, waiting in the far corner of the tent. He rushed over, bowed again, then took the book from Akkar and placed it again on its velvet pillow before exiting the tent.

"So you see, Nephew, we are a people of *fire*, a jealous people, a passionate people. It is our responsibility to ensure all who walk the earth know about the glory and might of Rhys, the one true god, and it's one we do not take lightly."

I had finished my glass of wine. That and the march made me weary, and I longed for the relative comfort of my cot. I wished he would just let me leave.

"Rhys prefers to woo people with the warmth of his words. But just as any flame can warm a home or cook a meal, it can also decimate a home or even an entire village, should it get out of control. Rhys is not afraid to use force to get his point across, and we mustn't be, either!"

"Yes, Uncle," I said as I turned to leave.

"Honey first, but vinegar always does the trick. That's my policy," Akkar added as I took my leave. "Rhys, be blessed!"

"Rhys, be praised," I replied, bowing to him and heading out into the night.

"So," Draven began when I entered our tent, "do we have our orders then?" Next to Draven sat Tygan, a fellow soldier I've known since we were boys. Both extended their arms to greet me when I sat down.

"We do, indeed," I replied. "We will march tomorrow, come sunset."

"Rhys, be praised!" Draven cried out joyously.

"Rhys, be blessed," we echoed.

Tygan handed me a cup of ale, which I pushed away. "I fear I've had my fill of drink tonight, and of stories, too."

"Did the Torch tell ya stories then? Good ones?" Draven asked.

"An interesting one," I replied, yawning and stretching.

Tygan seemed to get the message that I wasn't interested in further elaboration, so he changed the subject. "You must be thrilled to get this campaign over with and return to your beautiful betrothed."

"Selise *is* beautiful, to be sure," I replied, running both hands through my shaggy hair to push it out of my face. "But..."

"But what?" Tygan asked.

"Well, we don't have much in common. She hates the outdoors and has no desire to see more of the world, and I don't much care for the endless parties and balls she wants to drag me to. I just... I wonder if we'll have much to talk about."

Draven let out a deep belly laugh. "Captain Lukin is worried he may not have anything to *talk* about with his betrothed!" Soon, he was cackling, throwing his head back in glee.

I shifted uncomfortably in my seat.

"I'm sorry, me boy," Draven said once he'd caught his breath, wiping tears from the corner of his eyes. "Maybe it's me old age, but honestly, tell me, what can a *woman* know about anything of consequence? Why would you need to *talk* to her about anything at all? Why, I don't think I've said more than a hundred words to me own wife these thirty years!"

I held my tongue. I'd more easily convince a bird to swim than persuade Draven to see things my way. He's as old as my father was when he passed last year, and just as stubborn.

"Women are for keeping your cock warm and giving ya sons, that's what I say," Draven said, taking another drink of ale. "Lady Selise is healthy enough to bear your babes, and she's as beautiful as a painting and wealthier than any of us could dream of being, to boot! Let that be enough, dear Lukin."

"Well, *I* don't blame you, Captain," Tygan put in. "My wife is a blessing to us. She keeps me well-fed and well-loved. She's a great mother to my children, too. And I love jesting with her and listening to her ideas. She's clever as anything!"

"A clever woman?!" Draven scoffed. "Lukin, listen to old Draven. Buy the lady whatever she wants, plow her well and often, smile at her from time to time, and you'll both be happy enough."

"I suppose you're right," I said. Because I couldn't tell them about the countless days I've spent in utter joy, just talking with Nora, or exploring the cairn and its grounds. I couldn't tell them how precocious she is or about how she cried when I told her my uncle had arranged my marriage to Selise or how she begged me to keep her as a mistress—something my father had made sure to prevent by sending her away as soon as he caught wind of our affair.

"A whore is a whore is a whore, son," my father said when he found me despondent after she was gone. "You'll marry the lady Selise and forget all about that kitchen wench. And once you've put a Velga boy in your wife's belly, you can have whatever whore you want!"

But Nora was no whore. She had been a servant in the cairn since I was a boy—just like her parents—and she was the first woman I'd ever savored when manhood awoke within me. Even now, I feel safe and warm and full when I think of her.

"'Course I'm right!" Draven said, slapping me on the thigh and bringing me back to the moment. "Now survive this bloody campaign and marry her. I promise you'll laugh at yourself later for these silly misgivings."

I thanked him for the advice, attempting to sound sincere.

"Think of it! Worried what he'd *talk* about with a woman!" Draven laughed.

That night, it took hours for all three hundred men to find a way up the cliffs. A few soldiers were scraped and bruised, but all were in one piece when we stood at the top and regrouped.

By the light of the moon and our torches, we marched inland. The flatlands beyond the cliff gave way to rolling meadows until we finally reached the Keno River. Several meters across, Keno's waters, though not rapid, run deep. Just past the river lay a small village laden with darkness. Beyond the village, a dark mountain rose high into the air, covered in pine trees—*Mount Zaria.* I could just barely make out the color of flames dancing atop it.

As the army began fording the river, Tygan caught up to me and pointed out something on the other side: a child, not older than ten, hiding in the reeds. He was carrying something shiny, reflecting the moonlight. It could have been a weapon, but he looked frightened and confused.

Perfect, I thought. *Just what we need—a child screaming and alerting the others.*

Before I could warn my men to ignore the boy, one of them fired a lighted arrow straight at him, hitting him deep in the chest. He cried out in pain just as the arrow pierced his skin, then fell into the river.

As I turned to see if anyone had been alerted by the child's cry, the mountaintop lit up with dozens of flames bobbing down the mountain toward us. So we forded the river, torches ablaze. I hoped that Akkar would still try his honey method.

4

Evryn

"Don't cry out," he says from behind me, holding his blade to my throat. His accent is thick and foreign. He smells of sea and smoke and sweat.

I freeze, raising my hands.

"Good," he says, lowering his blade. "You are Evryn Korina, yes?"

I try to slow my breathing and think. He isn't Kenozarian; that much is clear. I've never heard an accent like his. Plus, I can't imagine anyone on the island being bold enough to invade us like this, not at the risk of challenging Korina Freya. So why is he here? What does he want with me? I could lie and risk angering him when he finds out the truth or disclose my identity and risk whatever he plans to do to Evryn Korina.

I nod.

"Now, listen. I'm going to tie your hands behind your back. Please don't cry out when I move my hand. I won't harm you. You have my word."

I obey and move my wrists behind my back.

Aunt Tabitha, what is happening? What should I do? I ask the ether. Still nothing.

He moves his hand from my mouth and sheathes his dagger, then begins briskly tying my wrists together with rope. After testing the knot's strength a few times, he helps me to my feet, and I turn to face him.

Before me stands a man, slightly taller than me, with a lithe, muscular build. A plumage of yellow, red, and orange feathers sits atop his helm. Beneath, he has hair the color of rust and a beard of the same hue, graying in places. His eyes are a deep green, like the leaves in mid-summer. A flame is emblazoned across his bronze breastplate. Beneath his armor, he's wearing a mustard tunic with fitted breeches and aged leather boots. Along with the dagger he held to my throat, he has a bow strung across his chest and a long, curved sword in its scabbard at his side.

I eye him suspiciously, unsure of what his next move is.

"Don't be afraid. I'm taking you down the mountain to the sea. My leader only wishes to speak with you."

To speak with me? *Me?*

He hooks his hand in the crook of my arm. "Is there another way down to the sea that doesn't pass by the village?"

I nod and start walking ahead of him, down and around the mountain's northwest side.

Moments turn to hours, and before I know it, we've reached the bottom of the northwestern ridge. As we leave the woods, we enter a wide clearing. The River Keno is not far off, and beyond that, the sea.

He's quietly scanning the horizon, obscured as it is by the morning mist.

"Who are you, anyway?" I ask after a beat.

He seems surprised to hear me finally speak. "My name is Lukin Velga. I'm the captain of the Branngardian army," he says, bowing his head, placing his right hand on his chest, and then extending it to me. *So he knows our customs.* "Why are you here, you and your army?" I ask, returning the greeting.

"We'll make camp here tonight," he says, not answering my question. He removes his cotton neck guard and wipes the sweat from his brow before opening his leather water bag and taking a few long drinks. Having quenched his thirst, he wipes his mouth with the backside of his fist and sighs in relief. "Water?" he offers.

I chuckle and turn to show him the rope binding my arms behind my back.

"Here, I'll help you. Come," he says.

When I step closer, he opens the water bag and tips it, pouring some water into my mouth, though most of it lands on my linen shirt.

"It's almost nightfall. We need to gather some firewood," he says.

"Again. Bound wrists."

"Right," he says, taking out his knife. "Turn around."

I eye him again.

"I'm not gonna hurt you. Just turn around."

I do, and he cuts the knot. I think he may free me, but then he ties my wrists together again in front of me.

"You kidnap me and then expect me to *help you?*" I ask as he tightens the new knot.

"It's up to you," he replies, shrugging. He briefly looks into my eyes before looking away. "The longer it takes to get this fire going, the longer we'll sit here freezing."

I'm frustrated, but he's right. Nightfall is near, and it gets cold this close to the sea. There's no point in freezing to spite him, so I head back into the woods.

The thought occurs to me that I could run, but I'm weary from the hike down the mountain and still have neither water nor food, plus my hands are bound and I don't want to test his marksmanship with that bow. So, I gather firewood and grumble to myself. It's not easy with bound wrists, but I manage to gather some dried grass and broken branches.

When I return, Lukin is sitting next to a ring of stones he set up for the campfire. I drop the kindling and branches in the center of the ring and clumsily attempt to sit on the ground. Lukin makes no attempt to help. Instead, he takes a flint from his knapsack and gets busy.

Before long, there is a crackling campfire before us. As he nurses it along, I get a better look at him. The sides and back of his head are shaved to the skin while the fiery red hair on top hangs long, past his ears. He stops from time to time to move it out of his face before finally tying it back with a bit of leather.

"What sort of game do you have around here?" he asks, interrupting my thoughts. He's rubbing his hands together over the fire to warm them. "I saw a few small rodents but not much else."

"The prairies on the other side of the island have more game than here. The biggest thing in these woods is a doe, maybe a buck, if you're up for the challenge," I reply.

He scratches his beard in thought. "I'll go see what I can find." He stands and picks up his bow and quiver of arrows. They're fletched with the same bright yellow, orange, and red of the plumage on his helm. "Please, don't flee. I'll just have to hunt you down again, and we're both too tired for that, yes?" With that, he turns and heads into the woods.

Finally left alone with my thoughts, I ponder what awaits me, awaits *us*. I have read enough to know what happens when a foreign army arrives unannounced. Whatever they're doing here, it can't be good news for Kenozaria.

And why have Aunt Tabitha and Papa gone quiet *now*, of all times? After having spent my life being guided by their wisdom and plagued by their unsolicited advice, it's unnerving to reach out and hear *nothing* when I need their guidance the most.

Before long, Lukin comes tramping back out of the woods, dragging a few large branches behind him. There's a small rabbit slung over his shoulder, its blood dripping down his armor. He drops the branches, sits next to the fire, and begins cleaning the rabbit. The silence between us—and from beyond the Veil—helps to enhance the sounds of the summer night. Toads near the river bellow their call, and owls come alive as the night sky darkens.

"Why have you come here? What do you want?" I ask him again.

Lukin slides the rabbit onto a stick and positions it on two y-branches above the fire, then gets to work chopping up the tree branches with a small ax he takes from his satchel.

"I thought you spoke my language?"

"As I said, I'm taking you to our leader, the Torch of Branngard. You can ask him all you wish to know when you meet him tomorrow."

"*Me?* It's my mother you should speak with."

He nods, adding the branches to the fire and sitting down to turn the spit. "She's nowhere to be found."

Nowhere to be found? Panic is burning in my chest.

"Your siblings weren't exactly helpful, so I was sent to find you in hopes you'd speak on your mother's behalf."

"And my siblings. Are they safe?"

"Oh, yes. Not to worry. No blood was spilled last night, I assure you."

"No blood was spilled? But we heard a child cry out—"

"Yes, I apologize," he says, cutting me off. "He was… collateral damage. My men mistook him for a lookout when they saw him in the reeds next to the river. He looked to be carrying a weapon."

Søren. It had to be Søren. The boy has a habit of strolling by the river late at night, searching for toads to capture, much to his parents' chagrin.

"He wasn't a lookout," I reply. "He was only a boy, probably hunting for toads. That was a *net* he carried."

Lukin sighs and turns the rabbit over. "I apologize. It wasn't intentional."

We sit in silence until the rabbit is finished cooking. Lukin pulls the spit out of the fire and lets the meat cool a bit before passing it to me. I'm starving, but I hesitate. It's rude to eat before the one who cooked the meal.

"Please, I insist," he says, pushing the steaming meat closer to me.

I am too hungry to refuse a second time, so I take it from him and eat my fill.

"I only have one tent, unfortunately," he says, pulling a big swath of fabric out of his satchel and shaking it out.

"It wouldn't be the first time I spent a night under the stars," I reply. Why would he be so generous with food but so stingy with shelter?

"What? No. I meant it's for you. *You* sleep in the tent. I don't mind sleeping in the open. It's safer that way," he continues, "in case we should have any unwanted guests in the night, I mean."

"We could always share the tent. You *are* a trustworthy person, aren't you?"

He coughs loudly like he's uncomfortable. "Ah, no. I mean, yes! I am! But... that's... I'm fine out here. Really."

"Well if you change your mind, there's plenty of room." It's entertaining to see this man, a seasoned warrior, acting so coy around a woman. I can't imagine what sort of place he comes from.

After he's set up the tent, he ushers me inside. "Sleep well," he says before turning to reclaim his spot beside the fire.

"You, too," I reply, stepping inside. He laid out a rough blanket for me to cover with and placed a folded, thick woolen shirt at the end as a pillow. One could almost call it *cozy*. I lie down and close my eyes, listening to the sounds of the fire crackling and Lukin humming to himself.

I'm running through the forest again, but Torek is with me this time. "Faster, Evryn!" he says, dragging me behind him.

As we run on, the temperature begins to drop as we get farther and farther from the mountain.

"We have to get to that fire! Just a bit farther," Torek cries, pointing at a light looming in the distance, like a campfire someone has left burning.

But when we arrive at the source of the light, it's not a fire at all, but a newborn girl lying on the ground in swaddling clothes, her skin radiating the same amber glow we all do during our Bright ceremonies. The cold does not seem to affect the child, who lies still, calmly surveying her surroundings.

Torek picks her up from the frozen ground, but I can't see what she looks like, because now she is glowing brighter than the sun.

"Evryn, the Light," she says, "you must focus on the Light. Make it grow!"

5

Lukin

Betweeen the cold and the strange noises of a strange place, sleep was all but a hopeless cause. So just before sunrise, I gave up and sat next to the smoldering fire, wrapped in my heavy cloak. The firewood pile was getting low, and I wanted to check the trap I'd set last night, so I headed back out into the woods.

Now, as I sit next to the fire cleaning the squirrel I found in the trap, I overhear Evryn climbing out of the tent.

"Good morning," I say. "Come, break your fast by the fire." She nods and comes to join me.

As Evryn eats, I busy myself with packing up the tent. I can't help but look at her from time to time, stealing glances when I can. Her dark auburn hair is messy from sleep. She's wearing a pine-green tunic, stained and torn, and some dark pants. She looks around at the morning scene and rubs her eyes, then stands to stretch after she's finished eating.

"We should get going," I say, dousing the fire and slinging my satchel across my shoulders. "Lead the way, Ms. Korina."

"Don't call me that," she half laughs. "It's Evryn. Just Evryn."

"I apologize," I say, bowing my head slightly. "Could you please guide us to the river, Evryn? I can find our way from there."

"That's better, Captain," she says, mockingly tipping her head at me and heading due west.

As we walk on, I think about what will happen when we arrive at camp. What will Akkar say to—or *do* to—Evryn? What's been happening in the village while I've been away? Is Akkar's honey method working, or has he switched to vinegar?

"You said you're taking me to meet your leader, the... what did you call him?" Evryn asks, interrupting my thoughts.

"The Torch of Branngard."

"Does he not have a name?"

I chuckle to myself. "Yes, his name is Akkar."

"So why do you call him 'the Torch'?"

"Because he's the head of our country and our faith. He speaks for our god, Rhys."

She seems surprised. "Your *god*? You only have one?"

I recall my conversation with Akkar that evening in his tent about how Rhys had killed off all the other gods in his rage. "Yes, well... there used to be many gods. But now, there is only Rhys. And the Torch speaks for Rhys."

"I see," she replies quietly.

"Do your gods speak to you?" I ask.

Evryn looks at me for a long moment. "Something like that," she says.

By mid-day, we're close to the Branngardian camp. All that stands between us is a few miles of grassland and the wide river. The air smells more and more like seawater the closer we come.

Evryn walks along beside me in silence. Were it Selise or even Nora by my side, I'd have been expected to entertain them incessantly. But

Evryn seems unfazed by me, uninterested in arousing my attention or keeping it at bay. It's almost as if I'm not even there.

My thoughts are interrupted by a tree branch snapping somewhere ahead of us. I look around for the source but see nothing. Evryn grabs my hand and points her chin at a group of trees and brush, so I follow her in that direction. We squat down in the underbrush, waiting. I slowly pull an arrow from my quiver and nock it against my bowstring.

Before long, a man comes strolling into the open grasslands. His breastplate bears the flame of Branngard, but I can't tell who he is. Soon, he's joined by two other men, arguing.

"Captain Lukin left days ago! He's not coming back! They've beheaded him or chopped off his cock for stew," one says.

"Nonsense!" Tygan replies. "Captain Lukin could best any man in Branngard, and you think a savage from this backwater has a chance?"

"Will you two half-wits shut your traps?!" the first man whisper-yells.

Draven. His voice is unmistakable.

"Those are my men. They're looking for us," I whisper to Evryn. She looks warily at the group of men but slowly rises with me anyway.

"What are you lot doing roaming these parts?" I ask, walking out of the treeline with Evryn by my side.

"Captain!" Tygan calls out when he sees me.

"You gave us a real scare!" Draven says, embracing me. "I'm so glad you're well. And it seems you've caught yourself a little captive, is it?"

"Not a captive, no. This is Evryn Korina, the daughter of the chief of Kenozaria. I'm accompanying her back to camp. Akkar wants to speak with her."

Draven smiles broadly. "Och, forgive me! It's a pleasure to make your acquaintance, me lady," he says in broken Kenozarian, bowing.

Evryn smiles in return but says nothing. I wonder if she's able to understand his thick accent.

"Let's get back to the camp," Tygan says, "if it please you, Captain."

"Yes, let's," I reply, giving Evryn a reassuring smile.

Within an hour, we've reached the great river, Keno. It moves as slowly as the night before and is just as wide and deep.

"Is there another spot we can cross?" I ask Evryn. "Somewhere narrower?"

Evryn shakes her head. "No, it's this wide or wider all the way to Salix."

"What do you think, Draven?" I sigh, wiping the sweat from my brow.

Draven looks at Evryn as if he doesn't trust what she's said. "If we had more time, I'd send these two to scout north and south for a narrower crossing. But we're losing daylight. I say we ford here."

"Are we going to cross or...?" Evryn asks, standing from where she had been squatting on her haunches while we conferred in Branngardian.

Draven shoots me a look, but I ignore him and follow Evryn as she steps into the river, with Draven, Tygan, and the other young soldier taking up the rear.

We are wading through the low, steady waters, balancing on the boulders in the riverbed. But when we are halfway across the river, the water suddenly rises and the current picks up rapidly, pulling us hard south. I look ahead for Evryn, worried she'll be carried away, but she is walking deftly through the rising current as easily as if it were solid ground.

"Lukin!" Draven cries out. "The lad!" I turn to see the young soldier bobbing in the water, struggling to find his footing.

Somehow, Evryn is the first to reach him. Her wrists are still bound in front of her, and he's twice her size and wearing armor, but she works against the current, pulling him up. We rush to her aid, helping the young soldier to his feet, then we link arms to get across to the other bank.

The young soldier falls to the ground when we get to the riverbank, coughing and spurting water.

"You're fine, lad. That's right. Take a deep breath. Good lad. You gave us a right scare!" Draven says, helping him remove his armor and slapping him hard on the back.

"What happened?" Tygan remarks. "How could the river just... *do that*?! It rose so quickly!"

"It happens," Evryn remarks, like it's perfectly normal for a river to suddenly rise above its banks and fall, just as quickly.

"You really saved the day back there. If you hadn't gotten to him so fast..." I say.

"Keno did not claim him because it is not his time," she responds simply, wringing water out of her tunic.

I'm speechless. Even when she saves a man's life, she declines to take credit.

We finally arrive at the edge of the Branngardian encampment just after nightfall. As we approach the barricade, the guards step aside to let us through. Then we are ushered into the large tent in the center of the camp, where the Torch of Branngard is waiting.

6

Evryn

When the guards lead us inside the Torch of Branngard's tent, I expect to see a king or a demigod, or at least an incredibly intimidating specimen of a man, from how Lukin had described him. Instead, there's only a little man sitting at a little desk, his dark head bent down in studying an open book.

When he sees us enter, the man looks up, taking a moment to assess the group of us gathered in his tent. He smiles and shouts something in his language, and the others echo it.

"May I introduce Evryn Korina," Lukin says in Kenozarian, bowing his head respectfully.

The little man approaches, smiling up at me. "Welcome! It is such a great honor to meet you, my dear," he says, inviting us to sit in a set of chairs arranged around a small table. "You didn't make it easy to find you, I must say!" His Kenozarian is even more impressive than Lukin's.

"It's a much larger island than we thought, Uncle," Lukin says, pouring three cups of steaming liquid from a pot on the table.

"Indeed," the Torch replies, handing me a cup before taking a quick sip from his own.

"I did not know I was wanted," I reply, taking a sip from my cup. It's a peculiarly spiced tea, rich and hot and sweet. It warms my entire body, which is a welcome change after the cold and stress of last night.

"What matters is you're here now, and we must speak about... well, our little situation here. I assume my nephew has told you about our country and my position as the Torch?"

I nod and take another sip before placing the cup back on the table. "Yes, he has. But I don't understand why I've been summoned, or why you and your army are here in the first place. You didn't send an envoy or my mother would have told us."

Akkar is taken aback. "What a direct young lady you are. Rhys, be praised! I like that. So, I'll be direct with you in return."

"Your Holiness," Lukin interrupts, "may I suggest we provide the lady with a change of clothes and a hot meal before we begin discussing such matters? It's been a long and arduous journey, with very little rest and even less food."

"You are most correct, Lukin!" Akkar says. "Please see that our guest is comfortably dressed and fed. Pomisha and her ladies will be happy to help Ms. Korina, I'm sure."

"Yes, Your Holiness," Lukin says, bowing.

"You'll have to forgive my poor manners," Akkar says, addressing me. "I shall see you in the morning. You will break your fast with me?" His tone makes it clear this is *not* an invitation.

"Yes, of course," I reply, then Lukin takes my arm and leads me out of the tent.

As we walk south across the camp, I see men walking and chatting together as other men sharpen their swords, and still others practice their archery skills. There are men arguing with one another, men grappling, men full-on fighting. There are men everywhere, but not a woman in sight.

41

"You said you're taking me to the women?" I ask.

"Yes, we're nearly there."

After some time, we come up to the southernmost edge of the encampment. Every other tent in the encampment is bleached a stark white, but these are wine-red. That's when I finally see the women.

A few dozen are milling about, and they do not look well. Two are fighting over what looks to be a chunk of bread, while another sits outside a tent, her clothing disheveled and filthy.

"What's *wrong* with them?" I ask.

"Oh, these women are the... *entertainment*," he replies uncomfortably.

I understand exactly what he means. Some in our society have made it their career to pleasure others, but it's always a choice they've made willingly. They find it healing to provide comfort and pleasure to other people, and they're respected and cared for members of the community. These women couldn't *possibly* have chosen this vocation, suffering as they are.

"But why are they so... *unwell?*"

"Akkar doesn't exactly approve of their presence. He says they are a shameful drain on our resources, so they depend on the soldiers to share their rations with them."

"And your uncle sent me *here* to rest and be fed?" I ask, worried. These women don't even have enough food for themselves, let alone more to spare for me.

"Oh, no! No, not *these* women. Pomisha's tent is just here," he says, pointing at a much larger tent, set some distance apart from the others, at the top of a hill.

As we approach, we are greeted by guards standing shoulder-to-shoulder around the perimeter of the tent. Whomever Pomisha is, the Torch is clearly dedicated to keeping her inside and everyone else out.

Lukin speaks briefly to one of the guards, who bows his head in acquiescence and moves aside, opening the tent for me to enter. I step inside, but Lukin lingers back.

"No men allowed," he says. "Pomisha will send for me in the morning when you're ready to break your fast with the Torch."

"You won't be joining us?"

"No, I'm afraid I have other matters to attend to. I'll escort you to him in the morning and then be on my way. Blessed eve," Lukin says curtly.

As he walks away, the guard he had spoken to calls into the tent, and a young woman adorned in a burgundy robe flits past me to talk with him, then heads back behind a curtain, leaving me standing there in the antechamber. A few moments later, she beckons me to follow her.

Soft fabrics adorn lush furniture all around the central chamber. Braziers burn in every corner of the tent, offering both heat and light, and heavy incense fills the air. Plates heaped with food sit on tables throughout the room. It's even more richly adorned than Akkar's tent.

On a chaise at the back of the chamber, I see a woman whom I can only assume must be Pomisha. Soft, bouncy ringlets frame her umber face and drip down her shoulders. On both wrists hang a plethora of golden bangles, and more gold hangs from her ears, nose, and throat. The light of the braziers reflects off her golden robe. She is incandescent.

Having noticed my entrance, her maidens stand in greeting. Pomisha stands then, too, her jewelry tinkling and her long robe swishing this way and that as she moves toward me. That's when I notice the heavy golden shackles on her ankles, with just enough length of chain between them to offer her the ability to take half a stride. Still, there is an elegance about the way she carries herself, an air of pride in her posture.

As she approaches, I get a better look at her. She seems to be roughly Mother's age, with fine lines wrinkling the space around her midnight eyes, which glow behind the heavy kohl that encircles them.

She begins to speak to me in a language I can't understand, one that doesn't sound like Lukin's language either. Her ladies snicker at the look of confusion on my face. She hushes them and orders something, causing one of her ladies to step forward, carrying a pitcher of water and a bowl.

The young woman takes me to a corner of the tent, full of pillows and rich, brocaded fabrics, and invites me to sit. She pours the water over my hands into the bowl. Having rinsed the dirt from my hands, I also splash some cool water on my face. Another of her ladies brings me a platter overflowing with fruit and nuts, some of which are native to the island and others I have never seen in my life.

All the while, Pomisha sits on her chaise, looking amused by the scene playing out before her. I wonder what she is thinking, what she imagines the Torch intended in sending me to her.

Having had my fill, I stand. "I need to relieve myself," I say. No one seems to understand what I'm saying, so I squat and put my hands on my stomach, scowling in pain while making grunting noises. They burst into laughter, but at least they understand now. Finally, one of them leads me to the entrance and explains the situation to a guard, who promptly leads me out to a section of the woods far enough away from the camp for privacy but not so far that I could easily escape.

I squat for a long while, thinking, begging someone, *anyone* to tell me what to do. Aunt Tabitha was clever as a fox. She'd know how to slip out in a hurry. Papa would counsel patience and careful action. My old friend, Moira—who died of a sudden fever when we were eight years old—would advise me to do whatever was most surprising, to keep them on their toes. Still, no one responds.

After I have relieved myself, I return to the tent and am, once more, invited to wash my hands. Having done so, I am ushered into the smaller chamber at the back of the tent—Pomisha's personal chamber. In the center of the room sits a large, plush bed, covered in pillows and animal skins and heavy woolen blankets. Pomisha's ladies are pouring pitchers of steaming water into a large washbasin to the right of the bed.

Pomisha turns to me and says something which must mean, *Get undressed*, because her ladies approach and gently begin helping me to remove my filthy clothing, which they then toss into the brazier. When I am stripped bare, Pomisha excuses her ladies, who bow and pass wordlessly back into the center chamber of the tent.

I step into the washbasin and slowly sit down in the hot water. It feels *heavenly*, like an embrace from a long-awaited friend. Mother has a washbasin in her room, but hot baths are a luxury reserved for special occasions, considering how much labor is required to haul water from the well and heat it in multiple pots on the stove. So more often than not, we bathe in the river, whose waters are never much above freezing. This bath is the height of luxury, all things considered.

"You must be exhausted," Pomisha says in perfect Kenozarian. Seeing the shock on my face, she laughs. "A lady has many secrets, sweet one."

I sit up in the washbasin, unsure how to respond. She could have been speaking to me in my own tongue all this time, could have rescued me from my embarrassment earlier, but chose not to. *What kind of game is she playing?* I silently ask Aunt Tabitha, who doesn't reply.

Pomisha reclines on her bed of furs. She's watching me, but I'm not sure what she expects me to do, so I lay my head back against the basin and relax in the water, massaging my aching muscles.

"You are a true beauty," she says, looking at me in her cool way from across the room. Her voice is sweet as honey, husky and warm.

"As are you," I reply.

"Do you know who I am?" she asks, cocking her head to the side and playing with one of the tendrils of hair dancing there.

"You are Pomisha?"

"Yes. I am Pomisha, of the Obsidian Isles. I am the Jewel of Branngard."

"It is an honor to meet you, then, Pomisha of the Obsidian Isles," I reply, bowing my head and placing my right hand on my chest.

"You are most welcome here, Evryn Korina," she offers with a wry grin. Noticing the surprise on my face, she continues. "I have heard nothing else from Akkar since we arrived on this land. 'We must find Evryn Korina! Bring me Evryn Korina!' he says, day and night, night and day." Her imitation of Akkar is humorously accurate, and I can't resist laughing. "And now, here you are, in my tent," Pomisha adds.

"And now, here I am," I reply, reaching for the pitcher on the side table.

Seeing this, Pomisha stands and walks to the basin, then takes a seat on the chair next to it. "Allow me?" she asks, taking the pitcher from me and filling it with water before pouring the water down the back of my head. After she's finished wetting my hair, she pours some sort of liquid into her hands from a vial on the table, then begins massaging it into my scalp. The sensation is delightful, and I relax even further.

"Are the Obsidian Isles part of Branngard?" I ask.

"No. They are far away, closer to here than there."

"I see. And how did you come to be... associated with Branngard?" I ask, carefully choosing my words.

"When I was a young girl, the Torch and his entourage came to my island one summer. Not Akkar, but his uncle, the Torch before him. Akkar was my age then, or a few years older."

46

"Oh? What brought them there?"

"The Obsidian Isles are known for their beauty, you see—both the landscape and the women," she says. "In that way, my island is not so very different from yours."

"It seems so," I reply.

"Akkar's father, the brother to the former Torch, befriended my papa when they were younger, and he would often bring Akkar to our home during his visits. There was nothing about him back then to signify greatness—aside from his bloodline, of course. He was weak and skinny and shy. To everyone else, he was a Velga boy, a prince. But to me, he was just Akkar, the annoying boy who threw rocks at my cat. But he also protected me when bigger, older boys picked on me, so we were something like friends."

As she speaks, she scrubs my skin with the cloth and rinses it with the pitcher of water.

"After some months, it was time for the Torch and his party to leave my island and return to Branngard. But before he left, Akkar's father paid my papa a handsome sum to take me with them. That's how I became one of the wards of the Torch, to be raised with Akkar and the other youths of the court at the capital, Rhys Domus. I never saw my family again."

I sit quietly listening as she pours water through my hair and down my back, rinsing out the suds.

"When I came of age, the Torch decreed that Rhys intended me to be the next Jewel of Branngard. So when Akkar's uncle died and Akkar came into power, I was officially set apart as the Jewel, his one and only permitted partner—or, the closest thing he will ever have to a partner." Here, she gestures to the chains on her ankles.

Somehow, I can't imagine Akkar having a concubine—especially not one as beautiful as Pomisha, considering how small and frail and unattractive he is—but I keep that thought to myself and try not to appear shocked. "I can't imagine it has been easy to be his lover, after having been raised alongside him. He's practically family, yes?"

"Yes, it was hard for me to make love to him at first," she says, faltering. "But, well, the Jewel does whatever she must to please the Torch."

"And it pleased him to teach you languages."

"Yes. It was important for me to know how to entertain foreign diplomats and other guests of Branngard, so he hired the best tutors for me. They taught me about the geography of the world and the customs of the people inhabiting the lands around us, as well as their languages. And I learned about the affairs of state, of war and strategy, among other things..." she says, trailing off.

Now, I understand the chains, the excess guards, the mystery maintained by the exclusion of men from her tent. Much more than a concubine, the Jewel of Branngard is a *weapon* of the Torch, one that must be both sharpened and sheathed until he has need of her. I begin to ponder on the deeper reasons he chose to send me to her instead of simply giving me a tent of my own for the night.

Pomisha stands and helps me out of the basin, then dries my body with a soft cloth. After I'm dry, she invites me to sit on the bed with her and begins massaging perfumed oils into my skin. Her hands are soft and supple, and her touch is electric. The energy emanating from her is intoxicating.

"You are to speak with Akkar in the morning?" she asks quietly as she begins to brush my hair.

I had nearly forgotten. "Yes," I reply. "I am hoping he will tell me why he has come to my island. And maybe he has more information on my mother's whereabouts."

Pomisha stops brushing my hair and leans close to me. "Do not trust him, sweetling," she whispers into my ear. "The Torch knows how to get what he wants, and I assure you, whatever he wants here is *not* in the best interests of your people."

I turn and look into her dark, sincere eyes. The comfort of our surroundings, the gold she wears, the luxurious fabrics she clothes herself with, the abundance of food and wine surrounding her and her ladies—none of it can make up for the fact that she is a prisoner, and has been since Akkar's father bought her from her own papa, so long ago.

"Thank you," I whisper.

Without another word, Pomisha stands and extinguishes the candles and lamps burning around the room. In the darkness, there's the swishing of fabric and the chinking of her gold jewelry. Then she lies down on the bed and tugs on my arm to pull me down too, wrapping me next to her under the furs. Her shackles, icy cold, knock against one another as she turns to face my back and embraces me. Her naked skin against mine is soft as silk, and she smells of exotic flowers.

For a little while, we lie together that way, breathing in unison. Then I feel her hot breath against my neck as she kisses the skin there. It's been six months since I've been touched like this, six months without the frenzy of desire burning within me now. I freeze, unsure how to respond. She is more enticing than any woman I've ever seen, but the thought occurs to me that this could all be an elaborate trap.

"I want you, Evryn Korina," she whispers, pressing her breasts into my back. As she kisses and caresses my neck and runs her hand down my body, I'm unable to resist.

I give in and turn to face her. She takes my face in her hands and kisses me, sweetly at first and then with more hunger. She lifts her thigh and moves my hand down her body, welcoming me. I slide my fingers up her thigh and find the warm spot there. She moans softly and presses herself against my hand. She sighs deeply as I take one heavy breast in hand and begin softly massaging the nipple.

As she relaxes further, I trail my tongue down her neck and find her nipple with my lips, sucking and tugging with my tongue as I continue massaging the skin around her throbbing yoni. She stops me and pulls my face up to hers, kissing me passionately and licking my lips playfully with her tongue, breathing heavily as I continue my rhythmic massaging. Then she flips me onto my back and pins my arms while she delicately kisses my thighs.

When she finds my sweet spot and begins gently licking and sucking, I forget all about Kenozaria and Mother and Akkar and Branngard and Torek. I fade into euphoria as I shake and moan with pleasure. I don't care whether she's a slave or a weapon or a trap or all three. I only know one thing: I want more of her.

I'm vaguely aware of her ladies in the next room, separated from us by a thin curtain, but she doesn't seem to mind, so I don't. We pass the night in each other's arms, eventually succumbing to divine exhaustion.

I awake just after sunrise, alone in Pomisha's bed. The guards outside the tent are shouting. More and more voices come running. Something is wrong.

I hastily throw on the clothing that has been laid out for me on the table next to the bed and head out into the bright morning air.

Mere feet from the tent lies the body of Pomisha of the Obsidian Isles, the Jewel of Branngard, with a dagger sticking out of her belly. Her blood is soaking into the earth, staining her golden robes the same wine-red as her tent.

7

Korina

Every muscle in my body aches. There's a dull pain rippling out from a scabbed-over gash in the thin skin of my temple. Though I feel chilled to the bone, a thin film of sweat hangs on my brow. My lips are chapped, and my tongue scrapes like sandpaper against the fleshy softness of my cheeks.

"Water," I call out to whoever is near, their face blurred in my vision.

My caretaker pours a cup of water from the metal flagon on the table near my bed and gently puts the cup to my lips, helping me to drink. Some water dribbles down my chin, so my companion wipes it away gently.

A flash of memory hits me. A child crying out in the village, scrambling down the mountain in the moonlight, searing pain, and then darkness. Nothing but darkness.

"Where are my children?" I ask anxiously.

"Safe at home, Korina," the voice says. At least they know who I am.

I relax back into the bed—someone's bed, somewhere, that I've been lying in for some indeterminate period of time.

"I'll just go gather some more firewood," my companion says.

I whimper in response and reach out to grab their arm but grasp only air.

"Relax," they reassure me. "I won't be gone long, and if you need anything, call out. One of the others will come to help you. They're just outside the door."

I drop my hand back to the bed and close my eyes. When I open them again sometime later, I can feel the fire in the hearth burning at the foot of my bed.

"Shall we try to eat? The stew is watery but filling. And it doesn't taste too bad, either."

As I feel the spoon against my lips, I suck the stew down, chewing on bits of meat and potato before swallowing. When I've had my fill, I turn my face away.

"Where am I?" I ask.

My caretaker stands and adds another log to the fire. "You're safe in Salix," he says.

Salix? Why on earth am I here, of all places? Salix is the *last* place I ever want to see again.

"What happened? Who—"

My caretaker cuts me off. "I'll explain everything in the morning. For now, rest."

And so I do.

When I awake—it could have been a day or ten that I lay sleeping, for all I know—my vision is much improved. The fever has dissipated, too.

I look around at the room I lie in. The furnishings are sparse, but personal touches are sprinkled throughout, and the furniture is well lived-in. In front of me, the fire in the hearth is burning gently. To my right stands a window hung with simple white curtains. Through it, I see the overcast sky full of thick, dark clouds pouring rain down on the verdant green beyond.

Someone opens the door and steps inside. "Good morning," he says, removing his overcoat and muddy boots. He carries a basket with a few tan eggs and some fresh bread. As he turns to approach me, my heart stops.

"*Torek?!*"

My mind races, trying to make sense of the situation. *Am I dead?* Yes, I must be dead. There's no other explanation.

"But how?"

He comes to my side, helping me sit up in bed. "I'll cook these eggs, and then let's enjoy our breakfast, yes? There will be time for explanations later."

I'm too weak to protest, so I close my eyes and travel back in time to that winter. I see Evryn's sorrowful face, the pit of grief that engulfed her and stole her light—all of it based on a lie. Here is Torek, in the flesh, cooking eggs in an iron skillet.

"Let's get some food in you," he says, scooting a chair next to my bed and offering me a bite of eggs.

I'm ravenous, so I drop the subject for the moment and eat both helpings, leaving only the bread for him.

As I finish my meal, the door opens, and in step several people—friends from Kenozaria.

"Oh, Korina!" Rayyan exclaims, smiling with tear-filled eyes. "You really gave us quite the scare. I'll never forgive you for it."

"Liar," I quip before she comes to the bed and leans over to embrace me.

Ayfa, Rayyan's eldest, stands with her, along with a few other Kenozarians.

"What are you all doing here? What happened?" I ask.

"There was an invasion," Rayyan says. "During the Bright Ceremony. When we were running down the mountain, you tripped and sliced your head open pretty badly."

"Invaders from where? And during a Bright Ceremony, no less? Who would dare?"

"They come from the land across the Syril Sea," says Ayfa. "I've never seen warriors like them."

"And you left my children there?!" I cry out, stirring from the bed.

"Korina, peace," Torek says. "You know no one here would put them in danger."

"*You* don't get to speak as if you care for my children," I snarl. "Not after what you've done."

Torek looks at the ground in defeat.

"Darling," Rayyan says, taking my hand in hers. "There was so much blood. We rushed you to the only place we knew you would be safe. We couldn't take any chances on these invaders finding you."

She's right. Much as I dislike it, Salix *is* the safest place for me outside of Kenozaria. "Have you heard from them? From Evryn and the others?"

Rayyan and Ayfa exchange a glance. "All are safe," Ayfa says, placing a hand on my arm. "But Evryn was taken."

Taken? A ferocity is growing within me at the mere thought of someone harming my child. "What do you mean, *taken?*" I ask, trying to steady myself. "And how can you say she is safe?"

"Ari sent a message a few days ago. Evryn was captured in the woods, running east. Branngard is holding her."

"*Branngard,*" I repeat. They're a relatively young country, just an upstart. There didn't seem to be any reason to fear them—until now, obviously. "And what of Kenozaria? What remains?" I ask, thinking of the villages on the eastern shores of my island that have been decimated by foreign invaders. Every Feast Day, I thank the gods for the mountains that protect our little village on the east and the river that protects it on the west.

"Kenozaria stands untouched," Rayyan replies. "The only loss was little Søren. They mistook him for a scout. But they paid blood money to Plana for his death."

"And they even bought some livestock!" Afya laughs. "Can you imagine? Invaders *buying* livestock!"

None of this makes sense. We've survived many ambushes at the hands of other villages on our island. But they'd always come to steal grain or livestock or claim revenge for some previous revenge killing, stretching back generations. Why would they invade and then... *do nothing?*

"But why have they come? What do they want?"

"They say they want to speak with you," Rayyan says. "*Only* you. And they refuse to release Evryn until you come."

"What are we waiting for?!" I say, again attempting to get out of bed, but Rayyan gently holds me back.

"We must get you healthy first, okay?"

"Yes. You won't be able to make the trip in this state," Torek adds. "We must focus on your healing so we can get you back to Kenozaria. For Evryn."

I eye Torek again but decide against wasting my little remaining energy on arguing with him.

Soon, my sister, Meryn, and her daughter, Tasia, arrive, bearing savory pies and fresh baked bread. It's been years since I saw her when her husband passed, and it's good to be in her company again. The warmth and geniality of the scene comfort me, and before I know it, I am falling asleep again to the sounds of the people I love talking and laughing.

* * *

Each morning for weeks now, Rayyan has been coming to my bedside, helping me dress, and walking with me around the little cottage I'm staying in.

"Why did he not send word? Where has he been? For six months, I watched my daughter drag through life, barely able to care for herself, and now he's here, fine and well! The nerve of him!" I say this morning as we finish dressing me.

Rayyan strokes my hand. "You are right to be angry. I know I was when I first saw him," she says. "But I really think you should let him explain. It's not my story to tell."

I scoff and look away.

"Anyway, you know my memory is bloody awful. I'd muck it all up," Rayyan adds.

"Yes, it really is." I laugh.

Later in the evening, as I sit enjoying the breeze and braiding grass lazily as the amber sun drops behind the mountains, Torek approaches and sits on the ground next to me. And this time, I don't ask him to leave.

I've been thinking of what Rayyan said and warming up to the idea, if only out of curiosity. Of course, it helps that he's been preparing my meals and feeding them to me each day, something I suspect Rayyan has arranged.

"Good evening," I offer.

Torek smiles. "Good evening to you, too. How's your head doing? Looks like the cut is healing nicely."

"Yes, I think so," I reply, touching the scar. "Thanks for asking."

"You should be well enough to travel soon, I think."

"Gods, I hope so."

We sit in silence for some time, until finally, I open the subject.

"I'm ready, Torek," I say. "Tell me everything."

He takes a deep breath and turns toward me. "I'd spent the day hunting in the eastern foothills, and I was exhausted. The village was quiet and dark like everyone had left town, perhaps for a wedding or funeral. There was a blizzard raging and I needed shelter, so I ducked into a house. I thought it was empty, but as I turned a corner, there he was, dagger at the ready. He plunged it deep into my belly and stole my armband," he says, showing me the scar on his abdomen.

"When he stabbed me, I fell backward and bumped into a candle, knocking it on the floor near the curtains. We fought one another as the fire began to engulf the room. Finally, I broke free and ran from the house, eventually collapsing in the woods. I must have passed out because when I awoke it was night and fire was spreading through the village. The man must have been trapped inside his house by falling debris."

"And that's why they thought it was you," I finish for him. "Because he was wearing your armband."

Torek nods. "An elderly widow from the village found me in the woods the next day. She patched up my wound and nursed me back to health," he continues. "But I had to hide in her home until it was safe to escape. She kept me in the cellar, only letting me out at night so I could get some fresh air and relieve myself."

Poor Torek. My anger is replaced by compassion for the boy I've watched grow from infancy, right alongside my own little ones. "I guess that explains your absence. But couldn't you have sent a message?" I ask.

Torek mindlessly tears off a piece of grass from the ground next to him and tosses it away. "I tried. I did. But she refused to allow me to send a message, insisting she would be killed for harboring an enemy if the message were intercepted. How could I repay her kindness with that sort of risk?"

He does have a point, I realize. "But how did you escape? And why did you come here instead of going home?"

"One night, the old woman came to me in the cellar and told me it was time. She said someone had invaded Kenozaria, so her people were distracted in fear of how far the invaders would come inland. She packed a small satchel with some food to last me a day or two, as well as some water in a leather bag, and she pointed me south.

"'There are scouts all along the road north,' she warned me. 'They're looking for a girl from Kenozaria, and if they catch you, they'll question you.'

"So, I followed the road south and east until I arrived here. I told my story to your sister, who agreed to give me shelter until I could make it to Kenozaria. I sent a message as soon as possible, but then you arrived, and we received that message from Ari. That's when I learned what happened to Evryn."

I hug him. In truth, I've loved him like my own son, and it broke my heart when I thought he was dead. But I never can tolerate sadness for very long before it congeals to anger in my gut.

"Torek, we have to rescue my daughter."

"Yes. We must," he agrees.

II

Autumn

8

Lukin

I'm sitting by the fire, mesmerized by the dancing flames, for the moment free of the bothersome worry I've been carrying since the night we arrived back at camp with Evryn in tow.

Akkar has been sending me to her tent every few days to see if she's changed her mind about confessing her "guilt"—and of course she hasn't. I've managed to convince him not to resort to his tried and true methods of coercion, up to now, but who knows how long that will last.

At first, I anticipated these meetings with dread, so I would get straight to the point so I could say I'd done my duty. But with time, I found myself *enjoying* her company, wrong as it is. A captive companion is hardly a *true* companion, but our conversations flow so easily that I find myself forgetting that she is a prisoner and I, one of her keepers.

Aside from informing her of any new happenings on the island or news from her family, we talk about everything from the stories she grew up listening to, to the many places I've visited in my journeys furthering Akkar's mission, to the minutiae of the plants and insects on the island. I've begun sneaking fruits and cakes to her when I come for my visits, just for the pleasure of watching her eyes light up when she sees me coming.

But Akkar is not one to allow these things to carry on long, and I worry about what will happen to her when his patience runs out. To even *harm* one of the Torch's slaves means a lifetime of enslavement in their place. But to kill the *Jewel of Branngard*? The punishment is death, and not a fast one. So I spend most days, between drills and strategy meetings, pondering on how I could help her to escape without putting her and her family in further danger.

The sound of coughing brings me back to the present. Draven approaches the fire and takes a seat near me, offering me a cup of ale. I take a long drag and hand the cup back.

"The girl is asking for ya. Won't eat until ya come and speak with her, she said."

I sigh and stand up, trying to hide my happiness; now she's *asking* for me, no longer waiting for Akkar to send me. "We can't have her dying on our watch, can we?"

Draven stands, too, and holds me by my shoulders, looking into my eyes with sincerity. "Lukin, son. You're not to blame. You've done as the Torch himself has instructed ya, and Rhys'll bless ya for it. Don't torture yourself so, aye?"

I offer a weak smile. "I'm fine, Draven."

"I've known ya since ya were still on your mother's teat, me boy. I know when something is weighing heavy on ya."

I thank him and take my leave before heading toward the black tent where Evryn is waiting.

The tent is dark, and the air inside is smothering. Evryn sits slumped against the center post, her arms bound in front of her and one ankle shackled to the post by a short chain. Her clothes are filthy and her hair matted, and she smells just as one would expect someone to smell when they haven't bathed in weeks. As I approach, she turns to face me, her eyes shining in the darkness.

"Took you long enough," she says, attempting to stand.

"They say you won't eat," I begin, pulling an apple from my satchel.

"Correction. I refused to eat until you graced me with your presence." She smiles. "And now you have, so..."

I chuckle, handing her the apple.

"Any news from my family?" Evryn asks between bites. "My mother?"

"Your siblings are fine. They're still camped just outside the encampment, refusing to leave until the Torch releases you. But there's still no word from your mother."

Evryn finishes the apple and sighs, wiping her mouth with the back of her hand. "This is the part where you ask me to confess to killing Pomisha, and I insist that I know nothing about her death," she says. "Now, that's done. So tell me when he will free me."

I know she's telling the truth. Even when Draven shook me awake that morning with the news, I knew beyond a shadow of a doubt *if* someone had killed Pomisha, it certainly wasn't Evryn.

"I promise you, I am doing all I can to have you released, but Akkar is adamant you must have been the culprit." I lean in and lower my voice so the guards outside can't hear. "You were with her *all night*. You slept in her bed with her—naked, if her ladies are to be believed! Even *if* you didn't kill her—" I say, stopping short. "Even *though* you didn't kill her, that alone is reason enough to arrest you. The Jewel of Branngard is the Torch's *property*, Evryn!"

Evryn holds her face in her hands and sighs in frustration. "Yes. I slept in her bed. But she invited me! How was I to know it was forbidden?"

Branngardians are prudish, this much is true. I've seen enough of the world to know that women often enjoy one another's company far more than the company of men, even and especially in bed.

"Lukin, I swear to you, I know nothing of her death!" she cries. "I can't stay in this tent forever!"

"Evryn, listen," I say, making the decision I have been dreading. "I am going to do what I can to find out what he's planning. Please, you have to trust me. I will not stand idly by and watch him execute you for a murder I know you didn't commit."

"Execute me?"

"Please, trust me," I say, looking into her eyes. "I'll do what I can."

Beyond the antechamber veil, Akkar is pacing his study.

"Lukin! How good of you to join me," he calls out when he realizes I am standing there. "Do come and sit. Tea?" His face is twisted in a frenzy of thought.

"Yes, Uncle. Thank you," I say, offering a slight bow.

After the tea has arrived, Akkar wastes no time getting to the point. "What did she say to you?"

So I tell him everything, except the part where I promised to find a way to have her released.

"Yes, this is good," Akkar says, stroking his beard. "She is becoming desperate, it seems."

"Desperate for her freedom, yes," I remark. "As would anyone be, in her position."

Akkar stands and calls out for one of the Shield.

"What will happen to her?" I ask, not wanting the moment to pass. "We can't keep her locked up like that forever, based on suspicion alone."

"*I* most certainly *can*," Akkar says sternly. "But I won't. She's too valuable to waste away like that." Before I can ask what he means by that, he calls out again for his Shield. "Please send for the soldier, the one from Roiland."

"Uncle, what should I tell her family? They are anxious for news of her. I fear if we continue to hold her, we risk creating more unrest among the villagers."

"Trust your uncle, Lukin. And trust Rhys. These heathens are no threat." With that, he dismisses me just as the Shield returns with the young soldier from Roiland.

I take my leave and begin walking to my tent, but curiosity gets the better of me, so I turn around, making a beeline for a tent not far from Akkar's and sidling around the back of it to listen.

"Branngard rewards loyalty, young man," Akkar says. "What you've done for Rhys and the Faith cannot be overlooked."

The young soldier from Roiland, whoever he is, thanks the Torch.

"Remember: tell no one. Everything Rhys intends for this island depends on that girl and her next moves. We mustn't allow anyone to derail things, yes?"

"Yes, Your Holiness," the young soldier replies. "And my family?"

"Your little children will be spared, and your ancestral home will be returned to your wife. Rhys loves to bless his humble servants," Akkar says.

I hear the soldier kiss Akkar's hand and stand before leaving the tent. When he is a good distance from the tent, I come up behind him and cup a hand over his mouth, dragging him behind the smithy.

"If you value your life and the lives of your children, you will tell me what you have done for the Torch," I whisper with my dagger at the man's throat.

"You wouldn't dare!" he replies gruffly.

I turn the man around to face me. His face is puffy and red, and he wears a patch to cover the hole where his right eye once was.

"Oh? Do you imagine the Torch would even suspect it was me, his beloved nephew?" I say. "And even if he does, he will hastily blame someone else for your death. You're a foot soldier and nothing more, certainly not worth tarnishing Velga family honor."

His remaining eye widens. He knows I'm right, but I press the blade harder into the thin flesh of his throat to drive the point home. "Okay! Okay. I only delivered a message, sir!" he cries as I press harder. "I delivered a note to the Jewel of Branngard. That's all, Captain, I swear!"

"What did the note say?"

"I don't know what it said! It was sealed! I wouldn't dare open it!"

"And you placed it directly into Pomisha's hand? Her Shield allowed you that close?"

"I didn't go inside! She met me at the entrance."

"And what happened?"

"I handed the note to her. She looked at the Torch's seal, broke it, read the note, and... I don't know... She seemed... sad. Then she dismissed me."

My mind is racing, trying to piece together the events that have transpired. "Okay. Okay, listen. When you were there, did you see Evryn, the islander they're accusing of the murder? Was she in the tent?"

He is hesitant to answer, so I flex my arm, ready with the blade again. "I can't say if it was her. I couldn't see fully because of the veils but... yes, someone was asleep in the Jewel's bed. Naked," he says. "Please, Captain. I know nothing else. I just wanted to save my family!"

"I understand. Thank you." There's nothing more I will learn from him, so I let him go.

As I watch him walk away, gimping hard on his left leg, I think about what the note could have said that would help make sense of Pomisha's death. But that's a hopeless cause. Pomisha would have burned it.

And how did the murderer get past the Shield? Their only

responsibility, night and day in shifts, is to keep watch of her and the women in her care within the tent. How could they have let someone slip inside and kill her? And her handmaids were sleeping when it happened, but surely one of them had to have seen or heard something when she was murdered. But all have been questioned and all report the same thing: the Jewel of Branngard stumbled out of the tent with the dagger in her belly.

It could have been one of her maids, maybe one she had a harsh word for that day. But then why wait until that night, *the same night* she spent with Evryn? Was it jealousy? Maybe one of them was envious of the intimacy they shared?

I know all the evidence seemingly points to Evryn, but it just doesn't sit right with me. Something tells me there is a piece of the puzzle missing—a piece I may never find.

9

Evryn

Akkar is standing in my face, nearly nose to nose. There's a sickly-sweet blend of spices I'm not familiar with emanating from his curly, dark hair. The smell catches in my throat and lingers. Between that and the sweltering heat radiating through the tent, I'm finding it hard to catch my breath.

"We have credible reason to believe your sister, Ziva Korina, infiltrated our camp and murdered the Jewel of Branngard in cold blood the same night you violated her."

Ziva? She wouldn't hurt a fly. She cried for a week when she accidentally killed a baby rat rummaging in her room one winter. No, Ziva loves me, but she's not capable of murder. And she's too intelligent to think such a plan would succeed.

"Where is she? What have you done to her?" I ask, fury burning in my chest.

"Oh, calm yourself. She is well! We are holding her in another tent, on the other side of camp, under heavy guard. But she's safe. We aren't barbarians!" Akkar laughs.

"I want to see her."

"That is quite impossible."

"Then how can I trust she's safe?"

"Well, I suppose you can't, can you?" he muses, walking around me in a circle. "That requires faith, something your people are sorely lacking, from my estimation."

"We have very different understandings of faith, *Your Holiness.*"

Akkar is not amused. "Let us not waste time. You can either submit to our justice, or we will mete it out to your sister. The choice is yours."

"You'll *kill her?*" I ask.

"Oh, of course not! That would be a terrible waste," Akkar says, scoffing. "No. She will make a fantastic new Jewel for me. So youthful and fresh and vibrant, your sister." He steps so close to me that we could be kissing if I bent down.

"She's a child! You'd make my twelve-year-old sister your concubine? What's wrong with you?"

"I pity you and your simple way of understanding your little world," he says. "Thankfully, Rhys loves to educate people, and He has chosen me as his... *particular tutor,*" he continues, running a knuckle down my cheek. I try to move away from him, but my back is firmly up against the pole in the center of the tent. Annoyed at my resistance, he gesticulates wildly. "It is a great honor, child! A greater honor than either of you could hope to receive without this tragedy."

Tragedy, he calls it. But Akkar doesn't seem to be mourning his lost love—the only woman he's ever lain with, who surely carried more than one of his fated offspring in her womb. On the contrary, he acts almost *delighted.*

"What do you want from me?" I ask.

"Don't act so ignorant. It's beneath you," he scolds me, stepping closer still and reaching to whisper into my ear. "I want what any man would want from you, my girl: merely the pleasure of your company and the warmth of your arms."

69

Now I understand why he gawked at me when Lukin first brought me to him. "And what will happen to Ziva if I agree to your deal? If I agree to take her place?" I ask, weighing my options.

"Oh, she will be safe, along with the rest of your family. As for your mother... well, I assume she must have died or been taken captive off the island. It has been such a long time for a mother to *voluntarily* keep away from her children, and during an invasion, no less! Your people are *savage*, though, so I suppose she may not think it odd."

I suck my breath through my teeth, narrowing my gaze on him. He knows nothing about my mother's whereabouts. That much is clear. "So you admit that's what's happening here? You're invading my island?"

Akkar takes a step back and analyzes his fine hands, playing with the rings. "An unfortunate turn of phrase on my part, I apologize. Rhys has sent us to do His good work of bringing the Light to your people, that is all. As you can see, the only blood that's been spilled here was at your sister's hands."

"Ziva did not kill your—She didn't kill Pomisha. I don't know who did. But it wasn't my sister, and it wasn't me."

Akkar calls to a guard, who enters the tent to receive his orders. "Please have our guest cleaned and properly fed and bring her to my tent afterward. She wants for comfort, it seems, and Branngard is *most hospitable*," he says, touching my cheek again. I turn my face as far away from him as my neck will allow.

"Do think on what we've talked about, my dear, hmm?" he says sweetly. "You're a clever girl. I worry your sister may not be as... *adaptable* as you seem to be, and my patience for silly, problematic girls is limited. Jewels go missing all the time, after all. And I am most curious to savor the taste of local meat," he whispers in my ear, then grabs my face and tries to kiss me.

"Savor this!" I spit at him.

I think he'll strike me, but he calmly wipes the spittle from his face with his finger and places it inside his mouth, closing his eyes in ecstasy.

"You're *wild*. I like a challenge. It will be a pleasure to break you in," he whispers, patting me on the cheek before leaving me alone in the tent. A few moments later, some guards take me back to Pomisha's tent.

Nothing looks the way it did weeks ago. Far from the hustle and bustle of before, now Pomisha's servants lounge around the tent, looking wanton and sorrowful. Their previously bright, colorful clothing has been replaced with black mourning clothes. No one makes eye contact with me.

I walk through the antechamber into Pomisha's room and sit on her bed. Two of her ladies come and prepare a bath for me, wordlessly. I remove the filthy rags I've been wearing and step into the basin. They scrub my body with more force than is necessary, and can I blame them? In their mind, I'm either the murderer of their lady and friend, or else I'm protecting the true culprit.

After they've washed and dressed me in extravagant finery, they bring out a looking glass. I've never before seen my own reflection, aside from when I stood above a still pond now and then. The image in the looking glass is striking. I stand, draped in a deep purple robe, covered in gold jewelry. They've braided my long auburn hair atop my head and interwoven sprigs of wildflowers throughout it.

I truly look the part now, and I know that was Akkar's plan: to give me a taste of the blessings he'd lavish on me if I sold myself to him in exchange for my sister's freedom.

They sit me down at a table and place a feast before me. As I sit eating, I try my best to forget my surroundings—this tent, that bed I shared with Pomisha, these grieving women who would, I know, cut my throat if they didn't fear reprisals from the Torch.

My mind drifts to the meeting I will have with Akkar tonight. Of course, there is no choice; there never was. I won't allow Ziva to suffer in my place. Will he allow me to see her before he sends her back to my family and shackles me the way he did Pomisha?

I wonder, for the hundredth time, where my mother is, and for a split second, I consider what Akkar said. *Is she dead?* I can't imagine anyone would have taken her captive, let alone killed her. She is beloved throughout our island, and no one would be bold enough to harm her or mindless enough to turn her away. But if not, where could she be?

As I finish my meal, I hear the guards outside Pomisha's tent speaking with someone, who clearly wants to come in. After a few moments, their voices die down, and in walks Lukin.

"Hello there," I say, casually taking a sip of wine. "I thought men weren't allowed in this tent?"

Upon seeing me in the finery they've dressed me in, Lukin stops short and seems dazed for a moment. "I... Akkar sent me. And there's no Jewel to protect any longer. Are you well?" he asks.

"It looks like I am far better than well, yes? Better than I was when you last saw me, I'd wager."

He sighs and sits down in the chair opposite me, pouring himself a cup of wine.

"Have you come to take me to your uncle? His loyal servant, as always."

Lukin says nothing.

"Oh, you're staying? Yes, let's have a feast together, Lukin Velga. Let us again play as if I am not a prisoner and you are not my keeper, shall we? That will be a fun game."

He takes a long drag of wine and sets the cup down, then relaxes back in the chair. His casual ease juxtaposes my own inner turmoil, and my resentment boils over.

"Tell me. Did you know this was his plan all along?"

"No, I swear it. I had no idea. I—" he begins, but I cut him off.

"Oh, good. That's a relief. So, surely this," I say, gesturing to our surroundings, "must be the result of all the hard work you did in advocating for me with your uncle? Slavery. A great upgrade over what... Death?"

Lukin drops his head for a moment before lifting his chin and looking me square in the face. "I am sorry. I did all that I could. Truly."

"That's a relief," I say, taking another long drink of the wine. My head is swimming, and I like it.

Lukin studies his hands as we both sit in silence.

"Have you seen my sister? Is she well?" I ask. Being angry with him is exhausting.

"No, not yet. But I am assured she is well."

I can't take it anymore, thinking of her chained to a pole in a tent, covered in her own filth and terrified. She is just a *child*. The sorrow is leaking out of my eyes now.

"At least she will be free soon. At least she will attend her own Bright Ceremony. I wish I could be there to see it!" I cry.

Lukin clears his throat and stands, then walks to my side of the table. "It's time to go," he says sternly, in a voice loud enough that the guards can hear. "I will take you to the Torch."

I think of begging him, pleading with him to let me go, but at this point, I'm certain they would only find me again—and, worse, the offer might not be on the table anymore. I can't risk Ziva's well-being, so I stand.

Lukin shackles my wrists behind my back and hooks his arm in mine.

"Trust me," he whispers. And then we walk out of the tent, into the light of the setting sun.

10

Lukin

Evryn stands next to me in the Branngardian garb Pomisha's attendants had dressed her in, ill at ease. To my right stands Draven—drunk, as usual. Tygan rounds out the party on Evryn's left, staring at the ground and saying nothing. A Branngardian priest, decked out in his ornate yellow, orange, and red ceremonial attire, stands before us, nervously speaking the words. It's clear no one in the room wants to be there.

"He is asking if you understand what's happening here," I say, addressing Evryn. When she doesn't answer, I turn to look at her squarely. "Evryn, please. You have to at least nod your head."

Evryn nods, and the priest continues the ceremony in High Branngardian—a language even I struggle to understand since it's reserved exclusively for sacred rituals. Like a wedding, for instance.

"Lukin Velga, son of Quentin, of Yarrow's Cairn, do you willingly enter into this union, taking this woman under your care? Do you swear by Rhys to protect Evryn and provide all her needs, to guide her and discipline her when she strays, to bless her with your seed, to honor her with kindness, and to die in service of her and the children she may bear you, if need be?"

"I do," I say.

"Evryn... erm. What was your father's name, girl?"

"Evryn Korina," I reply for her, deciding it's not the right time to explain the Kenozarian naming system to the elderly priest.

"Evryn Korina," the priest continues. "Do you willingly enter into this union, submitting yourself to this man? Do you swear by Rhys to honor Lukin, to obey him in all things, to keep his secrets, to display your beauty and share your body only with him, to maintain his home according to his standards, to care for any children Rhys blesses you with, and to give your life in service of him and the children you may bear for him, if need be?"

Evryn would never agree to such a list of demands. And why should she? She barely knows me, after all. So, when I'm translating the oath for her, I choose much more general words, ones less offensive to her cultural sensibilities.

"I do," she says, keeping her focus on the ground.

The priest takes Evryn's hand and slits the palm with a small dagger, causing her to wince in pain, then he does the same to mine. Squeezing some of the blood from both into his own palm, he mixes the blood together and rubs a few drops on our lips, earlobes, and foreheads.

"Oh Rhys, Blessed Lightbringer," he prays, "we ask you to protect this union and to bless this man and this woman with long life and many children. We ask you to guide them on the path of righteousness, the narrow path that leads to Paradise, and we ask that their union be a badge of honor for Branngard, your chosen people, and a light in the darkness of the world."

Turning back to us, he continues. "With your blood and these sacred rings I bind this marriage," he says, placing a silver bracelet on my right wrist and a gold one on Evryn's. And with that, the ceremony is over.

Evryn stands silently, unblinking, staring down at the gold bracelet the priest placed on her wrist.

"I'll just walk them back to their tents," I say, venturing to place a careful hand on her shoulder.

She looks up into my eyes, and I can see the fear she carries there.

"Yes, okay. I'll just... wait here," she says, looking around at the various trappings of my tent.

"I'll hurry back," I assure her.

Draven hands the priest a bag, heavy with gold. "Now, ya aren't to say a word to anyone, priest, understand? Ya know it wouldn't be in your best interest to admit you've administered a marriage without Himself's blessings, now would it?"

The elderly priest takes the bag and bows genially to all before pulling off his ceremonial garb and stuffing it into a knapsack, then donning the heavy, black-hooded cloak he typically wears on his rounds of the camp. And then he's gone.

"You should tell the Torch tonight," Draven says when the priest is some distance from us. "You know as well as I do that this cannot remain hidden for long, no matter how much gold we paid that priest."

"I fear you're right," I reply, anxiously rubbing my fingers through my beard.

"Who can tell what the Torch'll do to ya when he finds out—or to me!"

I smile and pat him on the back. "You are a loyal friend, Draven. You both are," I say, looking at him and Tygan. "And I assure you, I will not allow my uncle to do anything to harm either of you. Captain's honor!"

"I'm glad for you, sir," Tygan says. "I hope you've found someone who can make you as happy as my Gwen makes me."

"*Happy?*" Draven guffaws.

Not again.

"What happiness can be had in angering both your god *and* your Torch—and uncle, to boot?!"

"Draven, you know why—" I begin, but he cuts me off.

"I know you've said you're doing this for the sake of the girl, Lukin. Ya said it many a time. But I... well, forgive me, but I think it's more likely you've done it to please yourself."

"I hope you know me well enough to know that no woman, no matter how clever and pretty, could tempt me to abandon my morals. Surely you don't think I'd put your lives and my own on the line for the sake of some... passing pleasure?"

Draven looks sorry now. "Forgive me, Lukin. I've had a dram too much to drink this night."

"There is nothing to forgive, my old friend. And let's be honest, you're right to worry. The Torch would never hurt me, but you two? You're fair game."

"Ya wee mongrel!" Draven laughs, slapping me on the shoulder. "Och I am sorry, though. This certainly isn't the wedding I imagined for ya, young Lukin. Nor the bride."

I give Draven a weak smile. "I'm sure she'll do just fine."

"She'd better, considering you've booted me out of me tent and burdened me with this animal and his snoring," he says, jabbing Tygan in the side.

"Hey!" Tygan laughs, holding his side. "That's nothing compared to your stench!"

After we've walked around the camp for a while, we turn back—Draven and Tygan to their tent, and I to confess to my uncle.

"You must be out of your mind, Nephew!" Akkar is screaming. "I... There are no words! There simply *are no words*. You must explain yourself!"

I study the silver bracelet now adorning my right wrist. I know there's nothing I could say that would assuage his wrath, so I say nothing.

"An answer, Lukin! I demand an answer! By Rhys and by the memory of your father, my brother—for whose sake I do not have you scourged this instant—I implore you!"

"Uncle—" I begin but think better of it. "Your Holiness, please forgive me. I didn't do this to spite you. It was the will of Rhys. I can say no more."

"*The will of Rhys*, you say? The will of Rhys?! *I* am the voice of Rhys! You obey *me*! Do you have any idea what you've done?"

I stand up straighter. "Yes, sir. I understand. And I am willing to take whatever punishment you deem fit."

"Don't play games with me, boy. You know full well my hands are tied." Akkar sits down, mopping his forehead before taking a sip of water. "We must announce this new development with the blessing of the Torch and Rhys himself, damn you! We can't have people thinking you disobeyed me."

I'm relieved but I try not to show it. "And the girl?" I venture to ask. "Evryn's sister, Ziva."

"Take some Shield and release her back to her family," Akkar says, rubbing his temples.

"Yes, Uncle."

"I'll deal with you in a few days when I have had time to collect my thoughts."

"Understood."

"In the meantime, you'd better get to work. The sooner you sow your seed in that girl, the better!" He shouts, dismissing me.

Ziva is bound and chained to the pole in the center of a black tent, just as Evryn had been. As I approach, she flinches.

"It's okay. I won't hurt you. My name is Lukin. I know your sister.

I am here to take you back to your family."

Ziva looks up into my eyes. "Evryn? Is she okay? I want to see her."

"I'm sorry I can't make that happen. But if you'll let me come closer, I will unchain you and lead you straight to your family. They're waiting for you."

Ziva struggles to stand, so I offer her a hand, then I release her from the shackles and tie her wrists in front of her.

When we reach the edge of the encampment, a young man is standing next to a tent on the other side of the barricade. He spots our approach and runs into the tent, bringing a young woman outside with him.

"Ari! Halline!" Ziva cries, running into their arms as soon as I loosen the knot on her wrist. The two of them embrace her and the whole party weeps with joy and relief. I feel uncomfortable witnessing such an intimate family moment and begin to turn back.

"Excuse me," Ari calls out. "Please, can you tell us anything about Evryn? Is she safe? When will you release her?"

"She is very well," I report. "She's no longer a prisoner."

"Then when will you bring her to us?" Halline asks.

I don't want to be having this conversation. There is no easy way to tell these people what I've done or to explain why. "Evryn won't be returning to Kenozaria."

"I don't understand. If she's not a prisoner anym—" Halline begins.

"Because we were married last night."

Ari's eyes widen and his jaw falls open. Ziva cries into his chest.

"This cannot be true. Evryn *cannot* have chosen this," Halline says with a hand on Ziva's back.

"I am sorry. But I promise you, she will want for nothing."

"I demand you let us speak to her!" Ari cries out, but Halline puts a careful hand on his shoulder.

"Thank you," she says.

"There is nothing to thank me for," I reply, turning to leave.

Evryn is sitting cross-legged in the corner of the tent, absentmindedly playing with the wildflowers in her hair. She has stripped off her finery in favor of a long, dark green cotton dress.

"How are you? I don't imagine this is how you hoped this night would end," I say, approaching her.

"The night is still young," she replies simply.

"Ah, yes. I suppose you're right," I say, sitting down a fair distance from her. I haven't a clue how to talk to this woman who is now my wife.

"How is my sister?"

"Akkar already released her back to your family. I made sure of it, personally," I assure her. "And I met your siblings, Ari and Halline."

Evryn's face lights up. It's the first time I've seen her come to life in weeks. "Are they well? What happened?"

"They seem well, yes. They were happy to see Ziva safe. And they asked about your well-being, which I assured them of." I decide not to tell her they know we're married.

"I wish I had been able to see Ziva before they released her," Evryn remarks sadly.

"I'm sorry. Akkar would never have allowed it. I hope you understand."

She nods.

"What matters is you're both safe now," I continue.

"How can you be so sure? Since he's lost me, what's to stop him from recapturing Ziva and making her his new Jewel?"

"Akkar cannot harm her now that we are married. He wouldn't dare. She is a member of my wife's family. His honor prevents it. Plus, Akkar never settles for second-best."

"What do you mean, 'second-best'?"

"I can't explain it, but I have a feeling this was his plan all along. I believe he framed her for Pomisha's murder because he knew you would volunteer to take her place as the new Jewel. He did it to get you in his claws."

"But how? He couldn't have known Pomisha would be murdered."

"I'm not convinced she *was* murdered. All we know for sure is that Akkar sent her a note, she read it, and then she was found dead a few hours later. I shudder to think of what he said in that note."

Evryn sits pondering what I said. "What a sick, cruel man. Why would your people respect and obey someone like him?"

"Fear. They believe he speaks on behalf of Rhys, whom they also worship out of fear. They know no other way of life."

"Yes. Fear is certainly a powerful motivator."

"Your people, do they fear your mother?"

"No. They love her, trust her," Evryn says. "They chose her as the chief of the Sanctum because she truly finds joy in serving the best interests of the community, even if it means sacrificing what's best for herself and her children. Our people feel safe under her leadership."

I'm speechless.

"So who will be his Jewel now?" Evryn asks, bringing the conversation back to the point at hand. "How will the Torch of Branngard fulfill his... baser needs?"

I'm uncomfortable even thinking of the Torch's *baser needs*. "He will go without, I suppose. Until a suitable option can be brought from Branngard."

"Or until they find one in my village to capture in my place."

I toss my hands in the air. "Look, I can't marry every girl in Kenozaria to protect them from Akkar. I did what I could do."

Her face softens. "Yes, I can see that, and I am grateful." She takes my hand briefly, then drops it again as a cloud of some other emotion passes across her face. "I suppose you think I am obligated to... express my gratitude to you?"

"What?" I ask. "No. No, please. You are not obligated to do *anything*. This wasn't a transaction."

She looks into my eyes. "And what if I *want* to consummate this union you've dragged me into?" she asks seductively.

"I didn't drag you. I—"

"What would *you* call it when a woman is captured on her own land and kept as a prisoner, and her only hope to escape enslavement is marrying a man she barely knows, or else letting her captors enslave her twelve-year-old sister instead?"

"Well, in that case, I'd say it's my duty to refuse your advances, to guard your virtue."

Evryn smiles flirtatiously. "Bold of you to assume I have virtue to guard, Lukin Velga."

I blush, unable to come up with a witty response. I notice she's playing with her necklace. "That's beautiful. Was it a gift from your mother?"

"No," she says, sorrow heavy in her voice. "It was a gift from Torek. He was my betrothed before he died last winter."

"I am sorry for your loss. I'm sorry for *all* of this."

Evryn looks down at the necklace and seems to be lost in thought for a moment. "I have a question."

"I'll do my best to answer."

"What *did* I promise you, in those vows?" she asks, removing the last wildflower from her hair.

I try to think quickly of something to say that isn't *quite* the truth but near enough. "You vowed to trust my judgment and to make yourself exclusively available to me."

"And? There was more, I'm sure."

"Yes, there was more. But it doesn't matter."

Evryn isn't satisfied. "Maybe your people are comfortable violating oaths, but it's not the way here. Words have power. Tell me the specifics. Please."

I do my best to repeat what she vowed. Evryn's eyes widen when I get to the part about obeying me. "Listen, I don't actually expect you to honor any of it. As you said, it wasn't really a choice for you."

"And what did you promise me?"

"I promised to always protect you, to honor you, to provide for you, and to die for you and our children, if need be," I reply, leaving a few things out.

Evryn sits in thought for a moment before turning her dark eyes back to mine. "Okay. I will do my best in all those things. All but one."

"Oh?"

"I don't... I'm not sure I can bear children," she says, fidgeting with the gold bangle on her wrist.

I can see the pain in her eyes. "Evryn—"

"No, I'm serious," she says, cutting me off. "If I were going to be a mother, it would have happened by now."

"Why would you think that way? You're so young."

"My mother is wise, and she seems sure it's not in the cards for me." Evryn drops her head.

"And do you *want* children?" I ask. "I mean, in a different circumstance, obviously."

"Yes, with all my heart," she says, choking back tears.

Moved by her emotion, I draw nearer to her and take her hand in mine. "Please, don't worry yourself. As I said, this is not a marriage, at least not like that. If we can enjoy happy companionship, that would be enough for me. And if you truly want to raise children, plenty need parents to look after them. I'd be happy to help you in raising them."

"But won't you have... needs? And don't you want a child of your own?"

In fact, she has no idea how important it is for me—not just personally, but politically. The next Torch must come from my direct bloodline, after all. But what people don't know won't hurt them. There's enough of a market for young boys—though, typically for more nefarious reasons. We could easily find an orphan that would fit the bill. We could go away for a few years and return with a lad that looked convincing enough, and no one would be the wiser.

"Those needs are unimportant in this equation," I reply. "What I need from you is your *mind*," I say, pointing at her head. "You would be an excellent military strategist, you know? I wouldn't like to face you on a battlefield, that's for sure."

Evryn smirks. "That's right, you wouldn't. Smart man."

11

Korina

Halline sets some water to boil for tea as the others bring fruit and cheese for us to eat.

"We're so glad you're home, both of you," she says, wrapping an arm around Torek.

"Me, too," I reply, pulling her in for a hug.

"It took you long enough," Ari says. "We were really starting to worry."

"Well, I don't have control of the weather, unfortunately," I reply. The trip lasted longer than usual, thanks to the unseasonable rains, and the slow gait of my donkey. "What news of Evryn?" I ask, taking a bite of an apple. "Have they allowed you to see her?"

"No, Mama," Halline says, playing with the corner of a napkin. "They report only that she is well. But they won't allow us to see her or even send her any messages."

"We thought they were only holding her until Korina could come to speak with them. Why would they imprison her? What on earth has she done?" asks Torek.

Halline and Ari exchange a look just as the tea kettle begins to whistle. Halline attends to it, returning to the table with five mugs of steaming tea. She adds milk and honey to my mug, just how I like it, then passes it to me. I blow on the tea and breathe in the vapors. The smell is comforting.

"Tell me," I say, placing my hand on Halline's.

So they tell me everything: Evryn was captured running east, for reasons we still don't know. They claimed to be holding her for questioning, in lieu of me, but then she was accused of murdering their leader's concubine. Then they captured Ziva, too, and accused *her* of having been the culprit all along.

"I can't believe it," I cry. "*Ziva?* They thought *you* killed a grown woman? You wouldn't dare! Did they harm you?" I ask her, stroking her cheek and turning her face to look for cuts and bruises.

"No, Mama," Ziva says. "They kept me chained up in a tent, and they asked me a bunch of questions about the lady who died, like if I knew anything about her death."

"What was Ziva even doing so close to their camp?" I ask Halline and Ari. "You were supposed to keep an eye on her. Was that really so much to ask?"

"She waited until we slept and snuck out that night," Ari says, eyes downcast.

I turn to look at my youngest child. "Is this true, Ziva?"

Ziva lowers her head in shame. "I just wanted to see her, Mama! I wanted to make sure she was okay, but I never found her. They caught me just before dawn and drug me to their leader."

I sigh and rub my forehead. A headache is pulsing behind my eyes.

"Wait. Why release Ziva but not Evryn?" Torek asks. "Do they really think Evryn killed the concubine?"

"Not quite, no. But there's more," Halline says. "About Evryn, I mean."

"What do you mean? Is she okay?" I ask. Sensing Halline's reticence, I push. "Just tell me, Halline. Is Evryn safe?"

"Yes, Mama. She's safe." Halline doesn't look up from her mug. "She's being treated very well now, apparently."

"*Now*, you say? What's changed?" Torek asks, sitting up in his seat.

"The night Ziva was released, we spoke with the captain of the army, a man named Lukin."

"And? What did he say?" I ask.

Halline stands up to transfer another pot of boiling water to the washbasin in my room while Ari and Ziva stare down into their own mugs, avoiding eye contact.

"Will someone please tell me what is going on?" I ask, frustrated.

"She married him, Mama," Ari finally says. "Evryn's not coming home."

I steady myself on the table while Torek slumps in his chair with his face in his hands.

"*Married?* Tell me this is a sick joke."

"We wouldn't joke about this," Halline says, placing another pot of water on the stove and then coming to join us at the table.

"Why would she do this?" Torek cries.

No one has an answer.

"I must go to her," I decide. "I must beg this captain to release her from their bond."

Halline takes my hand. "Please don't. I'm afraid they'll imprison you, too."

"I cannot leave her there, Halline. She belongs here, with us, with her people, among the trees. Being his wife is just another kind of prison for her."

"At least don't go alone," Ari says. "Take a few warriors with you."

"No, we cannot be seen as a threat. I am just a mother, going to appeal for the return of my daughter. There is no reason to endanger anyone else. I wish I could stay here with you all, too. But I have to try, for Evryn. You know I'd do the same for any of you."

"We understand, Mama," Ziva says, hugging me.

"I will come with you, Korina," Torek says as he stands.

"I doubt your parents will ever let you leave their sight again. I know I wouldn't if I were them."

"I'm sure they'll understand."

"I'm grateful for your help, then. We will leave at first light tomorrow."

"First light," Torek says, finishing the contents of his mug before heading home.

"Where has Torek been all this time, Mama?" Ari asks after Torek has gone. "Lyra and their family and Evryn and all of us... we mourned him. We buried him! And now he's here, alive and well?"

"Well, he wasn't dead. Obviously," Ziva says. Halline and Ari eye her severely. "Sorry."

"I assure you, he didn't intentionally do it," I say, and then I decide to relay Torek's story to them, leaving nothing out.

"Something doesn't seem right," Halline says when I've finished. "I can't put my finger on it, but... I don't know if I believe his story."

"Does it really matter where he was?" Ziva asks. "I, for one, am glad he's alive and well."

"True. Though, I imagine he doesn't feel as happy to be back in Kenozaria now that Evryn is..." Ari says, his words trailing off.

"We will bring her home," I assure them as I stand up to finally head to the comfort of my room. I'm exhausted from travel and the shock of this news. My bones are aching for a bath and bed. "All will be well again."

As I sit in my washbasin, listening to the fire crackling in the hearth and enjoying the warmth of the water as it soothes my sore muscles, I reflect on the past few weeks' events.

They *must* have coerced her or threatened her. Evryn is many things, but she's not a traitor to her people. Never. But how can my rebellious, headstrong daughter have been coerced into marrying that man?

Then again, I'm no stranger to the power of coercion. I was only fourteen years old when Ronar Tara came to ask my father for my hand almost twenty-five years ago.

* * *

He was a tradesman that had recently come to Salix from Kenozaria. He had quickly made a name for himself as a reasonable, calm man who was true to his word. He was a widower of some years who had recently lost his adult daughter, too. Having watched me helping my mother in our tailoring stall for a few weeks, he'd become enthralled with me and gone to my mother to seek my hand in marriage.

My first reaction was violent, passionate refusal. For one thing, he was the same age as my father, with a full gray beard and drooping eyes. Plus, I secretly hoped to marry the stable boy who worked with my father's horses.

That night, my father beat me bloody while my mother watched.

"You should be honored such a man would want you, you ungrateful little bitch! He will guarantee your future!" my mother shouted.

"You will stay in this room without food or water until you've had time to reconsider. Maybe it will give you a taste of what your life will be like if you refuse this good man's hand," Father said, closing the door behind him.

I cried all night, begging all the gods to save me. And just before dawn, I realized that's *exactly* what they were attempting to do in bringing him to our shop that day. Being his wife would mean I was no longer subject to Mother's iron rule and to Father's drunken rages. And more than anything, it meant I could go home to Kenozaria.

Though I had been born there, just as my parents had, I couldn't remember my time in Kenozaria. My family had been exiled from the village when I was three years old, apparently because of Father's drinking habit—something I wasn't supposed to know, but I overheard many arguments in the night, and Mother never failed to place the blame where it belonged.

I had heard that Kenozaria was governed by a body of elders made up exclusively of women, and that daughters were valued members of society. It seemed like a magical place, so different from Salix, where daughters were treated like burdens to be pushed onto someone else as soon as they reached marriageable age.

I had nothing to lose. So when my mother came to wake me in the morning, I made a show of apologizing for my stubbornness and happily accepted the offer. Ronar and I were married in the spring of my fifteenth year and departed for Kenozaria not long after.

That Autumn, I discovered that I had fallen pregnant. I was still so young, and my mother hadn't told me what to expect. I was terrified. So, in a moment of weakness, I turned to my husband's sister, Tabitha, who knew all about herbal remedies and concoctions. She made a dram of some concoction that was supposed to release his seed from my womb.

"I had to be careful to get the dosage just right," she said, handing me the vial. "Too little, and you'll just have a bellyache. Too much, and you'll have a brief but horrendously painful death."

It was so bitter that I nearly couldn't swallow it, but I was willing to try anything. She must have given me too little, because aside from some severe tummy pain and a case of watery stools that lasted a full day and night, the herbs didn't do much, and Evryn came squalling into the world the following summer.

From the moment she was born, I knew I wasn't up to the task of mothering her. Freya hadn't exactly been a supportive, nurturing mother to me, so I worried about the type of mother I'd become. I asked Ronar to hire a wet nurse rather than feed her myself because the feeling of holding her frail little body frightened me, young and inexperienced as I was.

Thankfully, Ronar turned out to be a gentle, kind husband and a caring father. Where I failed, he made up for my weaknesses. Having already raised a child himself, he knew what it took. He was patient with the children, offering them a warm place to nuzzle when their mother's icy countenance repelled them.

I didn't *want* to be so icy. On the contrary, I envied my children's bond with their father. But I felt incapable of offering them what had never been given to me.

Thankfully, though, with each passing year and each new child, mothering came more and more naturally to me. Somehow, though, this created even more distance between Evryn and me. She developed a deep sense of envy over the love she saw me giving her younger siblings, believing, it seemed, that I had simply *chosen* not to love her.

As Evryn grew, she reminded me of rue, the yellow flowering bush that lives in ample supply among the rocks and hills surrounding the village. It can survive with very little water and thrives in the rockiest soil. Like Evryn, all it needs is plenty of sunshine and space to grow. Like rue, Evryn thrived despite her environment and the poor roots she'd inherited. And so I took to calling her Rue as a pet name—one she hates.

When Ronar died, there was nothing left in me to offer my children. The bloom of joy that we'd cultivated together in our simple, contented life shriveled up and died the moment my husband drew his last breath, leaving me feeling just as I had before he'd scooped me up in Salix all those years ago—barely a shell of a person.

Thankfully, Tabitha and Evryn had a strong bond. Ronar and his sister were two halves of a whole, and Evryn did so love her papa.

So, Tabitha mothered Evryn, and the two of them mothered Halline, Ari, and Ziva—at least until Tabitha died just after Evryn's Bright Ceremony, leaving Evryn, once more, without a tender hand to guide her.

By that time, I was carrying more and more responsibility as the new chief of the Sanctum, and it was easier to commit myself to my duties in Kenozaria than to my children. Leadership came more naturally to me than motherhood ever had; The people in our little community were grateful for my guidance, while Evryn resisted me at every turn, rebelling sometimes out of sheer spite, it seemed.

As Evryn came closer to the age I had been when I was forced into marriage, I became more and more nervous. Every little mistake she made grated against my frayed nerves. I saw with stark clarity how my own lack of a loving mother had crippled my ability to offer the same to my daughter, and I worried Evryn would repeat the pattern, but I hadn't a clue how to remedy matters.

So when Minara's eldest son, Torek, showed an interest in Evryn, I was more anxious than ever before. After all, Evryn was still a young girl, just eighteen when the two of them agreed to marry.

Of course, Kenozaria was not Salix, and I was not like my mother. I'd never force Evryn to marry someone against her will, and I wouldn't stop her from marrying someone she truly loved. But *Torek*? The boy was far from ready for marriage, that much was certain, and it took years for him to convince me that his dedication to Evryn was sincere. With time, though, I warmed to him.

When Ari began spending more time with Torek's little sister, Lyra, I decided it was time to get to know their mother, Minara, and her family better. She was also a member of the Sanctum, and as I got to know her, I realized she and her husband were good people. I believe they would be good to my children, should our two families come to share this double bond.

And then Torek disappeared, leaving Evryn with a broken heart that I well understood, having survived the loss of my Ronar. I could have advised her, guided her down that dark path. But when I tried to comfort her, there was an icy chill between us, this time radiating from Evryn. It was as if she was lost in an abyss of hurt she could not translate into words. So Halline took over the job of comforting Evryn, continuing the trend of my children mothering one another in the face of my inability to do so.

But now, it's me that Evryn needs—only me. I *must* not fail her now.

Standing up from the washbasin and drying off my pruned skin, I'm so tired I nearly don't make it to my bed.

"I'm coming, Rue," I whisper as I fall asleep.

12

Torek

I've imagined a thousand times what it would be like to see Evryn again, to smell the scent of her hair, to feel the warmth of her skin against mine. Many a night, I've lain awake trying to remember what her voice sounded like, or imagining her reaction when we were finally reunited.

Now, as Korina and I walk toward the Branngardian camp, all my hopes are dashed.

"She will be overjoyed to see you, Torek," Korina says as if she's been reading my mind.

"I certainly hope so."

"She'll be shocked, sure. But you're the love of her life. You know she won't turn you away," she says, patting me on the shoulder.

"Except for the fact that she married another man."

Korina's smile fades. "Yes, there's that. But let's not give up hope just yet."

As we approach the Keno River, I step in first, giving Korina a hand and guiding her across the slippery rocks in the riverbed. After we climb out of the river onto the western embankment, we rest for a few minutes, eating some of the berries and nuts we packed for the trip. Then, we continue on.

We finally arrive at the edge of the Branngardian encampment just as the sun has begun its slow descent across the western sky.

"I am Korina Freya, Chief of the Sanctum of Kenozaria," Korina says, addressing the soldiers who are standing guard in front of a wooden barricade, blocking the path ahead. "I'm here to negotiate for my daughter's release."

The guards appear confused. They confer briefly in a foreign tongue, then one of them breaks away and runs back toward the camp. When he returns, he has an older man with him, wearing an ornate red, orange, and yellow dress.

"You're here to see the Torch?" he asks in broken Kenozarian.

"Yes. I was invited. I am the chief of the Sanctum in Kenozaria. Your leader is expecting me."

"And who are you?" he asks, addressing me.

"This is my guard, Torek Minara," Korina says on my behalf. "He is escorting me." *Guard?* I can hold my own in a fight, sure, but I'm certainly no guard, and she doesn't need one; She could beat *me* in combat any day, even at her age. But Korina Freya doesn't do anything without reason, so I don't ask questions.

The Branngardians speak with one another briefly. "Fine," the priest says. "You'll have to surrender your weapons."

"We carry no weapons," Korina replies, holding her hands up.

The soldiers eye us suspiciously, clearly trying to assess whether we could be concealing anything deadly. They decide we're harmless and wave us on, around the wooden barricade. And it's good because had they attempted to check, they'd have found the dagger I've strapped high up on my thigh, just in case.

We are escorted to a massive tent, larger than any I've ever seen, that sits at the center of the camp. As we approach, the guards at the entrance check us once more for weapons, as if we could have somehow acquired some on the way. Thankfully, they're not very thorough. Having found nothing, they lead us inside.

Sitting before us in a plush chair is an unremarkable man, dressed in a wine-red tunic. He stands to greet us when we enter.

"What an honor it is to finally meet you," he says cheerily, addressing Korina in Kenozarian. He invites us to sit in the chairs opposite his. "I am the Torch of Branngard, but you may call me Akkar. This is Draven Firon, my master-at-arms."

"Pleased to meet you, me lady," Draven says with a slight bow, his own Kenozarian nearly impossible to understand.

"Thank you for admitting us," Korina says, addressing the Torch. "I am Korina Freya, and this is my guard, Torek. We come on behalf of my daughter, Evryn."

"Ah, Evryn. Sweet girl, your daughter," Akkar says, waving over a servant who carries wine and fruit. "We're glad you've finally come! We were beginning to think you'd left the island, or..." he says, trailing off.

Korina smiles uncomfortably. "No. I wouldn't leave my children like that—not willingly, anyway. I was unwell, recovering in a relative's home in a distant town. I got here as soon as I could."

"Well, then. I'm sure your daughter will be overjoyed to know you're recovered."

"May we speak with Evryn?"

The Torch takes a long drink of water. "Alas, you've arrived a mite too late," he says casually.

"Too late?" Korina asks, anxiety rippling in her voice. "What do you mean? Last we knew, she was married to the captain of your army and doing quite well."

"Yes, she *is* happily married to my nephew, Lukin, a development which I am most pleased with. They do make the most darling couple. Imagine their children!"

I shift in my chair. "Where is Evryn? You promised to release her if Korina came to speak with you."

"*I did* make that promise, but when my nephew came to me and confessed his ardent wish to marry the girl, I couldn't turn him down. I do so love him, and he has an unfortunate tendency to capitalize on that weakness from time to time. Not that I understand why he'd choose her over one of our own fine ladies back home, but alas... the follies of youth!"

"Yes, I imagine that *would* be hard for you to understand," Korina remarks, unfazed by his insult.

"Ah, well. We may as well make the most of it, hmm? Such a marriage can be the foundation of a strong alliance between our two countries."

"I demand to speak with my daughter," Korina says, standing up from her chair. "Now."

Akkar stands, too, and a few of his guards step inside the tent, having heard the tension in her voice. Akkar raises a hand to stop the guards from coming closer.

"As I said, you have come too late. My nephew has been called away to Branngard on some personal family business and taken his new bride with him."

I start forward, but Korina places an arm in front of me to stop me. "And when will they be returning?" she asks.

"Oh, there is no telling, my lady. Maybe never? Branngard is such a beautiful place, you see. Modern and flourishing, as I hope we can one day make Kenozaria, together!"

Korina drops her arm. "If you will excuse us, we'll be returning to our homes."

"Oh, but you mustn't go now, not like this," Akkar says, circling around to stand between us and the entrance to the tent. "We are neighbors now! Let us make an effort to regard one another with the same respect you hold for the leaders of the other tribes on the island. We have no qualms with your people, I assure you!"

"She said we'll be leaving now," I say, stepping closer to him. "If you'd like to arrange for a more formal meeting with the chief, you may send word to our village. But now, we are going."

Akkar bites his lip in frustration but motions his guards to back down. "I see. Well, I wouldn't dare hold you. But do look out for my invitation, won't you? We have much to discuss regarding the future of *our island*."

With that, he steps out of the way, and we leave the tent.

Korina and I are walking back to Kenozaria, and I can tell that she's in no mood to talk with me, but I can't stop myself.

"I can't believe this. I refuse to. You know Evryn wouldn't willingly leave the island like this. That's not like her. This is her *home*."

Korina looks across the horizon for a moment. "I'm not sure I know what Evryn would do, Torek. And if she truly has left the island, there's not much we can do about it."

I'm taken aback. "You don't mean that."

"What can be done? We don't have the naval power to go after her, not while we wait to see what he intends to do to Kenozaria. I have a responsibility to our people, to protect our home, to defend the mountain."

"We cannot let them take her! How can you just... give up?"

"I am not *giving up*. But we cannot abandon Kenozaria to chase my daughter. Evryn is a grown woman, and she is strong. If she truly doesn't want this marriage, she will find a way back home. At this point, it is out of our hands."

"And the village? What of us? You are too smart to believe that Branngard will stop at this arbitrary line in the sand. We must raise the banners and call our allies to our aid. We must be ready!"

"That would be seen as an act of war by Branngard, and they'd be right!" she says, frustrated. "If we spread this news across the island, there *will* be outright war, and not everyone will side with us. Believe me, child, you don't want to witness that kind of war. No. You let *me* worry about how best to protect Kenozaria."

With that, she turns and walks on ahead, leaving me to trail behind her, alone with my tortured thoughts.

* * *

Falling in love with Evryn wasn't something that happened overnight. It was more of a long, slow cascade than a fall. But I do remember the day I knew I wanted her for life.

It happened during the summer of my fifteenth year. Mama and Father had been fighting again, about what I can't recall, so Lyra ran to Korina's house, as she often did when she was afraid.

I went there to find her and bring her home after the chaos had died down, and I found her playing—not with Ari, as she usually did, but with Evryn. The two were sitting together and Evryn was braiding Lyra's hair, and Evryn was humming a tune she'd heard from some traveling musicians over the summer. As I stood watching, out of their sight, Lyra turned and looked at Evryn.

"Does every couple fight like Mama and Papa?" Lyra asked.

Evryn finished Lyra's braid and brushed a finger across her cheek. "Well, not quite so passionately, no," she said. "People who love each other shouldn't hurt one another as much as they do. But everyone has disagreements."

"Well, I'm *never* getting married."

"You don't have to, you know," Evryn replied.

"I don't?" Lyra asked, turning to look into her eyes.

"No, of course not. You could love lots and lots of people in your life and never find one you wanted to build a family with. But maybe you'll find someone who just… feels like *home*."

"You mean like you and Torek? You never argue!"

Evryn laughed. "Oh, believe me, we do. But we always apologize if we've hurt each other, and we work hard to prevent such issues. Your brother makes me feel safe to be myself and he accepts my flaws. So I'm patient with his."

Lyra sat for some time, playing with the end of her braid, like she was thinking about what Evryn said. "Okay, well… if it's someone like *that*, I guess I'll think about it."

That day, seeing Evryn with my sister—offering Lyra an honest, balanced perspective on what love truly looks like—I knew Evryn was my home. The knowledge settled into my heart, and I haven't questioned it since.

But then, I guess that's not *quite* true. I've never wondered if Evryn was the best partner for me, but I *have* entertained the idea of exploring other options. It didn't happen on purpose, of course.

I was betrothed to Evryn the night I was stabbed, and all I wanted was to get home safely, back into her arms. But the gods had other plans for me.

* * *

When she found me in the forest that winter night, I thought I'd died and she was an ancient one, come to welcome me to the trees atop Mount Zaria. It could have been the fever, but she appeared to me as a being of pure light.

That fever gripped me for many days more, and it took a week before I was able to eat solid food again without pain and retching. After two weeks, I was finally well enough to leave bed.

"You'll need to take your time," she said from the hearth, where she sat stirring a stew of deer, carrot, and wild greens.

"Thank you for your hospitality," I said.

"Of course," she replied, helping me into a chair next to the hearth. "You would have died otherwise. If not the fever, my men would have made easy business of you."

"Your men?"

She stood back up, having helped me sit in the chair. "Yes, my men," she said, ladling some stew into a bowl and handing it to me.

I took a deep breath, savoring the vapor. "Who are you to have your own men?" I took a careful bite, and it tasted as good as it smelled.

"I am Nerys Beretta," she said, greeting me. "And they're my husbands, each one."

I choked on the stew. "I... I'm not hungry, after all."

She laughed a deep, hearty laugh. "Oh, calm yourself. If I wanted to kill you, I'd have left you to the wolves. Or the fever, or the men."

I couldn't believe it. Everyone knew Nerys Beretta was an old crone who used her powers to punish young men who turned down her advances. She'd refused to take part in her Bright Ceremony decades ago, claiming she didn't need the guidance of the ancestors to help her live well, and had chosen to make her own way in life, far from the mountain, behind the massive walls of her stronghold in the east.

The bitterness and loneliness had caused her to grow ugly and misshapen as the years went by, legend told. There was *no way* this was her. This woman looked maybe ten years older than me, with soft hazel eyes and golden hair, like woven silk.

"You're safe here, but you're welcome to leave anytime you like. My men know to leave you be," she assured me as we sat together at her hearth. But with each day that passed, I found myself less and less inclined to rush back to Kenozaria.

Being with Nerys was a consummate pleasure. Her company was a healing balm. She took me all around the woods outside her fort, showing me flowers I'd never seen before, teaching me about mushrooms that could kill a man with one bite, and others that could bring him to ecstasy. The first night she climbed into my bed, I felt a twinge of guilt rise in me as my body responded to her touch. But when her lips met mine, I found myself unable to resist.

And so time dragged on this way, night after night, day after day. Before I knew it, it was summer. Eventually, all that had happened before she found me in the woods faded into a distant memory and I knew only Nerys. Her fort was my only home, her people my people, her heart my heart.

Then one early summer night, as we worked in her garden, tearing out the weeds and tending to the grapevines, a messenger arrived, handing her a parchment.

"Kenozaria has been invaded," she read. Her face was troubled.

Kenozaria. It sounded familiar, like someone I once loved.

"Chief Korina Freya has been taken to Salix," she continued reading. "And her daughter, Evryn, is missing."

Suddenly, all the memories began to pour over me. Evryn and Lyra in the bedroom talking. Evryn skin-to-skin with me in the meadow, the smell of pine and mountain lavender in her hair. Evryn and my mother, cooking a meal together. I had to return to her, to them, without delay.

The next morning, I set off.

"We shall see one another again, Torek Minara," Nerys whispered, pressing her forehead against mine. "Go, be well, and remember this time we shared."

"Thank you, again, for saving my life. And for your kindness and hospitality," I said, turning south toward Salix.

"It was my honor," she said, stepping back behind the wooden gates, which shut between us.

I knew I would have to come up with a story that would explain my absence and it would have to be convincing enough to win over Korina. Because as much as Evryn tries to distance herself from her mother, she relies on her mother's guidance, even as she resists it. If I could get Korina on my side, maybe she could sway Evryn to give me a chance.

When I arrived in Salix, I was ready with my story, and somehow, against all odds, they bought it—all but Rayyan. She took a bit of convincing, but eventually, I won her over, too. It was she who suggested I should be the one to look after Korina, and thank the gods she did.

* * *

After arriving back in Kenozaria, I say my goodbyes at Korina's house and head home to my family. They are waiting for me with open arms and some of my favorite foods. When I finish eating, I go to my bedroom and attempt to sleep, to no avail. I lie awake well into the night, unable to sleep.

I can't stop the images that flash across my mind—that man caressing the skin I worshiped, loving the woman the gods destined for me. If I ever *do* see him, I'll make sure he knows who I am and what he took from me.

III

Winter

13

Evryn

When they dropped the sails and the Nightengale caught the wind, I turned to see my homeland drifting farther and farther behind me. My heart shattered.

Kenozaria was even more beautiful from afar than I could have known, lost as I was in her forests and hills. The rich, dark green of the pines stood in stark contrast against the white granite peak of Mount Zaria, all of it surrounded by sparkling blue-green waters.

Every ounce of me wanted to jump overboard and swim back, come what may. As the sea spray swept against my face and neck, whipping my loose hair around, I cried silent tears, alongside Lukin, who stood stone-faced next to me with his hand on mine on the deck rail.

Mere days after our wedding, Akkar had insisted that Lukin was needed back in Branngard, to raise support for the ongoing work of bringing us "savages" to heel. And, as Lukin put it, Akkar wanted to "ensure the safety of the Jewel of Kenozaria." In other words: keep me as far away from my people as possible.

The Jewel of Kenozaria. He's taken to calling me that as a mockery and a threat, so I never forget the thin line that protects me from him. "Jewels go missing all the time," he'd said that day in the tent when he gave me that impossible choice, and now he's made sure I remember the precariousness of my situation.

After a week of seasick days and awkward nights lying next to Lukin in our tiny cabin, attempting to sleep, we docked in Marpum.

My senses are assaulted by a thousand unfamiliar sights, sounds, and smells. There are more people in Marpum than in all the villages in Kenozaria combined. The men wear various shades of gray, brown, and red, while the few women I see are covered head to toe in thick black swaths of fabric that cascade down past their ankles, dragging behind them in the dust of the road.

The buildings, too, are odd. Made of heavy gray stones and red clay bricks, they are tall and magnificent, with huge windows and ornate roofs. Everywhere I look, I see the sigil of Branngard—flying on flags, painted on the sides of buildings, beaten into the armor of the soldiers all around the docks.

The smell of a thousand people and livestock and the dust from the road clog my passageways, causing me to cough and sneeze. I hope Lukin's home is far from this place, and greener. I don't understand how people could live in such a place, with no access to fresh air or room to roam free.

As we walk down the gangplank, people begin to take notice of me, and soon, we're surrounded by a crowd, pointing and whispering. Lukin takes my hand in his as our retinue of Shield—a "gift" from Akkar—surrounds us and pushes people away.

"Our carriage should be here by now," Lukin says, looking around anxiously.

"Carriage?"

He laughs under his breath. "Yes, it's like a cart, but large and luxurious, and drawn by horses instead of donkeys."

"Horses?"

He points one out, across the street. It looks like an enormous donkey, but more graceful and *much* more powerful. And now I see them everywhere. Some are trotting along with single riders, some nibble on piles of hay, slapping their long tails around to keep the flies away, and others are pulling carts of vegetables or barrels bound for the bellies of the ships along the dock.

Just then, what I assume is our carriage arrives. The four black horses who pull it tower over me, huffing and snorting with impatience. They are *magnificent*. The carriage itself is also black as night. Emblazoned alongside each other on both doors is a phoenix, engulfed in flames, and the flame sigil of Branngard.

As the carriage comes to a stop, a young woman with Lukin's same red hair and green eyes steps out, followed by a stocky soldier who steps down from his seat in front of the carriage.

"Evryn Korina, meet my sister, Lady Navya Qaronin, and Sir Orlo Barex, our resident knight," Lukin says in Kenozarian, then introduces me to them in Branngardian. I'm not sure what he says about me, but his sister seems unimpressed. She bows to him before responding in Branngardian.

"Navya says my family and the servants are happy to welcome me back home, and she is pleased to meet you."

At this, Navya bows to me, too, without meeting my gaze.

I greet her in the way of my people, to which she responds with a simple nod and a clearing of her throat. She turns again to Lukin, and the two of them briefly speak before Lukin opens the door of the carriage and ushers us in. He and Sir Orlo load our few belongings atop it before Lukin climbs inside and Sir Orlo takes his seat next to the driver in front. I turn to see our retinue of Shield climb atop several horses and pull up, two ahead of the carriage and two behind.

The carriage is even more spacious than it looked from the outside, large enough to hold my entire family. The seats are adorned with soft red velvet, detailed in gold. The door handles and edging glimmer in the soft glow of morning sunlight that filters through the curtains on the carriage windows.

"How far are we from your home?" I ask.

"We should reach the cairn by nightfall. And it's *our* home." He smiles.

As the carriage starts moving, we are jolted forward. Beyond the docks, we pass through a bustling neighborhood, full of people selling sweets and pastries and baubles. Children chase each other through the alleys as the salespeople swat them with brooms and canes and others close up their wares and flee from the rain that begins to fall. The women in this part of the city wear more colorful clothing, and less of it in general.

Eventually, the carriage pulls out of the city and onto a rougher road, surrounded by rolling moors. The sky is overcast in winter gloom, and the brown moors are covered in frost.

"Come spring, this will all be green and vibrant," Lukin says, watching me as I look out the window at the landscape.

Now and then, we drive past a small home or a modest farm, and more than once we are waylaid by a flock of sheep crossing the road behind their shepherd, with dogs nipping at their heels.

As the carriage bumps along north and west, Lukin and Navya carry on in Branngardian. Occasionally, Lukin translates a snippet or two, but for the most part, I am left to my thoughts.

As the hours wear on and the sun moves in her arc across the sky, I find myself struggling to stay awake. Each time I doze off and wake again, there is a new landscape flying by outside the window of the carriage. Now it's soft rolling hills, now a stone bridge across a raging river, now craggy climbs speckled with wiry pines. Soon we are crawling up, up, up into the mountains.

After what feels like forever, the carriage comes to a stop, jolting me awake for the final time. When I look out the window, I see a massive, dark building looming ahead of us. It is the largest building I have ever seen in my life, towering over the tallest trees. Candles light some of the windows, but most are dark. It looks like it's been standing there, hidden in the mist, for thousands of years.

Someone steps forward and opens the carriage door. Lukin exits before helping Navya and me down. We are greeted by a retinue of servants. Unlike the women closer to the docks or the women in the city, these women wear black linen tunics over matching trousers, and their heads are covered in red cloth. It's unclear if they're trying to hide their hair or keep it out of their faces.

After bowing to us, an older woman approaches Lukin and signs something to him.

"This is our dear Banu," Lukin explains, smiling warmly. "Our Head of House. She keeps this place running like clockwork. She says it's an honor to finally meet the beautiful new lady of Yarrow's Cairn."

This isn't a title I realized I'd have, and it makes me uncomfortable, but I smile anyway. I turn to the younger women standing with Banu and greet them with a bow, as Banu had greeted me.

Navya, watching the scene, clears her throat in what sounds almost like a laugh, confusing me.

"You don't bow to *anyone*," Lukin whispers. "They're showing you honor, as their lady."

"Oh," I remark. "How should I respond then?"

"Smile and nod," he says. So I do.

"Why aren't they saying anything?" I ask Lukin as we walk through the open door of the castle.

"Servant women have their tongues cut out when they enter service," he whispers.

I'm mortified. "It's a wonder you *have* any servants then. And why only the women?"

"They didn't *choose* this life. They're born into it. And when they come of age, they're… initiated. It's an honor, my father always said. They are proud to be in our service."

"You don't believe that, do you? And again… why only the women?"

Lukin sighs. "Because *Rhysvox* declared that slave women were only good for two things: serving the needs of the household and the needs of their lord, and neither requires a tongue."

Now I understand what he meant by the women not choosing to serve but being born into it; Branngardian lords get a two-for-one deal: free pleasure *and* the chance of acquiring a new slave in roughly nine months.

It bothers me, but I decide to drop the subject for now and follow him through the long, cavernous corridors.

"Are you hungry?" Lukin asks as we enter a dining room with a dark wooden table long enough to feed every man, woman, and child in Kenozaria, and laden with enough food to feed all of them. The walls are covered in the same heavy velvet as the carriage, and the Velga family crest is emblazoned on tapestries along the walls.

"I think I need to sleep," I reply.

Lukin says something to the servants, who cover the food and take it away. "Of course. I'll show you to our rooms," he says, leading me up a big flight of stairs to the second floor.

The lord of Yarrow's Cairn requires a full *floor* of rooms, apparently, each the size of an entire home back in Kenozaria. Dark and gloomy, the walls and furniture seem to be coated in a hundred years of dust.

"Here's our sleeping chamber," he says, taking me into the largest of the rooms.

There, in the center, stands a massive, dark bed with four posts holding up a canopy. The windows are hung with heavy fabric that doesn't permit any light. Lukin immediately gets to work building a cot on the far side of the bed.

"What are you doing?" I ask.

"Making a bed for myself."

"This bed is more than big enough for the both of us." I laugh. "And the rest of your family, I'd wager."

Lukin makes a curious face and drops the blanket he'd been folding. "I assumed you'd like to sleep alone."

"We shared a cabin aboard the ship, Lukin. I know you don't bite."

Lukin laughs. "Well, we didn't have much of a choice in the matter there, but here, we have more privacy."

"And what do you think the servants will say when they come in each morning and see the lord of Yarrow's Cairn, Lukin Velga himself, sleeping on a pile of blankets on the floor?"

"Easy!" he says before grabbing the whole pile, walking over to the window seat, lifting the top, and throwing the lot inside. Then he barrels over to the bed and climbs under the blankets. The whole process takes him but a moment. "They'll never suspect a thing."

"You've clearly had practice with that," I laugh.

Lukin smiles slyly and invites me under the covers. I collapse next to him, fully clothed, and don't wake until the following afternoon.

14

Lukin

"Is she *still* sleeping?" Navya asks, adding more bacon to her plate.

"She's exhausted, sister. It was a long journey, and this is all a lot for her to take in. She's never left her island before."

"*Clearly.*" Navya laughs.

"Now, stop that," Mother scolds Navya as she takes her own seat at the table. "She's your brother's wife, after all, and the new lady of the cairn, and you'll show her the proper respect."

"Mmhmm." Navya rolls her eyes dramatically as she takes a drink of orange juice.

"I wish you'd been here to greet us last night," I say.

Mother smiles and thanks the servant who brings her an egg to crack into her cup. "Oh, darling, I *am* sorry about that. We didn't return from Rhys Domus until an hour or so before you arrived, and I was simply too tired to stay awake."

"Too *drunk*, more like it," Navya remarks under her breath.

Mother narrows her eyes on Navya. "Why are you still *here*? You have a home of your own, you know. Hasn't your husband asked for you?"

"*Someone* had to greet the good lord of Yarrow's Cairn at the docks since the dowager lady was *indisposed*," she says. "And anyway, my husband probably hasn't noticed my absence. He has plenty of other… *activities* to keep him distracted."

Mother throws back the concoction in her cup and groans. "It is *your responsibility* to make sure his focus stays on you and your duties to each other, daughter."

"Yes, Mother," Navya says, haughtily.

"Navya, don't tire me this way. You've been married for a year now! If he doesn't get you with child soon, eyebrows will wag."

"Yes, Mother."

"Now, back to our new dear lady. What was her name again? Eleven?"

"*Evryn*," I correct her. "Evryn Korina."

"Interesting name," Mother replies. "And tell me: what is it about this *Evryn* that was so good you had to break your engagement with that darling, wealthy Brailen girl? The servants say she looks plain, so I doubt it's about her looks."

"I explained in my letter; we had no choice."

"Oh, you had a choice, all right," Navya says. "Me? Now that was a *no-choice* sort of situation, but you? You're *Lord Lukin Velga of Yarrow's Cairn*! You have all the choice in the world."

I sigh and take a bite of egg and spread some marmalade on my crust of bread. "Yes, I suppose you're right. I *did* have a choice, and I am proud of the one I made. Evryn is a good woman. You'll see."

Mother smiles and reaches across the table to take my hand in hers. "Yes, Lukin. I am sure she is. It's not how we'd have *preferred* your life to go, but I am sure she is a delight, and we will do all we can to ease her transition here."

"I, for one, don't understand why we have to host four Shield, with their clanking armor and loud boots echoing through the halls, day and night," Navya whines.

"Now, Navya. Let's be grateful for your uncle's generosity," Mother replies. "They're here to protect us."

"They're here to protect *her*," Navya says. "The precious womb that will bear the next Torch mustn't be left unguarded."

"No one likes it less than we do," I reply, wiping my mouth and hands with the napkin.

We eat in silence until we are interrupted by Banu, bringing me a note.

"Duty calls," I say, standing and excusing myself from the table.

Out in the parlor, I greet Sir Timur Wexley with a warm embrace.

"Finally, the lord of Yarrow's Cairn graces us with his presence!" He laughs as we turn toward the side entrance. I grab my heavy cloak and leather gloves from a hook on the wall before we head out into the gardens. The snow from the night before has melted, leaving the landscape brown and the air musty.

"What an honor to have my breakfast interrupted by the new Sir Wexley," I reply, clapping him on the back as we walk.

Timur beams with joy, and for a moment I see the lad I met so long ago in the training grounds at Rhys Domus.

"I may have been knighted, but you brought home a *wife*, good Lukin!" He says, eyeing me playfully. "What's it like?"

"Which part?" I ask. "Being the Lord or being married?"

"Both!"

I was only made the lord of the cairn a few weeks before we embarked for Kenozaria, just after my father passed, so it's not something I've had time to adjust to—much like my new status as Evryn's husband.

"It's... There's a lot to learn."

"Oh, I'd imagine so. And I'd love to hear how you've managed to leave the cairn engaged to the illustrious Lady Selise Brailen and come home with a heathen for a wife!"

For the present, I decide not to argue with him about which of the two women is more civilized than the other. "It's a long story," I reply.

"Oh, I don't doubt it! One doesn't simply break one's engagement with a Brailen girl, after all. An interesting story indeed!"

I chuckle under my breath. There is no way to make Timur understand Evryn's appeal.

"And how fares my little brother?" Timur asks.

"Tygan is doing quite well," I reply. "He follows Draven around everywhere, but that's to be expected."

"Yes, I suppose you're right," Timur says, "I'm just glad he's keeping out of trouble."

I nod, blowing on my gloved hands to warm them.

"And where is the new lady of the cairn?" Timur asks. "Is your mother keeping her busy with some urgent embroidery project?"

"Evryn hates sewing. She's recovering from the trip."

"Well, I hope we shall all finally get to see Her Grace at the feast?"

"Feast?"

"You hadn't heard? The moment your mother received word you'd be returning home, and with a wife no less, she scheduled a massive affair to welcome you both."

Of course she did. Far be it from my mother to do anything quietly and privately. "And when shall I be hosting this feast?"

"In some weeks, I believe," he says, scanning the gloomy horizon.

I nod in agreement and wrap my cloak tighter around me.

"She will be there, no doubt," Timur says, stuffing his hands into his pockets.

"She?" He eyes me severely and it dawns on me: my mother invited Selise. "She wouldn't dare. She is too decent to bring us that sort of embarrassment."

"My apologies. My cousin's wife *would* lie to me about Miss Brailen coming for a fitting this morning for a dazzling new dress that she says needs tailored for an important feast coming up. But there are plenty of feasts!"

"Indeed. Well, we shall handle it with respect and courtesy, if she does show."

A few weeks later, I'm in a hurry, rushing Navya and Mother to finish their shopping, when I see her in an alleyway. I almost miss her, but the sunlight gleaming on her golden hair grabs my attention.

Nora stands begging on the side of the road in filthy, torn rags. As she readjusts her hood, I see that her left eye is encircled in a large purplish-blue bruise. She's carrying a baby who can't be older than a few months. After ushering the ladies into the carriage, I send them on their way in the care of Sir Orlo and make an excuse to stay behind.

She sees me as the carriage pulls away and instantly drops her head to avoid my gaze, but it's too late. I approach her and lead her down another dark alley, farther from the bustling crowd.

"Nora, I..." I begin, unsure what to say next. It's been ten years since my father banished her from the cairn to stop me from getting her with a bastard.

She readjusts the hood of her cloak over her head and tries to pull away from me. I can see the shame in her eyes, and it breaks my heart.

"Why are you out here, on the streets like this? It's freezing! You must get your baby inside," I say, removing my cloak and tossing it over her own threadbare one. "I'm so sorry for this. I had no idea..."

I open my purse to give her all of the spare coins I have, handing my coin purse to her, but she closes my fist around the purse and looks into my eyes. I sigh and open her palm, placing the purse there and closing her fingers around it.

"I would take you home with me and give you all that I have, if I could. You and your baby," I say, gently taking her cheek in my gloved hand. "But I am married now. And even if I *could* bring you back, my mother wouldn't allow your child on our grounds. And that's for the best. You know what they would do to her as soon as she could speak..."

Nora looks frustrated. She knows I'm right. She moves away from me, removing my cloak from around her shoulders and handing it back to me before turning to go, slipping through an alleyway and out of my sight.

I curse Rhys and Keno and Zaria and all the other gods I have discovered on my travels, then tie my cloak back around my own shoulders and head back to the main road to find a carriage back to the cairn.

15

Evryn

Gray water spills out of the bucket and onto the ground, wetting my boots as I sit scrubbing our clothes. Lukin has tried several times to convince me to let Banu and the servants handle it, insisting that it's below my station to wash our laundry.

But I feel like a caged-in animal, desperate for something to do with my hands and to escape my mind—and the Shield, my constant shadows, except when I'm in my bedchamber and when I come to do the washing. Apparently, they don't believe I'm in much danger among women.

It's odd how much comfort I find in the act of washing our clothes. If Mother could see me now, she'd die of shock. I've always hated it, often bargaining with Halline and Ari to trade places. It didn't help that Mother always found the stains I'd missed. Now, though, I find myself enjoying the rhythmic feeling of the clothes spinning and tumbling against my hands in the water.

After I've wrung out the laundry, I toss it into the wicker basket beside me and stand, carrying it to the line. After I hang the clothes, I realize that I'm covered in soap suds and dirty water, so I head upstairs to change.

Having changed into clean, dry clothes, I head down to the dining room to eat brunch with the household. As always, I do my best to pick up on their conversation. I've learned a few words and phrases here and there in the past several months, but I'm still incapable of carrying on a conversation. Lukin does his best to include me by translating the words I don't understand, but much is lost in translation, I'm sure.

A ruckus breaks out in the snowy courtyard below, so we rush to the window to see what's happening. Two guards are arguing heatedly, one of them brandishing a war hammer at the other, his eyes wild with rage.

"What now?" Lukin asks frustrated, dropping his napkin on the table and rushing down to the scene with Sir Orlo.

Men. It doesn't matter whether they're young or old, Branngardian or Kenozarian, they never seem to tire of picking fights with one another. The men back home typically settle things before first blood, but these men seem ready and willing to kill each other if their perceived honor requires it.

When they get down to the two quarrelsome men, Lukin and Sir Orlo cajole them into a friendly handshake, and the scene dissolves.

Quick to fire, quick to ash, as Mother says.

Now I'm thinking of Mother and Halline and Ari and Ziva, and that makes me think of the trees, and now I am thinking of Torek and Papa and Tabitha in the Bright Lands. Panic and sorrow creep up my throat and into my eyes.

"Not helpful," I say under my breath to bring myself back to the present. The dowager and Navya look at me, puzzled, so I apologize and excuse myself. I need a walk. I need to get some fresh mountain air in my lungs. I head down to the mud room and bundle up.

Outside, the Shield follow behind far enough to make me feel like I'm free, but close enough to save my life, thanks to Lukin's insistence that they stop crowding me so much. It's odd to be in such close association with these men and still know nothing about them—not even their names.

As I walk along the eastern edge of the grounds, snow begins falling more heavily. Soon, the rocky crags around the cairn are laden with silver ice and a layer of fresh snow. If I weren't essentially a prisoner, it would be a beautiful sight to behold.

I can't help but think about what Halline and the others must be up to. They will have just celebrated the start of winter—Zaria's season of cold and storms, when whole families gather together to keep our bodies warm and our spirits uplifted... If they still celebrate these things, that is.

I long to send them a letter, to explain myself, to get news of what's happening back home, but Lukin says finding someone trustworthy to bring the letter to them instead of delivering it straight to Akkar would be nearly impossible.

"But what would be so wrong with me communicating with my family?" I asked him once when I brought up the subject.

"Akkar would assume you were spying for your mother and speaking in code. He'd confiscate the letters and send even more Shield here to keep an eye on you."

The idea of being watched more closely than I already am in a place that was supposed to be my home seemed unbearable. "Please, Lukin," I implored him. "Please, try to find someone. Maybe Timur?"

Lukin laughed. "Timur would be the first to report to Akkar, letter in hand."

"Some friend he is."

"No one, absolutely *no one*, is more loyal to their friends than to their own necks. Akkar would have him killed in a slow, bloody way if he were caught. That's too much to ask of anyone."

I could sense the sincerity in his words, so I dropped the subject and did my best to ease into my new life. I willed myself to think only of the future, to forget that I ever was Evryn Korina, daughter of the chief of the Sanctum and betrothed of Torek Minara. Now I am Lady Evryn Velga, Honorable Wife of Captain Lukin Velga, the Lord of Yarrow's Cairn. And Ziva is safe.

By the time I return to our rooms, it's mid-day and I'm exhausted and ready for a nap. Lukin, it appears, has beaten me to it. He is splayed out on the bed, snoring away, while the cat that has made our rooms his personal lair stalks around the room, no doubt chasing a mouse.

I smile at the simplicity of the scene and sit before the hearth, removing my muddy boots and changing into dry clothes, then go to lie in the bed next to Lukin. After an early morning scare some weeks ago—when a servant forgot to knock and found him asleep on his cot on the floor—Lukin had to come up with some elaborate story to explain himself. So he has given up on sleeping on the little cot, and we pass most nights lying mere inches from each other in our bed, never touching.

As I lie next to him, watching his back rise and fall as he snores away on his stomach, I realize that he's just as much a prisoner as I am. His duties as the lord of the cairn, his responsibility to his mother and sister, to the soldiers in his care, to me—he is not any freer than I am to pursue his own interests. He can't even pursue true love, or something like it.

At least my cellmate is handsome and kind. It's not love I feel for him, not even close, but I have to admit I have come to enjoy his companionship. Our conversations about his travels and my experiences in Kenozaria are a pleasant distraction from reality, and he makes me feel safe in an otherwise strange and sometimes frightening new world. I guess one could call it *friendship,* and that's more than some couples ever find, so I'm grateful.

Before long, I fall asleep, lulled by his rhythmic breathing and the sound of the wind blowing across the moors.

When I awake again, it's dark. The cat now occupies the warm spot where Lukin slept, enjoying his own snooze.

I walk back down to the dining hall only to find Lukin and his men happily drinking and singing some sort of sea shanty in a tired, sloppy-drunk fashion. As I approach, Lukin smiles and stretches out an arm.

"Wife!" he says, inviting me to sit on the bench between him and one of the other soldiers. "Did you enjoy your nap?"

"I would have if you hadn't snored so loudly," I laugh, poking him in the chest.

"I bet ya *were* exhausted from all the… ahem… *work* he's been making ya do, aye?" one of the soldiers jests, winking and taking another drink of ale.

"Hey!" Lukin yells, not seriously. "I'll thank you to keep such talk away from our lady's ears!" He's obviously deep in his cups.

"I'll just go see what Banu is up to in the kitchen," I say, trying to find an excuse to leave. I'd much prefer the comparative comfort of our sitting room, with a good book beside the fire. Even if I can't understand the language yet, the books are better company than this drunken lot—and safer, too.

Lukin smiles at me genially before his men start taunting him again.

"You'd better go after her!" one of them laughs. "We know how you love to chase your prey!" Everyone roars with laughter.

As I walk back to our rooms, I pass through a long glass corridor and look up to see that there's a full moon tonight. It hits me that several girls back home will be experiencing their Bright Ceremony tonight, and the realization almost brings me to my knees with longing.

16

Korina

The morning air is crisp. Gentle snow is beginning to fall. Rayyan, Minara, and the other Sanctum members sit alongside me under the tent, waiting for Branngard's arrival. After the fourth time they sent a messenger requesting an audience with the Sanctum, we finally relented. They were supposed to have arrived before midday, but the sun has risen high in the sky and they are nowhere to be seen.

"Not exactly starting off on the right foot, these people," Rayyan says as she wraps a shawl more tightly around her elderly mother's shoulders.

"Maybe he died on the way here?" Minara quips. The group erupts in laughter, and I can't help but join in.

Finally, well after high noon, their little caravan arrives. A hundred soldiers accompany Akkar's litter, all decked out in their finery. When the litter stops, the men carrying it carefully lower it to the ground and several others come to the side of it, sweeping the heavy, brocaded curtains to the side.

Climbing out of his litter with the assistance of his man, Akkar wears a golden crown and carries a massive staff with a crystal atop.

His men behave as if he were a god of sorts, bowing and kneeling before him and never looking him in the eye. It's a pathetic display of submission, and for a man who hardly deserves it, from my estimation.

"That *cannot* be him," Rayyan mumbles as Akkar is lifted out of his litter. "He's what... fourteen?" I stifle a laugh and give her a serious look.

"What a pleasure it is to meet you again, Korina," Akkar says as he approaches my chair, acting as if we're old friends, meeting to catch up over a cup of tea.

"Welcome to Kenozaria." I bow my head, then place my right hand on my chest and extend it to him.

Akkar shakes my hand and then wipes his hand on his clothes. "And these must be your fellow committee members?" he asks, gesturing to the other women.

"The Sanctum," I correct him. "I may be the chief of the Sanctum, but I am only one voice."

"Yes, yes," he replies, waving away my correction. "Shall we begin?"

"You'll see that my guards have stood a distance off," I remark, nodding toward the small group of Kenozarian warriors who wait some feet away from the gathering. "It would make us all more comfortable if you'd ask yours to do the same."

Akkar turns, addressing his retinue, most of whom bow and back up several paces away from the proceedings. One remains.

"I hope you understand if I keep the one guard. Draven here *is* indeed a brave warrior, but he's not in his prime, you see?"

Minara coughs. "Let's proceed," I say, getting the message.

"Perfect!" Akkar replies cheerfully. "Firstly, let me formally thank you for inviting us to this diplomatic meeting. We are most honored by your invitation."

"As you have requested this meeting several times, we are curious as to what you'd like to discuss with us."

"Yes!" he says, turning to Draven, who pulls a rolled-up parchment from his knapsack and hands it to Akkar. "We have several *requests*," he says, raising his eyes to mine and emphasizing the last word.

"Go on."

"First, we request that Kenozaria formally recognize the autonomy of the settlement of Rhysland," Akkar says as if he had asked for a glass of water. "We also ask that Kenozaria formally ally with Rhysland, should any tribes from elsewhere on the island decide to attack us."

His arrogant entitlement makes me chafe with nervousness. Men like him never stop once they've been allowed to cross a boundary, but he isn't the first man to assume that Kenozaria is weak because it's run by women.

"Is there anything else?" I ask.

"Yes, one last thing," he says calmly, folding his hands over one another in his lap. "We ask that Kenozaria host one hundred inhabitants of Rhysland, to teach them your language and your customs and to learn ours from them. I think you can agree that two nations who understand each other better will naturally coexist better."

I glance over at Rayyan, whose jaw is set. Minara looks confused. Plera, Rayyan's mother, looks on with a furrowed brow.

There's no way our people will ever agree to that last request. If we are willing to allow armed strangers to sleep in our homes alongside our children, they've already won: full-scale colonization is underway.

"These are high demands," Rayyan remarks. "One wonders what Branngard is offering in return."

Akkar smiles and hands the parchment to Draven, then stands up from his seat and walks slowly around the tent. He makes a point to stay well away from us, seeing our guardsmen come to attention when he stands.

"This is truly a beautiful land," he says, gesturing to the surrounding landscape. "Rhys be blessed, I have truly never seen a more perfect place. There is fertile soil, mountains to the east for protection, and clean, fresh water in the river. One couldn't ask for more!"

"Yes, we are grateful for our home."

"Branngard is also beautiful, but it's nothing like Kenozaria. The soil is hopelessly rocky, you see. Very little food grows there, unfortunately, and as Rhys has blessed us with more and more people over the years, we have found ourselves struggling to feed everyone."

"A most unfortunate situation," Minara replies.

"Indeed," Akkar says, his face downcast. "It would be a tragedy for so many people to die senselessly. Rhys has made more than enough resources for all His people! And we are *all* His people." He stands in thought for a moment, gazing off into the distance. "If you'll allow me to speak frankly?"

"Of course," I reply.

"It's as simple as this. If you agree to our terms, we may live together peaceably as allies and friends. Our people may intermarry and exchange the bounties we've each been uniquely gifted with."

"And if not?"

"If you refuse to help us in our endeavors to settle here, there can only be one response: Rhys and his soldiers will utterly decimate this land. Everyone you know and love will die a *most gruesome* death." Akkar says all this as if he were speaking of the weather, or what he plans to eat for breakfast.

We all sit speechlessly, taken aback at his audacity.

"Come now! This is a *good* thing!" Akkar continues.

"You realize this is our home? We have knowledge of the land, and the might of the rest of the island would stand beside us. And yet you threaten us with impunity?" Rayyan asks, astonished.

"Indeed, I do know this. And yet, you do not know our god. You people are accustomed to the puny, weak gods you worship—gods who *clearly* cannot protect you from an invading army. Rhys has *never* allowed anyone to successfully invade Branngard, or any of our settlements abroad."

I sit up straighter in my chair, weighing his words. "We wish to convene in private and will return here when we are finished discussing your terms," I say calmly, as the rest of the Sanctum stands and begins moving away from their chairs.

"Of course!" Akkar replies, cheerfully.

"We cannot agree to his terms," I say once we are alone.

"Yes," Plera says. "Out of the question."

"But how will we fight them? We may have the numbers, but we've seen their warriors," Rayyan remarks. "These men are warriors *for life*. They have no other trade, no family, *nothing* distracting them from war. They've been training all their lives for this." Several Sanctum members agree. "Even if we can gather forces from across the island, our people are farmers, healers, blacksmiths. They've got families and lands to protect."

I listen as they speak back and forth. "We should send messengers to the other villages on the island and beg for assistance," Rayyan says.

"It's winter!" one of the other Sanctum members speaks up. "How can we expect our allies to march to our aid now?"

I nod. "We will need to gather forces as quickly as possible. There's no telling when they will attack. All we can do is try. May Keno and Zaria protect our people and this sacred land."

17

Evryn

The wind is howling outside our sitting room window, so I add a few logs to the fire and order some tea. As I sit sipping and staring into the flames, I ponder what I'll do with my time tomorrow. I've already read the books I can understand in the library, and there's not much else to do to entertain oneself in this massive place.

I look down at my threadbare socks. I need a new pair or two. My knitting skills aren't what they should be, though, so I consider asking Banu to buy some thicker socks for me at the market.

After some time, I hear Lukin and Timur's footsteps coming up the stairs, so I head to our bedchamber. I lie down in bed, hoping they'll finish their conversation soon so that I can to sleep, where at least I can dream of home. But the conversation drags on and on. I can't understand what they're saying, but it's clear that Lukin is surprised by whatever Timur has just said. Their voices continue to rise, Lukin sounding increasingly angry and Timur increasingly apologetic. Then Timur says something I *know* I haven't misheard: "Evryn's mother."

Some moments later, the two men quiet down. I hear Timur's

footsteps heading down the stairs just as Lukin comes into our bedchamber. After adding another few logs to the fire in the hearth, he sits down on the bench at the edge of our bed, removing his boots and rubbing his sore feet.

"I'm sorry, we must have kept you awake," he says, not looking at me.

I sit in silence, glaring at him, waiting.

"Is everything okay?" he asks, turning to meet my gaze.

"What did Timur say about my mother?" I ask, directly.

"That she is alive and well."

"And?"

Lukin sighs. "And she came to the encampment looking for you the night before we sailed for Branngard. She thinks you are still a prisoner."

She's right. Though I know he wouldn't stop me from going if I wanted to, I am not free. I've sworn an oath to Lukin, for one thing, and I feel beholden to him. He saved both my life and my sister's, after all, and I can't in good conscience leave him now, knowing how he'd be mocked and ridiculed for it by his men—and, worse: his uncle, the Torch. And at least here, I have my own space, free of Mother's preening and criticism, free of the expectations the village has of me as her eldest daughter. And I have Lukin, for what he's worth.

But now, hearing that she'd come looking for me, an old familiar feeling creeps through me again, something older and deeper than either my affection for Lukin or my sense of obligation to him or even my sense of relief at not living under Mother's iron fist—a longing that doesn't care that my mother has failed me in all the ways that matter from the day I was born, a part of me that simply wants to be near her.

"Did you know?" I ask. "That she had come for me, I mean."

"No. Tonight was the first I'd heard of it. I'm fairly certain Timur wasn't supposed to tell me, but he's loose in the lips when he's drunk."

"How did he get this information?" I ask.

"His younger brother, Tygan, wrote to him. He's a good lad."

"Yes, I remember him. But what did Akkar say to convince my mother to leave? It's not like her to give up that easily."

"He told her we had already sailed to Branngard." Of course he did. Akkar was desperate to keep me as far away from my family and my homeland as he could, for reasons I still don't understand.

As we sit together in the darkness, a thought occurs to me. "Why do you think Akkar framed us for Pomisha's murder in the first place?" I ask him. Somehow, we've never discussed it.

He scratches his beard. "As far as I can tell, he needed to use you as bait to get your mother to the encampment, I assume to discuss matters diplomatically. But then when she came, they only spoke of your whereabouts. Timur heard that she outright refused to discuss anything else once she realized she wouldn't be able to speak with you."

"Why do I matter so much to him? Kenozaria is not like Branngard; I will *not* be my mother's successor."

Lukin shrugs. "It seems as if Akkar set his mind on securing a union between your family and Branngard almost as soon as we arrived. And he must believe that you were the best bargaining chip."

"Is that why you married me? Because Akkar wanted you to?"

"Of course not. For one thing, he was none too pleased when he found out," he says. "And you know I married you to save you from that impossible choice, and to protect Ziva and the rest of your family."

I believe him. I have no reason not to. "But why did he see me as a bargaining chip? I am worthless to him, I assure you."

"That's not true. Ask yourself: if your daughter was suddenly married to the captain of an army that invaded your home, wouldn't you do everything in your power to keep the peace between your people and their people, for her sake?"

I laugh out loud. "As I said, he has it all wrong. He should have married Halline off to you or else waited for Ziva to come of age—anyone but me."

"What do you mean?"

"Korina wouldn't go to war for me. Her first commitment is always to the people of Kenozaria. I am *not* the prize Akkar thinks I am."

"Well, she has refused to speak with him again, no matter how many times he's invited her. So you must mean something to her."

"Sounds like her," I say. Mother is known for her ability to endure uncomfortable conditions for much longer than your typical person when she sets her mind to it. "What will he do if she never agrees?"

"It's hard to say," Lukin says, stretching his arms above his head and yawning. "We've been planning that settlement since I was a young boy. That's how I understand your customs, your language. The Torch and my father worked hard to prepare me for this. I can say this, though: Akkar always gets his way in the end."

"And what does Akkar want with Kenozaria?" I ask. "He was supposed to discuss it with me the morning after we arrived at the encampment, but then... Pomisha... "

"I'm not sure, to be honest. But I know that he sees it as our *responsibility as Rhys's chosen people to spread his worship throughout the land*," he says, imitating Akkar.

"And he does that how? By kidnapping and enslaving young women?"

"It's worked out well for him thus far," Lukin shrugs.

"And the people of Branngard approve of this? How could anyone support such tactics?"

"People don't ask too many questions when their coffers are overflowing and their children are thriving. And the farther Akkar spreads Rhys's worship, the more the realm benefits."

I laugh under my breath. "The most valuable thing on Kenozaria can't be mined or harvested. I'm afraid he's going to be very disappointed."

Lukin stands and walks into his office next to our bedchamber, pulling open a drawer. When he returns, he's holding a rolled-up scroll.

"Have you seen a map of our world?" he asks, unrolling the scroll and laying it on our bed, settling the four corners with some decorative pillows.

I look at the ancient, watermarked piece of parchment with various green and brownish shapes cast about in a sea of blue.

"That is Kenozaria," he says, pointing at a misshapen oval no bigger than my thumb. There is a tiny dot in the upper left quadrant of the island, with a mountain next to it and a river winding from the northwest corner to the southeast.

"Home," I whisper.

"And this," he says, drawing his finger northwest from my island, "is Branngard."

The brown shape of Branngard is at least five times larger than Kenozaria, and the map is much more detailed. There are city names and mountains galore, with forts marked out.

I look at the other shapes spread across the map, the other lands Mother surely tried to teach me about at some point while I was focused elsewhere. One, even larger than Branngard, looms to the east of Kenozaria. It is green and vibrant.

"What's this one?" I ask, pointing to it.

"That large one there is Volander, home of the fairy king, they call him."

"Fairy?" I ask. "You can't be serious."

Lukin laughs. "He's not a fairy, obviously. It's a nickname. My mother is from Volander, thus the red hair and green eyes. And the water there is sweeter and more refreshing than any on earth. See all these rivers?" he asks, pointing. There are at least a dozen rivers marked, stretching out like fingers across the land.

"And what about this one?" I ask, pointing at a brown piece of land, east of Branngard.

"That's Tarsh," Lukin says. "They're good people, humble people, like Kenozarians. It's a dry, rough place. Very hard to survive there, but there are gems buried beneath the soil. Akkar has worked to conquer it for some time, to mine them."

"What is it with men and conquering things?"

"You mean aside from the allure of unimaginable wealth and the unlimited greed of men?" he asks. "Well, I can't say much for other men, but for Akkar, he believes it's about fulfilling his duty to the Branngardian people, to our family, and to Rhys."

"And what do you think, Lukin Velga? Should everyone worship your god?"

"He's not *my god*," Lukin says. "I have only ever worshiped two things, and they have much in common: the sea and women."

"Women? Tell me, wise one: what do the sea and women have in common?"

"They're both endless, full of possibility and an equal measure of danger," he says. "And I love them, the sea and women, both. Heart, body, and soul—nothing is more worthy of worship than a woman."

"Curious that you chose me, then..."

"Oh?"

"My heart is like the woods you found me in. You may not understand all the secrets, but it's not some unknowable mystery like the ocean. It just takes some knowledge of the terrain."

Lukin looks at me curiously. "And what if, in theory, I wanted to learn to navigate your heart?"

"In that case, I'd be happy to guide you." I smile. "At least, in theory."

Lukin smiles, too. "You *are* a prize, Evryn," he says.

"What?" I ask.

"You said you're not the prize that Akkar thinks you are, but you're wrong. You are a blessing and a joy. I am very grateful to have you in my life, in whatever capacity I am able." With that, Lukin kisses one of my hands, then stands to replace the map in the office drawer before walking around to his side of the bed.

I wish he'd stayed and embraced me, but the moment has passed. He lies down on his side of the bed and within a few minutes, his breathing becomes steady and slow.

I wait for sleep to overtake me, too, but like so many nights before, I lie awake, my eyes scanning the canopy of our bed. Finally, I can't take it anymore, so I get dressed and step outside into the hall.

Walking the halls of the cairn, candle in hand, I ponder on our conversation.

Zaria stands strong, protecting us from danger and offering us a place to commune with the spirits of our ancestors, and Keno shares the blessings of the water with every living thing on our land, impartially and without demands. Naturally, we are grateful for their bounty. But who would worship a god like Rhys, whose power I've never seen displayed, beyond the fear his name instills in the people who bow to the Torch?

They will stop at nothing to spread their way of life to my people—to all people, whether they want it or not. That much is clear. But from what I've seen, Branngardian men are raucous and crass and quick to anger, while the common women are either neglected or essentially imprisoned for male pleasure and entertainment, and the wealthier are kept pacified with opulent parties and balls and feasts—extravagant, competitive displays of their wealth and prestige.

No one in Branngard—aside from Akkar, maybe—seems truly

happy.

Eventually, I tire myself out and head back to our bedchamber. As I am walking past Navya's rooms, it sounds as if she is crying. Her voice is muffled, but it's clear she is talking to someone—a man.

I stop in my tracks. I know I should walk away, up the stairs to our rooms, but I can't help but hesitate a bit longer. *Who* could be in his sister's room this late—a *man*, one she is crying to, one who most certainly is *not* her lord husband, or else we'd have met him when he arrived?

As I stand trying to contemplate what to do, I hear the man's footfalls coming toward the door, so I flee around a corner. I see him crack the door just enough to look around, making sure there's no one around to see him. I cannot make out his features in the darkness, but he is very well-dressed. When he is convinced it's safe, he slips out and closes the door quietly behind him before walking down the long corridor toward the eastern staircase.

18

Lukin

Evryn and Selise sit awkwardly side-by-side in the places my mother assigned them. From my spot across the table, seeing them next to one another like that, there is no comparison. Selise is the most alluring creature in Branngard—and lord knows I've seen them all, rebellious and desperate as I was to escape my family's plans for me. She speaks several languages and carries herself with grace and poise. And, of course, there's her family's astonishing wealth, which would have come into my possession—wealth that far exceeds that of even our own Velga family estate.

But Selise Brailen, in all her pomp and finery, pales in comparison to Evryn's effortlessly astonishing beauty. The way her auburn hair falls into her eyes. The way she looks about the room, trying not to make it too obvious that she hasn't a clue what she's supposed to do with all that silverware. *Especially* the way she smiles at me, with that one dimple on her right cheek.

"Doesn't she speak?" Selise asks, interrupting my thoughts. "Or have you married a servant?"

"She is still learning our tongue," I reply. "Believe me, she's very talkative in her own."

Evryn eyes me from across the table, so I translate for her. In response, Evryn attempts to greet Selise in Branngardian.

"What an adorable creature!" Selise laughs, *not* returning Evryn's greeting.

"Indeed!" Timur agrees, lifting his wineglass. "Let us toast to the new Lady Velga!"

"To Evryn," I say, motioning her to stand. Evryn smiles uncomfortably and stands before taking a sip of her wine and sitting again.

"Where are the musicians?" Mother asks from her seat. She's been drinking since the moment she awoke, and it's obvious. "Let's hear some music!" Having been located, the four musicians sit at their spots in the corner of the hall and strike up a classic Branngardian folk song, one about Ilaria's betrayal of Rhys.

"Would the new Lady Velga mind if I took the lord for a walk about the room?" Selise asks Evryn, who looks back and forth between us, confused.

"She wants to talk with me," I explain to Evryn. "Do you mind?"

"Not in the least," Evryn says, turning to Selise and smiling, then she rises from her chair and walks toward the roaring fire in the hearth, wineglass in hand.

"What a... peculiar young thing," Selise says as she takes my arm. "I do wish I understood the allure."

"Yes, I can see why you would struggle to understand."

Unfazed, Selise carries on. "Your dear sister, Navya, is here, yes? I wonder what she thinks of her."

"Indeed. I believe she is upstairs, still getting ready."

Selise chuckles. "Yes, that sounds like Navya. It's a wonder she's been so long away from her own home. I do hope all is well with Lord Qaronin?"

"We are making up for lost time, my sister and I," I reply, looking around the room. Timur and Sir Orlo are speaking to each other in one corner while my mother seems to be trying to communicate something to Evryn by the hearth. "If you'll excuse me, Miss Brailen," I say, but she doesn't release my arm.

"Oh, surely we're not on *those* terms, are we, Lukin?" she asks, smiling sweetly. "Whatever has transpired, we are still old friends, yes?"

"Of course we are," I reply, releasing myself from her grip. "And I see that my wife needs me."

Selise smiles sardonically. "Yes, she *certainly* needs you." With that, she turns to find my mother and strikes up a conversation with her.

I head toward the hearth but see that Evryn has returned to her seat at the table. Just then, Navya comes down the stairs, looking radiant as ever.

"Sister," I say, approaching her. "I was beginning to think you'd run back to Lord Qaronin."

Navya chuckles. "Never," she says under her breath before turning her attention to a few of the ladies gathered around the table, so I take my seat, across from Evryn.

"You're doing a wonderful job," I say under my breath, smiling warmly.

"Those guards are doing a wonderful job of monitoring my every move," she replies, rolling her eyes and motioning toward our group of Shield, who stand in the corner of the room, watching her with eagle eyes. "And your *mother*... Of all the seats, she placed Miss Brailen in the chair *right next to mine*. And here I thought *my* mother was the tactician of the family."

"Yes, she does have her moments," I reply, laughing. "Don't take it to heart. She's a bored old woman with nothing to occupy her time but court gossip and trouble-making."

"And planning feasts, apparently," she says, gesturing to the room.

"Ah, that was all Banu."

Evryn takes a sip of wine. "And why isn't she here to enjoy her hard work?"

I am not sure how to respond. The obvious answer is that, much as we love her, Banu is still a servant. Sure, she has worked her way up through the ranks and she enjoys the benefits of her elevated station, but she would still *never* be permitted to attend such an event. But I know this won't make sense to Evryn. "I assume she is tired," I reply instead.

Evryn doesn't buy it for a minute, but chooses to drop the subject, it seems.

Selise and Mother return to the table, followed by the rest of the guests, and soon, the servants bring out the next course and more wine.

"Tell us, Lady Velga," Selise says, slightly slurring her words before taking another sip of wine. "How did you and Lord Velga meet? I understand he was tasked with capturing you and this... somehow lead to love?"

"Quite the peculiar story!" one of the other ladies quips from her spot farther down the table.

"Yes," I reply for Evryn, realizing that everyone in the room must have already heard the story, one way or the other. "There was more to it than that, but that's the general story."

"Do they not *eat* where you come from, girl?" Mother asks Evryn, too loudly. Evryn looks at me, confused.

"She's asking if you like the food?" I ask her. She smiles and takes a bite of the stewed greens in front of her, but struggles to swallow them. "This is a new place with new foods," I explain on her behalf.

"I shall ask Banu to make some frogs and crickets for her breakfast tomorrow," Navya quips as her friends laugh.

Evryn looks around at the women at the table and then directs her gaze at me. She may not understand what was said, but she knows when she's being laughed at.

"I believe she will do just fine," Timur says, coming to my rescue. "My own wife is from the Fire Isles, and it took some time for her to adjust, too."

"Yes, I have full confidence in my wife," I say, extending a hand to her across the table. Evryn takes my hand and smiles.

"Speaking of... wherever she is from, I have some news," Selise says, taking a bite of duck.

"Oh?" I ask.

"Apparently, the chief of the savages, Korina—a *woman*, if you can believe it—is creating problems for us, and the Torch is losing his patience. War is on the horizon after all," Selise says, faking sympathy. "They say he is planning a full-scale invasion soon."

"What did she say?" Evryn asks, looking concerned. "I heard her say my mother's name."

I take a deep breath. "It was nothing of consequence." This could all be Selise's attempts to unnerve Evryn, or it could be baseless gossip. And if it *is* true, what's the point in telling her about something she and I are helpless to stop?

"I see. So, you won't tell me. That must mean it's very bad news," Evryn replies, setting her napkin down on the table.

"Please, don't give any stock to her words. She is trying to intimidate you."

"Will you two stop blabbering on in that horrendous language?" Mother calls out from her spot. "Keep your bedroom talk for the bedroom!" The group erupts in laughter.

"To Lord Velga," Selise says, lifting her glass. "And to... *wiser matches.*"

"To wiser matches," I reply, unsmiling. She has no idea how right she is.

Eventually, the party dies down and the guests begin to leave. I escort Evryn up to our room and make my excuses, promising to come right back. There is something I must do.

When I come back downstairs, only Selise and Timur remain as Banu is ordering servants around to begin cleaning up after the feast.

"I'll escort Lady Selise to her carriage," Timur says, throwing his cloak over his shoulder and pulling on his gloves.

"Yes, that's a good idea. But may I have a word before you go?" I ask Selise.

"Oh, but of course! Anything for Lord Velga," Selise says, tripping on the hem of her dress.

When I have gotten her out of earshot of Timur and Banu and the servants, I place my hands on her shoulders and look down into her eyes. "You are not to return to the cairn *ever* again. This is the home of the Velga family, and my wife, Lady Velga, will be honored in her own home."

"You jest!" Selise laughs until she realizes I am serious. "Lukin, really! You *cannot* be happy like this! *I* could have made you happy. You don't have to lose out on us," she says, trying to pull me closer.

"You are the last woman alive who could have made me happy, Miss Brailen," I remark. "And there never has been an 'us' to lose out on."

"Don't be so self-righteous, Lord Velga. Even you with all your lofty morals have *needs*, needs I am happy to fill, from time to time…" she says in a husky voice.

"Good evening to you, Miss Brailen," I reply, turning to leave.

Evryn is lying in bed when I enter our bedchamber. "Please forgive my delay," I say, sitting down in a chair by the hearth to remove my boots.

"The lord of the cairn has many responsibilities," Evryn remarks dryly.

"Yes, unfortunately."

I stand by the hearth, looking into the fire and pondering the events of the night. Selise attempting to lure me into her bed, Evryn's bold confidence in the face of their jeers, my mother embarrassing us as always...

"What did she *really* say, Lukin?" Evryn asks, bringing me back to the present.

I sigh heavily. "She said some pretty hurtful things about your home, that's all," I lie. "I didn't want to tell you because it would hurt you unnecessarily."

"How can such a beautiful woman have such an ugly spirit?"

"I couldn't have said it better myself. But most people here aren't very astute when it comes to these things."

"Yes, it seems so. If only Tabitha were here..."

"Tabitha?" I ask.

"My late aunt, my father's sister. She knew how to read someone's spirit before they even walked into the room," she says, smiling. "I miss her."

"You know, here, when someone loses a loved one, we say, 'May Rhys warm them.' Because death is so cold, so final."

"Not back home. Tabitha is still very much alive, just not in the way she was before. She lives with our ancestors among the trees atop Mount Zaria."

"That's a comforting thought," I say, unsure how to explain that neither her ghost stories nor my uncle's elaborate myths hold any weight in my scales. "Speaking of being cold, it's chilly in here. I'll send for more firewood."

"Good idea," Evryn remarks, rubbing her shoulders and wrapping herself in the blanket.

"Come, join me by the fire."

"Or you could come to join me in bed," Evryn says, lifting the blanket and inviting me closer. I am unsure how to respond. She's never initiated any sort of intimacy. It could be the wine, but she didn't drink much. Frozen by indecision, I continue unlacing my boots in silence. "Or not," she says, dropping the blanket and rolling onto her side.

I decide to head down and gather the firewood myself from the hall. When I return, she is still curled up in the blanket, awake, staring at me.

"Please don't be offended," I say. "This is a new experience for me, too."

"I am not offended," she says, "but I am cold." With that, she stands up from the bed, still wrapped in the blanket, and approaches the fire as I add a few logs. I am expecting her to sit down on the bench at the foot of the bed, but she approaches me, just as I am turning to grab another log to add to the fire. I bump into her, causing her to trip and fall backward onto the bed, bringing me with her. We both erupt in a fit of laughter.

"Well, this is one way to get things started," she laughs.

I clamber off of her and sit on the edge of the bed, laughing all the way, too. "My apologies," I say once I've finally caught my breath.

"There's no need," she says, smiling. "I *am* your wife, after all."

"Technically, yes. But…" I say, unsure how to maneuver the situation. I want her so badly sometimes that I can taste it, but I find myself unable to respond to her advances when I recall *how* she came to be my wife.

"It's no problem. I'm not one to force myself on a man. I know when I'm not wanted," she says.

"It's not that—of *course* you're wanted," I begin.

"Just not by you?" she asks.

I can't will myself to speak.

Evryn takes my hand and looks directly into my eyes. "I know what you want, Lukin."

"Oh?" I ask, feeling myself beginning to warm up. I can't tell if it's the fire in the hearth or the one in her eyes, but either way, it's working.

"Yes," she says, smiling coyly. "You want some of that *fantastic* cake Banu baked for us." She stands up from the bed and walks over to the table in the sitting room, bringing me a plate with a small piece of moist, chocolate cake.

"You know me so well, wife," I say, awkwardly taking the plate from her.

IV

Spring

19

Evryn

It's obvious to me, but I doubt anyone else in the cairn knows; the signs are hard to detect for the untrained eye. If it weren't for Tabitha's careful instruction, I would be in the dark, too.

Her tired eyes, the pallor in her face, the slight swelling beneath her skirts—Navya is with child. Worse, she hasn't seen Lord Qaronin since last summer, and I'd wager she's three months gone.

As the carriage bumps along toward Rhys Domus, she vomits into a metal canister for the second time this morning. "This damnable road," she says, dabbing her forehead with a handkerchief. "Makes me toss up my meal every time."

"There's a tea for that," I say, smiling warmly.

She looks at me askance, as if she's not sure whether I'm offering her tea for her nausea or for the *true* reason she feels like tossing up her breakfast. "Yes," she says, sighing deeply and looking out at the southern sky.

Spring is flowering around us, new life bursting forth on the mountains. The purple flowers of the wisteria trees that line the road tantalize us with their sweet scent.

I can't believe it's been more than six months since I arrived on this land—even longer without Halline's smile or Ziva's embrace or Ari's laughter, without a walk through the pines or a visit to the mountain or a dip in the healing waters of the River Keno. More than six months without being reprimanded by Mother.

My thoughts stop just outside the city limits of Rhys Domus when the carriage comes to a halt and Sir Orlo knocks on the carriage door.

"Oh, what is it *now*?!" Navya half shouts at him.

"Sorry to disturb, my lady," he says to me, ignoring Navya. "They need to search the carriage. Protocol, that's all." Then he helps us down out of the carriage.

As we stand on the side of the road, watching the soldiers examine every nook and cranny of the carriage, Lukin comes riding up, alongside Timur.

"It's a fine day for a stroll," he says, climbing down from his horse and handing the reigns to the footman of the carriage.

"I couldn't agree more," I say, taking his hand and leaving Navya to rant and rave. "Is it always this tense coming into the capital?" I ask. Our attaché of Shield follows closely behind us, as always.

"They've stepped up security in recent days. Apparently, the Torch is coming to visit tomorrow."

At the mention of him, my stomach churns, recalling the sickly-sweet smell of his beard in the sweltering heart of the tent, and the disturbing way he savored my spittle. "Oh? Is there a special occasion?"

Lukin shrugs, looking out across the eastern sky as the sun climbs higher. "I'm sure we will find out when he summons us."

"Surely he won't be attending the ball?"

"On the contrary, Akkar can't resist a ball. He enjoys the fanfare of it all, the excitement." Now that he's said it, I see it. Akkar *must* live vicariously through others in many ways, forbidden as he is from enjoying the baser pleasures of lesser men.

"We should get back on the road," Lukin says, then leans closer. "Does Navya seem... *off* to you?"

I swallow hard. I consider being honest about my suspicions but think better of it. I know Lukin well enough by now to hope he would respond well, but this is new territory. "I think she may have caught a chill, that's all. Plus, this 'damnable road,' as she calls it," I reply.

He laughs and takes my hand, leading me back to the carriage.

Navya is pulling me through the bustling city center, searching for a tiara for me, for the ball. She is on a mission to find this *one specific shop* she swears has the best-quality materials. My feet are killing me, but I push on, for her sake. I imagine it's a kind of distraction from her woes, so I let her have this one small mercy.

All along the sides of the road, people are hawking their wares. Dried and salted fish, fresh flowers, rope, mousetraps, and more are dangled in front of us as we pass through the crowds. Men, women, and children of all ages and in various stages of illness and squalor call out to us, their eyes hungry and yellowing. They reach out their hands and ask, some with words and others through sign language, for whatever we can give them. Sir Orlo and two Shield walk ahead of us, and the other two Shield walk behind us, dodging requests from those who tried us first with no luck.

"I apologize for the path," Navya says, pulling me closer. "The alleys here are too narrow for the carriage, but this is the most direct route. Just don't let them touch you."

I'm astonished by the cold way she snarls at them. How is she not moved to tears by their suffering? Of course, there are people in Kenozaria who are hurting from time to time, but none like these poor souls, who look as if they've never known a good night's sleep or eaten a full meal, perhaps in their entire lives. We would never stand by idly while a fellow human suffered as they do.

"Why doesn't anyone do something? Doesn't the Torch help them?"

Navya throws her head back and laughs. "Help them? Why?! Rhys has decreed this as their lot in life, and there's no doubt they deserve it." When I say nothing, she strokes my hand. "Lukin did say you're from a primitive place, but really, Evryn..."

I ponder on what Dowager Lady Velga would say if she were here. She seems to be more merciful than Navya, but I'm beginning to think this is just the way things are here. Most people eke out a miserable existence right alongside the opulence and excess of a few of their neighbors, and no one bats an eye.

We finally find the shop she's been searching for and step inside. The scene from the street outside can't be further from the one within. Incense burns in a corner, filling the room with a heady oud that makes me feel like I've entered a whole new world. The dresses on display are extravagant in their finery, covered in ornate patterns and dripping with glittering gems, each costing more than it would take to feed one of the orphans in the alley for a year.

Notably, the Shield don't follow us inside. They *really* don't fear what could happen to me at the hands of other women. I fantasize about seeing them come up against Ayfa or my cousin, Tasia, in hand-to-hand combat.

"My lady Qaronin!" The shopkeeper greets us with a bow, bringing me back to the moment. "How can I be of service?"

Navya smiles in return and asks for a few chairs and some tea for us while we recover from the walk. Having brought them out, the shopkeeper shoos her attendants away and begins plucking ribbons and lace and jewels from behind her counter.

"And what can you be seeking today?" the shopkeeper asks.

"My good sister here requires a tiara for the ball tonight, Trudy," Navya says, smiling. "I know you must have something perfect for Lady Velga."

Trudy calls out to one of her attendants, who comes rushing to receive her orders before bustling back to the back of the shop. "Oh, I have *just* the thing, my lady," Trudy says as her attendant returns, carrying a pillow with a delicate crown of crystal and gold. "I believe it will be the perfect fit," she says, placing it atop my head and adjusting my hair around it.

Navya gasps with pleasure. "Oh, you've done it again, Trudy, you brilliant girl! It's perfect!"

Trudy hands me a looking glass. Just as I had been in Pomisha's tent after her ladies dressed me in her fine dresses and gems, I sit stunned by the image before me, who looks something like me but not at all like myself.

"This will go perfectly with your dress tonight," Navya smiles, proudly.

"It's truly a work of art," I say, gazing at myself in the looking glass. "I worry, though, that I may damage it somehow. What if it falls off? It looks so fragile."

"The sweet thing worries she may *damage* the tiara," Navya laughs. "Why, it's worth less than any of the chairs in the cairn!"

Trudy and Navya and even the attendant laugh at this. "Oh, you needn't worry about that. We'll make sure it stays put," Trudy says.

After paying the deposit on the tiara, Navya hands the box to Sir Orlo and turns to head out of the shop, pulling me behind her.

Once inside the carriage, Navya immediately retches into a metal canister beneath her seat before hurling the contents of it out the window onto the street. I wish with all my heart that I could say something, but I lack both the courage and the language to convey what I wish to: that she needn't suffer this burden, especially considering how early it is and the risk she's taking carrying a child that is not her husband's.

"You should be the one retching into a metal can," Navya says.

"Aren't you due to give my brother an heir soon?"

"As Rhys wills," I reply, unsure what else to say. The truth is, there's *no way* I will be giving him an heir soon, or maybe ever unless the gods decide to perform a miracle within me. There's a core component missing from the equation, considering Lukin hasn't so much as kissed me, let alone *"blessed me with his seed,"* as the Priests say here.

"As far as I can tell, it has less to do with Rhys and more to do with *desire,*" Navya says. I turn away from the window and look at her now, struck by her directness. "My brother made a *love* match, lucky him. A son is sure to arrive to you two in no time."

"Didn't you also choose Lord Qaronin?" I ask, confused.

"*Pffttt.*" Navya chuckles. "*No one* would choose that man."

"I'm sorry. I had no idea."

"Yes, you have no idea about *most* things." I am curious to know more about her story, but not enough to subject myself to her incessant patronizing. But Navya doesn't care whether I want to hear it or not. "My parents betrothed me to him when I was nine years old and he was forty. He is Branngard's Keeper of Coin, and no one could ask for a purer bloodline—outside my own, of course. He used to bring me sweets and dolls when he would come to visit my father at the cairn."

Here, she stops the story to take a deep breath, and it looks like she may need to retch again, so I motion toward the metal canister, but she shakes her head. "I should be grateful that he had the decency to wait until my first blood to consummate the marriage. And he was clever enough to wait until my father died to start beating me."

"Navya, I'm so sorry," I say. I cannot imagine what it would be like to have only ever known one man, one lover, and to be so unhappy with him.

"I've lost two babies now, two babies he didn't care to mourn with me. They were girls, both. They were so tiny, but it was clear," she says, wiping a tear away from the corner of her eye.

"Is there any hope of escaping him?"

"*This* is my escape," she says, gesturing to the carriage. "He can't stop me from visiting my family, especially since my brother is home now to look after me."

"Look after you?" I ask, confused. "You've got to be nearly my age."

"Yes, and I'm a woman. Rhys created me *deficient*, in need of a man to *guide* me," she says sarcastically, rolling her eyes.

"If this were Kenozaria and this happened to me, my mother would have brought an army to kill him the moment she learned what he was doing to me," I reply.

Navya chuckles. "My mother has no army, and if she did she would send it to reinforce my prison bars."

We drop the conversation there and ride the rest of the way to the capitol in relative silence—except for the sound of her retching into the metal canister.

20

Evryn

The banquet hall at Rhys Domus is larger and more impressive than I could have imagined. Massive golden and crystalline candelabras hang from the ceiling, holding hundreds of candles.

The giant windows are hung with delicately embroidered draperies, and there are dozens of life-sized paintings adorning the walls—portraits of former Torches, according to the plaques nailed to the wall beneath them. I take note that Akkar's diminutive frame is not a Velga family trait.

Against the far wall stands a throne fashioned out of coiled and polished reams of gold, beat into the shape of flames—no doubt Akkar's seat for the affair. Behind it hangs a tapestry bearing the flame sigil of Branngard. The entire scene makes the magnificence of Yarrow's Cairn look *cute* in comparison.

Couples dressed in fine garb are spread throughout the room, as the men toss and scoot and twirl their partners around in circles. It's a wonder none of them runs into the others. While I sit at a table, sipping wine and watching the couples, Lukin is busy entertaining Navya, who is, he says, at risk of tarnishing the family name.

Since her second glass of wine, she's been making a spectacle of herself. At one point, we looked up to see her laughing loudly in the face of a baron and his wife, who slapped her hard across the face before storming off, drawing sounds of approbation from the crowd. So Lukin has made it his mission, and that of Sir Orlo, to keep her away from other dancing partners.

"Where is her husband?" I asked Lukin when he told me his plan to protect her. Lord Qaronin was supposed to have come to the ball to finally collect his wife.

"Wherever he is, he won't have a wife much longer if she continues this way," Lukin whispered. "Branngardians don't look kindly on women who 'shame their families with public displays of lewdness,' as Akkar would put it."

It seems to me that Branngard doesn't much value the precious blood it claims to work so hard to protect. Back home, a person has to be such a menace to society—so unsafe that they can't be trusted to keep on living—before Mother or any of the other chiefs on the island would approve an execution. Here, looking at the wrong person in the wrong way warrants a blade to the throat, it seems.

"She *has* to be tired by now," I say when Lukin swings Navya back around to our table as the music quiets down.

After sitting her down and putting a glass of water in front of her, Lukin whispers something to Sir Orlo before turning his attention to me. "Come, wife," Lukin says, taking my hand and whisking me around to a spot in the fray. As the music strikes up again, a slower ballad, Lukin looks down into my eyes briefly before pulling me in closer. "I do apologize for my sister's behavior," he says quietly. "This isn't what I hoped for you at your first official Branngardian ball."

"Oh, it's not so bad," I reply with a smile. "At least she hasn't vomited on anyone yet..."

Lukin looks at me with a quizzical brow. "She *has* been quite sick lately. I'll call the doctor to the cairn when we return."

"No, I'm sure it's nothing," I reply, trying to appear normal. It would take a trained healer mere moments to discover what ails Lady Qaronin, and that wouldn't be in her best interest. "And I'm enjoying myself. Have you *seen* my partner? Fabulous dancer."

Lukin laughs. "I had hoped to have some time alone with you tonight after we get her into bed."

My ears perk up. "Oh?"

"Yes, so we can... discuss the plans for the new addition to the library. Banu has hired a few builders to come around next week, and I thought you may have some ideas."

And just like that, the excitement is gone. "Yes! The library. Of course. I'd love to." Lukin seems to notice the change in my mood but dances on like nothing is amiss. "Lukin—" I begin, gathering the courage to ask him to maybe spend some *alone time* with me tonight, unrelated to the ongoing library renovation. He looks into my eyes, but before I can continue my thought, the music comes to a halt and there is a blast of trumpets.

"His Holiness, the Torch of Branngard and the Keeper of *Rhysvox*, Akkar Velga!" the announcer says, thumping his staff on the ground three times. After he steps out of the way, the attendants behind him begin rolling out a golden carpet, leading from the entrance straight up to the throne of golden flames.

With another flourish, Akkar steps forward, adorned in gold and dripping in rubies. I'm surprised he doesn't topple over under the weight of it all. He walks with his head held high under the crown, his face set in stone, with a permanent scowl of serious intent.

I watch the crowd, watching him. Every last face is awestruck. Some even wipe tears from their eyes. I still cannot understand what it is about him that creates such awe and respect in these people. All I see is an angry little man wearing his hoard of stolen treasures and marching toward a chair that's far too big for him.

Trailing behind Akkar are several priests, decked out in simple red robes. One of them carries a velvet pillow with an ancient book atop. I am shocked to see that the people bow even lower as this book passes than they did for Akkar.

Having arrived at the throne, Akkar clambers up the stairs then turns and sits, red-faced and exhausted. "Thank you all for attending this grand affair. Rhys, be praised!" he says, smiling broadly.

"Rhys, be blessed!" the people call out in response. I look over at Lukin to see that he has repeated the words, too, but with less fervor than the others. He seems annoyed.

"Let the festivities begin!" Akkar calls out—as if he hadn't arrived *in the middle* of the festivities.

"Shall we?" Lukin asks, offering me his hand.

"But Navya—" I begin.

"Sir Orlo will see to her," he says, spinning me around in a circle.

And so I dance with him, losing myself in the joy of the moment. His laughing eyes, the sound of the music, the taste of the mead in my cup, which Lukin fills again and again for me. Before I know it, the band is winding down for the night, the guests are dispersing, and my mind is swimming.

Leading me back to my chair, Lukin leans in and whispers, "Here he comes." Before I can stand at the ready, His Holiness approaches.

"Well, now. Look at this miracle of miracles! Can you be the same spunky little barbarian my nephew scooped up from the ignorance and squalor of Kenozaria? Why—you almost look the part of a *lady*, Miss Evryn!"

Lukin coughs. "Your Holiness, may I present my wife, the Lady Evryn Velga of Yarrow's Cairn."

Akkar grabs my hand with both of his, kissing it dramatically. "And what an *honor* to be in your presence, Lady Velga!" I try to pull my hand away, but he pulls me closer to him, turning us both away from Lukin. "Let us take a turn about the room, hmm?"

I look over my shoulder at Lukin, who stands helpless, seemingly caught between two very different courses of action.

"I hope you had a good journey," I say, trying not to slur my speech.

"Oh, dreadful! It really is *such* a long way!"

I walk alongside him, his arm hooked in mine, watching as every eye in the banquet hall follows us. Surely, it's no small thing for the Torch of Branngard to walk arm-in-arm with someone, but the honor is wasted on me.

"I have enjoyed the pleasure of your mother's company this past winter, I thought you should know," he says, looking at me intently like he is waiting to see how I respond. I want to remind him that he's met her once before but stop myself.

"That's excellent news," I say instead. "Is she well? And my family?"

Akkar looks at the ground solemnly for so long that I begin to think the worst. "They are well, so far as I can tell. But your mother... I worry about her mind."

"Oh?"

"Women are not designed to hold such power. Naturally, she struggles to see sense."

"Curious," I say, willing myself to hold my tongue.

"I do not savor war and bloodshed, truly. The whole bloody affair puts me off. Rhys loves to forgive, but alas... some people simply won't be led with kindness."

"What are you saying?"

Akkar smiles and pats my hand. "Rhys has much bigger plans than any man could fathom. He wants to see your people *flourishing*! But your mother seems intent on holding back that progress."

"We were doing just fine..." I say, my words trailing off. "And it is my mother's responsibility to look out for the best interests of her people. She is simply doing her job."

"Nonetheless, Rhys has His will, and I am but a humble servant."

"May I have your leave to return to my husband?" I ask between clenched teeth.

"Oh, of course! You must *long* for your husband's embrace," he says, knowingly. "Tell me, when can we expect the news of a son?"

I blush, against my will, as we walk toward Lukin. "As you've said, Rhys has His will."

"Indeed! But we cannot accomplish His will if we do not… use the *tools* at our disposal."

I stop in my tracks and look down at him, hard. "Tell me, Your Holiness, how long were you blessed with the pleasure of Pomisha's company before she gave you a son?"

The veins in his neck are bulging. "Yes, well… Pomisha was clearly not fit to bear the blessed Velga seed. But my new Jewel will not fail me thus." At this, he nods toward a group of women at the corner of the room. In the center of them stands a girl, not older than Ziva, with golden hair and porcelain skin. She stares back at me, like a fawn, and I see the fear in her summer-sky eyes.

"Perhaps my nephew needs some lessons in the art of wooing a woman into his bed," Akkar whispers, biting his lower lip in insinuation.

"It requires neither knowledge nor skill to order your men to steal a young girl from her nursemaid and imprison her in your bedchamber," I say. "Blessed evening, Your Holiness." Without another word, I release myself from his grip and walk toward Lukin, who begins walking toward me, too.

"It's getting cold," Lukin says, throwing his cloak over my shoulders and wrapping his arm around me when we meet.

"Yes," I reply, walking with him out of the banquet hall to our waiting carriage.

21

Lukin

"Dowager," the doctor says, "if I may…"

"What more can you have to say this night, Doctor Harod?" Mother asks, sighing dramatically.

The old doctor sits in a maroon armchair next to the fireplace, puffing on his pipe nervously as the great clock in the library chimes again. He's been here since the morning, and now as darkness pours over the cairn, it seems he will be here longer still.

"The lady Qaronin is… I worry for her, in her state," he says, haltingly. "I've watched her grow from a babe and I tell you, she is unlike herself."

"Shocking!" Mother yells, causing Evryn to flinch beside me. "I can't imagine why that would be. Can you, Lukin?"

"What are you suggesting we do, Doctor?" I ask him, ignoring my mother.

"A convent, my lord. One of the smaller ones in the north, the Daughters of the Flame, perhaps. She could receive the care she deserves, with dignity. And the child will be well cared for."

"The *care she deserves*?" Mother shouts again. "*Dignity?!* There can be no dignity in a whore like that girl!"

"She can hear you, Mother," I say quietly. "She is still your daughter."

At this, Mother laughs and takes a final long sip of her wine before dashing the rest of it, glass and all, into the flames in the fireplace. "I have no daughter."

I look over at Evryn, who sits silent, her eyes wide and questioning. I have no way of making her understand, using any language known to man, the events that are about to unfold.

"And what of the knight in question?" Doctor Harod asks.

"I will deal with Sir Orlo," I say.

"*You* will do nothing of the sort," Mother pipes up from the hearth where she is leaning. "I will take the matter up with the Torch himself on the morrow. He'll ensure justice is had."

At this, the door of the library bursts open, and Navya tears into the room, with nails and teeth bared, headed straight for Mother.

"Someone get this beast under control!" Mother shouts, dodging Navya. I step between the two of them, holding Navya off as the Shield attempt to restrain her.

"*You* are the only beast I see!" Navya screams, tears pouring from her eyes. "That man has shown me the only kindness I have ever known, and you can't *stand* it! You can't *stand* seeing me *happy*! You can't bear the thought that I could have *love*, unlike you!*"

"I want to see you *alive*, you ungrateful wretch!" Mother shouts back.

Evryn gives me a sideways look, then follows the group carrying Navya off to her rooms, leaving me alone with Mother and the doctor.

"You cannot blame her like this, Mother. It's unfair and premature," I say after some moments. "How can you know what took place between them?"

Mother laughs under her breath, looking into the flames. "I may be old but I'm not senile. We *both* know what took place between them, right under our damned noses. And *honestly*, Lukin, don't play the fool. I know you love your sister, but it's unmanly of you to defend her so."

"Whatever happened, Navya will have to carry and birth this child you intend to take from her. Isn't that punishment enough?"

Mother rolls her eyes and scoffs. "That girl will suffer through some months of discomfort in the privacy of the cairn, and then be free of her *burden*. Meanwhile, the best knight in the realm will lose his head within the fortnight, all because your sister couldn't keep her legs closed."

"There must be some way out of this, something we haven't thought of."

"My blessed, naive boy," Mother says, softening now. "Will you never accept the ways of the world? Women have an evil in them that even the best men struggle to resist."

"How can you be so sure it was not the other way around, hmm? Sir Orlo is *twice* her age, and he's been in our service since she was freshly blooming. It's more likely *he* was the one who seduced *her*."

"Sir Orlo has proven himself a man of honor and renown! He wouldn't *dare* have seduced a woman in his care, let alone a married one. I won't hear of it, Lukin!"

Here, Doctor Harod clears his throat. "Once more, I must advocate for the young lady. She needs a quiet, safe place to recover, far away from the stresses of the cairn. I worry for her sanity if you keep her locked in that room for months."

Mother muses quietly for a moment, then promptly turns toward us. "Lady Qaronin should remain here, in her ancestral home, where the best doctors and healers in the land can tend to her these next months," she says. "But, of course, I entrust my son, the lord, to do what he sees fit." With this, she leaves us alone in the library.

"I am most grateful for your service, as always, Doctor Harod," I say, paying him his fee.

"I have known your family since my father was their physician, Lord Velga," he says, placing the pouch into his bag. "Believe me when I say I *wish* I hadn't learned what I learned tonight. Your sister has suffered enough in her brief life."

"It is such a pity, for all involved."

Doctor Harod stands, picking up his bag. "I do wish the dowager would look on Lady Qaronin with more mercy."

"We could all use a little more mercy," I say, seeing him out of the library.

After walking Doctor Harod to his waiting carriage, I climb the stairs to go and check on Evryn and Navya, but as I am headed to Navya's rooms, Mother approaches me in the hallway.

"Can we trust him?" she asks, eyeing the carriage as it drives away into the darkness.

"Doctor Harod?!" She looks at me condescendingly, and I can tell she is preparing yet another speech about how simple-minded I am. "Yes, Mother, I believe Doctor Harod to be a man of his word, a man of honor, who genuinely cares for this family."

"Good," she says. "It would be a tragedy to lose yet another good Branngardian man because of your sister's foolishness." I nod in agreement and turn to head toward Navya's rooms. "I do hope you gave him a heavier purse, to help secure his lips," Mother adds as I walk away.

When I enter Navya's bedchamber, I find a scene of such relative comfort and serenity that one could easily believe the entire row in the library to be a bad dream. Navya sleeps soundly as Evryn sits next to her bed, dabbing her forehead with a cool towel.

When she sees me enter, Evryn shushes me. "She just fell asleep," she says, looking at Navya with concern.

I take her hand and lead her to one of Navya's sitting rooms, then pour us both a glass of wine.

"What is going on, Lukin?"

"Navya is with child."

"Yes. And?" Evryn replies.

"What do you mean, 'Yes, and'? Did she tell you?"

"Of course not. I just… know these things." I eye her for a moment before taking a long drink of the wine.

"I see."

"From what I could gather, your mother intends to force Navya to carry the baby, then take it away from her?"

"There is no other way."

"That's just something men say to justify the inexcusable things they do to protect their honor."

"Evryn, you don't understand our ways—" I begin, but she cuts me off.

"I understand plenty well enough, Lukin. Your sister was forced to tolerate a man she can't stand, then when she finally found love, she is being punished for it by losing not only that man but the baby they created together." I say nothing. "What *I* don't understand is why you do nothing to stop it."

"I cannot oppose a ruling of the Torch, however much I hate it."

"And do you hate it, Lukin?"

"Yes!" I shout, louder than I mean to. Remembering Navya sleeping in the next room, I lower my voice. "Yes, I hate it. I don't want my sister to suffer. I don't want that man to die, a man who has served us loyally for as long as I've been alive. I hate this entire situation. But what can be done? Akkar will not show mercy, regardless of who is involved. It's one of the highest crimes in Branngard, to violate another man's wife."

Evryn throws her hands in the air. "Navya is *not* a man's *anything*. She is a *human being*, and she's afraid! At least let her go to the convent.

You are the lord, not your mother! How is Navya supposed to give birth to a healthy baby when she's trapped in that room? She needs fresh air, sunlight, and some semblance of normalcy!"

"I know she's afraid. But in this rare case, my mother is right. I can't guarantee someone won't hurt her there, some religious zealot bent on making things even worse for her."

Evryn sighs. "If Akkar were wise, he'd send these Shield to protect her, not stalk me."

"You are far more valuable to him than my sister, unfortunately," I say.

"Correction: what he hopes I may one day carry in *my womb* is more valuable to him, and only because it will have come *from you.*"

"Yes."

Evryn softens. "I wish we could get her to Kenozaria. She would be safe there. No one would care who the father of her child is; no one ever cares. What is *wrong* with this country? What is wrong with your mother? Has she no mercy for her own daughter?"

"I wish we could all have the type of life your people do. I wish that more than anything."

"And yet, you lead the army of the man who wants to make sure *no one* gets to live free."

"What army?" I ask. "I gave up my army the moment I chose to marry you, Evryn. Men I have known all my life. Because I..."

"Because you what? Say it. Why did you make that choice?"

"I'm going to sleep," I mutter, unable to tolerate another moment of this conversation.

Evryn doesn't acknowledge my words, so I walk out of the room, down the hall, and up the stairs to our rooms.

When I enter our bedchamber, I sit down and remove my coat and boots, and do my best not to think about what Evryn said, but it's a losing fight.

Can I blame her for believing I have the power to rescue everyone I care about? That's precisely what I have done for her and her family. How could I protect them but not my own sister? From her perspective, it must seem senseless.

But she doesn't know me as well as she thinks she does. Whether it was Nora, helpless on the street with her baby, or the pain in Navya's wild eyes tonight, or the fear in my mother's voice throughout my childhood, begging my father to stop beating her when he became enraged at some squire or other and took it out on her, I've never been able to protect the women I love. And it's killing me.

For a moment, I allow my mind to wander around the possibility of helping Navya escape to Kenozaria. But almost as soon as the thoughts begin to churn, they hit a brick wall: Navya couldn't survive there. With the ease and comfort of the life she's accustomed to, even if Kenozaria *were* an option, I feel certain she'd choose her current lot.

Eventually, I tire myself out and fall asleep. I wake at some point when I hear Evryn come in. She climbs into bed, careful to avoid touching me, even "accidentally," as we sometimes do.

22

Evryn

Rain is pelting the crowd of hundreds gathered in the courtyard square at Rhys Domus. Before us, on a wooden stage, stands a cross that must have been erected overnight. On each side of the stage stands a giant brazier, whose flames lick at the wood within them, unaffected by the rain.

Akkar walks toward the stage, covered by a canopy to protect him from the rain. He is adorned in black from head to toe, all but his golden crown and staff.

"Justice!" the crowd howls. "Bring him out! Make him pay!"

The Torch approaches the stage just as a servant places a small set of wooden stairs in front of him. As he climbs onto the stage, the crowd howls even louder.

"Rhys, have vengeance! Let His justice be had!"

Akkar stands before the crowd, patiently waiting for them to quiet down.

"Let the Torch speak!" someone finally calls out.

"Oh, people of Branngard, keepers of the flame!" Akkar cries. "Rhys has heard your prayers for vengeance and will answer them!" The crowd cries out in bloodlust. "Rhys loves to see justice paid out to those who violate His most sacred laws. And there can be nothing more sacred than the divine right of a man over his wife." Here, Akkar gestures to a seat to the right of the stage where a bulbous, sallow-faced man, whom I assume is Lord Qaronin, sits with a look of rage permanently plastered on his face.

"We are gathered here today to witness said vengeance on the life of one man, a formerly knighted soldier of Branngard, Orlo Barex, who shamelessly violated the honor of Lord Qaronin by forcing himself on the lord's wife, Lady Navya."

Forced himself, they call it, to justify murdering a man whose only crime was loving a woman who loved him in return, by her own admission. And the only way to protect Navya's life, according to Lukin, is if the entire affair is painted as rape.

A door opens into the courtyard and Sir Orlo—or the creature who once was known as such—is dragged out in chains. His battered face is unrecognizable and his back is a mass of mottled flesh. He is covered in a mixture of dried blood and the dung and spittle the crowd is throwing at him. He is completely naked.

As he is taken up onto the platform, a woman rushes forward and falls to her knees before the retinue of Shield who encircle the stage. "Have mercy on my son!" she cries. "He is a good man, an honorable man! He would never violate someone's wife! Please, Your Holiness! Have mercy!"

Akkar smiles warmly at the woman before gesturing to his Shield to remove her. "Let Rhys's justice be had!" he calls out before walking down the stage and joining the other lords sitting alongside Lord Qaronin.

"You shouldn't watch this," Lukin whispers to me. "Please, let me take you back to the carriage."

"No." I can't make him understand why, because even *I* don't understand what keeps me glued in place, unable to look away.

The hooded figures haul Sir Orlo onto the cross. He is too weak to resist them, so he moans, pleading for his life. Lukin flinches next to me when they nail Sir Orlo's wrist to the board. His screams echo through the square to the chorus of the crowd's cheers. They nail his other wrist in place as the rain begins to let up. The men holding him down step aside so the crowd can get a better view. Their cheers grow wild with frenzy.

"Open him!" they cry.

After some minutes of his agonizing screams, one of the hooded figures lifts a short scythe from the table atop the stage. The second hooded figure roughly grasps Sir Orlo's manhood, root and stem, as the first man slices through the flesh slowly. Sir Orlo howls in pain. Somewhere in the crowd, his family weeps and begs for mercy, but their voices are drowned out by the crowd.

"Zaria, have mercy," I whisper to myself, clutching Lukin's arm tighter.

Dropping the severed bits into a bowl on the stage, one of the hooded figures stretches the skin of Sir Orlo's abdomen taut as the other tears into the delicate skin just above what used to be his manhood. With one swift slash upward, Orlo's innards fall out of him, splashing onto the stage.

The horror of the sight takes my breath away, causing my legs to shake beneath me. A terrible chill is running up and down my spine. I focus my attention on a small boy, not much older than five, who looks on at the gruesome scene from his father's shoulders. He keeps trying to get his father to take him down, to hold him, but his father insists he watch.

Several members of the audience scream for joy as the hooded figures approach Sir Orlo's body again. They then remove his eyes, ears, nose, and fingers, lobbing his bits into the crowd, including his cock and balls.

"We're leaving, Evryn. Enough," Lukin says, taking my hand and pulling me through the crowd.

"He isn't dead," I say, my voice shaking as Lukin helps me into the carriage.

"No, he isn't," Lukin says coolly, settling into his seat across from me and looking out the window as the rain continues falling. "They will leave him there to die."

"And what of his body? Will they at least return it to his family for a proper burial... or what's left of it?"

"We do not bury bodies here. The soil is too rocky," Lukin says as the carriage pulls away. "They will throw his body onto the side of a mountain outside the capital and let the scavengers eat him. Had he died with honor, his body would be burned."

"But he didn't," I say to no one as the carriage drives on toward Yarrow's Cairn.

"No, not in their eyes," Lukin replies.

As the sky darkens to night and the carriage bobs along toward the cairn, I can feel Lukin's eyes burrowing into me from his spot on the seat across from mine.

"Go on," I invite him. "It's clear you want to say something."

Lukin sighs and leans on his knees, reaching for my hands.

"I'm worried about you. What a horrific thing to have witnessed."

"Yes," I say, mindlessly. The only way I've learned to survive these moments—so frequent here in Branngard—when facing what previously would have been unimaginable, is to step outside my body. I imagine myself as a spirit in the trees atop Mount Zaria, looking down on the whole affair from a safe distance, unaffected.

"I wish you had listened to me and stayed at the cairn."

"So that I could listen to your sister howling in pain and begging to be released from her prison? Is that somehow less horrific?" I ask, looking at him directly.

"I'm sorry for the entire bloody affair. I wish there was something—" he begins.

"Something you could have done to stop it?" I ask, cutting him off. "Yes, I understand you were incapable of saving Sir Orlo's life, but you can still help Navya."

"We've *talked* about this," he says. "She is safest in the cairn."

"Then let her *live* in the cairn, at least. Don't let your mother keep her locked up like that. What are you afraid of? That she will run? To *where?*"

He sits in silence for a moment, contemplating my words. "You're right. I will speak with my mother."

"Good," I say, and decide not to press the topic any further at present.

As the night rolls on and we come ever closer to the cairn, I eventually nod off into something like sleep, but it feels more like a trance. I can still hear and feel and smell everything around me, but it all feels dim, like I'm wrapped up in a warm cloud.

I imagine Navya in her prison chamber of a bedroom, looking out of her bolted window. The weeping has ceased finally and she sits, as silent as death, resigned to her fate. Her sorrow moves me, inexplicably. She hasn't shown me an iota of kindness, but somehow I feel for her, woman to woman. I wish there were something I could do to free her.

There is a warm Light glowing within me, the one I've carried all my life, so I focus all my attention on it. I can feel the energy coursing upward from the bottom of my spine, rising higher and higher out of the top of my head. Then I direct the column of light toward Navya. I imagine her warm, happy, and free, frolicking with her baby through the moors that surround the cairn.

Then a heavy fog begins rolling down from the mountains in my vision, cloaking the cairn in a thick haze. I imagine the guards outside her room falling asleep, one by one, until everyone in the cairn is sleeping, save Navya.

As we pull up to the cairn, I am snapped out of my trance by the sound of a loud crash and Lukin shouting for help before barreling out of the moving carriage.

There, just outside the steps to the entrance, lies Navya's broken body. The windows just below her bedroom stand open, curtains flapping wildly in the wind.

23

Lukin

As they lay Navya's body on the pyre in the courtyard of the cairn, Mother stands beside me looking on blankly, as if she were watching some gardeners cut down a withered tree. She reeks of wine and spirits, but that's nothing new.

The priest steps forward to begin the ceremony. "We have come together on this dark day to begin mourning the loss of our dearly beloved daughter, Lady Navya Qaronin," he says. "Taken from us too soon, Lady Navya will be remembered for her generous nature and warm spirit."

Generous nature? Warm spirit?! They're not even *trying* to make it sound like Navya.

"When one of Rhys's devoted servants dies in such a way, Rhys promises a reward in the Hereafter beyond one's wildest imaginings," he says. "Were His Holiness, the Torch, here, he could read to you from *Rhysvox* the detailed descriptions of all that awaits our beloved daughter, Navya. Let this be enough for now: she will never shed another tear."

The notable absence of His Holiness, the Torch, and that of the good lord Qaronin, is intentional; Mother arranged everything as soon as possible on purpose, in fact, to prevent their attendance—for reasons she refused to elaborate on.

Mother clears her throat as if to say, *Get on with it.*

"Here today to send her off with honor is her brother, Captain Lukin Velga, Lord of Yarrow's Cairn," he says, gesturing for me to come to stand alongside him.

I release Evryn's hand from my own and join him in front of the small crowd.

"Would you like to say anything about your beloved sister, Captain Lukin?" the priest asks.

I stand speechless, scanning the memories in my mind for one I could speak about openly that wouldn't shame my sister or the family. I wish I could say something *true,* like the way she taunted me as a young boy, making fun of my poor swordsmanship, or the way she tortured Banu and the servants, leaving frogs in their stew and hiding spiders in their bed sheets when they were busy cleaning up her messes. But none of that will do.

"Nayva died with love in her heart" is all I can muster, and it's not untrue. The love she bore Sir Orlo was as undeniable as the truth that she certainly didn't *fall* out of that window. "She will be greatly missed by all."

I look at Mother one final time, willing her to stand, to say *something,* to show *any* emotion toward her daughter before it's too late, but she continues staring at me blankly, a look of impatience on her face, no doubt wondering when she can return to her bottle.

"Rhys has brought us to life, breathing fire into our mother's wombs, and it is to the fire we return," the priest says. I signal the soldier nearest to the pyre. He and the others who had placed her body on the pyre grab their torches and light them in the brazier burning next to the priest. "May Rhys accept Lady Navya with fanfare and reward her for her service as a Branngardian daughter, wife, and sister," the priest says as the soldiers toss their torches into the blaze.

Before long, the flames consume her body. The air is so thick with smoke that it's hard to breathe. As the crowd begins to disperse, I take Evryn into the cairn before ensuring that all the windows are closed to keep the smoke out. When I return to the courtyard, everyone has left but Mother, who stands silently before the flames.

"Let's get inside," I say, wrapping an arm around her shoulders, but she won't move.

"Let her ashes choke me to death so I may join her," she says calmly, staring into the flames.

I don't want to push her, but the smoke is so thick now that I am struggling to breathe. "We must go, Mother," I say, coughing.

"No!" The storm finally gathers in her eyes, and she crumbles to the ground, weeping into her hands. "My girl! My only girl!" she cries out, reaching toward the flame. She is shaking with grief, racking her body with coughs and spurts as she sucks in more of the toxic smoke.

Banu and several of the other servants come out to help me get her inside. She initially resists them but is finally persuaded to go inside and take a hot bath to get the smoke and stench off of her.

* * *

"There's nothing like a good hunt to clear the head and energize the body," Timur says as our horses slow to a trot.

"You're right," I say, pulling up my reigns before readjusting the leather strap that holds back my unruly hair. Navya has been dead for two weeks and I've hardly left Mother's side. Evryn, too, seems to be operating in her own inner world, no doubt trying to make sense of the recent events. A good hunt was exactly what I needed.

As we are returning, we see Akkar's carriage headed toward the cairn.

"You'd better hurry back," Timur says. "Wouldn't want to keep him waiting."

"I need to get to Evryn."

"Yes, I imagine you must be very eager to return to your wife."

"No, I… I meant I need to warn her that Akkar is coming. It's not exactly a pleasant experience for her to see him, after everything…"

"All the more reason for you to *comfort her*," he says, grinning mischievously.

I take a deep breath and lean forward to stroke the side of my mare. "That is the *last* thing on my mind, Timur—or Evryn's, for that matter."

"Understandable," he says, turning his steed toward his estate.

I take my leave and gallop toward the stables. As I ride, I think about what he's said.

Truth be told, I'm in agony. The more time I spend with Evryn, the more I long for her. Not in the empty way I hungered for Nora or the self-seeking way I yearned to finally marry Selise and inherit her father's fortune. My desire for Evryn is more simple than all that, purer even. She's my friend, my *dear* friend, whom I also *desperately* want to have my way with.

It's her intelligence, her sensitive spirit, that sets my heart alight. It's her tenacity, the way she can silence me with a single glance when she's set on proving me wrong. And I'm so often wrong, now that I think of it. Damn my education and all my travels, this woman from a tiny, isolated island knows more about what *truly* matters than I could ever fathom.

Sometimes, though, as I watch her going about her day in the cairn, or as I pass her on my way to this or that lordly duty and see the way the sun glints off her auburn hair or the way she smiles at me like we have a secret no one else could understand—it makes me want her, truly *want* her, body and soul.

But the closest I've ever come to enjoying Evryn was a brief moment last winter when we'd embraced after a long day and she allowed my face to linger alongside hers, cheek to cheek, longer than usual. As I pulled away and looked into her dark eyes, I wanted so much to kiss her but lost the courage.

Every time I think about savoring her, I remember that Evryn didn't *choose* me. How can I enjoy myself with a woman who would just have willingly married Draven if it would have saved her life and that of her sister? So I simmer with longing, alone in my hunger for her, unable to express the complexities of my feelings for her even if she gave me the chance.

As I head into the cairn, I send a servant with a message to Banu to do all they can to prepare some sort of lunch for Akkar. I can imagine her spitting with rage at the inconvenience of it all.

Evryn is sitting by the fire in her favorite chair in our sitting room, nervously fumbling with a shirt of mine, apparently attempting to sew a patch onto a hole I've torn. Her eyes are narrowed on her work, and she seems frustrated.

"Good afternoon," I say as I enter the room and sit in my chair next to hers. "How goes it?"

Evryn glares at me. "The thread may have won the battle today, but I'll win the war," she says with determination. "If only Halline were here. She's so much better at sewing than I am."

"I have full confidence in you," I say, placing a hand on her shoulder. "But there is more pressing business to attend to."

"Oh?" she asks, putting the shirt down and brushing her hair out of her face.

"Akkar is nearly here. We spotted his carriage on the way back from the hunt."

"I thought I smelled something rank," she says. "And I don't mean the deer blood on you."

I can't help but laugh at her wit.

"How long do we have?"

"I'd say about half an hour."

"I suggest you get Banu to prepare your bath then, Lord Lukin," she says, stepping into her closet to find something more suitable to wear.

"My dear nephew," Akkar says, embracing me and offering his hand after I help him down from his carriage. I kiss it, then invite Evryn to greet him. She does so in the Kenozarian fashion, causing Akkar to wrinkle up his nose and give me a look of dismay.

As Evryn and Banu and the other servants walk inside ahead of us, Akkar pulls me aside. "Let us sit and talk as men tonight, hmm?"

"Of course, Uncle," I say, inviting him to lead the way to the banquet hall.

"I apologize, Your Holiness," Mother says when she sees him enter the hall. "Had we known you were coming, we would have prepared a more appropriate welcoming party."

"Nonsense, sister," Akkar says. "I come not as the Torch, but as your brother-in-law, brokenhearted at your recent loss. And after so much hardship already, the poor thing! I do wish you'd informed us of her demise sooner, so we could have been in attendance."

Mother takes another sip of her wine. "Yes, well. It's over and done with now, isn't it? We do our best to move forward."

"Yes, that is all that can be done now, I fear," Akkar says, taking the seat Banu offers him. "At least she died with honor."

I can see Evryn's internal wheels turning as we take our seats at the table. *Not now, Evryn, please.*

"Yes, with honor," Mother says blankly.

"And how are you handling things now, as the lady of the cairn?" Akkar asks Evryn.

"As well as can be expected," Mother answers for her. "She is such a queer little creature, but she does her best."

"Yes, *queer* is a good word to describe her, I'd say," Akkar replies, smiling at Evryn.

"My wife is a fabulous homemaker," I say, taking her hand in mine across the table. "She has brought much-needed light and warmth to these cold halls."

"Well, now, isn't that *delightful*," Akkar says, taking a sip of the hot tea Banu has placed before him.

Soon, the food is brought out and conversation around the table ebbs and flows.

"Are you enjoying yourself?" I ask Evryn when there's a lull.

"Doing my best." She smiles.

"To doing our best, then," I reply, raising my glass to her.

"Indeed," she says, clinking her glass against mine.

When everyone has finished eating and the table has been cleared, Akkar excuses himself to the library, inviting me to come with him.

"I pray you enjoy the rest of your evening, ladies," I say, closing the door behind us. Evryn glares at me from behind the door as it shuts.

My stomach is churning as I take a seat next to the hearth, inviting Akkar to take the other. It's clear that he wants to talk to me about *something*, and I can't think what. Even as a boy, I've dreaded such exchanges with my uncle, who always seems to have plans that will make my life harder in some way.

"How are you, Uncle?" I ask.

"Rhys be praised, I am well, Nephew! I am pleased to see how well you're managing the cairn." He seems cheery, but his serene countenance is often nothing more than a thin veneer hiding a sea of rage that frightens me.

"I'll take your praise to Evryn, and to Banu and the servants," I reply. "It is they who keep this place running smoothly."

"Indeed," Akkar smiles. "Now, sit with me awhile, and let us speak of other affairs." He snaps at a servant, who brings us a platter of tea and cakes.

"How are things in the encampment?" I ask. This may be my only chance to learn what's *truly* happening in Kenozaria, beyond empty gossip. "Is Draven keeping the men in line?"

"Oh, he's a trusty little hound," Akkar says. "Nothing like you, of course, but then you've got other responsibilities."

"Yes," I say.

"Speaking of those *other responsibilities,* how *is* your wife, really?" Akkar asks. "I hear she still insists on washing her own laundry among the servants?"

Of course he's been spying on us. His "gift" of an attaché of Shield has obviously been doing double duty. "Yes. Evryn is quite a self-reliant woman. It's something she enjoys, she says. So, I don't stop her." *Where is this going?*

"It's not about whether she enjoys it or not, Lukin. It's about the *propriety* of it," he begins. "The lady of Yarrow's Cairn should not be seen doing such menial tasks." I open my mouth to respond, but he cuts me off. "And speaking of clothing, I hear she insists on wearing the same sort of simple tunics she wore back on the island. But I am sure you've provided her a rich wardrobe!"

I shift in my seat and place my teacup on the saucer before me. "She prefers to wear the clothing she has been accustomed to all her life, and I can't see the harm in allowing her that small comfort. It reminds her of her home, of her land."

At this, Akkar's face becomes still and serious. "Kenozaria is *Rhys's* land, Nephew. All the earth belongs to Rhys, and by extension to Branngard, as the stewards of the land."

My heart is pounding in my chest, part anger, part fear. "Yes, Uncle. You are right. Forgive me. I will speak with her about it." I know better than to argue with him when he turns into the Torch instead of Uncle Akkar.

"Good, then!" he replies cheerfully before taking a sip of tea. "And tell me: how are things coming along in the bedroom?"

Why are so many people taking such a keen interest in my marriage bed? "All is well. Rhys, be praised," I reply. My heart races harder and my face turns punch red.

"Rhys, be blessed! Good, good. However, it *has* been many, *many* moons since your wedding, and well... it worries people when a pregnancy has still not taken after so long. Are you *sure* all is well?"

"These things happen in their own time."

"Yes, you are right," he says, looking down at his delicate fingers. "However... there are times when the issue at hand is not simple biology but a... *spiritual* obstruction." *Here it comes.* Akkar always has a way of finding a deeply meaningful explanation for even the simplest of matters. "And in such cases, the solution is often a spiritual one. *Rhysvox* holds wisdom for every ailment under the sun."

"Of course," I say. I have no choice but to listen.

"'And come into your wives as you deem fit, as often as you please, be it from any direction. Seek not your own pleasure alone but seek to bring her to ecstasy, as such matters quicken the heart and ready the soil for planting,'" he recites from memory.

"I assure you, my wife is pleased with me," I say defensively. And in my mind, it's not untrue. That pleasure isn't of a *sexual* nature, sure, but she seems happy with me, nonetheless.

"I am sure you are doing all you can! But, the fact remains that she has not conceived, and I think you understand the gravity of our situation. The Torch of Branngard can only be born of the Velga bloodline, and as Rhys didn't see fit to grant me sons and my Pomisha is... no more," he says falteringly, "you and that girl are our best hope for the succession."

"But your new Jewel is young and vibrant. I am sure she will bless

183

you with a son in no time."

"Perhaps, but I am an old man and not so virile as you, Nephew," Akkar replies, swirling the tea in his cup.

"I am doing the best I can, Uncle, for our family and Branngard."

"I don't doubt it! And I appreciate your efforts!" I take a final sip of the tea in my cup and begin to stand, but Akkar stops me. "In such times as these, Rhys has given us a way to ensure that the deed gets done..."

"Oh?" I ask, sure I don't want to hear the answer.

"As you are a young man, and no doubt schooled in the ways of pleasing a woman, I won't insult you by suggesting that your wife is... *dissatisfied* in the bedroom," he says. "But, *just in case* that is the issue at hand, you should know that in the old days, the Torch and the high priests of Branngard used to have a practice of... *observing* the sacred deed, to help guide the man who had failed to properly plant his seed."

I stop breathing. "You want to *watch me making love to my wife?*"

"Oh, it's not like that, Lukin! It's not some *voyeuristic endeavor*, I assure you! It's simply a matter of confirming that a man is properly preparing his wife for the sowing, that's all!"

"And what if my wife does not want to be watched like that?"

"Women do not know what is best for them, Lukin," he says, annoyed. "I thought several months of marriage would have taught you this. The continuation of the Torch's bloodline is, I think you can agree, of more consequence than the feeble feelings of a silly heathen girl."

"Lady Evryn," I begin, "is my wife." Hot anger is reddening my cheeks. "I thank you to speak about her in a more respectful way."

Akkar is taken aback. I have *never* deigned to speak to him in such a way, and I can see the lake of fury burning in his eyes ever hotter. But he says nothing. So I stand and bow to him, and without another word, I turn to leave the library.

"We shall look in on your relations tomorrow night," Akkar calls out to me as I close the door behind me.

24

Evryn

"We must hurry," Lukin says grabbing me by the arm and shoveling some of my clothes into a leather satchel.

"Why, Lukin? What's happening?" I ask. "Where are we going?"

Lukin doesn't look at me as he continues throwing my few belongings into the bag. "*We* aren't going anywhere. *You* are going back to Kenozaria, to your mother's family, in Salix."

"*Salix*?" I ask, confused. When he still doesn't answer my question, I stop in my tracks. "Lukin! You're scaring me. Tell me what's happening!"

Lukin shushes me and shuts the door of our bedchamber behind him. "Evryn, listen to me," he says. "I made an oath that I would protect you. And I promised never to touch you without your consent. Yes?"

"Yes…" I begin, unsure where he's going with this.

"Akkar is coming here, to our bedchamber, tomorrow night with his priests, to *watch* us, to make sure I am… pleasing you, in bed…"

My mouth is dry and a chill is creeping down my spine. "Your uncle wants to watch us make love? But why?"

"He's concerned because you're still not pregnant. We have to get you out of here."

"What about the Shield? How are you going to get past them?"

"I have had Banu give them a sleeping dram in their wine. They will be out until tomorrow afternoon, easily."

"But won't he know you helped me escape?" I ask, concerned for him.

"It doesn't matter. I'll deal with the consequences. I cannot violate you like this. You don't deserve that. I—" he begins but stops himself. "I... care for you, deeply."

I can see the pain in his eyes and I know, in an instant, what he *isn't* saying. "But why won't you come with me to Salix?" I ask gently.

"He will chase us to the ends of the earth if I come with you. I am the last of the Velga line. He can't just let me go. But he will eventually give up on you."

"There must be another way."

"Do you want me to do this, to let this happen? Is that what you want?"

"I don't want it like this, but I... I want *you*," I say, stepping closer.

"Evryn, they want to *watch*! How can I...?" Lukin cries, collapsing into a chair. I stand above him and brush his hair out of his face, allowing my hand to linger on his cheek longer than usual. In an instant, he stands and embraces me. "Evryn," he whispers. "You're everything to me. You must know. You must. I'm sorry. I can't do this."

"It won't be forced, Lukin," I whisper, "Not if I want it." Then I take his face in my hands and kiss his lips gently. The moment our lips touch, a hunger overtakes me—one that has been building for weeks. But now, seeing his tender heart and the way he is fighting with himself to avoid causing me any harm makes me long for him all the more.

Lukin pulls me closer to him, kissing my mouth, my forehead, my cheeks, my eyelids. The passion that's been building begins to overflow and we are both panting, tearing at each other's clothes.

"I want you," he whispers into my neck. "I want you so goddamned bad, Evryn," he moans.

"Then have me," I whisper, moving my hand down his abdomen toward his pants. "I'm yours."

In an instant, Lukin stops and pulls himself away from me. "No. No, I'm... I'm sorry I lost control. I can't. Not like this."

"You could. Right now, you could have me. He's not here now. It's just you and I," I say. I pull him closer and kiss his lips, then his neck. "I *want* you inside me, Lukin," I whisper into his ear. He shudders with pleasure and I can feel him hardening on my thigh.

"What if a child came of this night, Evryn?" he says, pulling away from me again. "How is this a good time to bring a child into the world, and in such an awful circumstance?"

"I told you. I can't have—" I begin, but he cuts me off.

"You can't know that! No, we will send you to Salix and I will deal with my uncle's wrath!" he cries out, readjusting himself in his pants and fixing his ruffled hair.

I try to protest, but it's clear he is set on his plan, so I give up.

It's just after nightfall and the crickets are chirping in the moors surrounding the cairn. Lukin is leading me by the hand. In any other circumstance, it would be a romantic night for stargazing.

Soon, a carriage pulls up. Lukin helps me inside and briefly speaks with the driver before turning to me again.

"The carriage will take you to the shipyard in Marpum. The ship should arrive off the coast of Salix within a week or so. Remember: you are a servant, headed on a voyage south to collect fabrics for your master. That is all. They will send you off in a dinghy, which you will need to row to shore. You can walk the rest of the way, right?"

"I know how to get to Salix," I reply. "Don't worry."

"There is enough food and supplies in here to last you three weeks, just in case. And there's some Branngardian coin, in case you need it," he says, handing me the satchel. "And take this dagger."

I throw the satchel over my shoulder, stuff the coin purse in my belt, and fit the dagger beside my ankle in my wool sock. As I'm doing this, the dagger clinks against the gold bangle on my arm. I begin to remove it.

"No, please keep it," Lukin says, stopping me. He takes my face in his hands, kissing my forehead. "I would not part with you under any other circumstance. I am so sorry for how we came to know each other, but I hope you know I have cared for you, in my way."

"I do know," I say, choking up. "I'll send word when I've arrived safely."

"No, we can't trust the messengers. I don't want Akkar to find out where you've gone."

"So... this is it? I will never see you again?" I ask.

"I hope these shall not be our last moments together. But if it is the last time we see each other, know this: you are the most *extraordinary* person I've ever known, and I love you, for what a soldier's love is worth."

"You are so much more than a soldier." I smile, caressing his cheek. "Much more. And your love is worth more than you can ever know. I wish I could convince you to change your mind."

"Never," he says, sternly. "Now, go. Please, be safe. And find happiness, Evryn Korina. You deserve it."

"As do you, Lukin Velga," I reply quietly as he slams the carriage door and slaps one of the horses to go.

Boarding the ship in Marpum, I am a walking corpse. There was no hope of sleeping in the carriage, and by now it's been more than two days since I've lain in a bed. As I board, I am careful to keep my hood up and my head down, avoiding eye contact with anyone.

I spend my nights awake, lying in my hard, lumpy bed, trying hard to quiet my mind. The sound of rats scurrying this way and that keeps me awake, and once a sailor mistakes my room for his own, bursting in before I leap out of bed, dagger drawn, and push him back out into the passage.

I spend my days alternately watching as the waters skim across the windows in my cabin and attempting to sleep off the worry and sadness of the night before. I leave my cabin only to collect my share of food and ale from the galley. I try not to think of what is happening to Lukin now, or what awaits me in Salix.

V

Summer

25

Lukin

A steady drip of water keeps time as I try in vain to get some sleep. A rat scurries too close for comfort, causing me to jump and kick it away, moaning as the pain in my back shoots through me.

I've lost track of how many days I've been here, rotting belowground in the dark cells of the Lighthouse, Branngard's prison for the worst offenders. There is a tiny slit high above my head that lets in some fresh air. Through it, a sliver of light moves across the walls and floor, telling me that the days are getting longer. The suffocating heat that worsens each day solidifies my perception that summer is in full swing.

As I lie in the corner of my tiny, damp cell, I pass the time with memories of Kenozaria—of the rich smell of earth that poured into my lungs, and the feeling of the tall grass against my hands as I walked the prairies. I think of the men I left behind, the men I'd trained with since I was a boy, the men I'd happily have died for.

But mostly, I think of Evryn. She haunts my waking thoughts and visits my dreams. I recall her face when she was concentrating, the sound of her voice as she sang quietly to herself while she worked on some task or other, oblivious to my presence. I petition all the gods I've ever learned about in my travels, pleading with them to protect her and allow me to see her again one day. I remember the last time I saw her eyes.

I recall all that transpired after she left.

* * *

I'd been hiding in my rooms all day when Timur came looking for me the day after I sent Evryn away.

"Are you ill?" he asked. "No one's seen you, or your wife for that matter, since last evening."

"We're fine," I replied simply, inviting Timur to take a seat next to the hearth in our sitting room.

"Well, that's a relief," he said. "Then maybe you can explain why you missed sparring this morning and lunch this afternoon if you're both so well as that?"

"We've been resting."

Timur sighed and took a drink of ale from the cup I had placed before him. "Right then. I'll leave you to… whatever it is you've been up to. But do let me know if either of you needs something," he said, standing up to leave.

"Wait," I said, knowing before I said a word that I was going to regret it later. "I need to talk to you."

Timur smiled and sat again, drawing his chair nearer to mine. "Good man," he said, patting me on the knee. "Tell your old friend what's troubling you."

"Evryn is gone," I said, fidgeting with the silver bracelet on my wrist.

Timur's eyes opened wide. "*Gone*, you say? What… you don't mean… ?"

"No, no. She's fine… or at least, I hope she is."

"So?"

And so I told him of my conversation with Akkar, of the horrible thing he'd asked of me, of the fear and sadness pooling in her deep brown eyes when I'd sent her away.

Timur sat for a long time thinking on what I'd told him.

"Well, say something," I said, anxious.

"I'd say you've leaped from the pot and into the fire, my friend."

"Yes. I'd say that's an accurate assessment of my dilemma."

"What will you do? I imagine Akkar won't be pleased when he sees you've misplaced your wife."

I ran my fingers through my hair nervously. "I'll have to face his wrath, I guess. But that's better than hurting her."

Timur scoffed. "You've allowed yourself to fall in *love* with the girl? She's a savage, Lukin! A barbarian! Rhys, be praised! It's like you've forgotten who you are!" I began to defend myself, but Timur cut me off. "No, I've held my peace since you arrived here with her. But I can't any longer."

So I sat, listening.

"You've sworn it was your noble virtue that drove you to take her to wife. Fine. Though for my money, I'd still say you did it for your own lust, and I don't blame you! I don't. She's certainly a beauty. But now, you've endangered yourself further, and the rest of your countrymen, too, by letting her get away!"

"What? I—How have I endangered anyone?"

"Don't you know she'll raise an army and slaughter every last Branngardian on her island, including your uncle?"

"She wouldn't. She's not like us. Her people aren't like us."

"I never took you for a fool," Timur said with disdain. "You don't truly imagine she *loves you*? Lukin, you invaded her homeland! You took her captive!"

"Listen—" I began, but Timur cut me off.

"She's a clever little minx, I tell you. She'll be the death of you and your line, and you've got no one to blame but yourself!"

With that, Timur stood and walked to the door, fuming.

"Timur, please," I said quietly, ashamed. "Don't tell Akkar. I will deal with him myself."

Timur laughed to himself, frustrated, and then left me behind, disappearing into the darkening night.

It could have been hours later or only moments, but when the knock came at the door, I had been sitting in the same spot Timur left me in and was no more prepared than I had been when he left me there.

"Welcome," I said, opening the door for Akkar and his priests and the few Shield he always traveled with.

"What pleasant rooms you have, Lukin!" Akkar said, sitting in a chair by the fire. "Your wife is certainly more domesticated than I imagined she would be!"

"Yes, Uncle," I said. "Shall I bring you and your men some tea? All I have at the moment is that or ale, and, well…"

"There's no need," Akkar replied simply. "Where is Lady Evryn?"

I stood up and moved closer to the door of our bedchamber. "Evryn is not here."

Akkar turned to face me. "Oh? Has she gone out, this late in the night? You really should keep a better eye on her, Lukin. These moors are dangerous at night—" he began, but I interrupted.

"No, she is not in Branngard. She is gone."

Akkar stood, walking closer to me. "She's escaped?! Oh, Lukin, I'm so sorry!" he said sympathetically. "We'll send some men to find her right away! And where are those useless Shield?!"

"No. She did not escape." My face was stone. "I released her. She is far from here now."

"You did *what*?" Akkar asked, close enough to me that I could smell his breath. "Surely you must be playing a clever trick on your uncle."

"I am not."

"I see," Akkar replied after a moment. "And you understand that this decision makes you a traitor to your own family, and an enemy of Branngard and Rhys Himself?"

"I do," I replied, thinking of what Timur had said earlier about the possibility of Evryn raising an army and coming back to kill us all.

"Good then," Akkar replied calmly. He motioned to one of his Shield, who had laid a hand on his sword in expectation. "No, that won't be necessary," he said calmly. "Though the typical sentence for such a choice would be death by beheading, as my nephew is the only male in the Velga line, we mustn't be wasteful of his precious blood."

"I don't understand," I replied. "My wife is gone. My blood is worthless to you without her."

"What wife?" Akkar replied, smiling. "As far as I recall, you are engaged to Lady Selise, of House Brailen."

I was speechless. "But I married Evryn. *She* is my wife, in the eyes of Rhys."

"*I speak for Rhys,*" Akkar said, narrowing his eyes at me. "And *I* say there was never any such marriage between you and Evryn Korina, and you'll be ready to marry the young Brailen girl presently—after an appropriately brief stint in the Lighthouse, of course."

I said nothing, looking down into his eyes.

"My nephew will need to be taken to the Lighthouse at first light," Akkar said, addressing his Shield. "Please ensure he is ready for his trip."

Two of the Shield moved toward me and tied my hands behind my back, then led me quietly down the hall to one of the cells beneath the cairn.

"Don't worry, Nephew," Akkar said quietly as the Shield were locking the iron gate. "I'll be sure to give Evryn your regards when we find her. She'll make a *perfect* Jewel."

I lurched at him, causing one of the Shield to slam his armored fist into my belly. I buckled over in pain.

"I'm sorry you're struggling to accept your new reality, Lukin, but every choice has consequences. It's time you learned this hard truth," Akkar said, brushing my hair from my face. "Perhaps Rhys will see fit to bless you with this wisdom as you wait to be released from the Lighthouse."

The next morning, I was tossed unceremoniously into a carriage. Akkar poked his head inside. "I have dispatched an urgent message to Draven and his men who, I am sure, will find her promptly, so that I may bring her to justice as soon as I arrive back in Rhysland."

"No!" I cried out before the Shield slammed the carriage door and sent me on my way to Rhys Domus.

It had all been in vain. They would find and entrap Evryn again, or else one of her sisters, and her family would be exposed to Akkar's greed without the thin veil of Velga family honor to hold him back now. It seemed that every decision I'd made to try and save Evryn and her family from hardship had led them ever closer to danger. I howled in pain, collapsing on the floor of the carriage.

26

Evryn

A week to the day after we pushed off from Marpum, the captain meets me at my cabin to tell me that Kenozaria has been sighted.

"I won't ask no questions, see, but I hope ye'll tell yer master how safe and comfortable yer journey aboard me ship has been."

I pass him some of the Branngardian coin Lukin has given me. "He will reward you further, I am sure," I reply before turning and stepping down the rope ladder into the waiting dinghy and rowing myself ashore.

I walk all night, climbing hills and traversing valleys. Just as the sun is coming up, I collapse on the ground, searching through my satchel for a water bag. Having found it, I drink deeply. I set up my tent in a valley between hills for the windbreak, as high winds are common this time of year this far south. I climb inside and relax for the first time in hours, and before long, I'm asleep.

When I awake again, the sun is high in the sky. I dress in a fresh set of clothes and get busy putting away the tent, electing to eat some dried meats and berries as I walk rather than stop to hunt; if I don't stop, I won't have time to think. When I am too tired to walk more, I set up camp on the prairie and get busy collecting firewood.

As I sit warming my hands before the fire, a familiar pain creeps through my chest. I ache for my family—for Halline and Ari and little Ziva and even my mother. And now I'm thinking of what must be happening to Lukin, now that they've surely discovered my disappearance.

I eat my dinner under the pitch-black canopy of night, every star overhead glistening in the cloudless sky. Then, I turn in for the night, hugging my legs to my chest for warmth.

The next morning, I rise and decamp, then head farther north and east. I can smell the marshes in the air now, so I know I am getting closer.

As I walk on, I wonder what my Aunt Meryn will say when I arrive in Salix, seeking shelter. How much does she know about what's happening in Kenozaria, about what I've done? Maybe she'll turn me away—or worse, send me back to Branngard, condemning me as a traitor.

I've only ever been to Salix once before when I spent a summer with Aunt Meryn when Mother was pregnant with Ari. I remember that there were too many mosquitoes, and I missed my friends back in Kenozaria. My grandfather was a stern, angry sort of man, but Meryn was a kind, plump woman who squeezed my cheeks too tight and fed me deliciously moist raisin cookies until I felt I would burst.

Some years later, Aunt Meryn's husband had come to Kenozaria, seeking warriors to help defend their land from a warring tribe. But Mother had refused their request.

"The warriors of Kenozaria belong in Kenozaria, not fighting for a distant land," she'd said. "And, frankly, we are not keen to die for a lost cause." In her mind, the warring tribes of the south would never stop warring, and she was right, but they were none too happy with her for it. I worry they may turn me away in recompense.

The sun moves along its path in the sky as I continue my trek, and I begin to get the feeling that someone is watching me. But every time I turn to look, I see only an empty landscape.

When I reach the edge of the prairie, I set up camp and then myself with building a fire as the sun goes down.

As I sit, warming my hands over the fire, I hear a snap and whip my head around, looking into the darkness but seeing nothing. I'm *sure* now that someone is following me. What I don't understand is why they are hanging back. Why the stealth?

When I lie down to sleep, I keep my dagger in hand, just in case, but neither man nor beast disturbs my sleep.

It's late into the next morning, and I'm standing by a dock at the edge of the marsh, paying a boatman to take me across to Salix. Taking note of my clothing and the stench that no doubt lingers around my person, he asks me a few questions about who I am and where I've come from.

"I'll pay double if you leave my business to me," I reply, flashing my coin at him. That silences him, and he pushes on.

As we glide through the marsh, I notice a hooded man in a boat ahead of us. His boatman is less motivated than mine, it seems, and we eventually overtake them. As we pass by, I try to get a better look at him, but his hood shades his face.

Having made it across the marshes, some hours later, I decide to camp for the night rather than show up in Salix at dark. Appealing to them in the middle of the night would certainly communicate my desperation, but I don't want to risk being refused entry at so late an hour.

After I've set up camp and gotten a fire going, I decide to scout around the area. That's when I see the same hooded man, walking ahead of me through the tall grasses, evidently with the same plan in mind.

I hunch down several paces behind him as he walks, curious about him and what brought him here to Salix. The thought occurs to me that he may be the same person I could feel following me since the second day of my journey.

Eventually, my curiosity gets the better of me, so I take my dagger in hand and approach him quietly. "What brings you to Salix?" I ask from behind him, dropping my voice lower than my typical register.

He stops in his tracks and drops the hood, his dark hair shining like a wet seal, catching the last rays of sunshine. "I am searching for something I lost," he says. I drop the dagger as he turns and looks me square in the face.

"Torek?!"

27

Torek

I wish, for the thousandth time in my life, that I knew what Evryn Korina was thinking. She hasn't said a word to me, and her face gives nothing away as she stares into the fire, lost in thought. After we've eaten in silence for a while, she suddenly speaks.

"How long have you been following me?"

"Two days."

"Thought so," she says, moving the embers around in the fire with a long stick.

"Are you okay?" I ask.

"As well as I could be, all things considered," she replies, taking a long drink of water from her flagon. "Though, maybe not, considering that I'm currently talking to a ghost."

"There's a lot to catch up on, it seems. You must have many questions for me, too," I reply, adding a larger log to the fire.

"No, not many. Only one."

"Oh?"

"Why? Why did you do it?"

I stand, looking up at the darkening sky and taking a deep breath. "Why what?" She looks into my soul with those knowing eyes, saying nothing. "I know my absence was hard for you, but I can explain."

"Hard? And how do you know this?"

"Your mother told me everything. I found her in Salix just before we came to find you."

Evryn nods. "Yes, I heard she'd come looking for me, briefly anyway. Before she abandoned me."

"Evryn, you married him. They said you sailed to Branngard with him. What did you expect her to do?"

"What did I expect her to do? Luk—" she begins but corrects herself. "Torek, I expected my mother to save me. I expected the chief of the Sanctum to *do something*. I expected her to work just as hard to find me as she would have if it were Halline or Ari or Ziva who'd been captured and then imprisoned and then—"

"And then married?"

"This is insane! You're here, alive! You were *dead*, and here you are!" she cries, staring at me as tears began to pool in her eyes.

She's right, and we both know it. "Do you want me to tell you what happened?" I ask.

Evryn nods wordlessly. So I tell her my story—or, rather, the false one I told Korina. "I swear to you, Evryn. I came as soon as I could," I say, pleading. "But by the time we arrived at the encampment, it was too late."

"It was," Evryn says quietly, looking at the ground. "Far too late."

We sit in silence for a while. The air is heavy with the pungent scent of the marshlands. Bullfrogs are croaking and a red-winged blackbird sits nearby, calling out to its mate.

"Why were you going to Salix?" I ask.

"You first."

I smile but try to hide it. Evryn is still herself, I can see. "Your mother sent me to Salix to ask her sister for help."

Evryn chuckles. "Mother must be losing her touch. And her wits."

"Oh?"

"I can't imagine Salix would send help her way when she denied them in their time of need."

"You *have* joined Branngard's side, haven't you? But then, can I blame you? You *did* marry the captain of their armies, after all…"

"What?" she asks, offended. And I'm glad she's offended. "Of course I haven't *joined their side*. But Akkar told me Mother was making things difficult for him. Has something happened?"

"No. Not yet. Your mother is gathering support, that's all. And Salix is her best hope."

Evryn nods, understanding. "Listen, I'm exhausted. I'm going to try and get some sleep," she says, standing up to head to the tent.

"That's it? I don't think so," I say, grabbing her by the arm. "I told you what brought me here. Now it's time you explain yourself, too."

"*Explain myself?*" Evryn asks, incredulous, staring down at my hand on her arm. "You don't get to demand answers from me! Not now!"

I let go of her arm. It would not serve either of us if I were to push her further and walk away with a broken wrist or a bloody nose. "Please," I ask, calmly. "I need to know."

"Fine," Evryn replies, wrapping her shawl tighter around her shoulders and sitting down next to the fire again. "What do you want to know?"

"The captain, the man you married. I know I don't have a right to you, not now. But I have to ask. Why did you do it? Did they force you? Why did you choose him over your family?"

Evryn says nothing for a long time, her jaw clenched. "I married him *because* I love my family, Torek."

"You didn't answer my question," I say, moving closer to her now. "Do you love him?"

"No," she says. "At least not in the way I have loved others." She leaves no room for questioning who those *others* may be. "If it's okay with you, I'll sleep now. It's been a long few days."

"Of course," I reply, moving away and watching her walk back to the tent. "Sleep well," I call out.

She doesn't respond.

I've been awake since dawn, waiting for Evryn to wake up and join me. But it's been several hours, the sun is rising higher and higher, and she still hasn't made so much as a sound. I know she was tired, but I am starting to worry about her.

"Evryn?" I say, tapping on the side of her tent, but there's no reply, so I open the front flap. She's gone.

I panic for a moment. She couldn't have gone off to relieve herself without me hearing her leave the tent, and she wouldn't have left camp and headed into Salix without waking me, no matter how angry she is. I notice her satchel sitting in the corner of the tent. My sense of panic builds. Salix is less than an hour's hike from here, but she wouldn't leave her satchel behind on purpose. Evryn is nothing if not practical.

I swiftly gather up my belongings and her satchel and decide to continue on the path to Salix, hoping that she acted out of character and headed that way without me before dawn. As I walk across the prairie, I look for signs that she's passed by but see nothing. It's as if she's vanished into thin air. So I walk on, calling out her name every so often in hopes she'll hear and respond.

Just as I'm coming up on the edge of Salix, I notice something brightly colored, dashing through the tall grasses. A man dressed in an orange tunic and bronze armor is chasing something, *or someone*, into the trees. *Branngard*, I think, recognizing the look of the armor and the color of the tunic. I dash toward him, bow in hand.

The Branngardian soldier has caught up to Evryn and now holds her arms behind her back as two other men attempt to tie a rope around her wrists.

"Let her go!" I cry out as I approach, arrow at the ready.

All turn to see who is addressing them. When Evryn whips her head around, there's a small gash above her right eyebrow, with blood slowly trickling from it.

"Let her go, or I swear I'll put this arrow through your neck!" I call out, not remembering for the moment that they can't understand what I'm saying. Still, my stance is clear enough to get the message across.

The older soldier smiles, baring his yellowed and rotten teeth, releasing Evryn into the hands of the other two soldiers. That's when I see that he's Draven, the same man who had been with Akkar when Korina and I came to the encampment to bring Evryn home. He approaches me slowly, smiling, speaking words I can't understand.

"Torek!" Evryn calls out, fighting off the soldiers who are trying to gag her. "Run! I'll be fine! Just run!" One of the men holding her slams his fist into her stomach and she keels over in pain.

Before I can react, Draven runs toward me, curved blade in hand, slashing wildly. I drop my bow and arrow and grab a long dagger from its sheath on my belt, all the while dodging and parrying his attacks. We chase one another round and round, bouncing from boulder to boulder, splashing into the marshy land surrounding us.

Jumping left to escape a hard slash at my groin, I whip around and get him into a choke hold, dragging him down to the ground and pulling him into an ever-tighter grip. But he throws his elbow hard into my ribs, causing me to gasp in pain, releasing him.

Now free of my grip, Draven finds his footing and his sword. He lifts his arm, ready to open my throat. That's when Evryn breaks free and runs full speed at him, stabbing him hard in the kidney. He stumbles forward before falling face-first into the marsh.

"Evryn!" I cry out, jumping to my feet and running toward her.

Hand-in-hand, we run as fast as our feet will carry us in the direction of Salix, without looking back.

28

Evryn

I collapse, my lungs burning as I try to catch my breath.

"Are you hurt?" Torek asks, taking my face in his hands and looking at the gash on my forehead.

"I'm fine," I say, taking the water bag out of my satchel and sucking back a long drink. "Do you think they're coming?" I scan the western horizon. We're safely within the limits of Salix, but Draven could be just behind us for all I know.

"I doubt we'll see him ever again," Torek replies, darkly.

People who had been going about their morning tasks now stop and stare at us. One, an elderly man, approaches us, offering to help.

"Please, tell Meryn Freya that we've come from Kenozaria to seek her help," I say.

"Of course," he says. "Kenozaria is our sister. You're most welcome here, my dear."

"Evryn," I say, greeting him properly. "Evryn Korina. And this is Torek Minara."

His eyes go wide when he hears my mother's name. "Oran Klintara," he says, greeting us.

"Can you show us where we may find shelter and a hot meal?" Torek asks.

"You are more than welcome to wait in my home," Oran says, leading us there.

When we step inside, his daughter looks up from a book she had been reading. After Oran explains the situation to her, she smiles warmly and offers us some oats and fruit.

"I'll just go and tell my son to send for Meryn," Oran says, stepping back outside.

"Thank you for your hospitality," I say to his daughter.

"Perhaps you'd like to ahh... wash up a bit before she arrives?" Oran says, coming back into the modest sitting room.

"Let them eat first, Papa," she says, looking embarrassed by her father. "They must be starving! Who knows how long they've been on the road."

"Oh, I can guess a few days, at least," he says, pointing at our disheveled, filthy clothes.

After we've had our fill, Oran's daughter takes us outside around to a room at the back of the house, with a separate entrance. Within, there is a bed and an oversize washbasin, full of steaming water. Several wooden shelves are hung on the wall next to the washbasin, laden with various ointments and salts.

"My father is... well, he's quite advanced in age and impolite at times," she says. "You'll have to forgive him."

"He's not wrong. We *have* been on the road awhile," I say. "We're grateful for your kindness to us... umm... sorry, we never got your name."

"Yvette," she says, greeting us with a smile. "Yvette Rava. My brother, Wotan, should be arriving soon with Meryn. Can I get you some fresh clothes?" she asks. "I think mine should fit you, and he looks to be about my brother's size."

"That's so kind of you," Torek replies. "We'd be most grateful."

After she's gone, Torek and I are left alone together for the first time since last night. I undress in silence, feeling his eyes on me. "What?" I ask finally as I slip into the hot water. It's *heavenly*. "It's nothing you haven't seen before."

"Can't a man enjoy looking at the woman he loves?" I don't know how to respond to this, so I ignore it.

Torek begins undressing and climbs into the basin in front of me. I carefully avoid his gaze, but he stares into my heart—or the pillow-soft flesh that hides it. I instinctively cover my chest.

"You've never been coy around me, Evryn Korina."

"The last time I saw *your* body, Torek Minara, it was naught but charred remains." That silences him well enough.

After a few moments, Yvette knocks on the door. "I've brought clean clothes. I'll just set them right outside for you to grab when you've finished," she says from behind the door.

"Thank you again," Torek calls out from the washbasin, keeping his gaze locked on me. Once she's gone, he continues. "Look, Evryn. I told you what happened. Is this how it's going to be between us now?"

I sit looking at him for a long time, wrestling with the hundreds of biting things I would like to say to him, and choosing not to say any of them. Because I know the anger I feel for him is a farce, a mask I have concocted to hide the sorrow I feel beneath it all. And then there's Lukin, taking up more space in my heart than I knew I had given him.

"Evryn?" Torek says.

"Yes, Torek. This is how it's going to be, at least for now. You cannot truly think we can just... pick up where we left off. Not after all that's happened."

"That's *exactly* what I hoped for," he says, watching as I stand up and grab one of the soap jars from the shelf next to me and begin scrubbing my body. "I only survived that ordeal because I knew you'd be waiting for me. I knew you'd be my wife, my home, like you were always meant to be."

"I made an oath to him."

"You did what you had to do to survive. No one—not me or your family or the people in Kenozaria or even the gods—expects you to honor that oath."

"It's not just the words I said, Torek... we *lived* together. We grew very close. I care about him, about his family. I can't just act like it didn't happen—play like you weren't dead, like I didn't bury a body I thought was yours and spend months mourning you."

"You could," he says, pouring some soap into his hand before lathering up his dark hair. "You could if you chose to. You could thank the gods for my safe return and open your heart to me again."

"Fine. I am not ready to choose that path," I say, taking the pitcher down from the shelf and filling it, then I pour some water on my head and lather up my unruly mane.

"Oh, that's okay with me. I'm a patient man," he says. "You'll come around. You always do."

"Okay, Torek," I say, before rinsing my hair and then sitting back against the washbasin. I know this conversation—and this issue—aren't going anywhere anytime soon, but there's nothing more to say for now.

"What will we do?" he asks as he's standing up from the basin. I can't help but stare at *his* naked flesh now, as the morning sun pours through the curtains onto his glistening skin, highlighting the dark hair that dapples the best bits of him.

"About?" I ask, forcing my gaze up to his face.

"Like what you see, eh?" He laughs. "It can be yours, for a modest price."

"Oh?"

"Just all of you—body, heart, and soul."

212

"Modest, indeed."

He laughs, throwing his head back as he dries it off with the towel. "I'm serious. Your aunt is surely waiting next to the hearth as we speak. What's our plan?"

I had forgotten all about her and about Mother and Kenozaria and even Lukin the moment he stood from the basin. "I... I don't have a plan. We'll tell her what's happened and beg for help."

"And? What kind of help? How much? When?"

"I'll think of something."

"Sure, you will. You're *Evryn Korina, heir to the chiefdom of Kenozaria,* after all. You can do no wrong!"

"You mock me?"

"I *toy* with you, my dear," he says, smiling wryly. "But really, your ability to come up with a plan on the spot is unrivaled." He has no idea it was Aunt Tabitha and Papa and my other passed-on loved ones guiding me all that time. But they're silent now, as they have been for a year now, ever since the night Branngard arrived, so who knows what I'll say when we meet Aunt Meryn in a matter of minutes.

I stand up from the washbasin, allowing him a long, lingering glance at all he wishes to see. Two can play at this game.

Torek stands still, quietly taking in the sight, then abruptly turns and cracks the door to collect the clothes Yvette left there. "You'll want to be clothed for this meeting, I think," he says, handing me the linen shirt and trousers Yvette lent to me.

Having dressed, the two of us head back into the main sitting room to find Aunt Meryn, my cousin Tasia, and two Salixian warriors waiting for us, alongside Oran and Yvette.

"We're sorry to have kept you waiting," I say, approaching Aunt Meryn to greet her.

"Oh, we understand. You've had quite an experience, I hear!" she says, standing and throwing her arms around me. She's just as warm and cushy as I remember, and she smells of cinnamon and cloves, like she's been baking all day.

"We didn't want to interrupt you and your partner," Yvette says.

"He's not my partner," I reply, "but yes, we did need the bath and the rest."

"And yet, you bathe together?" Tasia asks. She's tall and fit, with the same large golden eyes Aunt Meryn has.

Torek coughs. "We were betrothed, before…" he begins, but seems unsure how to continue.

"Oh, don't pay any mind to Tasia," Aunt Meryn says, shooting her daughter a scolding look. "We're glad you're here and you're safe! Oran here has been telling us what happened to the two of you. What a time you've had!"

"Yes," I reply. "We're grateful he welcomed us into his home, and for your willingness to come here and meet us."

"You're welcome in our home, as long as you need to stay," a young man sitting next to Tasia says.

"This is my brother, Wotan Rava," Yvette says.

"We are honored to have you here," Wotan says, smiling and greeting us in the customary way.

Torek and I return the greeting before we are all invited to sit down and sip tea.

"I understand things have gotten worse in Kenozaria," Tasia says. "Our scouts say Branngard has established a rather robust settlement on the west coast. And they have many fighting men ready to invade Kenozaria any day."

"Didn't their leader offer Korina Freya terms of peace?" Wotan asks.

"Hardly," Torek answers. "He demanded nothing short of complete submission. Quartering soldiers in our homes, allying with Branngard against their enemies, and more."

"Yes, I see what you mean," Aunt Meryn says, looking troubled.

"Korina Freya sent me to seek your aid. She asks that you unite with Kenozaria to stand against Branngard, should war become unavoidable."

No one says a thing, but there's a smirk moving across Tasia's mouth.

"I have witnessed, firsthand, the sort of 'civilization' these people want to enforce here, and there is no good in it," I say. "The destruction of our holy sites and rituals, the murder of innocents, the subjugation of our people, a deep hatred of the feminine..." The image of Navya's broken body, splayed on the cobblestones at the bottom of the cairn, flashes before my eyes, death being her only haven from the torture she knew was awaiting her. "These people *cannot* be allowed to accomplish their goals here. They cannot," I say, my voice quivering with emotion. "We *must* stop them. For our children, for our future."

Aunt Meryn stands, a look of solemnity on her face. "We are glad you've arrived safely. We will convene with our council and give you our answer in a few days. Unfortunately, my home is in disrepair after a recent storm, but it should be guest-ready soon. In the meantime, you are both welcome to stay here with Oran and his family," she says, looking to them for confirmation.

"Of course, you are welcome," Wotan says. "I speak for my family when I say we are honored to host Evryn Korina and her... fellow Kenozarian."

"Torek," I say, again.

"Yes, Torek," Wotan says, smiling as everyone stands to leave.

"We'll await your answer," I say as they head out the door into the afternoon sun.

"That went about as well as one could have hoped," Torek says after they've gone.

I nod.

"I apologize for my assumption earlier."

"Please, don't. It's nothing," I reply. "I understand why you thought so."

"We've only got the one spare room. I hope you don't mind sharing a bed?" Yvette asks me.

"We are grateful," Torek answers for me. "We'll make do."

When we close the door behind us in the spare room, I lie down without a word to Torek and fall into a deep, dreamless sleep.

When I awake, it's well after dark. Everyone in the house is sleeping, from the sounds of it—everyone but Torek, anyway. His side of the bed is empty. I lie in the darkness for a time but find myself unable to sleep, wondering where he's gone. So I climb out of bed and slip my shoes on to go find him.

A quick look around the sitting room shows me he's not inside, so I step back out into the garden, shutting the front door behind me quietly, thinking maybe he went out to relieve himself.

I find him leaning against a tree, bathed in the moonlight. He looks like a god, come down from the mountains for a holiday in the southern marshes.

"Couldn't sleep?" he asks when he sees me approaching.

"I guess it's contagious."

He chuckles and looks up at the full moon. "Who do you think is celebrating their Bright Ceremony tonight? Jeran? Who else?"

"Inas and Gwen."

We stand together under the tree for some time, neither saying anything. An owl hoots from a tree nearby and a bat flies across our vision.

"I owe you an apology," Torek continues. "I was... Look, you were naked and I'm a living, breathing man, okay?"

"Is this an apology or a justification? Because I can tell you now: I've met men who are perfectly capable of controlling themselves in the presence of a naked woman."

"Oh? Do Branngardian men not have cocks, then? Is *that* why he never put a baby in you?"

"Your apology is going *shockingly* well, I'd say."

He laughs and looks down into my eyes now. "No, I mean it. I respect you, I do. I care for you. I never stopped loving you, and it hurts me, this distance between us."

"Do you think it doesn't hurt me, Torek?" I ask. "I thought you were dead, and I lived a whole lifetime, it feels like, without you, in a strange place that I came to love. And then I had to leave that place suddenly, and then you *weren't* dead, and then we had to run for our lives! I haven't had but a few hours around you to even begin to process my new reality, okay?"

Torek takes in a sharp breath. "You're right," he says. "You *have* had one hell of a year, and I'm not making it easier. We have more important things to worry about now."

"Apology accepted," I say, wrapping my arms around my shoulders against the chill.

"Let's get back inside?"

When we crawl into bed again, this time I turn to face him. For the first time in more than a year, I can touch him, see his eyes, smell him, embrace him if I wanted to… and yet I resist, for reasons even I can't explain.

"I would offer to hold you, to warm you up, but…" he says.

"I know you, Torek Minara," I say, snuggling deeper under the quilts. "You stay on your side of the bed, now."

"Yes, *ma'am!*" he says seriously. "You know, I love a strong woman."

I stifle my laughter and slap his arm. "*Shhh!* They're going to throw us out on the street."

"Okay, okay," he says before reaching out a hand and moving my hair out of my face. "Let's get some sleep."

I let my gaze linger on his face longer than I should, and suddenly, the fires within me that used to burn round the clock for him are ignited, so I roll over to face the wall instead, inching away from him.

"Goodnight, Torek," I say.

"Sweet dreams, Evryn," he replies.

29

Torek

I want her. I *want* her, and she's right next to me, asleep, as she has been every night for a week. I could take her, now. If I wanted to, I could have Evryn and be rid of this burning hunger that fills my belly and pours into my loins.

She wants it too, I know. I could tell from the look in her eyes over dinner tonight. There was a moment when no one else was looking. She smiled in that old way she used to, that smile that said, *no one here knows us like we do.*

I roll away from her and try to sleep, but the hunger is burning me alive and I can't take it anymore. I turn toward her again, pushing myself against her and moving my hands up her torso, kissing her neck.

She stirs then and turns toward me, mumbling. My lips are on hers in an instant.

"Torek, what are you doing?" she asks, shocked, pushing me away from her.

"What? I thought..."

"You thought that the fact I'd forgiven you for your behavior means you're allowed to thrust yourself on me, without even so much as a request?"

I can't believe she's behaving this way. "Evryn, you're being ridiculous. It's me, Torek! Remember?"

"I haven't forgotten a thing. Not a damn thing, Torek."

"What's that supposed to mean?"

"You really expect me to believe that an old woman had you trapped in a cellar for almost a year? And then, the moment she released you, you ran straight to Salix instead of coming to Kenozaria to find me? The Torek I knew would *never* run from a fight."

I'm speechless. I thought my story was watertight.

"You died! And I don't know who... this is," she says, gesturing to me, "but it's not the man I loved. The man I was going to spend my life with is dead."

A rage is boiling just below the surface of my skin, and I can't take it anymore. I take her in my arms and pin her against the wall. I grab a handful of her hair and pull her head back as I kiss her neck and rub myself against her thighs.

"Torek, stop!" she's crying, so I let go of her hair and hold my hand on her mouth.

"Shhh," I whisper. "I'm not going to hurt you. I w*ant* you, Evryn. I know you feel it, too." She struggles against me, crying out against my hand and trying to bite me, but there's nowhere for her to go.

Somehow, her resistance makes it all the sweeter, and I wonder why we've never played at this before now. It's definitely a game. Evryn wouldn't *truly* resist me. She may be angry, sure, she may be shocked, but Evryn loves me and always has. She wants me as badly as I want her.

My hands seem to be moving of their own accord, tearing her nightdress up and my pants down. And then I'm inside her and it's ecstasy. I thrust into her, five times, six times, as hard as I can. She's whimpering, and I know it's because she's waited so long for this moment, too.

The smell of her hair, the taste of her skin, the warmth of her... it's too much and I lose myself in euphoria, collapsing against her, limp and sweating.

When I pull away from her, she's silent. I expect her to jump out of the bed, to strangle me, to cry for help, but she does nothing, says nothing.

"Evryn," I say, willing her to look at me, but she doesn't. She fixes her nightdress and wipes the tears out of her eyes and sits up in the bed, then stands and walks out of the room, into the darkness. I start to follow her, but she turns and looks at me with eyes that leave no room for questioning what she would do if I did.

The next morning, when I come to greet her and share breakfast, she doesn't even seem to register my presence when I sit down.

"Good morning," I say, pouring us both some hot tea.

"Mmhmm," she says, not at me—more like a general acknowledgment that it is, in fact, morning.

"I hope you slept well?" I ask.

This time, she doesn't respond at all.

"Evryn, I—" I begin, but she cuts me off.

"Aunt Meryn has sent her messengers throughout the island, and soldiers are beginning to arrive. We should talk strategy with her this morning."

I can't believe she's acting like nothing happened last night! "Sure, let's talk strategy," I say. "But is everything... okay between us?"

She sits very still, sipping her tea, collecting her thoughts. "Let me make one thing clear, Torek," she says, setting her teacup down on the table and looking fiercely into my eyes. "There is no *us*. You are my fellow Kenozarian, and we will work together to defeat Branngard's forces. That is as far as our connection goes."

She can't be serious. But she looks very serious. "But, Evryn. I... Look, I know last night didn't go how we'd have hoped, but..."

She looks out the window, across the horizon, dead to me and the present moment again. "As I said. We will work together to save our home. But if you so much as lay a finger on me ever again, I will kill you, and it won't be quick."

With that, she stands and leaves me at the table alone.

VI

Autumn

30

Evryn

We've been back in Kenozaria for a few weeks now. I'm grateful to be home, to be close to Halline and the others, but my attempts to re-adjust to life here have not gone as well as I'd hoped.

In some ways, I fear I'll never quite be the same. The Evryn who went to Branngard, the Evryn I was with Lukin, the Evryn I was before that night in Salix when Torek did what he did—they're dead and gone, and I don't yet know this new, raw version of me.

I wanted to kill him, to throw an ax through his skull and revel in watching him twitch before he died. I wanted to tell Aunt Meryn and send a messenger to Mother. I wanted to watch as every person across the island came to participate in his execution, the way the Branngardians had for poor Sir Orlo. I wanted to slake my thirst for vengeance with the honey-sweet sound of him crying in pain, the way he'd made me cry that night.

But I don't do any of those things. I smile and act like all is well between us. I share a small cottage with him, not far from Mother's. I let everyone think I am overjoyed by his return to the land of the living. In public, we are a united front. Because we need a united front to save our home and our people. We cannot afford the distraction it would create were I to give him his just rewards.

So I bite my tongue. I smile. I let him sit next to me at public gatherings. But he *knows* the truth: he has lost me forever, *truly* lost me.

Branngard has expanded its encampment to include parts of the river now, driving us further north to seek out water. They've even begun building another encampment along the river south of us, between here and Salix, to cut off our supply train. Each day we hear more news about the raids and destruction they are reaping on any and every village they come across.

Meanwhile, the seasons march on, unfazed by the scrambling and bickering of men.

The afternoon sun warms my skin as I lie relaxing on a grassy knoll. The trees are beginning to change color and there's the smell of rain and sleep that hangs in the air this time of year.

I can't smell autumn without thinking of Papa. He used to take me into the mountains each year to hunt for elk and deer. We'd hole up in a little shanty his father, my grandfather, built for the purpose. We'd hunt in the mornings and warm ourselves by the fire in the evenings as he told me stories from his life and tales from our ancestors. That's how I learned about Keno and Zaria and their love that had created the world and everything in it.

And now thinking of love has me thinking of my love—the one I left to his fate. The guilt creeps up on me as quickly as the longing. Who knows what Akkar did to Lukin after they discovered my absence? I could have sentenced him to death the minute I set foot on the ship. It's hard enough knowing I'll never see him again, but to imagine *no one* will? It's too much.

So I fight it, pushing him and Navya and Banu and Lukin's mother and my entire life at the cairn, both the bitter and the sweet of it, out of my mind. I throw myself into the task at hand—raising an army to defend Kenozaria. But the harder I try, the worse it gets. At the most inconvenient times, Lukin's face will flash across my mind, or I'll remember something he used to say or a face he'd make or the sound of his laugh, and I'm right back there beside him.

My thoughts are interrupted by Torek's labored breathing coming up behind me as he removes his armor and lays down his weapons.

"Did you kill anyone?" I ask.

"One or two. But they didn't go down without a fight," he says, pointing at a deep red scratch running across his left leg.

"I'm disappointed. You were supposed to 'mow down an army, single-handedly,' as I recall."

Torek laughs as he lies down next to me, keeping ample space between us.

"So the training is going well, then?"

"We'll get them ready in no time."

"Have the tribes from Lofy arrived? I thought I'd heard they were about a day's march away yesterday."

"They arrived at dawn. Two hundred warriors."

With the new arrivals, we'll be six hundred strong. Branngard has around half that number, but they have more sophisticated weapons. I can only hope our numbers and our knowledge of the lay of the land will be enough.

"I'm *famished*," Torek whines. "I hear the eldest daughter of Korina makes a mean stew."

"The eldest daughter of Korina is ready for a nap," I say, leaning on my haunches to stand up.

Torek sighs dramatically. "Fine. I'll make the stew and when you wake from your nap, you can insult my cooking skills. How does that sound?"

"Perfect."

When I awake, Torek is gone, but he's left the stew simmering on the embers. I ladle some into a bowl and sit at the table, blowing on it. I'm starving, but the smell is overpowering, even for Torek's cooking.

"How old is this meat?" I ask no one as my stomach begins to churn. I run from the room just in time to vomit into a bucket that has been collecting a steady leak in the corner of our room.

There's a rap at the door, and it's Aunt Meryn's high-pitched voice calling from behind it. "Evryn! Are you well? It's Auntie Meryn, dear." She had insisted on coming with us back to Kenozaria, to assist mother and Halline, should the need arise, and we were all grateful for her presence.

I wipe the sweat from my brow and slosh some water around in my mouth before spitting it, too, into the bucket. "Coming!" I call and walk to the door to open it.

When she steps inside, she takes one look at me and grimaces. "You look as if you've seen a ghost! You're so pale!" she says. "What ails you? And what is that *awful* smell?"

I wave her concern away. "Torek ails me, as always. This time, it's his stew."

"Oh?" she asks, walking toward the pot hanging in the hearth. She removes the iron lid and takes a big whiff. "It smells good!" She begins walking through the house, sniffing out the source of the smell. Having located the vomit, she turns and looks at me, concerned.

"I'm fine," I reply, wishing she'd leave me alone so I could rest. Suddenly, my thoughts are invaded by an old familiar voice.

Should have taken the herbs, Aunt Tabitha whispers, clear as day.

"What?!" I ask aloud.

"I didn't say anything," Aunt Meryn says. "You do seem ill, Evryn. First the vomit, and now you're hearing things? Should I fetch the healer?"

"No, no. I'm fine. So many new people in town, you know? I'm sure something is going around."

Aunt Meryn looks at me severely for a second and then breaks her gaze from me, picks up the basket she'd been carrying, and turns to head for the door again. "Well, if you change your mind, send Torek to the healer. She's a clever old witch. She'll know what to do."

"Yes, thank you," I say, closing the door behind her and falling back in bed.

Had I imagined Aunt Tabitha's voice? I haven't heard from anyone in the Bright Lands since the night Branngard arrived, and I can't understand why they'd start up again now—not when I pleaded for their guidance when I was a prisoner, not when I needed their help when I was running from Draven, not when it would have counted most. *Now.*

A few moments later, Torek comes through the door. "I ran into your aunt on the path," he says, removing his cloak and hanging it on the hook next to the door. "She says you're ill?"

"I'm fine. It's just a bug, I'm sure."

"Okay..." he says, his words trailing off. "What's wrong, exactly?"

"Your stew tried to kill me."

"And? That's nothing new."

"I don't know. I'm dizzy. My thoughts are... clouded? And I'm *so* tired, no matter how much I sleep."

He realizes it at the same moment I do.

"Evryn," he says, calmly approaching me. "You haven't bled since we arrived from Salix..."

The boy's smart, I hear Aunt Tabitha whisper.

I sit up in bed. "It *can't* be. It... it's not *possible*."

Torek beams, his eyes bright with possibility. "*Of course* it's possible!"

The bile is rising in my throat again, so I run to the bucket, but I don't make it in time, spilling the remainder of my lunch on the wooden floor. Torek comes to help me clean up, but I push him away.

"Evryn—" he begins, but I silence him with a look.

"If Keno and Zaria have blessed me with new life, you are nothing to us. *Nothing.* I will carry this life, I will birth this life, I will raise this life. You live because it serves our people for me to keep up this façade. As soon as we have expelled these invaders from our land, you are welcome to go back to wherever you were all that time. I have no use for you... *we* will have no use for you. Do you understand?"

He looks down, defeated. "Yes."

"Good," I say, hurling again. I don't miss this time.

31

Lukin

A light rapping on my cell door wakes me from my fitful sleep. "A letter for you," the guard says, handing a folded message through the tiny grated window he'd opened in the door. The seal has been broken, of course, but there's a clear indentation of Akkar's stamp on the dark red wax.

"On decree of the Torch of Branngard," I read aloud, "Captain Lukin Velga is to be released from the Lighthouse after serving his full sentence in the Dark Cells. He is reinstated as lord of Yarrow's Cairn, and his titles and lands are returned to him and his line."

"Step away from the door," the guard says, opening it on the squeaking, ancient hinges. "This way."

And with that, I'm freed from the Lighthouse, stepping into the sunlight for the first time in months. I'm placed in my carriage, which drives me straight home.

32

Evryn

Mother has just finished up another meeting with another small tribal leader, and she looks exhausted.

"You could let Halline handle some of these war council meetings," I say, bringing her a mug of warm cider. She takes a few quick sips and then hugs the mug to her chest, breathing in the warm vapor.

I still haven't gotten used to the easy way we have been getting along since I returned from Branngard. It could be that she's just grateful for my safety, but part of me knows it's more than likely a product of my pregnancy. Somehow, she seems to see me as her equal now, deserving of her respect. It's a start.

"Your sister is more than capable," she says. "But these men have a hard enough time taking *me* seriously, let alone a girl her age, wise as she is."

"It's a wonder to me that you were elected in the first place," I reply, taking a seat at the table in our kitchen.

"Well, thank you for your vote of confidence."

"No, I meant... how did Kenozaria become so open to this way of life when so many of the other villages on the island are... well, *not?*"

"It's a good story, actually," she replies, taking another sip of her cider.

"We have time," I smile just as Ari comes in and adds another log to the fire.

"Mama is telling *stories*?" he asks, excitedly pulling up a seat at the table.

"Your sister wants to know why our people elected me Chief," she says.

"Booorrinnnggg," Ari says, standing up again to go back outside. Mother slaps him on the side as he slips past her.

"Well, if you really want to know..." she begins.

"I do," I reply, taking a sip of my own cider.

"Well, like most things in life for a woman, I was only able to acquire this position by appealing to a man," she begins.

"Father?"

"That's right," she smiles. "But, not in the way you'd think. When we came back to Kenozaria, your father's mother, Hannah, was Chief of the Sanctum. And she took a special liking to me. She was warm and patient with me."

I don't remember much about my father's parents, since both died when I was so young, but I *do* recall the warmth and tenderness she showed to Mother and us children.

"She took me under her wing and began introducing me to other leaders around the island, so people began to take me more seriously. I can't have been much older than Ari is now, so that was a feat. When she passed not too long after Ari was born, the village unanimously chose me as her successor."

"Didn't Aunt Tabitha want to be chief after her mother passed?"

"Oh, no. Tabitha was never cut out for the life of a politician. She preferred her animals and trees," she says, smiling. "Sound familiar?"

I chuckle and take another sip of my cider. "I miss her."

"I do, too," Mother says.

"As I recall, the two of you weren't exactly *friends*," I say.

"We were very different sorts of people, Tabitha and I, it's true," she replies. "But she did such a good job of raising you, especially when your Papa left us for the Bright Lands. I respected her for that, and I was devastated when she passed."

"Mother, *you* and Papa raised us. Aunt Tabitha just helped," I say, sincerely.

"You're being generous," Mother says. "I did my best, but I am not unaware of the impact my absences had on you."

I look down into my mug, unsure how to respond. I have been waiting for this conversation all my life, longing for the chance to hear my mother simply *acknowledge* how much it hurt me when she disappeared for entire lengths of time—either physically or mentally. Now that it's arrived, I am unsure how to feel.

"You aren't absent now," I reply, taking her hand across the table. "I'm glad you'll be here with me when my baby arrives."

Mother beams and tears begin to fill her eyes. "Evryn," she begins, but stops herself as the tears start to fall.

"It's okay. We don't have to talk about this now."

"No," she says, firmly. "We only have now, really. It's that sort of 'later, later, later' thinking that got us into this mess. I kept thinking I would be a better mother to you when you were older, but the more you grew, the less prepared I was to guide you. Time slipped away from me."

"I didn't need you to guide me. I just needed you to *be* with me. I needed you to *see* me. I just wanted you to love me like you loved Ari and the others."

"My sweet girl," Mother says, wiping tears from the corners of her eyes. "Do you know why I am so attached to your brother?"

I shake my head.

"Ari nearly killed me when he was born. You were in Salix, so I doubt you remember that time, but it was horrifying. The midwives said they didn't think he'd make it. Rayyan had just given birth to Ayfa, so she nursed him for me because my milk wouldn't come in. It was just a very hard time, and it bonded us. Plus, I was only sixteen when you were born. You were just learning to walk when I had my Bright Ceremony. I had *no idea* how to be a mother to you."

I nod, understanding. My own impending arrival has me thinking about all the ways I am sorely unprepared to be a mother, and I am much older than she was when I was born. There is a sort of mercy growing in me for her, in step with my growing baby.

"By the time Ari was born, I was nearly a decade older, and I'd had plenty of practice raising you and Halline."

"You're saying I was your *practice child*?!" I ask, laughing. "I need to write that down so I can use that line on this little one."

"That's *my* job as their grandma!" Mother laughs before finishing off her cider. "I have to tell them all about how hard you've worked to be a better mother than the one you had."

I take her hand across the table and, for the first time in my life, I feel *warmth* radiating between the two of us. The frost is melting and the thorns are falling from the vine.

"I can only dream of being half of the woman you are," I say before Ayfa interrupts us, announcing that another tribal leader has arrived to talk with Mother.

VII

Winter

33

Korina

War drums reverberate through my chest. The morning air carries the cries of my people. Most of the houses in the village are still burning, and ashes fill the air, making it hard to take a breath.

Standing on the western edge of the mountain, I watch the long, steady line of Branngardian soldiers following behind their leader, marching through the rubble that used to be Kenozaria. I desperately will myself elsewhere, to another time where this isn't happening to the only home I've ever known—to my children.

Halline and Ziva are with Lyra and the other younger Kenozarians in the medic tent. Torek and I convinced Evryn to stay behind, for the sake of her child. I tried in vain to convince Ari to stay behind at the camp with his sisters, but he insisted on coming along.

"What are your orders?" a young warrior asks, interrupting my thoughts.

"Please, see to the survivors. Take a few men with you to escort them higher up, on the eastern ridge. We will do our best to hold the line and prevent Branngard from getting around to them."

"Yes, Chief," he says, running back down the mountain to help gather survivors.

I remember Torek's advice when we'd left Branngard's encampment that Autumn evening a year ago, to call up the banners as soon as possible. I curse myself for my damned hesitation.

Zaria, aid your people, I pray. *Keno, stop them in their tracks. Ancestors, save us and this blessed place.*

The sun has fallen behind the horizon. Hundreds of corpses lay strewn about the land they'd loved. Only twenty or so warriors remain by my side. We fight on, slogging through the muddy, steep trail. Branngard has pushed us further up the path that winds around to the eastern ridge.

"Please, send for Ari," I say to the warrior next to me. He runs east to where Ari's contingent is waiting, the last barrier between the rest of our people and utter destruction.

When he comes back with the warrior, Ari looks to me to be nothing but a boy—scared and longing for comfort. I pull him close to me and bury my face in his hair.

"Listen to me, Ari. There isn't much time. I need you to do something for me, okay?" He looks into my eyes, his own eyes dancing in fear. "Will you look out for Ziva, and make sure she is safe and well? Take her and run to Salix. You will both be safe there."

"But... how can we leave you behind? And Halline and Evryn? And Lyra?"

I smile and brush the hair out of his eyes. "My love, you must do as I say. Halline and Evryn are big girls, more than capable of caring for themselves. And Lyra will be needed here, to help her mother and the other healers. You can come for her as soon as it's safe."

Ari sighs in exhaustion, rubbing the ashes and mud from his face. "Come with us, Mama! We can all go to Salix!"

"Ari, we cannot leave the sick and old and the children here to fend for themselves, and they're too weak to move quickly. I must stay, to see if I can still negotiate a peace treaty with Branngard."

He pulls me in for an embrace, and I can feel him choking back tears. "I wish Evryn were here," he says. "She would know what to do. She always knows what to do."

"She really does," I say, willing myself not to think of her, or I'll lose my will here and now. "I need you to be brave."

"Yes, Mama," he says, drying his tears.

"Go now. Hurry. Stop only when you must, and don't look back. I will come to you or send word as soon as it's safe."

He turns and runs back east, and not a moment too soon. When I look down again, I see Akkar's personal guard at the head of his army, climbing up over the western ridge. Soon, they encircle us.

"It is not too late, Korina! You can still save your people," Akkar says, pointing his staff at me. "Surrender! Dedicate yourself and this ground to Rhys and He will free you and save your children!"

"To hell with you and to hell with your god!" I roar.

"Have it your way," he says calmly. "I'll make sure your daughters find strong husbands to break them in, stronger than my disgrace of a nephew. They'll be good Branngardian wives in no time, unlike Evryn!"

In a flash, I grab an ax from the belt of one of my men and lunge at Akkar, throwing it at him with all my might. The heavy blade lands, piercing through the armor with a moist thud.

The guard who jumped in front of Akkar buckles at the knees as dark, hot blood pours from the gash in his belly and he collapses on the ground.

Akkar's retinue of guards closes in on my men. Several flee, and the rest don't stand a chance. In a matter of moments, I stand alone, surrounded by my dead countrymen.

I know what must be done.

I pull a vial of pale yellow-green liquid from my pocket and uncork it, tossing the contents down my throat. Within seconds, my insides are alight with agony, dropping me to my knees. I fall to the ground, writhing in pain and expelling the contents of my stomach and guts. Hot blood is leaking from my eyes and nose, and I'm coughing up a stream of it.

Time stands still as I close my eyes and see the lives of my children flashing across my vision. I imagine them alive and well and cry a silent prayer, imploring the gods to protect them and my new grandchild.

As my limbs become heavier and fog creeps through my mind, I see Evryn—all the versions of her I have loved and failed.

"I'm so proud of you, Evryn," I whisper, mustering the last of my strength as my spirit lifts from the fleshy prison I've worn for forty-three years and settles into the trees atop Mount Zaria, who look at the carnage below and sigh in sorrow.

34

Evryn

I'm so proud of you, Evryn, Mother whispers.

I sit upright in my cot and hold my face in my hands. I'm covered in a film of sweat and my heart is racing.

The tent is dark and silent, but I can hear the sounds of warfare on the other side of the mountain.

I must be dreaming. How else would I have heard mother calling to me?

I stifle a wail, realizing what it must mean.

35

Lukin

"Too loose. We'll have to take it in a bit here and here," the tailor says, taking his piece of chalk out to mark the coat. "You were thinking royal blue? Such a good color for a winter wedding!"

"Hmm?" I ask, lost in thought.

"I asked if you'd like your coat for the ceremony to be royal blue, my lord?"

"Ah, yes," I say, stepping down from the dais. "Whatever Lady Selise has requested will do fine."

"You need to come back to reality, my friend," Timur remarks from the chair he sits in, watching. "You've been distant these past days."

"I've been *busy*. Planning a wedding is a time-consuming affair."

"Look, I've known you all my life, Lukin. I don't think it's just the wedding. You're not yourself since…"

I sigh. "I want things to be perfect for Selise," I say, avoiding his gaze as I look into the mirror.

"Mmhmm, I imagine that's *exactly* who's keeping you up at night, Lukin," he says, cocking his head to the side. "Are you sure it's not a certain buxom servant who I hear has been entertaining the lord of

Yarrow's Cairn nightly?"

I laugh, removing the tailor's coat and donning my own.

"Your wedding is a fortnight away, man. Surely you don't plan to carry on this little dalliance so brazenly?"

"I'll take care of it," I remark, handing the tailor his fee and turning to leave the shop.

"Alright," Timur says, standing and following me outside.

The cacophony of the street in stark contrast to the relative quiet of the shop bothers me. I can't wait to get back home to the stony silence of the cairn.

"I'll see you tonight, then?" Timur asks as he mounts his horse.

"Tonight?" I ask, climbing onto my own.

"Yes! Tonight! You can't just skip *your own betrothal ball*," he says, shaking his head in frustration. "You're already running late."

"Right. Yes. I'll see you there." I nod, turning my horse west.

"You are looking well, my lord," Selise says, smiling. The grand ballroom of Yarrow's Cairn is decorated with wintry flora, and she looks like part of the backdrop, coming to life. Her golden curls cascade down one shoulder, falling onto a deep maroon dress, her neck dripping with diamonds. She wears a lavish, snow-white fur around her shoulders to complete the look.

"As are you, Lady Selise. As always," I reply, bowing slightly. "Shall we take a walk through the gardens?" I ask, extending my gloved hand to her.

"I'd relish the chance." She smiles, taking my arm as I lead her out through the garden doors.

The snow piling up outside the cairn reflects the light pouring out from the windows as moonlight dapples the land beyond. The smell of cold rushes into my lungs, rejuvenating me. It's almost enough to make me forget my own inner darkness.

"You danced exquisitely tonight," I say. "I hope you've saved one for me."

"I suppose I'll make room in my card," she says, smiling. "Though, you really *should* have been my first, if rights were given as they should have done."

"My apology, my lady."

"You have your responsibilities, my lord," she replies. "Duties I am happy to support you in when I become the lady of this castle."

When she pulls me in for a secret kiss as we turn a corner and find ourselves alone, I am repulsed. Still, she is to be my bride, come what may, so I kiss her anyway before heading back toward the castle.

"I know we're not supposed to speak of it," she whispers as I open the ballroom doors, "but I hope you will be more satisfied with me than you were with… the *previous* Lady Lukin Velga. I would *never* leave you as she did."

"I don't want to talk about her," I say, leading her inside.

Hours later, when the last guests have gone, I help Selise into her carriage and send her on her way, back to her family estate for the last time before our wedding. Then I rush back to my favorite distraction, who lies in my bed at the opposite end of the castle, waiting patiently for me to return.

Nora is massaging the knots in my shoulders after we've washed up.

The moment I had my lands and titles reinstated, I hurried to arrange to have her brought back to Yarrow's Cairn. We've spent nearly every night together for the past several months. She is my midnight snack, the warm place I go to hide from the pressures of my station, from the demons in my mind.

She comes around the front of me and takes my face in her hands, looking concerned.

"I'm tired, that's all, darling. Could you leave me? I need rest tonight." She stands and drops her head demurely before dressing and leaving.

As Nora pads quietly back down to the servants' quarters below, an old familiar feeling washes over me—just as it does every moment I'm left alone with my thoughts.

Far from the cold, quick death I believed I'd chosen the night I sent Evryn into the darkness, or the long, lonely, painful death I worried I'd face in the Lighthouse, the relative brilliance of my future, panning out before me, is too much to handle at times. Golden though my life is, I am keenly aware it's a gilded cage. Akkar knows as well as I do that my freedom is contingent on my good behavior.

And so I stand at the windows in my bedchamber—in *our* bedchamber, the one I shared with Evryn—as I so often do, looking toward Kenozaria and thinking of her. I try to imagine her running through her beloved woods—strong and alive and surrounded by the people she loves. And *free*. But since Draven has refused to accept any of my letters, returning them unopened, I have no way of knowing what may have happened to her, or what else is transpiring across the sea. Still, I can hope.

My wedding to Lady Selise will be a glamorous, state affair, attended by dignitaries from across the world. Akkar himself will be returning for the event, to give his public blessing to our union. It seems as if Evryn has never existed in the minds and hearts of anyone but me. So I find comfort and entertainment in the arms of Nora, and distraction in my social events with Selise on my arm, doing all I can to simultaneously forget Evryn and keep her memory alive in my heart.

I head out early for a ride to clear my mind. The rolling moors, contrasted as they are by the dark mountains looming beyond, are a soothing balm I often seek out when nothing else helps. Out here, I am the lord of nothing, brother and son to no one, engaged to no one.

As I return to the stables, my groom approaches and takes the reins of my horse.

"You'd better get inside, my lord," he says quietly, stroking the side of my stallion and eyeing the Shield riding up behind me. "There's a letter for you."

"Oh?" I ask, removing my riding gloves and handing them to him. "From whom?"

"There is no sigil on the seal, my lord."

As I enter my study, I find the small letter, folded and sealed, lying on my desk. Curious, I open it to find one single line, with no signature.

"Kenozaria has fallen."

Evryn, I think, throwing the letter into the fire and packing a bag.

By nightfall, I am aboard the *Nightengale*, heading southeast.

36

Evryn

"Ari and Ziva were captured," Halline says as she helps me stand up from my cot. "We must move further east, into the mountains."

"Captured?" I ask. "Who took them?"

"Who do you think?" Halline asks, grabbing my cloak and boots and helping me into them. "They were running south, to Salix, and Branngard captured them. Torek and the others are gathering some scouts to find them. But for now, we have to focus on saving the rest of the people."

"Halline," I say, realizing she may not know yet. "What about Mother?"

Halline sniffs and wipes her nose on her sleeve. "She's gone, Evryn."

Somehow, having it confirmed breaks me worse than the initial realization. I crumble back down onto the cot, racking my body with weeping.

"Help me get her up," Halline says as Torek comes running into the tent. "We have to move, quickly."

"Yes, okay," he replies, taking my arm in his and helping me to stand. I can sense the fear in him as our skin touches, but I am too exhausted to care.

When we get to the clearing on the east side of the mountain pass, everyone gets busy setting up tents. The wind and the snow don't seem to care that we are already hungry and exhausted, and many are wounded and ill. By the time everyone is sheltered and fed, it's well into the night.

"Bring your mother and the others," Halline says to Ayfa. "We must convene the Sanctum immediately."

As Rayyan, Minara, and the others file into Halline's tent, each still covered in sweat and soot, Halline clears her throat. "I am not entitled to speak in this space," she says, "but Evryn and I come in place of my mother, Korina Freya, and ask that you convene this Sanctum to make an emergency decision."

"There is nothing to discuss," Rayyan says, wiping off her face with a handkerchief. "Korina Freya is gone. We are not in any position to seek guidance from her and the ancestors, but she always wanted you to follow in her footsteps."

All nod in agreement.

"By rights, my sister, Evryn, should be offered the position before me, as she is the elder," Halline says.

"I am happy to follow you, the wisest among us children of Korina Freya," I reply, squeezing her hand.

"It is decided then," Minara says, smiling.

"Now," Rayyan says, taking a drink of water from a flagon at her waist, "can we get to the matter of how we will survive these monsters?"

"Yes, let's," Halline says, taking a seat. "One hundred villagers, most of whom are children and elderly, are in need of our protection. Our first priority is keeping them alive and well."

"Yes," Rayyan agrees.

"We must seek allies," Minara says.

"We have already gathered every tribe on the island who is willing to come," Rayyan replies. "Where else will we find allies?"

"There is always..." Minara begins, letting her words trail off.

"No," Rayyan replies. "Not her."

"Yes, her," Rayyan's mother, Plera, remarks. "She may be our best hope."

"Mama—" Rayyan begins, but her mother silences her with a hand in the air.

"Nerys Beretta is no one to trust, I agree, but she has what we need now—warriors and a stronghold even Branngard would struggle to break."

"Plera speaks true," Halline says. "Does anyone have a *real* reason we shouldn't at least ask her?"

"Aside from the fact that she turned her back on her own people and built up a fort in order to *really* get across the message that she wanted nothing to do with us?" Rayyan asks, frustrated.

"Desperate times, desperate measures," Minara replies.

"Let us send a party to her under a flag of emergency," Halline suggests. "The worst she can do is say no."

"She can do *far worse*," Rayyan retorts.

Ignoring Rayyan, Halline arranges for a group of us to seek Nerys's help: Torek, Ayfa, and a few other Kenozarian warriors are to set out at first light.

"Ask her to shelter the villagers," Halline says. "That's all we ask. And extend to her our sincerest thanks and assurances that we *will* assist her in her time of need, should she ever call on us."

With that, the first Sanctum meeting under Chief Halline Korina is closed and all are sent on their way.

* * *

"Ari and Ziva should be here with us," I say as I pull the razor carefully across Halline's scalp. The morning sun warms us as we sit together on the floor of her tent.

"Ziva would certainly cut me less than you have," Halline winces.

"Sorry."

"You're doing your best," Halline says, wiping her head off with the cloth that I hand to her.

"We *all* are," I say, pulling her in for a hug.

"Your turn," Halline says, inviting me to sit in front of her now.

I eye her suspiciously. "Have mercy on me, Chief Halline."

Halline laughs and places a towel on my shoulders, then pulls my long auburn hair behind me and cuts the length of it off. Slowly, she cuts chunks out, dropping them in piles next to me.

We sit together in silence for a long time, listening to the sound of her scissors slicing across one another, punctuating the silence. It's been a long time since I have been able to enjoy time alone with my sister and I'm savoring the experience, heavy as it is with the reality of *why* we're getting this time together.

"Remember when Mama cut Papa's hair after Grandma Hannah passed?" Halline asks.

"Of course," I reply. "I'm surprised you do. You were so young."

"Papa's head looked like an egg, a badly misshapen egg!" She laughs.

"Yes, it did." I laugh with her.

"At least we look a bit better."

"Speak for yourself, Chief. I don't have a looking glass handy, and you're just getting started with that razor."

"You can trust me, sister. I won't let you down."

After Halline has finished shaving my head, she offers me a clean towel and helps me wipe away the last remains of loose hair and shaving cream from my ears and neck. I help her clean up the hair from around the room, and we both change into clean, warm clothes.

"I'll grab us some tea," I say, tossing a shawl over my head for warmth and stepping out into the blustery morning air.

Fresh snow is falling heavily, and I can't help but wonder what has happened to Torek and the rest of the party. It's been a week since they set out to Nerys's stronghold and we still haven't received word.

When I step back into Halline's tent, warm tea in hand, she reaches out to take her mug and helps me sit down next to her.

"Perfect," she muses as she takes a sip. "Just like Mother used to make."

"She taught us well," I reply, "though I'd wager yours is better."

We sit together, drinking our tea and alternately laughing or crying at our shared stories about Mother.

"Your baby is going to be the most beautiful baby ever," Halline says then, laying her head on my thigh and rubbing my belly.

"She'd better be, to make up for all the pain she's putting me through."

Halline looks up at me across the horizon of my belly. "You do know there's *much* more pain to come, right?"

"Now you're just being hurtful."

"I'm being honest."

"As long as she takes after me, I guess it's worth it."

"Hey, Torek is handsome!" Halline remarks. "And he could be a boy, you know."

"Nope. Definitely a girl." I groan, readjusting my aching hips. "And let's not talk about him."

"Him? You mean Torek, the father of your child and the love of your life?"

"Halline—" I begin, unsure how to even open the subject, or whether it's the right time. I decide to wait. "Yeah, I guess you're right. But really, I am sure it's a girl."

"I'd wager against you, but I'm light on coin at the moment. Wars are expensive affairs, it turns out."

"That, and you'd lose, anyway."

We lie next to each other for a while then, watching as the light dances through the trees, casting shadows on the fabric of the tent.

"I've missed you, little sister," I say, snuggling into her. "Speaking of little sisters, do we have any word on Ziva's whereabouts?"

"We are still searching for her. We can't get close enough to the village to get a good look, but we have some ideas."

"I can't imagine how she must be feeling."

"We will bring her home, soon," Halline says. "And Ari, too. He and Lyra will marry as soon as this war is finished. She will make him happy, I think."

"And you, Hal? Are you happy? Chiefdom seems to suit you," I say, brushing some hair from her face. "But what about *life*? Love?"

"It's hard to think of all that in the face of... all *this*," she says, gesturing around us.

"I understand."

"And Ayfa..."

"Yes?" I ask.

"She has some maturing to do, that's all."

"Halline, compared to you, we *all* have some maturing to do."

Halline laughs. She knows I'm right. "Anyway, I'll leave you to rest now," she says, sighing and standing up from the cot.

"Stay," I reply, motioning her to sit back down. "I want to talk with you more. Soon we won't have as many uninterrupted conversations."

Halline stops and sits down again. "What do you want to talk about?"

"I know you've been trying to protect me, Hal, but I need to know. What happened to her, exactly? To Mother."

"Mama died as she lived, my darling," Halline says sighing and taking my hand in hers. "With tenacity and grit, sacrificing all for her people."

"What are you saying, Halline?" I ask. "How did she die?"

"Rue."

One word. *Rue.* That's all she needs to say, and I understand instantly. It's too poetic to be true—the herb that had failed her more than twenty-five years ago finally worked.

"Why would she do this? Why abandon us like this?" I cry.

"She didn't abandon us, Evy," she says, stroking my head. "Mama was cornered and alone, and she knew Akkar wouldn't kill her. He would have taken her hostage."

"What? Why?"

"Imagine what we would be willing to accept if only to keep Mama safe. Think of what the rest of the island would tolerate if only to avoid having Korina Freya's blood on their hands."

Of course. She took her own life to avoid putting us in that predicament. Mother was nothing if not strategic.

"You really *must* get some rest now," Halline says, standing up to go.

"I'll try," I reply, rolling over and pulling the heavy blanket over my head. Before long, the tears fall hot and heavy.

37

Torek

Snow is falling so heavily I begin to worry we will lose the path, but Afya has it all in hand. It takes us a full day and night, but eventually, we stumble out of the foothills and see it looming against the eastern horizon: Nerys's stronghold, sighing under the weight of snow piling ever higher.

I have been struggling with myself since the moment Halline asked me, *ordered* me, to go with Ayfa and the others. I couldn't refuse without explaining myself, and that was *not* an option. As far as Ayfa and the others know, I have never met her. As far as they know, she is an ancient, crumbling crone of a witch.

When we approach the giant wooden gates, the archers pull their bows taut. "Who goes there?" one calls out.

"Torek Minara and Ayfa Rayyan," I call out. "We come on behalf of Chief Halline Korina, of Kenozaria. We come in peace."

"What brings you here?"

"We seek the mercy of the great Nerys Beretta," Ayfa calls out. "Or at least a fire to warm our freezing asses."

There is chuckling behind the gate. "Wait there," someone calls out. After what feels like an hour, the gate creaks open, and we are invited in.

Nerys sits at a long table, alongside a few of her favorite husbands, while the rest of them sit on benches around the room.

"Well, I didn't expect to see you back so soon, Torek Minara," she says.

Afya and the others look at me, confused.

"Thank you for welcoming us," I reply, deciding to deal with Ayfa later, after we've taken care of the business at hand.

"What brings you here?"

"We seek your mercy and shelter," Afya says, stepping forward and bowing slightly. "Kenozaria is in ruins and our children and elderly need protection."

"And your men are incapable of protecting you?" Nerys asks, smirking. Several men in the room laugh.

"We have lost many warriors already. Our people are freezing in the mountains and we are short on supplies. We will not last the winter without your help."

Nerys stands and walks toward our group. "Perhaps you have assumed that because I was generous with you, my help is something you can count on?"

"Not at all—" I begin, but she cuts me off.

"I helped you because doing so served my interests," Nerys says, matter-of-factly. "Tell me: how would helping this new chief of Kenozaria, the village of ash, serve me now? Does she even offer me tribute?"

"Please, may we warm ourselves before a fire and get something in our bellies? If you decide to send us back on our way after that, this is your right. But at least show us that mercy before we go back to our deaths."

"I am nothing if not hospitable!" Nerys says. "Get these people something to eat."

We are seated at a table near the giant stone fireplace on the left side of the room. Plates of mutton and deer are passed around, along with warm cups of spiced cider and goat milk.

After a while, Nerys approaches me. "You have many secrets it seems," she says, taking me by the arm and leading me away from the group.

"Aren't we all entitled to a bit of privacy?" I ask.

"Oh, indeed," she says, walking me back toward her private chamber. With that, something hard thumps across the back of my head, and all is darkness.

When I come to, I am tied to Nerys's bed.

"What is the meaning of this?!" I ask, pulling at the ropes that chafe against my wrists and ankles.

"Everyone is entitled to their privacy, as you said, and I intend to enjoy my private time with you," she says, sharpening a knife.

"No!" I cry as she comes walking toward me. "Please don't kill me! I am going to be a father!"

"Dumping your seed into a helpless woman doesn't make you a father."

"How can you possib—" I begin.

Nerys laughs, cutting me off. "How can I know that you raped a woman who trusted you? I know that and *much more*, Torek Minara."

I begin to cry with fear as she flashes the knife mere inches from my face.

"I will give you a choice," she says, grabbing my cock with her free hand. "Your cock or your people."

"What?!" I scream, trying desperately to pull away from her, but the ropes won't give.

"You have already fathered the only child you will ever have, and therefore have no more need for this," she says, playing with my flaccid member. "She certainly doesn't want to make love to you, and no one else will when I am done with you."

"Please, please. Don't do this! Please, there must be a way I can help you!"

"I've already enjoyed what was good in you," Nerys says, smiling. "Now, decide: will you damn your people—and your unborn child—to a brutal death, or will you let me take a piece of you for a prize?"

I piss myself in fear, and she laughs at the scene.

"Oh, poor little man! Okay, I guess I *could* release you and tell them what you've done to her and let them have their justice on you—if they can survive the winter and the war."

I hesitate, and with each passing moment I hate myself further. Only a monster would even weigh his options in this case, but I am too overcome with cowardice to speak.

So she makes the decision for me. I feel white-hot pain and a brief jerk, and then I'm gone again, into the darkness.

A week later, our party is walking back to our camp in the hills, alongside fifty of Nerys's men who have come along to help us transport the people back to the fort.

I struggle to walk as the pain in my groin throbs up through the top of my head and down to my toes, but I try my best to hide it. If anyone finds out what she has done to me, I will have more problems on my hands than a missing member. Such a punishment would not be meted out without just cause, everyone knows.

"We will never be able to repay you," Ayfa says, walking alongside me. "I don't know what you said, or *did*, in that chamber, but you may have just saved us all."

"It's nothing."

"And because I am grateful to you, I won't ask how you know her or why she was so eager to negotiate with you, alone," she says, more quietly, "but I can't promise no one else will start to ask questions or pass the word along to Halline or Evryn."

"We will live. This is what matters. I thank you for your discretion."

VIII

Spring

38

Lukin

I arrive beneath an overcast spring sky. I had bribed the captain of the *Nightengale* to go around the northwestern tip of the island, taking care to stay as far from shore as possible, so a few days were added to my journey, but it was a necessary step. I can't risk Akkar finding out I'm here.

I've brought only the clothes on my back and a small satchel of food and provisions for the road, enough to last a week or so. I don't know how, but I must find a way to help Evryn and her family.

First, though, I need men. Not a few Branngardian soldiers are more loyal to me than they ever could be to Akkar, brothers in war I've fought alongside for decades. One of them, surely, was the author of the letter informing me of Kenozaria's demise.

The question of how to send word to them without Akkar finding out plagues me as I walk through the mountain pass on the northern edge of the village, careful not to be spotted by even a shepherd.

I come to a clearing in the pines where there's a smoldering bonfire, encircled with large stones. A young woman lies beside the embers, asleep, wearing nothing but her shift. I approach her quietly and nudge her leg with my boot.

She opens her eyes and jumps to her feet. "Stay away from me!"

"I mean you no harm," I reply with my hands in the air, turning my head and closing my eyes to respect her modesty.

"You are a soldier of Branngard, I can tell by your accent," she says warily.

"May I?" I ask, removing my cloak and handing it out to her. "I assure you, I will not hurt you."

She takes the cloak and thanks me. "What are you doing here, then? This is sacred ground."

"Searching for my—" I begin but stop myself. "I'm trying to find Korina Freya and her family. I believe they are in danger."

"Yes, they *are* in danger," the young woman replies. "But you've come too late."

My stomach drops. "Too late? What has happened?"

"Korina Freya is dead," she replies. "She was killed the night of Dam Praya."

"*Dam Praya?*"

"The river of blood."

"My god. I... I had no idea. And what of her children?"

"Ari and Ziva have been captured. Halline is the new chief of the Sanctum, and she's working to free them from Branngard's grasp."

"And Evryn?" I ask, desperately hoping the news is somehow good.

She smiles broadly. "Evryn lives. She and Torek have built us an army."

"*Torek Minara?* I thought he was dead."

"So did we all."

A thousand thoughts flash through my mind in an instant, all culminating in two resounding truths: Evryn is alive, and I've lost her forever.

"I am so sorry," I say. "I didn't think the Torch would do this."

"Then you are a fool," the girl says, tossing my cloak to me and donning the woolen dress she'd stashed in her satchel, which lay behind a rock not far from the bonfire. She pulls the satchel across her chest and laces up her boots. After she is dressed, she turns to me. "Let's get this over with. I've got to take you to Halline."

"Lead the way," I say, extending my arm toward the path.

As she walks on ahead of me, she turns and looks at me curiously. "Who are you, anyway?"

"Lukin Velga," I say, greeting her in the Kenozarian fashion.

"Lukin Velga?" she asks. "Well, that's unexpected."

"Oh?"

"You look nothing like how I imagined you."

I chuckle. "Thank you? Or... I'm sorry?"

She smiles. "I'm Lyra, Torek's sister. Ari told me all about you."

"Did he?" What on earth could Ari have known about me, considering we'd only met once, and briefly?

"I know you were the captain of the Branngardian army and you married Evryn to protect her and Ziva from the Torch," she says.

"Yes, that's about the sum of it, although many don't believe those were my motives."

"Ziva does," she says simply. "And Ari always sides with Ziva."

"You said Ari was captured?"

"Yes. He's being held in the garrison in what used to be Kenozaria village."

"Used to be? Where is everyone?"

"They're taking shelter in a stronghold in the east."

"I am sorry," I say. "Truly sorry."

"Don't be. He will escape and return to me, I know it."

"I am sure he will. And Ziva? What's become of her?"

Lyra looks at the ground, sadly. "She's been sold to a Branngardian soldier, someone close to the Torch."

I rack my brain trying to think of who among his inner circle would willingly take a child slave, but no one comes to mind.

As we turn a corner on the trail, we come upon a massive fort, built of solid wood, standing dark against the morning sky.

"Welcome to New Kenozaria," Lyra says.

As we approach the gates, several warriors spot us and take up their weapons, but when they see it's Lyra with me, they lower them and someone comes to open the massive doors.

"Just let me do the talking," Lyra says as the gate opens.

"Who is this?" one of the warriors asks as he approaches me, eyeing me suspiciously.

"He's with me," Lyra says. "I'm taking him to speak with the chief and Nerys."

"He will have to leave his weapons with us," the warrior says warily, looking me up and down. "And he will need to be blindfolded."

I remove the short dagger at my thigh, lift my bow from across my chest and the quiver of arrows from my back, then take my curved blade from its scabbard, handing all three to the warriors. One of them turns me around and throws a bag of sackcloth over my head, placing my hand in Lyra's.

When we enter the room, the group inside goes quiet.

"Remove the bag," a woman says. "Let us see what Lyra has brought back for us."

When the bag is removed and my eyes adjust to the dimness of the tent, I see Halline, seated behind a large table, surrounded by several Kenozarian warriors and elders, and alongside a woman I've never seen before.

Halline looks ten years older than she did when I saw last saw her, and her hair is shaved close to the scalp. "What an unexpected treat," she says.

"Lukin found me on the mountain, by accident. He only asks for an audience with you," Lyra says.

"It's an honor to see you again, Chief Halline," I say, customarily greeting her and the woman beside her, but neither return the greeting.

"Can someone explain who this man is?" the other woman asks dryly.

"My name is Lukin Velga—" I begin.

"And you are Branngardian, from your accent, so why are you standing before us alive?"

I swallow and approach the table. "I understand why you'd be wary of me."

"Explain," Halline says calmly, motioning to a seat at the table and placing her hands on her lap.

"First, let me offer my most sincere condolences on the loss of your mother and the suffering of your siblings and the rest of your people," I say, taking the seat she proffered.

"Condolences received. Please, continue," she says plainly.

"I received word Akkar had invaded the village, so I got on the first ship here."

"Why?" she asks. "Why, after all this time, did you feel the need to return to our island?"

I can see this is going to be harder than I'd imagined. "I'm here to offer my assistance, in any way I can. I loved your sister, and I—" I begin, but Halline cuts me off with a wave of her hand.

"Those who love us do not leave us to our own devices in a dangerous situation," she replies. "Sentiments aside, what do you want?"

I am unsure how to proceed. Clearly, Evryn has not told Halline the details of the events that led to her flight from Branngard. "I... I don't want *anything*, Chief Halline. I came to help Evryn and your family, to protect her if I can."

"And *you* intend to protect us, all on your own?" the other woman asks, amused. Several people scattered throughout the tent snicker.

"Meet Nerys Beretta," Halline says, "who has so generously offered us shelter and assistance in her home while we rebuild our armies."

I greet Nerys in the customary way, and this time she nods in acknowledgment.

"There are many in the army who do not support Akkar's methods," I say. "If I can get word to some of my trusted friends among them, they will join our side. I am sure of it."

"Not his methods, perhaps, but they agree with him and you and the rest of them. You all believe we're a heathen people in need of Branngard's... *civilizing* guidance," Nerys says, sneering.

My face burns with shame. "I understand your hesitation, I really do. But not all Branngardians see things the way the Torch does, I assure you."

"You are his nephew, yes?" Halline asks.

"Yes."

"So you want us to believe that you, the *nephew of the Torch of Branngard*, and former captain of his armies, do not agree with his politics?"

"I do not." When she says nothing in response, I continue. "I've had the chance to get to know the common people in so many different places across the world. Unlike my uncle, I've been able to appreciate the many ways people can live a good life. And the people of Kenozaria are some of the most dignified people I've come across."

"And you arrived at this conclusion based on... what? A few months of playing house with my sister?" she asks, clearly unimpressed.

I take a deep breath. "Your sister is unlike any person alive, and I know she didn't become as she is by accident. It was the work of her people, her society, shaping her. No barbarian could raise a woman as incredible and kind and brilliant as your sister."

"If you believe Evryn Korina can be shaped, you don't know her half so well as you think you do, Captain," Halline retorts.

"It's Lukin, please," I say. "And I don't blame you for your suspicion. It is wise of you to be cautious. Please, let me prove my sincerity."

Halline and Nerys look at one another for a moment, clearly weighing their options.

"Look, if you send me away, I will just come back. Again and again and again. But if Akkar finds me before then, you'll lose your only chance to bring some of his forces to your side."

"Fine," Halline remarks. "Let's give the good captain a tent and a few guardsmen, to keep watch. Let us see how valuable he will prove himself to be."

"I don't need protection," I reply. "I'm sure your men are needed elsewhere."

"They're not for your protection," Nerys says, sending me and my keepers out of the room.

As we walk through the courtyard of the fort, I swear I see Evryn stepping out of a tent. I stand motionless, watching her. That's when I see her engorged belly and my breath catches in my throat. When she turns in my direction, I look the other way. If it *is* her, I don't want this to be our first reunion, among all these people who surely wouldn't understand the scene that would likely unfold before them.

39

Torek

"Can I have a word?" Ayfa says, wrapping an arm around my shoulder.

It's been a long day of hunting, and every muscle in my body cries for rest. "Go on then," I say, turning to face her.

"Captain Lukin Velga, Evryn's... *husband*. He's just arrived."

My mouth is dry. "I thought he was in Branngard."

"As soon as he heard about Dam Praya, he jumped on a ship to come help," she says. "I wanted you to hear it from me, so you could be prepared. If you'd like, I can introduce the two of you. But only if you promise not to throttle him."

I chuckle. "Somehow, I don't imagine Halline would approve."

"Or Evryn, for that matter."

"Speaking of Evryn, I don't know how she will handle it when she sees him," I say. The only thing worse than the cold way she treats me would be witnessing the warmth she may show him.

Ayfa's eyes widen and she grits her teeth. "Yeahhhhh... that's going to be an interesting reunion, to be sure."

"Well, let me know when you'd like me to introduce the two of you," Ayfa says, then turns to go.

Later, I'm walking down to the creek just outside of the fort to splash some cool water on my face and relieve myself. I have to sneak away to wash and to urinate, for fear of someone seeing the mangled mess Nerys left for me. As I am heading back toward the camp, Ayfa, her younger brother Björn, and some other Kenozarian warriors come walking toward me, into the woods.

"Hunting party?" I ask.

"There's a buck not far from here," Ayfa replies. "You're more than welcome to come with us. Though Lukin will be along shortly…"

I weigh my options. "The more the merrier. Let's see if Branngardian men are as good with the bow as they are with the sword."

Just then, a Branngardian soldier with red hair and a graying beard appears behind the group.

"Torek Minara, meet Lord Lukin Velga, captain of the Branngardian army," Ayfa says.

"*Former* captain. Now I'm just a humble traitor, remember," Lukin says. "It's an honor to meet you finally, Torek."

He extends his hand to me, so I take it and clasp his arm, taking the measure of his strength. "Back from the dead," I reply, smiling.

"If you two ladies are done getting acquainted, what say we find our dinner, eh?" Björn says as the group heads deeper into the woods.

As we walk on, I take stock of Lukin. He's larger than I imagined, and stronger, too. He carries a bow, having left his curved blade back at camp, I assume.

"I hear you did Evryn a great service," I whisper as we search for the buck's trail.

Lukin tightens his jaw. "I did what any man of honor would have done. What you'd have done if the tables were turned, I'm sure."

"Perhaps," I reply. "Nonetheless, we're all grateful."

Lukin smiles and continues on, following the band of hunters as quietly as he can, his bronze armor clanking softly.

"I'm glad she has you," he offers. "Again, I mean. She was devastated by your loss."

"I'm sorry to have hurt her. It was a rough situation."

"Ah, well. You two seem to have worked it out, well enough to build an army together."

He has no idea how wrong he is. "We manage."

"We are all going to bed hungry if you two don't shut your traps," Ayfa whispers.

"Sorry," I reply.

The group walks ahead of us, and I find myself alone with Lukin for the first time. The thought occurs to me that I could kill him, here and now, and no one would be the wiser. I could claim he threatened me or even Evryn. I could say he was spying for Branngard. I could come up with any of a dozen stories to justify it, and never again have to feel the bitter jealousy pooling in my gut now.

But that would break Evryn's heart, and she'd never forgive me, regardless of the excuses I could come up with. Then, nothing would stop her from having me murdered. Not now that we've got the armies here. I know it's a matter of time before she turns me away, and no one will come to my aid. Aside from what I did to her in Salix, I'm sure that killing the man who saved her life and protected her sister from slavery, helped her escape on pain of death, then came back from exile to help protect her homeland would ensure that *no one* would side with me, not even my dear mama.

A few paces later, Lukin nudges my shoulder, bringing me back to the present. Not far from us stands a large, elder buck. He grazes lazily through the woods, nibbling on the tasty spring grasses.

I stop, nocking an arrow and pulling the bowstring back. I take a breath, then release my arrow. Just as it chips the bark of a tree and skitters across the ground, Lukin's yellow-and-red-fletched arrow lands square in the buck's neck, dropping it dead.

"I noticed your trembling elbow," Lukin remarks when I turn to look at him.

At the sound of the buck falling, the rest of the band comes running. "Good shot, Lukin!" one of them remarks.

"Oh, this was all his doing," Lukin says, gesturing to me.

I look at Lukin, confused.

"Now you're shooting with Branngardian arrows?" Ayfa asks, mocking me. "Have you joined the enemy?"

"His needed sharpening, so I lent him some of mine," Lukin lies for me.

"Let's get this big guy cleaned up and drag him back to the fort," Ayfa replies, pulling out her knife. "I'm starving."

After we arrive back at the fort and wash up, I grab a couple of horns of ale and head toward the fire. Lukin is there already, turning the spit slowly.

"Good shot," I offer, handing him a horn of ale.

"We all needed to eat," Lukin says, taking a drink.

"Still. You could have taken credit."

"It wasn't important."

"You're a better man than me."

Lukin waves away the compliment before sitting down next to the fire as another of the warriors takes his place turning the spit. "I meant to congratulate you on the impending birth of your child," Lukin says, lifting his horn in the air. "I saw Evryn briefly earlier, though I don't think she saw me."

"Thank you," I reply, lifting my own horn. "Do you have children, back in Branngard?"

"No, I don't."

"At least, not that you know of, am I right?"

Lukin laughs. "You're not wrong."

"I thought you Branngardian types were chaste before marriage?"

"Not everyone," Lukin replies. "Especially those of us who've lived elsewhere."

I take another drink of ale, savoring the taste. "Here's to winning the war and getting you back to Branngard, where you belong, so you can make plenty of babies."

"To winning the war," Lukin replies, tapping his horn against mine.

The two of us sit together for a while, staring into the fire. Soon, Björn, Ayfa, Lyra and some other warriors join us at the fire, and within a few hours, the venison is ready to eat, and all are deep in their cups.

Having eaten his fill, Lukin stands, wobbling slightly. "I believe I will head to the stream. I need some water."

"And sleep!" I call after him as he walks away.

Just then, Evryn approaches the fire and sits down next to me, rescuing me.

40

Evryn

Nerys Baretta is *nothing* like I thought she would be. For one thing, she is more beautiful than even Pomisha had been, and she looks as if she hasn't aged a day beyond seventeen, though I know she must be easily as old as Rayyan.

"I can't believe she's been here all this time, right here, and none of us knew what she *really* looked like," I remark to Halline as she walks alongside me in the warm afternoon air. My belly is heavy, causing my hips and my lower back to ache, but walking helps.

"My thoughts exactly," Halline replies. "And I still don't understand exactly why she accepted us here so readily. Torek *must* have promised her something, but I can't seem to get it out of him."

He hasn't been the same since the day they arrived to bring us back with them. He has stopped sleeping in our bed, even when I've invited him closer for warmth. Whatever happened between the two of them, we are safe here behind Nerys's walls, and he's given me the space I need, so I don't ask questions.

"Listen, there is something you should know," Halline says, stopping my thoughts.

"Oh?"

"Yes. It's about Lukin."

"*Lukin?*" I ask, stopping. "Have you received word from him?"

"Evryn, he's here, in the fort. He came the moment he got word of Branngard's attack. He arrived yesterday."

I'm speechless. She can't be serious.

"Do you think we should trust him?" she asks.

"Yes," I reply, lost in thought as my mind wanders back in time to our last shared moments outside the cairn. "He is nothing if not good, to the core."

"I wanted to prepare you in case you saw him or heard he was here."

"Thanks," I reply, still not fully present in the moment.

"Ayfa is going to introduce him to Torek, to break the ice. Do you think that's a good idea? Will Torek lash out at him? I can't have skirmishes breaking out."

To Torek, Lukin is as good as dead, and to Lukin, Torek *is* dead. For them to encounter each other is less than ideal, but I can't imagine either of them becoming violent.

"I think it'll be fine. They're both men of honor, in their own way."

"And both love you," she replies softly.

I turn my face away, unable to handle the way my mind presses in on itself when I think of them, both here. The warmth and longing I feel for Lukin and the icy rage I feel for Torek crash into me, stopping my breath.

"So, they wouldn't do anything to hurt you, and both understand that to kill or otherwise maim each other wouldn't exactly make you happy."

"Indeed." In truth, I would pay good money to watch Lukin disembowel Torek, but I can't entertain such thoughts, not now.

We have made our way back to the tent when Halline turns to go. "I'll just go and check in with Ayfa, then I'll come back and rest here with you. Shall I send Torek in if he comes?"

"No. Tell him I need some sleep. I just... I need some time to myself, I think."

"Understood." She kisses me on the forehead and turns away, leaving me alone with my thoughts.

I step into my tent and collapse onto my cot—too exhausted, in every sense, to tolerate another moment awake.

When I awake, it's past nightfall and there's a gentle rain falling. My hair has begun to grow in now, but not enough to protect me from the rain, so I wrap my shawl around me and venture out into the camp.

As I approach the central fire, I see Lyra and Ayfa sitting together with Tasia and a few warriors.

"Fancy seeing you here," I remark taking a seat. "You come here often?"

"Oh, you know. On occasion," Ayfa replies, smiling and pulling me in for a hug.

"Strawberry mead for you," Lyra says, handing me a horn. "I watered it down. Because of the baby, I mean."

I thank her and take a sip, enjoying the sweetness as it explodes across my tongue.

"Your baby will come in the summer?" Lyra asks.

"That's what the healers say, yes," I smile, rubbing my aching belly. "Have you seen Torek?"

"They're over there," Tasia nods in the direction of another fire nearby.

"*They?*" I turn and see Torek sitting before the fire. Several others sit with him, their backs to me.

"Yep. Both of them."

"Ah," I say, tension rising in my stomach, realizing Lukin must be one of them.

"It'll be *fine*," Ayfa replies, laying a hand on my shoulder. "One of them is your husband, and the other one fathered your unborn child. What could go wrong?"

The group erupts in laughter.

"You want me to walk over there with you?" Tasia offers.

Be a big girl, Aunt Tabitha whispers.

"No, I can handle it," I say, and then turn to walk toward the man I love.

As it turns out, the man facing Torek isn't Lukin, but Ayfa's younger brother, Björn. When he sees me approach, he stands to greet me.

"Did you enjoy your rest?" Torek asks, inviting me to sit.

"I did," I reply, slowly taking a seat before warming my hands in front of the fire.

"Here, eat something," Torek says, handing me a small platter heaped with venison.

"Thank you," I reply, taking a bigger bite than I mean to. "Have you… Did you see Lukin?" I ask, not wanting to delay the inevitable any longer.

"I did. We went on the hunt together. Good man."

I breathe a sigh of relief. "Well, I'm glad that's over with. I wasn't sure how it would go."

"Yeah, we got along fine until I killed him," Torek replies casually, taking a sip of ale. I half believe him until his burst of laughter gives him away. "No, he turned in early for the night, I think."

They went into the woods. Together. With *weapons*. And both returned alive and intact. I don't know whether to be disappointed or relieved.

He's waiting for you near the stream, Papa whispers.

My heart is split. I never imagined I would see Lukin again, and I'm sure he didn't think he'd run into me in such circumstances—on the same side of a war against his people, me pregnant with a dead man's baby. But I have to take the chance if it could be my last.

"I'm just gonna go relieve myself," I say.

"You want me to come with you?" Torek asks, clearly drunk by now.

"No, it's fine. I'll stay close to the fort."

"Okay. But take your dagger. I'd feel better knowing you were armed."

"Already have it," I reply, lifting my skirt enough to show him the dagger strapped to the inside of my thigh, then turning to head into the woods.

41

Lukin

A light rain shower falls as I stand in the glade just outside the fort. My hands are freezing as I close my breeches and head toward the stream to clean up.

I'm thinking, once again, of Evryn. She's within shouting distance and yet she's further from me than she's ever been before, a gaping chasm named Torek standing between us.

What did I expect would happen when I helped her to escape Branngard? Evryn is young, beautiful, charming, and clever; she was bound to find a partner, sooner or later. I wished her happiness, and I meant it. I just never imagined I'd have to witness the fruits my sacrifice had produced—and with a man who I thought was dead, no less.

But Torek is from among her people, born on the land she loves so much. They have a history I can't pretend to understand, and now she's carrying his child. There really is *no* hope.

When I arrive at the stream, I scoop some water into my hands and rinse them, then cup more to splash on my face. A branch snaps in the woods behind me, so I rotate toward the sound, bowstring drawn taut.

She glares at me from the darkness of the woods, where she stands hooded, still as night, with her dagger drawn. The ferocity in her eyes takes my breath away.

"You're on Kenozarian land," she says darkly, stepping into the glade. I'm frozen in place by the sight of her. Her skin glows silver in the moonlight. She looks ethereal and ancient in the falling rain.

"I've come to help the cause," I reply, raising my arms in surrender.

"Which cause?" she asks as she steps closer.

"The Kenozarian one."

"The Lukin Velga I knew was captain of the Branngardian army. Are you not him?"

"I am. But I've defected to the enemy."

"And why would you do such a thing?"

I stop to think for a moment. "Because their women are more beautiful."

Evryn drops her arm and laughs aloud, her laughter rippling across the woods. "Good answer," she replies, smiling as she sheaths her blade and approaches the stream. She bends down awkwardly to drink some water before turning to face me again.

"It's good to see you," I remark, awkwardly. What else can be said?

"What happened to you after I left?" she asks. So, I tell her the truth, minus the part about being engaged to Selise again.

"I'm so sorry," she says. "How horrible!"

"Ah, it wasn't so bad," I remark, scratching the skin beneath my beard. "I've endured worse accommodations."

"Worse than rotting alone in a sweltering underground cell, imprisoned by your own uncle?"

I chuckle under my breath. "I wasn't *entirely* alone. I had some friends. Sure, they were four-legged rodents who tried to eat my toes and ears off, but one can't be picky."

"That's a rude way to describe your friends."

I laugh. "I am happy to see you so well." We find a downed tree and I spread my cloak out so we can sit on it.

"I've been better," she remarks, adjusting herself on the log and stroking her belly. "This animal gives me no rest." I notice that she is still wearing the golden wedding bangle I gave to her on our wedding night. My heart aches with pointless hope.

"I hear things don't much improve in that arena, once the baby arrives."

"Yeah, that's the rumor."

"What happened when you arrived back on the island? Aside from the obvious," I say, gesturing toward her belly.

"I headed toward Salix, like you told me to, and I ran into Torek on the way. We met with some trouble on the road and he saved me. And then…"

"You picked up where you'd left off?" I offer.

"Something like that," she says, looking past me into the dark woods.

"So I guess he wasn't dead after all," I laugh.

"I suppose not."

The cold and dampness are beginning to seep into my bones. I rub my hands together and blow into them. "I was sorry to hear of your mother's passing."

"Thank you." She looks weary, as if she's aged ten years in the span of one. "How is your mother? Don't think I have forgotten you or her or Branngard or the oath I made to you, which I have clearly broken."

"No, please—" I begin.

"I mean it. I know you don't hold me accountable. If this war weren't happening and I wasn't… as I am…"

"I understand. And I'm glad I proved you wrong, about being able to carry children, I mean."

Evryn looks up now into my eyes, provokingly. "I'd say Torek proved me wrong."

"Right," I reply, ashamed.

"Of course, you could have done it, if you'd taken the chance."

"What chance? Surely you don't mean—"

"You had months before Akkar forced us into that situation, entire *months* where you could have made a move, Lukin."

"I... I didn't know you wanted me to."

"Then you are blind," she says, staring into my soul. "I wanted it *very much.*"

I force myself to break our gaze and look out at the landscape. The rain is falling harder now. We'll have to head back to camp soon, or people will begin to worry. The last thing I need is someone accusing me of kidnapping Evryn Korina and her unborn babe.

"I loved you, as best I could, Evryn," I say, taking the last chance I may ever have. "I'm sorry for how this all unfolded. If things had been different—"

"And I loved you," she says, cutting me off and looking into my eyes again before placing her hand on my cheek.

I draw nearer to her, leaning my forehead against hers. Her skin on mine makes me forget all else. I want to pass the rest of my days here, to never leave these woods as long as I live, if only to keep her near me.

Damn it all to hell. I move close enough to feel her breath on my lips.

Just then, over her shoulder, I see Torek stepping through the trees, quietly. It's clear he doesn't want to disturb us. So, I do the unthinkable—I move away from Evryn.

"We have to get back," I say, my voice breaking. I stand and then offer her a hand before shaking out my cloak and wrapping it around my shoulders.

"Yes," she says quietly.

As we walk toward camp, Torek comes toward us and tosses his cloak over her. "I was worried about you. I went back to the tent and you weren't there, so I came looking for you," he says. "I was headed back just now to gather a search party."

"I'm fine," Evryn replies. "Lukin and I were just catching up, and we lost track of time." Something about the way they interact doesn't seem right, but I'm sure it's in my head. He's the father of her child, after all, the love of her life.

"Yes, it seems so," Torek replies, looking at me hard.

"My apologies," I say, taking my leave.

As I walk on, leaving them walking behind me, my face burns with shame. My hunger for her burns down to embers as I turn over in my mind, again and again, the moment we'd gotten lost in one another's eyes, knowing for certain it will be the moment I'll spend the rest of my life remembering—that spring night in the mountains of Kenozaria, Evryn still within arm's reach.

42

Torek

When we arrive back at the tent, we remove our soaked clothes and put on fresh ones. Evryn is careful to hide behind the inner walls of the tent, so I can see only the outline of her body.

"I was worried about you tonight," I say after she steps out from behind the inner wall.

"You don't think I can fend for myself?" she asks.

"Of course I do... normally. But these aren't normal times, and you," I say, gesturing to her belly, "aren't in your normal condition."

"I am not yours to worry about, Torek, nor is this baby."

I can say nothing more. By all the laws of Kenozaria, she is right. I should be dead now, *truly* dead this time. What I did was inexcusable.

Evryn lays down on her cot and soon I can tell from her breathing that she's sleeping. I know sleep won't come easily for me tonight, so I head back out into the night.

All the campfires in the fort have been extinguished—all but one. Lukin sits before it, huddled under his cloak, warming his hands on the embers.

"Couldn't sleep either?" I ask as I take a seat next to him.

Lukin turns and looks at me, seeming to instantly understand.

"I know you saw me, in the woods tonight," I continue. "I can't help but wonder what you'd have done if I hadn't interrupted."

Lukin sighs, stirring the embers with a stick. "I understand why you're angry. I had no right. I respect that Evryn is your partner now."

"Evryn has *always* been my partner."

"Respectfully, Torek, you were *dead*. You can hardly blame her for—"

"I don't blame Evryn," I say, interrupting him. "And, in truth, I don't blame you, not for what happened in Branngard. As I understand, you never even consummated the marriage. And you've acted with honor, time and time again."

"Then what is your issue with me?"

"I *have* no issue with you," I remark, slapping him hard on the shoulder. "I just want you to remember that *Evryn chose me*. After this war, I don't care where you go, Lukin, but it won't be Kenozaria," I say in a tone that leaves no room for argument.

Lukin shakes my arm from his shoulder, then stands up and tosses the hood of his cloak over his head, as more rain has begun to fall.

"I will not disrespect you, not here, not this night. We are on the *same side* of this war. We both want what's best for Kenozaria, for Evryn, for her family," he says, turning to go. "And *you* are her family."

With that, he walks away, leaving me alone with my thoughts.

IX

Summer

43

Lukin

For weeks, I have kept my head down and done my best to help out where I could. I keep myself busy with hunting, trapping, cleaning, cooking, and even caring for the animals—anything to keep myself out of sight of Evryn or Torek.

It seems to be working. For a moment, I thought everyone may have forgotten I was here at all, which was fine by me. I came to ensure Evryn was safe, and she seems as safe as she can be, all things considered. But then I was summoned to Chief Halline's tent.

"How shall we gather these men you claimed would come to our aid?" she asks.

"We need to send them a message. Can anyone get in or out to deliver one?"

"If I may," an older woman cuts in. "I could send Ayfa to deliver a message. She has sneaked in and out without their noticing before."

"Yes, this is a good idea, Rayyan," Halline remarks. "But who would she deliver the message to?" she asks me.

Draven is out of the question. He'd report the news to Akkar like the good dog he is. Tygan wouldn't hesitate to come to our aid, but he is never far from Draven's side. Suddenly, I remember the soldier from Roiland who had helped deliver the note to Pomisha.

"How much do you have in the way of gold or silver, or anything we could use as a bribe?" I ask.

"Who are we bribing?"

"A soldier, one I know to be without honor but happy to do what he's told when there's coin to be had."

Halline sits in thought for a moment. "It's a risk, but it's our best bet."

"You'll know it's him by the eye patch and the limp," I tell Afya as she prepares to leave that evening. "Just say my name and hand him the letter and the coins."

Ayfa sets out for Kenozaria at sundown, and we wait in the hills, cautiously hopeful.

When she returns to the fort in the morning, she looks worse for wear.

"Did you find him and give him the message?" Halline asks as Ayfa removes her armor and takes a seat by the fire.

"Better than that," Ayfa replies, smiling and wiping sweat from her brow. "We rounded up fifty men who agreed to join us here when the time is right."

"How?!" I ask.

"I snuck around the back of the village hall and watched for a while. Eventually, I saw the man with the eye patch, hobbling into the hall and sitting down to drink some ale. I waited until he was ready to leave and followed him back to his cabin. I approached quietly and held a knife to his throat, offered him the letter and the coin purse, and slowly backed away. He seemed frustrated when he read it, but he invited me inside."

"And you just... walked into a house with a man twice your age, who was a skilled fighter, no less?" Rayyan asks. "Ayfa, have I taught you *nothing?*"

"Hey, it turned out fine!"

"Go on," I say. "What happened once you went into the house with him?"

"There were four other soldiers gathered around the hearth."

"Zaria, be good," Rayyan prays.

"He told them what the letter said, I guess. I couldn't understand a word he said, but a few minutes later, the four soldiers left us alone for a while, then an hour or so later, he took me out to an open spot where around forty other soldiers were waiting."

The tension is thick enough to cut with a knife, and Rayyan looks as if she may faint.

"They brought out a priest who spoke a bit of Kenozarian and translated for me. One of the soldiers—I think he said his name was Tiger or something?—asked for proof the message had come from you, and since I had none, I described your appearance, which seemed to appease them."

"Yes, Tygan is a good friend of mine. What happened then?"

"They agreed to join our side!"

Rayyan breathes a sigh of relief.

"And there's more," Ayfa says, looking at Halline. "I know where they're keeping Ziva."

Halline's eyes open wife. "Where? Who is holding her captive?"

"His name is Draven, the men said. He is the second-in-command, now."

"*Draven?*" I ask. "No, no. Draven is a good man, maybe too loyal to Akkar, but he'd never enslave a child. No, you must have heard wrong."

"They gave me more details of what he's done to her, but...just...We must get her out of there as soon as possible."

Halline covers her face with her hands.

"Any word of Ari?" Lyra asks from her perch behind the group.

"They have him under heavy guard, at the garrison."

"My people have brought so much hurt here," I say. "Please, let me lead the party in freeing them."

"Listen, you don't have to beg us for the chance to risk your life saving my siblings," Halline replies. "But you won't be able to do it alone."

"Already ahead of you," Ayfa remarks. "Several of the soldiers are prepared to help us…"

"If?"

"If we will grant them immunity and shelter them from Branngard."

"Done," Halline replies.

"Tomorrow night they will free both Ari and Ziva, and wait for us in the same open field at midnight."

"It could be a trap," I remark. "I hate to say it, but I wouldn't put it past Akkar."

Halline weighs her options. "You're right. But we have to try."

44

Evryn

I awake to intense cramping and pressure, causing me to cry out. Torek wakes up and turns toward me.

"Is everything okay? You don't look well."

"I don't know," I reply, grimacing in pain.

Ask him to find some red raspberry leaves, Aunt Tabitha whispers.

"I need you to find some red raspberry leaves. They will stop the cramps."

"Yes! Okay. Yes," Torek says in a panicked voice, throwing his clothes and boots on and running out of the tent into the night.

Before long, he returns with a handful. I make some tea from the leaves and drink it slowly as the moon rises higher in the sky. It does offer some relief, but not much.

Long after Torek has fallen asleep again, my mind is alight with worry, for good reason. We're in the middle of a war and I'm mere weeks from being a mother, something I don't feel prepared for in the least. I decide to walk around outside in hopes it will tire me out.

As I wander around the area outside our tent, I reminisce about Mother's birth experience with Ziva. I had only been two years old when Halline was born, so I can't remember much about it, and when

Ari was born, I was in Salix, visiting my aunt. But the night of Ziva's birth is clear as day in my mind.

* * *

Mother wailed in pain for a full day and night, and I thought it would never end. As the midwives came and went in shifts, their faces set with worry, I was kept occupied with Aunt Tabitha, turning mountains of leaves into powders and teas and tinctures to help relieve Mother's pain and aid the delivery. Once Ziva was finally born, the midwives left our home, covered in blood. I was terrified.

"Don't worry, darling," Aunt Tabitha said, patting my hand. "These herbs will have her right as rain in no time."

People came and went that day, checking on Mother and Ziva. After everyone left the house, my curiosity got the best of me. I snuck to the doorway of Mother and Papa's room, hiding just out of sight in the darkness. I saw the two of them sitting in bed together, looking down at my new baby sister.

"How are the children?" Mother asked Papa.

"Oh, they're fine, my dear," he said, smiling and kissing her hand. "Ari slept through it. Halline is with him now."

"And Evryn?"

Papa took Ziva from Mother's arms, kissing her little head. "She will be fine."

"Ronar," Mother said, calling Papa by his first name, something she never did. "Tell me."

"She was frightened. Tabitha stayed with her, though, and kept her busy. I'm sure she will recover."

"Oh, Rue. I do wonder if she will ever mature."

"Nonsense," Papa smiled, handing Ziva back to Mother. "She's still young. She has plenty of time."

"Yes, but look at Halline! Younger than Evryn but with such a nurturing spirit and a strong countenance. Evryn shouldn't be so easily scared at her age."

"The children will be fine, Korina," Papa replied, stroking Mother's cheek. "Don't worry about them, my love. Rest now."

Mother's preference for Halline would only grow as she did. She was always so proper, always knew just what to say. And even *I* had to admit she was much more nurturing than I was. But a year after Ziva was born, when Papa died and Mother gave up on living, it wasn't Halline they turned to. It was me, and I did the best I could, young as I was.

* * *

Thinking of those days, and of Mother, causes tears to burn in my eyes. I feel a void of darkness opening within me, threatening to swallow me whole. Every good memory I've shared with her, few and far between as they were, flashes before my eyes without warning when I am going about my day, sometimes buckling me over in sorrow.

I think back to the conversation we had in our cottage mere weeks before Dam Praya. She was so excited to welcome my baby into the world. What would she have been like as a grandmother? She said she wanted to be a good one, but maybe she would have lacked the patience necessary.

These thoughts make the cool night air around me seem much colder, and I wrap my shawl around me more tightly. As a cold gust of air rushes past me, I stop, frozen in place, as if in a trance.

I see Ari, standing in a cell, his clothes filthy and his hair matted. A few houses away from him, in the house Torek grew up in, Ziva is huddled in a corner. She is crying as a man stands over her with his fist raised.

"No!" I cry out into the night. I try to focus my attention on the light within me, to calm myself. I imagine a heavy fog, rolling down off the mountain and enveloping the village—just like the fog that enveloped the cairn the night Navya leaped to her death. But this time, I imagine Ari and Ziva escaping and finding one another, and returning safely to us.

When I open my eyes again, all is just as it had been.

"Where've you been?" Torek asks without opening his eyes when I lie down on my cot.

"Just couldn't sleep," I say.

"The pain?"

"No, it's much better now."

"Then what's bothering you? Are you afraid? I promise I won't let anything happen to you or the baby."

"That's kind of you. We'll be fine. This baby isn't coming for another month, easy."

"Good, good," he says, sighing. "Evryn, if we could just—" he begins, but I cut him off.

"No. The answer is no."

45

Lukin

When we arrive at the meeting spot, I'm surprised to see several of my fellow Branngardian comrades. I half expected them not to show.

"Tygan!" I cry out when I see him, throwing my arms around my old friend.

"We couldn't believe you'd returned. But then, you often do unexpected things," he says with a wink.

I laugh. "I'm glad you're here. You've taken a great risk in helping us like this. I won't forget it."

"It's nothing. An adventure to liven up the night!"

"What happened? How did you free them?"

"It's the weirdest thing. Just before we were set to head out, most everyone in the village just... fell asleep."

"Fell asleep?"

"Guards, Shield, soldiers, even Akkar himself, I heard! Everyone but us four," Tygan continues. "We just... walked into Draven's house and found Ziva awake and tied up, so we released her."

"And Ari?"

"Awake, but the guards at the garrison were snoring! Can you

297

believe it?"

The ease with which the rescue took place serves to unnerve me further. While Akkar is not averse to letting an ant slip from his grasp in his efforts to trap a dog, I find it unlikely that such a daring rescue could truly have gone unnoticed.

I turn my attention to Ari and Ziva, who are huddled together. "Are you well?" I ask Ziva, who wears a Branngardian cloak with the hood pulled down, covering her face. In the moonlight, I can just make out her bruised eye and the dried blood standing on a cut on her lip.

"My sister will be fine," Ari responds, moving to stand between the two of us.

"I am sorry for what you've suffered," I say.

Ari stands up straighter. "Thank you for your help in rescuing us. I am sure Chief Halline will reward you and your men handsomely."

"Please. There is no need. We are relieved you're safe."

"Thank you," Ziva says meekly. "For what you've done for us all, for me and Evryn and now Ari, too."

I smile, unsure how to respond.

"We should get going," Ayfa says. "The men may be missed soon."

"Where are the others?" I ask her. "You said there were fifty soldiers ready to defect. I only see four."

"They're waiting for the war," Tygan says. "When they get the chance, they'll kill their commanders and come to our side."

"Okay, yes," I agree. "That's a good idea."

With that, the party begins walking up the mountain.

As the group enters the gates of Nerys's stronghold, Ari breaks into a run and takes Lyra into his arms, burying his face in her neck. Ziva walks slowly toward Halline before falling at her feet. I can hear her crying quietly. Evryn is absent, which I find odd. But then, she's not my concern any longer, I have to remind myself.

After the reunions, I sit by a fire and listen as my men recount all that has happened in the months I was away.

"Akkar's speeches became more intense," Tygan says. "All about bringing glory to Rhys and spreading His Light farther inland."

"I don't know why I ever expected less," I reply. "I was a fool."

"None of us thought he'd invade the village as he did," one of the others says.

"Tell me about that night. *Dam Praya*, they call it."

Tygan glances at the other soldiers and takes a deep breath.

"Please."

He takes a long swig of the ale in his mug and begins the story. "Akkar gathered us together at sunset. He said the chief of the village had threatened to destroy our camp and kill us all if we didn't leave her island. So he said we had to march on them, to save ourselves."

"That doesn't sound like something Korina would do," I remark. "Evryn said her mother was peace-loving. She would do anything to avoid bloodshed. There must have been some sort of miscommunication."

Tygan shrugs. "I wasn't in the vanguard, but I heard she tried to kill Akkar and then poisoned herself."

"*Poisoned* herself?"

"I was there," one of the others speaks up. "She drank something from a vial and died, almost instantly, in a pool of blood and bile. It was an awful thing to witness, I tell ya," he says. "The stuff of nightmares."

"I can't imagine," I reply. "But why did Akkar stop? Why didn't the army continue into the mountains and kill everyone?"

"More worshipers for Rhys," Tygan replies, rolling his eyes. "Akkar said they'd eventually see the error of their ways once they'd suffered enough starvation and disease, trapped in the mountains behind our blockade in the south and west, the sea to the north, and the heavy snows in the east."

"I guess he didn't know about the stronghold," I reply.

"He put us to work rebuilding the village, and we've been there, ever since," one of the other soldiers says. "He renamed it 'Rhysland.'"

Just then, I feel a tap on my shoulder and turn to see Halline. "If you are quite done entertaining the captain with the story of my people's demise," she says to Tygan and the others, "I'd like a word with him, in private."

"Of course," I say, blushing and standing up to join her.

As we walk, she looks out at the landscape and sighs. "My people have endured so much over the years. Famine, drought, disease. We've even dealt with an invasion or two. But this?" she says, dropping her eyes to the ground. "This is new territory."

"Akkar makes sport of conquering such places," I reply. "I'm sorry your beautiful home lay in his path."

"Indeed," she remarks. "Nonetheless, what you and Ayfa have done, what your men have done for my siblings... It can never be repaid."

"There is nothing to repay. It is the least we can do. Are they well?" I ask, nodding my head in the direction of Halline's tent.

"I believe they will heal, in time," she replies.

"Let's hope so."

"Thank you again, Lukin," she says. "My sister was blessed to know you."

"The honor was mine, Chief," I reply solemnly. "I only hope she has found happiness."

Halline smiles. "Yes. Trust me. We'll make sure Torek deserves her."

Later, as I lie in my tent, I am full of mixed emotions. On the one hand, the day was a success. At least we saved them—if nothing else, we saved them. And I'm glad Evryn is safe and, by all accounts, well.

But I don't know what's next. I can't stay here forever, watching her live out her life with him, but there is nothing for me back in Branngard but another prison cell—if I am so lucky. And I can't leave yet, not until I know she is safe.

Akkar may have taken a pause, but I know him too well to imagine he will stop now that he's captured their tiny village. He wants *souls*, not empty walls. Once he discovers Ari and Ziva missing, he will know something is amiss, and there's no way to predict how he will react.

Eventually, I drift off to sleep, listening to the sounds of the camp.

46

Evryn

"So… what's the plan?" Halline asks. Nerys's hall is full of people, all members of Halline's war council, as well as the Sanctum and, of course, Nerys herself.

I adjust myself in my chair. My hips are aching and the muscles around my belly are painfully tight.

"We want to maintain the high ground, so we need to lure them up into the mountains," Torek begins.

"But how?" Tasia asks.

"Bait," Torek remarks, looking over at Lukin. "Tonight, the Branngardian defectors will run down to the village first. They'll claim they were kidnapped the same night Ari and Ziva escaped. They'll report that we've taken Lukin hostage. Akkar won't be able to resist sending his forces after him."

"If I may," Ari puts in, "Somehow, I doubt Akkar will be willing to send so many of his soldiers here to save Lukin. He imprisoned him for months, after all, according to Lukin's story."

Lukin coughs. "With respect, you underestimate my value to him. Yes, he imprisoned me, but he ensured I didn't die."

"And?" Ayfa asks.

"And, I am the last of the bloodline of the Velga family. The next Torch *must* be born of my blood. Akkar depends on me to sire a legitimate son, something I haven't done since I... don't have a wife any longer."

I feel several sets of eyes on me, and my face reddens.

"Let's say this works and a good portion of the Branngardian army comes up the mountain. What then?" asks Rayyan.

"While the Branngardian defectors go to spin their tale for Akkar, we'll send a small party of warriors down the mountain in secret, to lie in wait," Torek replies.

"We only need around fifteen men," Lukin says.

"Why? What will they do?" Minara asks.

Lukin doesn't reply.

He's planning to kill his uncle, Papa whispers.

"You're going to kill Akkar," I say. "You need those men to help you kill his Shield." Murmurs erupt around the room.

"He's threatening the well-being of a people and place I have come to love," he says. "And he won't stop with your village. Akkar won't be happy until every living person is worshiping Rhys and living as Branngardians do."

"Someone has to stop him," Ziva pipes up. "I don't want anyone else to suffer as we have... as I have."

"We will avenge you, Ziva," Ari says, reaching out a hand to comfort her.

"You're saying the entire Branngardian army will just drop their weapons the minute they hear of his death?" Nerys asks Lukin.

"These men have nothing in common with one another beyond their devotion to the Torch—and to one another. They depend on his guidance. Without him, they have no reason to be here," Lukin says. "Once they see that we're winning, many will surrender and join our ranks. The remaining soldiers will not be eager to spill one another's blood for a lost cause."

"What will we do with them when it's all over? With the soldiers who come to our side?" Halline asks.

"That is a decision I leave to you," Lukin remarks, bowing his head slightly at Halline and the other Sanctum members.

Halline sits in thought for a moment. "It's a good plan, albeit a risky one."

"With respect, our key advantage is our position behind the fort, and our knowledge of the lay of the land," Ayfa says. "With this plan, we would be throwing ourselves in harm's way and leaving those in the fort with less protection. Isn't that *too* risky?"

"Believe me, this fort will not fall," Nerys pipes up from her seat next to Halline. "We have held this stronghold for nigh on thirty years, long before your puny little band of warriors arrived."

"The army will wait atop Mount Zaria to protect the mountain and stop Branngard's forces, while the smaller group goes down to kill Akar and retake the village."

"But you'll be *sacrificing* them if Branngard doesn't take the bait," I say.

"We are sacrificing ourselves," Lukin says. "The smaller group will be made up of me, Ayfa, Tygan, and a dozen or so other warriors."

"By dawn, we will either be reunited with our ancestors or else free of these scum," Ari says. "Either way, we will have victory!"

"Everyone, head back to your tent and prepare for the night," Halline says, breaking up the meeting.

After the men have left the tent, the women sit together, discussing what is to come next.

"I'm so worried about Torek," Lyra says, her head resting on Minara's shoulder. "He just came back from the dead. I don't know if I can survive losing him again. Or Ari!"

"We won't lose them, not this night," Rayyan replies, patting Lyra's thigh.

The tightening sensation in my belly suddenly gets much worse. I slouch over and moan in pain, gripping the side of the table for support.

"Are you okay, Evryn?" Halline asks, rising from her chair to assist me.

It's happening, Aunt Tabitha whispers.

No. Not now, not like this.

47

Lukin

"Thank you for this," I say, hugging the two Branngardian soldiers as they begin preparing to head down the mountain to report to Akkar.

"It's what we owe one another," one of them says.

I place my forehead on his, recalling the many battles we've fought beside each other.

"Let's go over what you'll say when you approach the village guard."

"We will look haggard, for one thing," the soldier replies.

"Oh, you've got that part of it down, I'd say." I laugh. "And then?"

"We'll hold up our hands, showing them we have no weapons, and say we'd been kidnapped by the Kenozarians when they came to rescue Ari and Ziva."

"*Steal*," I correct him. "Words matter to Akkar, you know this. He wouldn't see their rescue as *rescue*, but as theft."

"We'll say you came to find your wife and were also kidnapped by their army."

Yes, this could work. "Well, I'd say, 'Rhys be with you,' but I doubt Rhys smiles on this endeavor."

"The sea is on our side, always," one of the other soldiers replies.

"She won't let us die here, not like this, not when she waits to claim us for herself."

"I'll see you in the morning, one way or another," I say, embracing them once more.

They turn to head down the mountain, leaving me alone. I look west at the land, radiant in her glory, as the sun begins to set, dappling the sea beyond with golden light. The sight takes my breath away, and I pray to all the gods, to anyone who is listening, that it won't be my last sunset.

An hour later, Ayfa and Tygan and our small band of warriors are ready to head down the mountain.

"Douse your torches," I say.

Tygan stands next to me, looking confused. "You want us to walk down this mountain in complete darkness?"

"Lukin is right. We don't want them to see us coming," Ayfa puts in. "Don't worry. We know these trails well. We could walk them blindfolded. Just follow us."

"Lead the way," I say, stepping off the narrow path so Ayfa and the others can walk ahead of us.

As we make our way down the mountain, I remember another night on another mountain in another land.

* * *

"You'll be the father of the next Torch of Branngard, son," my father remarked as we hiked up Mount Firens, near the capitol at Rhy Domus. "It's important for you to understand your place."

"Yes, Father," I replied. I was twelve years old at the time and I still thought my father was the epitome of manhood. All I wanted in the world was for him to look kindly on me, to be proud of me.

"If you survive the next three nights out here, you'll return to us a *man*," my father continued, handing me my trusty bow—an aged little thing I'd been using since I first learned to shoot. "And *if* you survive, I'll replace that old bow with a new one, and a sword," my father continued as we reached the summit. Gentle snow had begun to fall, and my father wrapped his cloak tightly around him.

"I'm afraid, Father," I recall saying as he prepared to head back down the mountain.

My father looked at me sternly. "Fear is for women and pissants," he replied. "You *are* the heir to Yarrow's Cairn, are you not?"

"Yes, F-f-father," I replied, shivering.

My father clapped me on the shoulder and bent down, looking into my eyes, with the slightest hint of compassion. "Good man," he said, handing me my satchel. "There's a day's worth of food there, and plenty of water. You'll have to hunt for food to last you the other two days, or go hungry."

"Yes, Father."

My father looked at me hard for a moment and seemed as if he had more to say, but stopped himself and turned to head back down the mountain. "See you in three days," he said.

I survived those three days and nights, and I made my father proud, or at least I like to imagine I did. Though he never said so, the look on his face when I stumbled into the courtyard at Yarrow's Cairn three days later, freezing and weak but otherwise intact, warmed me.

As I venture down Mount Zaria on the way to kill my uncle, the man I've been raised to protect and honor, I try not to reflect on what my father would think of me now.

* * *

As we enter the land just south of the village, our group creeps along the dark prairie, grateful for the tall summer grasses. In the distance, we can hear shouts and the sounds of an army preparing to march.

"Looks like the plan worked," I remark to Ayfa. "Let's head toward Akkar's cottage."

"This way," Tygan says, leading the group.

When we arrive, we sit on our haunches, hidden by the darkness and the tall prairie grasses, waiting for the right moment. It doesn't take but another half hour before the bulk of the Branngardian army starts moving slowly up the mountain, torches ablaze.

I almost can't believe how well it's all gone. I get that old familiar feeling of worry, knowing Akkar is a cleverer man than most, and I begin for a moment to doubt our plan. My thoughts are interrupted by Tygan tapping me on the shoulder.

"It's time, Captain."

"Yes," I reply. "Each of you will pair up and take on one of the Shield. Tygan, you stay with me."

Ayfa and the others nod, readying their weapons.

The group slowly advances toward the cottage, as quietly as possible. But as we creep closer, someone trips on a clod of grass, falling with a clamor.

"*Dammit*," Ayfa whispers, noticing one of the Shield outside the cottage turning to see what caused the sound. We drop low, but it's too late. He's seen us, and he's alerting the others. It's now or never.

"Now!" I cry.

In a flash, we're on the Shield. Two warriors fall almost instantly, a dagger in one's eye and a gash in the other's neck. I stay as close as I can to Tygan, protecting his flank. I strike down a stocky Shield I've known since I was a new soldier, his tongue lolling in his mouth as blood spurts from his throat.

The whole thing is over in a matter of minutes, but the sound surely alerted Akkar to our presence. Standing to clean my blade, I assess the damage.

Six of our warriors are lost and two more are badly injured, but all the Shield are dead. Ayfa takes the wounded soldiers and heads back up the mountain, taking the southern route to avoid the melee.

Tygan and I slowly enter the dark cottage, weapons drawn. Candles burn around the room, and a cup of tea sits steaming on a desk in his office, but Akkar is nowhere to be found.

"Where could he be?" Tygan whispers. "He can't have gone with the army, can he? Why would his Shield be here if he isn't?"

I think of all the possibilities, but none of them makes sense. Akkar doesn't go *anywhere* without at least a few Shield, and unless he has added to their number, each one of them is dead now.

"I don't know," I reply, unsure what to do next, but then we hear footsteps approaching, just outside. The two of us run to opposite ends of the cottage and hide in the shadows—me behind Akkar's tall armoire and Tygan beneath his bed.

"It can't be! What happened?!" Akkar cries out as he approaches the cottage, accompanied by more Shield. "You two, move the bodies. You, search the cottage and then scout around the area to see if you can spot any tracks. You, stay with me. Kenozaria must have sent some men ahead to kill me, but they've failed. Rhys, be praised!"

"Rhys, be blessed," the remaining Shield replies.

"We must find my nephew," Akkar says.

"I'm sure Draven will take care of him," the Shield replies. "He'll pay for what he's done."

"No, you *buffoon!*" Akkar cries in frustration. "I need him *alive!*"

The Shield lowers his head in shame.

"He can't truly have joined their ranks, I know it," Akkar muses. "Lukin has disappointed me, it's true. But he would never turn his back on his countrymen."

"He is a loyal and brave captain, to be sure," the Shield replies.

"Let us hope he is recovered safely," Akkar says as he and the Shield step into the cottage.

Tygan is wiggling out from under the bed, just out of their line of vision. I want to cry out, to tell him to stop, but as he finally moves out from under the bed, his foot slams hard against the leg of the frame, causing Akkar and his Shield to look around in the darkness.

"Who's there?!" Akkar cries out, grabbing his staff. "Lukin? Is that you?"

I make a snap decision and step out of my hiding place, giving Tygan enough time to jump to his feet and meet the Shield who heads his way.

"Hello again, Uncle," I say, pulling my bowstring taut.

48

Evryn

"Let's get you more comfortable," Aunt Meryn suggests, leading me to my cot. "You just need some rest, maybe some water."

"This isn't like before," I reply, feeling my baby rotate painfully lower. "It hurts, much worse!"

Aunt Meryn helps me take a few sips of water.

"Let's see if some rest helps," Halline insists. "Rayyan, can you call a healer to come and check on her?"

"I'll go with her," Aunt Meryn says, and the two head out, leaving us alone.

"I'm so scared," I cry to Halline, as another wave of pain washes over me. "This can't be happening, not now. It's too early. The war—" I begin, but Halline cuts me off.

"Mama always said the one thing you can trust your children to do is surprise you," she says, rubbing my lower back. "Maybe your little one wants to get a head start."

"I guess I shouldn't be surprised," I say, "considering her parents."

"Hey, you said it. Not me," Halline chuckles under her breath.

Rayyan and Aunt Meryn return with the healer, who sits down at the foot of the cot as Rayyan brings a basin of water so she can wash her hands. Having washed and dried them, the healer raises my skirts and parts my lower lips.

"It seems you've busted your waters, my dear," she remarks, her eyes focused on the top of the tent as she feels around.

"What?!" I ask. "But I have another month! And I didn't feel any sort of gush!"

"Babies come when they're ready, my dear. And you could have been leaking for days," she replies, readjusting my skirts and washing her hands again. "We can only beg Zaria and Keno to strengthen you and your child."

"But—"

"You focus your energy here," Halline says, pointing at my belly. "Someone send word to Torek. He needs to know."

49

Torek

I walk as quickly as I can up the steep path to join my men. As if worrying about Evryn's safety wasn't enough to cloud my mind right when I need to think clearly, now I have the welfare of my soon-to-be-born child to worry about.

"Everything okay?" Ari asks when I approach.

"Not exactly," I reply, stopping to take a long drink of water from my bag. "Evryn's in labor."

Ari's eyes widen. *"Now?"*

"I said the same thing," I reply. "Though, I suppose it's not as if one can plan these things."

"Good point," Ari says. "And anyway, *of course* your child would be problematic right from the start."

I punch him in the arm, laughing. He has no idea that this child will likely never even know my name if Evryn's threats are to be believed.

We come up on the far western edge of the mountain, where the bulk of our forces is stationed, ready for Branngard to come our way.

"All going as planned?" I ask.

"Seems so," Tasia replies. "The Branngardian defectors left two hours ago to report to Akkar, and Lukin and Ayfa's party headed down soon after."

"Good," I reply, looking out at the night sky. From this far up the mountain, all looks normal in the village below. "Where are they?" I ask. "I don't see any torches."

Ari spits out the piece of long grass he'd been chewing on. "They doused them before they left the mountain. Safer that way."

"So now we wait?" I say, blowing into my hands and rubbing them together.

"Now we wait," Ari replies.

"Do you think it's enough?" Tasia asks, gesturing to the band of warriors behind us.

I can't tell her what I am *really* thinking as I look down at the village. Branngard has half our number, sure, but they are trained, experienced soldiers with advanced weapons and strong bronze armor.

"With Keno and Zaria and the help of our ancestors, I'm confident we'll win," I say instead. And it isn't a lie, not exactly.

"So, if we get out of this, there will be a wedding soon, hmm?" I ask Ari.

"Yes, that's the plan."

I smile, saying nothing.

"Why do you ask? Do you object? Because if we're going to start the whole 'You had better be good to my sister!' game, well..."

I pull Ari into a headlock. "You're right." I laugh, ruffling his hair when he breaks free.

Ari fixes his hair and scowls at me. "You'd better live long enough to attend," he says. "You and Evryn and my new little niece or nephew."

"Bet on it."

"And when are *you* going to marry *my* sister?" Ari asks, pointedly.

"I think it's pretty clear that we're partners," I reply, wishing he would drop the subject.

"Impregnating a woman hardly makes her your partner," Tasia pipes up.

Just then, hundreds of torches light up in a burst of flame down near the village.

"Looks like we've got action," I remark.

In a matter of moments, there are three columns of torches moving in the direction of the mountain. As we look on, a ruckus breaks out near the middle of the Branngardian line. A group of torches is plowing up the mountain, faster than the rest of the army. They look like a swarm of fireflies, devouring their comrades, whose torches drop and are extinguished soon after. It almost looks like...

"*Mutiny!*" Tasia completes my thought. "The other Branngardian soldiers, the ones promised to Lukin. They're keeping their word!"

"They'll be here soon!" I shout, turning to the warriors gathered on the mountain. "These are not like any warriors you've ever encountered, so you must be smart, and *always* keep the high ground!"

"For Lyra!" Ari calls out.

"For Korina!" another cries aloud.

"For Kenozaria!" one shouts, throwing her blade in the air.

"Archers, to the front!" Tasia calls out.

A hundred warriors step forward and form a line on the edge of the cliff, bows at the ready. As we stand waiting and listening to the sounds of the Branngardian defectors thrashing their way through their own men, time seems to stand still. The air is full of smoke and the metallic scent of blood.

By the time they arrive at the top of the mountain, the Branngardian defectors number only twenty.

"Welcome," I say, thanking them.

The soldiers smile, wiping the blood from their faces and blades and moving back into the ranks of our warriors, who greet them with shouts of victory. The drums start up, mimicking the throbbing hearts in our chests, beating faster and faster as the Branngardian army approaches the cliffs.

Moments later, they arrive in full force.

50

Evryn

I am dying. I'm certain of it.

The pain tearing through me is unlike anything I've ever known, and nothing the healer offers me dulls it, even a little.

"You must slow your breathing, Evryn," Aunt Meryn says, massaging the lower part of my back as Halline dabs the sweat from my brow with a wet cloth.

"I can't do this!" I cry out as wave after wave of pain travels from my abdomen through my thighs and hips, all the way down to my feet.

"It won't be long now," the healer comforts me. "You're nearly there."

I pace inside the tent, squatting to relieve some of the pressure on my lower back. When another wave of pain squeezes my abdomen so hard it feels like a rock, I lean against Rayyan for support.

"We're so proud of you," she says, massaging the tense muscles in my shoulders as I lie against her, panting. "Your mother would be proud, too."

"Is there... any... news?" I ask breathlessly between waves of pain.

"No news, Evy," Halline replies.

I am in too much pain to press her for more information, so I focus my energy down and in.

That's my girl, Aunt Tabitha whispers. *Find your center.*

I slow my breathing and try my best to ignore the sounds around me. I imagine what my baby will look like. Will she have my auburn hair or Torek's midnight locks? Will she have his gray eyes or my darker ones? How will I be able to look at her every day if she looks like him?

When another wave of pain hits, I feel less moved by it, less terrified. I breathe through it and soon, it passes.

You're doing a wonderful job, sweetheart, Papa whispers.

"Water, please," I call out, and one of the healer's assistants offers a flagon. I thank Keno for the gift as the cool water washes down my throat and splashes onto my chest.

As another wave of pain washes over me, I squat lower and grabbed onto the tent's center pole for support. The pressure is unbearable. It feels as if I will be split in two. I begin to grunt as my body takes over, pushing hard.

"Good work," the healer says, squatting next to me and letting me lean against her. "Just a few more and your baby will be here."

I close my eyes and imagine myself opening, wider and wider, welcoming her into our world. I imagine watching her play with her cousins in the fields outside the village, splashing in the river, or ice fishing in the winter.

As I continue focusing inward, I feel my body beginning to warm, as if lava is pumping through my veins rather than blood. When I open my eyes, my body is glowing, just as it did during my Bright Ceremony.

"Evryn?" Halline says, alarm in her voice. "What's happening?"

"I've never seen anything like it!" Rayyan remarks in awe.

You're going to be such a wonderful mother, Mother whispers, and it buckles me over with a longing I never knew I felt for her. I wish she was here with me, to meet her first grandchild. The sorrow of missing her and the joy of knowing what awaits me mix and drive me to tears.

You're so close, Papa whispers, and it is almost as if I feel his hand cupping my cheek.

I bear down again, grunting with the force of it, feeling my baby twist and turn into place within me. As I wait for another wave of pain and strength to come, I close my eyes again, remembering what Aunt Tabitha told me about the moment of delivery.

"When a new life enters this world," she'd said, "the ancestors come nearer to the mother than they are at any other point in her life. They almost *inhabit* her."

I can feel them, moving through me—all the women in my line pushing with me, lending me their strength, encouraging me. Energy pulses through me as I open my eyes again. The light in my veins is glowing even brighter, filling the tent with white light.

With the next wave of pain, I zero in and speak to my baby.

"You are so beloved, my sweet one," I say aloud. "You are welcome here. We want you here. So many people here love you already and are ready to protect you and guide you."

51

Torek

I feel as if I have been fighting this battle all my life. It never seems to end, the trail of Branngardian soldiers climbing onto the cliff's edge. Even as the archers pick them off, more pour ahead. It's nearly dawn. I'm exhausted and desperately thirsty.

As I slice through another soldier's neck, splattering the man's hot blood across my face, I move on, deeper and deeper into the fray.

From the corner of my eye, I see Ari, engaged with a soldier twice his size. The man is screaming in Branngardian, slashing with his mighty curved blade, hard on Ari—who is thankfully fast as lightning, dancing circles around the man, dodging his blows and using his weight against him.

I run toward Ari to help him, and that's when I notice the man's profile. It's Draven. Rage and vengeance burn in the pit of my stomach, radiating out through my sinews. Draven knocks Ari to the ground just as I approach, so I lunge at him, knocking him off-balance.

"Come get me, you worthless piece of shit!" I scream at him.

Draven corrects his steps, swaying and wiping the blood and sweat from his brow. Then he charges at me, slamming the full weight of his body into my stomach and knocking the wind out of me. He screams something at me, spittle and blood landing on my face. I try to steady myself, but he knocks me to the ground with a hard backhanded slap across my cheek.

He's got me pinned, with his hands around my neck. I desperately grasp for my blade, but it's just out of my reach. I am starting to feel faint, so I muster all my strength to whip my hips hard to the left, turning as hard as I can and slamming my thigh into Draven's groin. He growls in pain as he falls off of me, so I jump up and grab my blade, ready to plunge it into his belly.

"For Evryn!" I scream, raising my blade.

I feel something slam into my back; it's as if someone has plunged white-hot iron into my flesh. I howl in pain and stumble forward, looking down at my belly in shock as blood pours from the blade's exit wound. I fall to my knees, cupping my abdomen.

"Torek!" I hear Ari screaming as more men come to my defense.

As my vision goes dark, I see Evryn in my mind's eye, holding our new daughter. "Forgive me," I whisper, raising my hand to stroke her dark hair. I can feel the first rays of sunlight falling across my face as I close my eyes for the final time.

52

Evryn

As another wave bears down on me, I take in a deep breath and push as hard as my body will allow. Searing pain tears me open as my baby's head emerges.

"Just one more push! You're almost there," Aunt Meryn says.

When another wave of pain washes over me, I am too weak to push. So, I squat there, leaning against Halline and relaxing my body as much as I can, letting it do the work.

And with that, Ksenia enters the world with a head full of hair, dark as the night, and my chestnut eyes.

Forgive me, Torek whispers. And I know what it means.

Hours after I have given birth to Ksenia, we still have no news of the war party.

Evryn, the Light, Aunt Tabitha whispers, *you must focus on the Light. Make it grow!*

She is echoing Ksenia's words from the dream, and now I understand what she means. I know what must be done.

"Halline, gather the women. We must go to the top of the mountain," I say, handing Ksenia to the healer.

"You want to *hike* to the top of the mountain, in the middle of a war, mere *hours* after you've given birth?"

"Halline, there is no other way. We cannot beat them on our own. We need help."

"But it's not even a full moon!" Rayyan says.

I look at Halline, pleading. Halline stands, looking hard at me for a moment. "Rayyan," she says, "gather the Sanctum and the other women. We are heading up the mountain. It seems we've been summoned."

53

Lukin

"What a pleasure to see you, Nephew," Akkar remarks, steadying himself against the back of his chair. "And looking so well!"

I ignore him, turning instead to Tygan, who's managed to strike down the remaining Shield and stands panting and cleaning his sword.

"Go and report to Halline that the Torch is dead."

"Yes, sir," Tygan replies, sheathing his blade. "It will be my pleasure."

"I always knew he'd be a disappointment, like the rest of his family," Akkar remarks as Tygan leaves.

"Stop speaking," I command him, holding my bow steady.

"That won't be necessary, Lukin. Let us talk about this, shall we? I am sure we can resolve this little issue."

"This isn't a *little* issue, and no amount of talking will fix it. You invaded this village and killed innocent people, all for your own glory."

"Lukin, you wound me! You know everything I do, I do for Rhys, for Branngard. I do it for our family, for Velga honor!"

"What Velga honor?!" I ask, taking another step closer. "What *honor* is there in abandoning one's daughter to an early grave, all because she fell in love with the wrong person? In imprisoning your own nephew to save your reputation? What *honor* is there in forcing people to comply in the face of death, in murdering children in front of their mothers, in destroying their way of life—all in the name of your god? Why would anyone want to worship a god like that?!"

Akkar puts a hand on his chest, seeming truly shocked. "Draven warned me you'd lost your faith, and I refused to believe him. But now I see you as you are."

"Yes, Draven has proven to be much more loyal to you than he ever was to his men."

Akkar reaches out for the flagon of wine on the other side of his desk, pouring himself a glass. "Let an old man enjoy a trifle, won't you? Even Rhys can forgive me this one sin," he says, taking a long drink of the wine.

"Drinking that wine is the least of your sins. You couldn't wash all the blood from your hands if you spent the rest of your life trying."

"Alas," he replies, setting the glass back on the desk and relaxing into the chair. "It seems I won't have much time left to try, will I?"

"No, you won't," I answer, stepping closer yet.

"You know, Lukin. I do have *one* question before you take my life—if you'll oblige me, that is?"

"Ask."

"Did you know who Evryn *really* was when you saved her from the tent that night, scooping her up and claiming her before I could make her my Jewel?"

I try not to lose my concentration, but my arm is aching and Akkar's question throws me off. "What do you mean who she *really* was?"

Akkar chuckles under his breath. "For as bright as you are, boy, you do miss quite a lot."

I lower the bow as my arm gives way under the strain, and lay a careful hand on my blade.

"She's a girl like every other girl, Lukin. She's not even all that beautiful, but she has a *way* about her, doesn't she?"

"She's nothing like any woman alive," I reply defensively.

"Oh, yes. Don't misunderstand me. We both know how much I wanted her for myself, after all. But don't imagine it was empty *lust*. No," he says, "Evryn... she has *power*, Lukin, power beyond anything I could ever hope to possess."

"You are the most powerful man on this side of the world!" I remark. "What power could she have?"

Akkar takes another drink of the wine. "Let's reflect, for example, on the day you and Draven and the others crossed the river with her, as you were bringing her back to me, hmm? According to Draven's report, the waters were slow and steady. And yet, when you were halfway across, the river rose suddenly, taking down our young comrade!"

"Yes, but you can't truly be suggesting *Evryn* caused the river to rise. She was in it with us! Even if she had such power, why would she put herself at risk? And, she *saved* him!"

"Fair enough." Akkar shrugs. "How about the night you married her? The sky was *cloudless*. The moon was full, pristine. We should have had plenty of light to see you sneaking her into your tent. And yet, where was the moon? I swear to you, I stepped into my tent under a full moon and stepped out into the night again, moments later when I received the news, and the moon was *gone*. Not hidden, Lukin—*Gone*."

"You're saying you believe Evryn can control *the planets*, Uncle? It's unlike you to be so superstitious."

"Do you think I would say these things and risk angering Rhys if I wasn't sure of what I saw? When have you known me to be a reckless man?"

"I don't see it."

"How about the night you and that band of savages broke into the village and stole her siblings from under our noses? Did it ever occur to you how *easily* that little mission had gone?"

"How could Evryn possibly have affected the mission to rescue her siblings? She was miles away!"

"That night, I felt *vivacious* with energy. I paced around my tent, coming up with ideas on how to… *motivate* the Kenozarians to come into the light. And then, suddenly, it felt as if I had walked into a thick fog that settled over me, causing me to feel deeply sleepy. The next thing I knew, they were gone! I'd slept through the whole thing!"

"And?"

"And so did Draven. And so did every soldier in the settlement and every guard who was assigned to the garrison that night. Even the camp followers dozed, I heard. And then everyone just suddenly awoke once they were out. Do you *truly* think that's a coincidence, Lukin?"

I recall how ill at ease I felt when the rescue mission happened without so much as a drop of bloodshed. And it didn't seem like a coincidence, but there was no explanation for it.

"As I said, Evryn was far away when the rescue mission happened, with…" I shout, but my words trail off.

"With her *lover*. Torek, yes? According to my spies, she is heavily pregnant with his child, meaning you either lacked the virility or the strength to get the job done yourself, as I suspected."

I step directly into Akkar's space now, holding my blade at his throat. "You know nothing of strength, Uncle," I growl at him.

"I suppose you're right." Akkar sighs. "I have never sired any children, myself, either—at least not so far as I know. Pomisha failed me in that way."

"Is that why you killed her?"

"I would never kill a soul!" he cries.

"No, you wouldn't soil your hands. You send your hounds to do the dirty work for you, coward."

Unfazed, he continues. "Pomisha had served me faithfully, but she was spent. And I couldn't very well make Evryn my Jewel with Pomisha in the way, now could I? So I simply sent her a message, thanking her for her service."

I almost laugh at myself for not seeing it before. "So you convinced her to *kill herself*, and then framed Evryn and Ziva for her death?"

"What transpired after she read the letter was all Rhys's doing. When the girl wandered into camp, I saw my chance. I knew entrapping her was the only way to get Evryn to consider my offer."

"You're a goddamn monster, you know that?"

"Can you blame me? Have you not walked these mountains, Lukin? Have you not listened as you stood among the trees? This land is *made* for Evryn—it *is* her! She and this land are *one*! I *had* to have her by my side if there was any hope of bringing the Light to these simpleminded people."

"You've had too much wine, Uncle."

"I understand why you followed her back here when you received that letter."

"What? How—" I begin, but Akkar cuts me off.

"Who do you think summoned you here, Lukin?"

I recall receiving the simple letter, sealed without a sigil. "I don't know who, nor do I know how you knew about it."

"Nephew, you do disappoint me at times. When are you going to learn? I know *everything* that happens in Yarrow's Cairn."

I am losing my patience with him. "But why? Why bring me here and make it that much harder for yourself? You had to have known I would do anything to protect her."

"Because I love a good game, Nephew!" Akkar laughs. "And really, your love for that girl is womanly and disturbing."

I raise my blade again.

"I know you are angry with me, Lukin, but remember: It was *I* who made you captain of my armies and sent you here. I ordered you, specifically *you*, to go find her when we arrived. I made sure *you* were the one to bring her food and water when she was imprisoned in the tent. Have you ever stopped to ask yourself why?" he whispers, his eyes wide with implication.

"You're not making any sense. You were *angry* with me for marrying her!"

"Because I wanted her for myself!" Akkar shouts. "But, of course, I knew she was unlikely to willingly give herself over to an old man like me. But you? Oh, you, Lukin... You were the *perfect* bait for our Evryn. With your youth and your soft heart and your ridiculous obsession with honor, how could she resist you? I knew that if I couldn't make her my Jewel, at least I could bring her under my control by baiting you both with one another."

"You are wasting your final breaths, old man."

"I suppose you'd better get this over with, hmm?" Akkar says, sighing and standing again from his chair to approach me. "Who knows what she will do when she learns of our meeting here? You wouldn't want to anger her, would you?"

"Evryn would never hurt me, or anyone she loves."

"And are you so sure she *does* love you, Lukin? She carries another man's child, after all..."

With that, I slice quickly across his throat. The blood pours hot and dark from his neck. He's actually *smiling* before his body falls forward, slumping against my thighs and jerking this way and that until finally, he goes still.

"Rhys, be praised," I say, wiping the blood from my blade and sheathing it again at my side.

54

Evryn

The thought has never occurred to me that I have any real *power*. Mother was strong and reliable and tenacious—the epitome of power. Halline, too, has power, and she displays it by being gentle and kind and wise, keeping her basest inclinations in check. Aunt Tabitha's power was manifested in the way she could harness the abundance of nature to heal—and to hurt.

But unlike Mother or Tabitha or Halline, my soul has always been a fickle thing, desperate to escape when things become uncomfortable. Until this morning, when Ksenia's screams as she tore out of me into the world of the living shook me awake from my long slumber, I have lived my life like a leaf, blowing in the wind—helplessly pushed this way and that by the winds of fate. So I have relied on my ancestors and those I've loved and lost to guide me, and they never lead me astray.

But as I stand here atop Mount Zaria, surrounded by the women who have been so instrumental in bringing me up to be the woman I've become, I realize that I have access to more power than I ever dreamed possible—not to take vengeance, as Aunt Tabitha did at times, nor to suppress feelings I'd rather not deal with, as Mother did, but to protect and defend the people and places I love, like Halline. And I can't do it alone.

I reflect on the message I've received from both my daughter and my Aunt: *Focus on the Light. Make it grow.* The only way to make this light grow beyond me is to bring these women alongside me and unify our Light, together. I close my eyes and try to focus on my breath.

"I hope we get word soon from Torek," I hear Minara say, and it brings me back to reality.

"I'm so sorry, Minara. But Torek is gone," I say, taking her hand in mine.

"How can you know that?!" Minara asks, pulling away from me and clutching at Lyra to steady herself.

"You must trust me. He has passed into the Bright Lands, and we will all join him soon if we do not take action now."

The women look at one another in panic.

"We came here to ask for help," Halline says after a moment. "Let's see what our ancestors have to tell us."

I close my eyes again, centering myself on the Light burning within me, then I speak the words aloud—the same words Mother chanted during every Bright Ceremony to invite our ancestors to commune with us. As I speak the words, the other women begin to walk slowly around the fire. Soon, the spirits begin to pull them, faster and faster, around the campfire, and they glow like so many dancing flames.

"Zaria, protect us! Keno, avenge us!" I cry out. "Ancestors, guide our steps!" I focus all my energy on making the fire within me grow. I imagine the Light forming a wall of protection around our people. "Zaria, look on your sons and daughters as they join their ancestors. Pour forth your tears on their murderers! Keno, rise and wash away the invaders who come to hurt and pillage your beautiful land!"

The fire grows larger and larger within me as goosebumps rise on my skin, and I deepen my breathing. Suddenly, it feels as if a pillar of light explodes from the top of my head, right up into the morning sky, uniting with the pillars of light emitting from the heads of all the women circling the fire.

That's when the rain begins to fall.

55

Lukin

Stepping out into the dawn, I am greeted by torrential rain and the entire Branngardian army, rushing down the mountain toward me.

At first, I think they must be retreating, but then there's a sound like thunder that seems to shake the very earth beneath us. I gaze up in horror as a landslide cascades down the mountain. Trees, rocks, and a river of mud come crashing down the foothills, oozing faster and faster in my direction.

War be damned, I find myself running alongside them. The mud is taking entire cottages right off their foundations, like a child playing with blocks, leveling the village. The sound is terrifying.

As I run from the mudslide toward the river, something causes me to stop suddenly in my tracks: ahead, the Keno River rages, higher and faster, spilling over its banks and rushing toward us. What has always been a slow, deep stream is now violent, rushing white water, swallowing everything in its path.

I start running south, surrounded by a cacophony of screams and the unholy sound of bodies cracking as they slam into tree trunks and houses. All the while, the rain continues to pour from the sky in a great torrent that never seems to let up.

My attention is diverted by the sound of a woman screaming behind me. One of the camp followers, she is clinging to a tree branch, ten feet from the ground, as the mud and river rage below her.

I make a snap decision to try to get to her, but just as I turn to head her way, I trip on an exposed tree root. In a flash, I am swept off my feet and carried with the current, which drags me south and east of the village.

I fight to stay afloat, but the harder I struggle, the more water I take in. I scramble, trying to find anything I can grab onto to help me stay above water, but the river is moving faster and faster, carrying cottage walls and trees older than Yarrow's Cairn past me.

Suddenly, I crash against something hard, ricocheting my head off of a large boulder on the other side of the riverbank.

Everything goes dark.

When I come to, it is broad daylight. There's not a cloud in the sky. I am lying on the bank of the river—which has, as if by magic, slowed and settled back into its banks. Looking around me, I see dozens of my fellow countrymen dead and dying. There are too many to count.

Pulling myself up, I stumble back toward the fort, to Evryn.

56

Evryn

"What have we done?!" Halline cries, looking out over the scene of destruction before us after the dust has settled. I stand, surveying the wreckage myself, trying to make sense of what has happened.

Before I can reply, a few warriors from Salix come up the eastern side of the mountain with Lukin hanging on their shoulders. "We found him south of here. He's in a bad way," one says.

"Lukin!" I cry, rushing to his side. He flinches when I touch his left arm, and there's an obvious lump on the back of his head.

"Where are the others?" Halline asks.

Lukin shakes his head. "I can't say, for sure. Tygan and Ayfa were alive, last I knew, and a few others, but most of our party were killed by Akkar's Shield."

"They arrived with two other Kenozarian warriors an hour ago," Ari says, approaching us. He's covered in mud and blood, though it's unclear whether it's his or someone else's.

Lyra throws her arms around Ari's neck. He embraces her, kissing the top of her head.

"It's all gone, Evryn," Halline says as we both turn west. "The whole village, everything... gone."

I wrap my arm around her, pulling her in. "But *we* are here, all of us, safe and sound. Buildings can be rebuilt, Hal. *This* is what matters," I say, gesturing to the people milling about us. "*These people are Kenozaria.*"

Halline smooths her hair back, composing herself. "We must get back to the fort and regroup."

"Agreed," I say, turning to walk down the mountain with her.

* * *

Several days later, as the members of the Sanctum sit around the table in Nerys's hall, Tygan and Lukin approach.

"We come before you to request an official decree to protect the Branngardians who defected to the Kenozarian cause," Lukin says. "These men risked their lives so they could join you in your fight. They are not your enemies."

Halline nods, considering. "Is this what you want? To live here among us?" she asks Tygan. "You don't want to go home?"

"Yes, my lady," Tygan replies. "I will miss my home, but we are not safe there, not now. And this land is rich with fertile soil. We wish to live here among you, peaceably."

"And what of your customs?" Rayyan asks. "As we understand it, you worship a fire god whose goal is to destroy anyone who doesn't worship him."

Tygan looks at the ground, unsure how to reply, from the looks of it.

"They do not worship Rhys," Lukin says. "At least not in the way Akkar did."

Halline stands. "You must understand. Kenozaria is a *sacred* place.

We want to live in peace—to raise our children, tend to our flocks and our lands, and honor our ancestors. For you to live among us, you'd have to pledge yourselves to fight and even die in defense of this land, and to inform me should any of your fellow Branngardians harbor contrary ambitions."

"We understand this, my lady," Tygan replies.

"And how many of you are there?" Rayyan asks.

"Fifteen, my lady. Only fifteen remain of the fifty who defected."

"And what of Akkar?" I ask, finally opening the topic we're all waiting to hear about.

"Dead," Lukin says simply. The room goes silent.

"I am sorry for your loss," Halline says, placing a hand on her heart.

Lukin looks down at his boots and back up at us, sighing. "Don't be," he says. "We're all better off without him."

"And Draven?" Halline asks Ari. "As I understand, he led the charge."

"Yes, and he was the reason for Torek's death," Lyra adds, indignantly.

"Torek is *dead*?" Lukin asks.

"Yes," I reply simply. "He is gone."

"Draven has escaped," Ari pipes up, frustrated. "In the chaos of the landslide, he got away."

Halline sighs, resting her hands on the table in front of her. "What do you think, Evryn?" she asks, turning to me.

"Me?" I ask, confused. "I am not a member of the Sanctum."

"Yes, you," she insists. "Your wisdom in guiding us to Mount Zaria, and showing us how we could connect with the ancestors' power anytime we wished, so long as we do it together—it saved our lives, our homeland."

I sit for a moment, weighing everything in my mind. "The men who defected to join us have proven themselves loyal. But Lukin is the best judge of their character, and he should be the one to vouch for them, should they turn on us."

Halline weighs my words. Then she stands, causing us all to stand in response. "Kenozaria is welcome to all who would honor her land and protect her beloved people. Your religion and customs are your own, and we have no intention of curbing them, so long as they do not impede on ours."

Tygan and Lukin nod in agreement.

"It will take time to rebuild our village, and we could use the extra hands. So, you will each be given a year to prove yourself a helpful, willing participant in our society, and after that, you may marry and establish a family here, if you like," she says. "If, however, you are unable to live here peaceably, we will expel you from the island, forever. What happens to you then is out of our hands. Are we all in agreement?" she asks, addressing the room.

All nod in agreement.

"And what about us?" Nerys Beretta asks. "What will you offer us in exchange for the hospitality we have shown you?"

Halline swallows hard. "We could never repay you, Nerys. You know this. But we shall try. What would you like?"

Nerys sits in thought for a moment. "We are safe here, behind our walls, but I am barren and my men are aging."

"Are you asking for *women*?" Halline asks, puzzled.

"Yes, and no," Nerys replies. "We wish to unite our two villages in marriage, so that we may keep our bond strong."

"And how do you propose we do that?"

"Let's start with her," she says, pointing her chin at me.

I sit straight up in my seat. "Me?"

"Out of the question," Korina replies.

"Before you reject the offer, hear me out," Nerys asks.

Halline looks at me. "Go on."

"Ari is already betrothed, Ziva is still too young, and I wouldn't dare suggest the great Chief of Kenozaria marry one of my former husbands, but Evryn? She's freshly widowed, as I understand it, and would make a good wife to one of the younger men in my care."

Halline looks at me for a response.

"I am already wed," I reply, looking across the room at Lukin.

"But—" Nerys begins.

"You heard my sister," Halline replies. "However, I believe your suggestion to unify is a sound one, and I would be happy to discuss it further with you, at a later time, if you will permit us?"

Nerys nods in agreement and the meeting is adjourned. I leave the hall as quickly as I can, to get Ksenia.

As I walk toward Aunt Meryn's tent, Lukin catches up to me. "Do you mind if I walk with you?" he asks.

I slow my pace to match his. He looks tired and worn. "You look like you could use some rest," I say, unsure how to speak to this man I previously conversed so easily with, whom I have just publicly claimed.

"I could say the same for you," he replies, glibly.

I chuckle under my breath. "My daughter doesn't much appreciate my need for sleep."

"They never do," he laughs. We walk in silence for a while before he speaks again. "Evryn, I… I just wanted to—I'm so sorry for your loss. You and your baby needed him."

"Thank you," I reply, because it's the simplest response. I don't know if I'll ever be ready to tell anyone the truth about what Torek did.

"Evryn, what you said back there… It's… Well, I don't want you to feel like—"

"I know," I say, cutting him off. I can tell he wants to talk to me about everything, and though I feel that old familiar longing for him creeping up in me, the idea of trying to sort through all these feelings is too much. Torek was my great love and my worst enemy, the source of so much grief but also the reason I have Ksenia. Trying to pick apart the individual strands of rage and sorrow and relief and gratitude I feel toward him requires more energy than I have at present.

"I need time," I say. "I just need time."

"Yes, of course you do," he replies, looking at the ground as we walk. "I didn't mean to intrude. I…" he starts, his words trailing off.

"Yes?" I ask, stopping to look at him.

He stands in the morning sunlight, looking down at me, and I can see the pain in his eyes. "I hope you and your baby are well and safe. Should you need anything at all, please let me know. I am here. I care. I don't expect you to… Well, I understand why you said what you said to the gathering, but I won't impose myself."

"That is kind of you, Lukin," I say. "You are not imposing in any place you aren't already welcome. I just need time."

With that, I continue on to Aunt Meryn's tent.

X

Autumn

57

Evryn

"Perfect weather for a wedding," Halline remarks as she comes in from the rain, smoothing down her hair.

"Oh, just *divine*," I reply dryly, wiping my soiled hands on the towel on my shoulder.

"I, for one, would *not* like rain on my wedding day," Ziva remarks, tickling Ksenia, who giggles joyfully from her spot in Ziva's lap.

"*Your* wedding day is far off in the distant future," I reply. "Let's get you prepared for your Bright Ceremony first, eh?"

"But why do I have to wait?" Ziva whines.

"Because you have to be mature enough to handle it," Halline replies, stirring the soup I'd been making when she entered. "Our ancestors want to give you as much time as possible to enjoy being a girl. There will be plenty of time to be a woman."

"Mmhmm, Halline is right," I add, smiling.

"I guess…" Ziva sighs and then returns to playing with Ksenia. "I can't wait to see what Lyra wears!"

"I'm sure Minara will have designed something perfect for her," Halline replies.

"Torek would have loved to see it all," Ziva says. At the mention of his name, the hair on the back of my arms stands on end.

"I'll just... go check on the preparations with Rayyan," I say, picking up Ksenia and excusing myself. As I walk out, I hear Halline comforting Ziva, who feels bad for mentioning Torek.

As we rush through the rain to Rayyan's cottage, I look around at the beginnings of our new village. All around us are cabins in various stages of construction. My cottage was finished only a month ago, alongside Halline and Ziva's. Ari and Lyra's cottage, across the way, was finished just last week.

"What a pleasant surprise!" Rayyan cries out when she sees us come in. Ksenia reaches out to her, so Rayyan takes her in her arms and kisses her cheeks. "Look at this perfect gem of a child!"

She's beautiful, like her mother, Torek whispers.

I have no response. Even in death, I am not free of him. I guess that means he loved me, in his own way—a complexity I may never make peace with.

"It looks like you're almost ready for the ceremony," I remark, looking around at the spread of dishes laid out on her table.

"Yes!" she replies, still looking at Ksenia. "I still have a pie in the oven, but it should be ready now. And what about you all? Is Ziva ready?"

"I believe she's never been more excited in her life," I reply, smiling. "Though I wonder how she will take it when Lyra's newlywed life keeps her... *busy.*"

Rayyan laughs and carries Ksenia back to me, grabbing the towel from her table and opening the oven to pull out the pie.

"I'm sure Ziva will find something to distract herself with," Rayyan says, setting the pie on the table. "How is she recovering?"

"She's getting better," I say, hoping it's true. She seems fine most of the time, but sometimes she will see or hear or even smell something, and it sends her spinning out of control, leaving her a bumbling, weeping mess for days. Several nights I've been awakened roughly by her, screaming like someone is scalding her with boiling water, waking Ksenia and sending us scurrying to Halline's cottage to check on her.

Once, a few weeks after the war, Halline mentioned having seen a few Branngardian soldiers working on a nearby house, absent-mindedly saying one looked too old to be working on a house, and Ziva—thinking it may have been Draven—went into a frenzy, unable to control her breathing. We had to find the healer and administer a calming tonic to help her sleep.

She *does* seem to be getting better, but when she falls into the void of sorrow and fear Draven opened in her when he stole her girlhood from her, sometimes I worry if she'll *ever* be healed.

"She just needs the healing love of her community," Rayyan says, cutting through my thoughts. "She will recover, in time. As we all will."

We *all* will.

"You know, she does look *so* much like him, all except those eyes," she says, looking over at Ksenia, who is pulling on a tendril of my hair and sucking on her other hand.

"That's what everyone says," I reply, the bittersweet truth of it mixing in my gut.

Sensing my discomfort, Rayyan comes over and cups my cheek. "You'll make it through this, my dear. I promise. And we're all here to support you, okay?"

"Thank you for all your help," I say, making my farewell and heading out with Ksenia.

The rain has stopped by the time we approach the burial mound just southwest of the village. Mother's tombstone gleams in the light of the setting sun. Ksenia gurgles next to me, reaching for a butterfly that lands on my shoulder.

"Let's greet your grandmama, honey," I say, squatting down next to the tombstone to read the inscription.

Beloved mother, respected leader, proud Kenozarian

I trace the letters with my fingers and reflect on the order of those titles, unsure still which of them she would have preferred to be placed first. Ksenia lays in the crook of my arm, pulling on my top and whining, so I take a seat on the heavy rock in front of Mother's grave and nurse Ksenia, who tugs on the fabric of my tunic happily as she suckles away. Soon, her eyelids flutter closed and she passes out, milk-drunk and content.

She's perfect, Mother whispers.

"Yes," I reply, smiling down at Ksenia. "Hopefully she won't give me as much trouble as I gave you."

The clouds are parting finally as the sun begins to set behind the mountains. Soon, we'll have to rush home and get dressed for the wedding. For now, though, I sit in peace, holding my sleeping baby and smelling the rich, wet earth I longed to smell for so long when I was in Branngard. I'm back in the home I thought I might never see again.

Thinking of Branngard has me thinking of Lukin. I wonder what he will wear to the ceremony. I left him sleeping in our bed this morning, but not before I nuzzled my face in the downy red hair of his chest and kissed the skin there that protects his heart—the heart I have come to love so deeply.

"My darling," he said sleepily, stroking my hair and pulling me closer. "I believe someone in this room has soiled themselves, and it's not me."

348

"That's your daughter," I replied, smiling and handing her to him. He laughed and stood up, got dressed, and then took her into his arms.

"I may have to hose you down this time, Kessy," he said, squeezing his nostrils shut as he carried her outside.

Several months ago, when I finally told him the truth of what had transpired between Torek and me, he held me in his arms and wept for me and with me. Then he gave me all the space and time I needed to process what had happened to me. He is my dearest friend, and from our friendship has blossomed a deep, passionate, enduring love.

Ksenia is snoring away when I stand and take one last look at Mother's burial mound.

"I wish you were here," I say, and I mean it.

I am always with you, she whispers. *Whether you like it or not.*

I chuckle to myself as I head back toward the village, tying Ksenia onto my chest.

By the time the ceremony begins, the clouds have parted, thankfully, giving us a spectacular view of the stars as we sit at the feasting tables, watching as Ari and Lyra prepare to make their vows.

Halline stands before them, officiating the ceremony, while Ksenia and I sit with the rest of our family.

"Oh, Zaria, protect their union from any who may wish them harm or disunity," she begins. "Keno, help them to trust each other and their fate, even when times are hard."

Ari smiles at Lyra, who beams back at him, radiant with joy.

"Ancestors, guide their mouths to speak truth and kindness to each other," Halline continues. "Guide their ears to hear love even in harsh words, and their minds to see the best in each other.

"Ari and Lyra, do you vow to honor each other, in public and in private?"

"Yes, we do," they say in unison as Ari wipes a tear from Lyra's cheek.

"And do you vow to protect each other from harm, even and especially from each other?"

Again, they nod in agreement.

"And do you vow to commit yourselves to each other's well-being, even and especially if it should require you to one day part ways as loving friends?"

"We do," they say.

Halline then wraps a thick rope around their wrists. "With the oaths being announced for all to hear, it is my honor to present you as partners. May Zaria keep you enthralled with each other, and may Keno keep your love strong, even when you're *not* as enthralled," she says, causing the whole assembly to chuckle.

They're going to be so happy together, Mother whispers.

"Yes," I reply under my breath.

"Lyra and Ari!" Halline cries, raising the couple's bound hands.

"Ari and Lyra!" we all reply, cheering and tossing our flowers in the air as the band strikes up their song.

Lyra and Ari untangle their hands and begin dancing, over the moon with joy. I look over and see Ayfa pulling Halline in for a sweet kiss. My heart warms with joy for them. I guess Ayfa has matured enough for the Great Halline. Soon, all are dancing in the clearing, just as we did at Lyra's Bright Ceremony.

Just then, there is a tap on my shoulder.

"You are the prettiest girl here," Lukin says, smiling as Ksenia reaches for his beard. "But it's your mother I came to speak to."

"And how can I be of assistance?" I ask, smiling.

"You can dance with me," Lukin replies, extending his hand, "and save me from these damsels."

"They couldn't handle you," I reply, looking around at the women who are, indeed, damseling in his direction.

"Oh?" he asks, handing Ksenia to Ziva and taking my hand to lead me to the dance circle. "Am I so bad?"

"Positively *villainous*," I reply, smirking. We move into position in the group of dancers as the musicians strike up an old ballad, about Keno's love for Zaria.

Lukin smiles, pulling me closer. In answer, I kiss him softly, savoring the feeling of his lips on mine. His love is a soothing balm, a welcome respite after so much heartache.

"You are looking particularly resplendent this evening, my dear," he says, looking down into my eyes.

He doesn't look too bad himself, Aunt Tabitha whispers, causing me to smile even more widely.

"It's because I am happy," I reply.

"I wonder if they'll expect us to make our own vows," he says, musing, "since we already have, I mean."

I smile. "Listen, those vows were made under duress, and you know it."

"Ah, but then you claimed me again! In public!"

"Again, duress. I couldn't very well marry one of Nerys Beretta's cast-offs, could I?"

"Semantics," he laughs, pulling me closer.

"Everyone knows you're my partner, oaths or not," I say, brushing some hair out of his face.

"I should hope so," he says, kissing my forehead. "But just in case, we could try for a boy?" he says, smirking and pointing over at Ksenia, who is giggling as she is passed from person to person around the wedding party.

"I'm up for the challenge if you are." I lay my head against his chest and close my eyes, listening as the music swells and the trees lean nearer, green and vibrant and *alive*.

Epilogue

Fifteen Years Later

The afternoon sun beats down on the old man as he stands along the parapet of Rhys Domus, looking out at the eastern horizon.

He takes out a worn, yellowed handkerchief and wipes the sweat from his brow as he watches the men below in the courtyard, sparring. He grimaces at their general lack of skill. He couldn't have gotten away with such laziness when he was their age, he thinks.

"The Torch will see you now," a Shield says, stepping out into the sunlight from under the veranda.

"Thank you," he replies, turning away from the sparring ground and following the Shield.

Within, the Torch of Branngard sits on his throne in all his splendor. Upon his brow sits a crown of purest gold, inlaid with diamonds and rubies, larger than his eyes. Of course, his eyes are quite small, considering he is not much older than fourteen.

"It is an honor to be in your presence, Your Holiness," the old man says, bowing as low as his old back will allow.

"I understand you've readied the armies?" the Torch asks. "And what of the armies of Tarsh? Are they ready, too?"

"They are mightier warriors than I've ever seen, Your Holiness," the old man replies. "Except ours, of course."

The young Torch stands from his throne. "And when will you be ready to sail?" he asks, stepping toward the old man, who lowers his eyes, respectfully.

"In a fortnight, I'd say," he replies. "So long as the ships are finished."

"They will be ready," the shipmaster replies from his seat against the far wall in the long hall.

"Good. We can't waste the sacrifice of my beloved great-uncle Akkar. Rhys, be praised."

"Rhys, be blessed!" the room echoes.

"The Torch before ya was a great man, a great leader. But you're giving him a run for his money, alright... Your Holiness, sir," the old man says, casting his gaze down again.

The young Torch smiles, turning to sit on his throne again. "My mother, Lady Selise, says my father was the greatest warrior who ever lived. What do you say, Draven Firon?"

Draven bites his lower lip until it bleeds. "He was, Your Holiness."

"Yes," the boy replies. "I know the heretics say my father was a traitor later in his life, but his noble blood runs strong in me, and I shall bring Branngard and the Velga line and Rhys the glory they deserve. Rhys, be blessed!"

"Rhys, be praised!" the congregation shouts in response.

"Yes, Your Holiness," Draven replies, taking his leave and backing away from the throne.

Out in the sunlight, he removes the flask from his belt and drinks deeply. "I'll find ya, Lukin Velga, and I'll make ya *wish* you'd died in that flood," he says under his breath as he leaves the castle and heads toward the shipyard.

Thank You!

Thank you for reading! I hope you enjoyed reading *Evryn, the Light*, and will leave an honest review at any of the following locations:

- Amazon
- Goodreads
- Personal blog
- Social media post—Please tag @kaighlarises on Instagram and TikTok, and Kaighla Rises Writing on Facebook.

Acknowledgments

This book would not have been possible without the support of my Patrons, friends, and family, and the work of several others.

To start, I'm deeply indebted to the work of my editor, Lynsey Griswold, for her eagle's eye and lion's heart in helping me to craft and mold this story.

I am blessed to have the friendship and guidance of several local authors and editors—Jenna Wilson, John R. McCool III, M.I.H. McCool, Karl Witsman, and Stuart Robbins. I thank you for your honest and helpful feedback and recommendations on this, my very first fiction book baby. I am also eternally grateful to my Beta-reading and ARC-reading teams for their valuable contributions.

For the inspiration behind Akkar and Branngard's methods, I relied heavily on the work of Joseph Campbell, Merlin Stone, and others, who wrote so eloquently about the process by which the Divine Feminine/Shaman came to be torn from her primordial pedestal by the careful and intentional work of upstart patriarchal, monotheistic religions.

I'm grateful to my sister, AJ, for her kind assessment of the alpha and beta versions of this book.

My friend Nicole's encouragement kept me going through the darkest moments, and her sensitive and kind way of calling me to a higher standard kept me centered.

I'd like to thank Kaitlin for the many post-school-run calls to go over this or that plot hole, and so much more, and Rachael, for her support, day and night, night and day, from across the pond.

I am particularly grateful to my children for their patience in listening to my rants and mad ravings along this writing journey. They left me to my own devices when I needed writing time, and they believed in me so fervently that I began to believe in myself. And, of course, they made sure I had my favorite writing snacks: chocolate-covered pretzels and cups of sweet tea.

Finally, I am deeply grateful for the love and never-ending support of my muse, companion, and partner in all things—SJon. Pinky promise, babe.

www.ingramcontent.com/pod-product-compliance
Lightning Source LLC
Chambersburg PA
CBHW021215260626
47172CB00002B/437